Frank Barnard  r a career in
journalism, publ AF novels, *Blue
Man Falling* and lers and hugely
acclaimed. He li

Praise for Frank Barnard:

'Fantastic writing . . . terrific, atmospheric. Every smell and sound
is authentic to the period, but his pace is as modern as it gets'
bestselling author Peter James

'A fascinating story told with verve and affection'
Historical Novels Review

'Engrossing . . . funny, tragic and utterly compelling . . . will
keep the reader gripped until the very end' *Good Book Guide*

'This is a fast moving story of wartime derring-do, full of high-
minded heroes and lovely villainesses and plenty of dicing with
death. It is an adventurous yarn and a good read, certainly, but
also a timely reminder of the great sacrifices made by the real-
life prototypes, more than a half a century ago, in defence of our
freedom'
Julian Fellowes, bestselling author of *Snobs* and Oscar
winning script writer of *Gosford Park*

'Truly authentic. A jolly good read' *Sunday Express*

'Admirable. A compelling and engrossing novel'
Newbury Weekly News

'A triumph. This is boys' own adventure stuff, Biggles on speed
– an excellent read' *York Evening Press*

By Frank Barnard and available from Headline

Blue Man Falling
Band of Eagles
To Play the Fox

TO PLAY THE FOX

FRANK BARNARD

headline
review

Copyright © 2008 Frank Barnard

The right of Frank Barnard to be identified as the Author of
the Work has been asserted by him in accordance with the
Copyright, Designs and Patents Act 1988.

Winston Churchill quotes reproduced with permission of Curtis Brown Ltd,
London, on behalf of The Estate of Winston Churchill.
Copyright Winston S. Churchill

First published in 2008 by HEADLINE REVIEW
An imprint of HEADLINE BOOK PUBLISHING

First published in paperback in 2009 by HEADLINE REVIEW
An imprint of HEADLINE PUBLISHING GROUP

1

Cataloguing in Publication Data is available from the British Library

ISBN 978 0 7553 3892 4

Typeset in Galliard by Palimpsest Book Production Limited,
Grangemouth, Stirlingshire.

Printed and bound in Great Britain by
CPI Mackays, Chatham ME5 8TD

Headline's policy is to use papers that are natural, renewable and recyclable
products and made from wood grown in sustainable forests.
The logging and manufacturing processes are expected
to conform to the environmental
regulations of the country of origin.

HEADLINE PUBLISHING GROUP
An Hachette Livre UK Company
338 Euston Road
London NW1 3BH

www.headline.co.uk
www.hachettelivre.co.uk

To Jan, again

'The Prince must be a lion but he must also know how to play the fox'

The Prince (1532), Niccolò Machiavelli (1469–1527)

'Success is not final, failure is not fatal. It is the courage to continue that counts'

Winston Churchill (1874–1965)

AUTHOR'S NOTE

This is a work of fiction, although the story is interwoven with real events connected with the pivotal battle of El Alamein. The circumstances surrounding the death of General Georg Stumme, who assumed command of the Afrika Korps during Field Marshal Erwin Rommel's absence in Germany, just before the Allied attack, have never been properly explained. Who is to say that something similar to the action portrayed in these pages did not occur? And there was such a unit as Holly Force, a group of Palestinian Jewish volunteers dressed as German soldiers who carried out clandestine operations behind enemy lines. In real life it was known as the Special Interrogation Group, the brainchild of its commander Captain Herbert 'Bertie' Buck MC, and forerunner of the British Army's Long Range Desert Group and, ultimately, the SAS.

I would also like to highlight the role of the Royal Air Force aircrew and ground-crew who served with the Photographic Reconnaissance Unit (PRU), as well as those responsible for ferrying a huge variety of aeroplanes from the west coast of Africa to the front in North Africa – the so-called Takoradi Run. Both played a crucial role in the successful battle against the Axis forces, the first defeat suffered by Rommel, the Desert Fox.

RAF v. GERMAN RANKS

AC2 . . . *Flieger, Gefreiter*
AC1 . . . *Obergefreiter*
LAC . . . *Hauptgefreiter*
Corporal or senior corporal . . . *Stabsgefreiter*
Sergeant . . . *Feldwebel*
Flight Sergeant and Warrant Officer . . . *Oberfeldwebel*
Pilot Officer . . . *Leutnant*
Flying Officer . . . *Oberleutnant*
Flight Lieutenant . . . *Hauptmann*
Squadron Leader . . . *Major*
Wing Commander . . . *Oberstleutnant*
Group Captain . . . *Oberst*
Air Commodore . . . *Generalmajor*
Air Vice Marshal . . . *Generalleutnant*
Air Marshal . . . *General*
Air Chief Marshal . . . *Generaloberst*
Marshal of the Royal Air Force . . . *Generalfeldmarschall*
Supreme Commander . . . *Reichsmarschall*

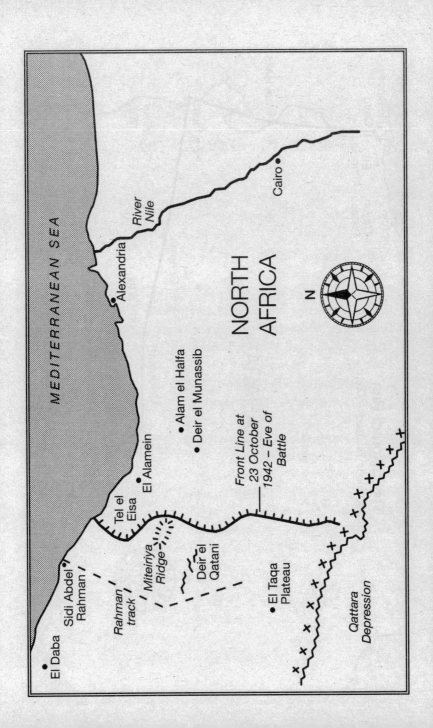

MEDITERRANEAN SEA

El Daba

Sidi Abdel
Rahman

Tel el
Eisa

El Alamein

Alexandria

River
Nile

Cairo

NORTH
AFRICA

N

Alam el Halfa

Deir el Munassib

Front Line at
23 October
1942 – Eve of
Battle

Rahman
track

Miteiriya
Ridge

Deir el
Qatani

El Taqa
Plateau

Qattara
Depression

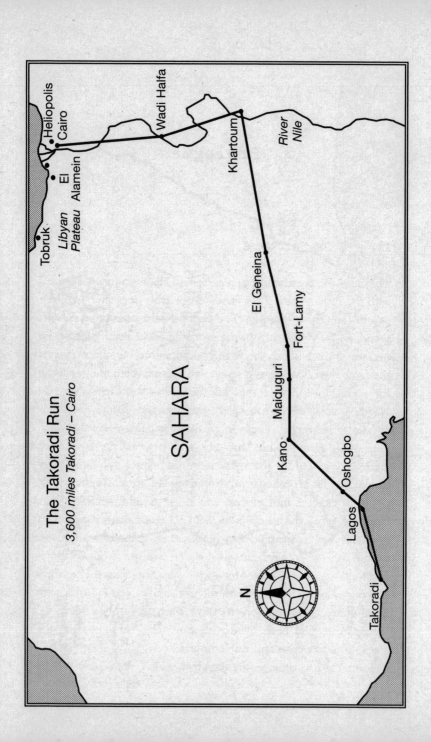

The Takoradi Run
3,600 miles Takoradi – Cairo

SAHARA

Heliopolis
Cairo
El Alamein
Tobruk
Libyan Plateau
Wadi Halfa
Khartoum
River Nile
El Geneina
Fort-Lamy
Maiduguri
Kano
Oshogbo
Lagos
Takoradi

N

Prologue

In a Kent orchard

The men were gathering apples. Their khaki uniforms blended with the brown and yellow leaves of the fruit trees that had been touched by an early autumn. The work was strenuous but welcome. Stationed a few miles from the farm, they had been training for overseas duty. Nobody knew their destination, but the regime at the camp was relentless and severe – to prepare them, they realised, for a great ordeal to come. The news was bad everywhere. In North Africa, Tobruk had fallen and Rommel's Afrika Korps was advancing on Egypt. The rumour in the regiment was that soon they would have sand in their boots. On the nearby farm, with labour scarce and his few workers falling behind, the farmer had watched as his crop began to drop from the trees, windfalls only good for cider. A hint of frost was in the air and, without much hope, he asked the soldiery for help. The company commander knew his men had earned a spell away from preparations for war. So now, in the orchard, the air was rich with the scent of apples and loud with the voices of men who were boys again. The fallers had been cleared from beneath the trees and placed in boxes with a handful of grass on top, to show they were to go for cider. Other boxes had been filled with fruit taken straight from the trees, firm and crisp and unblemished.

From time to time, as the days had passed, the soldier pickers had paused, easing down onto the long, damp grass, propping themselves against the stacked boxes and rough-barked trees, or stretching out, like picnickers before the war, taking in the smells and sounds and prospect of the green-gold English countryside. The cookhouse had filled their haversacks with rations and they quietly munched their wedges of white bread and cheese, brewing tea in billycans set over small fires of fragrant apple-tree twigs and drinking from enamel mugs.

But this was their last day in the orchard. Until now, the regiment had given their labour free. But today, Sunday, their time was their own and the farmer had agreed to pay them sixpence a box to get the orchard cleared. Better still, instead of haversack rations, they were presented with a spread of sandwiches and cakes and bottles of beer, set out on a table with a gingham tablecloth, near the gateway that led from the farmyard to the orchard. There, busy behind the table, were the farmer's wife and two young daughters, smiling and shy. The soldiers looked at them for long moments as they collected their food, saying little, smiling too, thinking of home while, amongst the trees, a faint mist gathered and hung above the ground, catching the rays of the low midday sun.

Then, as the men ate and drank, they heard, through the golden mist, the clangour of bells from the Norman church in the distant village. No bells had been rung for three years, struck dumb by war, only to be tolled to herald invasion. But these peals sent a message of hope. Soon news came that Rommel's advance had been halted, at an obscure spot on the Egyptian coast called Alamein, only sixty miles from Alexandria, home to Britain's Mediterranean fleet, with Suez, gateway to the Far East, not so far beyond.

It was the first time that the Wehrmacht, with its Italian allies, had been defeated in the field. The myth of Rommel, the invincible Desert Fox, had also been destroyed. And Hitler was denied his vision of two spearheads meeting in Iran, Rommel's Afrika

Korps driving through Egypt and General von Bock's army slicing south through the Caucasus, before turning east together, bound for India, to await the Japanese, already in possession of the coast of China, the East Indies, Malaya and Burma.

Once united, went the Führer's plan, German production and Japanese raw materials would be combined and the populations of Europe, Asia and Africa would be engulfed in a new Dark Age. No wonder, then, that Prime Minister Churchill ordered the ringing of the bells. After years of privation and setback, with invasion a constant threat, he told his cabinet: 'The people need something to celebrate.' Later, he was to observe of Hitler's first humiliation: 'Now this is not the end. It is not even the beginning of the end. But it is, perhaps, the end of the beginning.' And later still: 'Before Alamein we never had a victory. After Alamein we never had a defeat.'

But in the Kent orchard on Sunday, 8 November 1942, the soldier apple-pickers and the farmer and his family knew only that a famous victory had been won. Ahead lay greater conflicts. Soon the Allies would face the battle for Tunis itself and the wholesale surrender of the Afrika Korps, with more than 80,000 of its best men dead on the battlefield and over a quarter of a million more, still proud, marching into captivity behind their military bands.

Many of the men in khaki standing in the Kent orchard, amid the boxes of freshly picked apples, with the mist being dispersed by a rising breeze from the south-west and the sun lowering in the glittering sky, would not hear the sound of English church bells again. For on Christmas Day they sailed from Liverpool for Algiers, where preparations were being made for the final conflict. Where Scipio had fought, and Hannibal, and great armies had been destroyed between the mountains and the sea, Rommel's army lay, pinned between the Eighth Army at Alamein to the east and the combined British, American and Free French forces holding the mountain ridge that ran close to the Tunisian border to the west and south.

The regiment would play its part, and although not all its men would return, the memory of the church bells on that golden day remained with those who, years later, would find themselves restored to England; a memory and a reminder of what the soldier apple-pickers, among so many thousands – millions – had chosen to defend.

Part one

Lightfoot

One

Kit Curtis was awake before dawn. The small tent that, as flight lieutenant in command of B Flight, he shared with Keeble the intelligence officer was pitched close to a patch of camel thorn that, here and there, pushed its way through the stretch of hard grey limestone that served as the Photo Reconnaissance Unit's forward airfield. Close by was the ridge of Alam el Halfa and, ten miles to the north-west, within sight of the Mediterranean, lay the railway halt named by the Egyptians after a small hill crowned with two stone cairns that rose between the tracks and the sea: El Alamein.

The pink light of the rising sun filtered through the gaps in the tent flap, portent of another day flying alone and high in the desert sky, but for the moment Kit lay under the coarse blanket, shivering from the night cold. Keeble began to yawn and stretch. Then he pushed away his blankets and sat sideways on his bed, rubbing his face with his hands. 'Good grief, who'd imagine you could be this parky in the desert. What's the time?'

'Coming up to six.'

'Ops will have their targets from Wing by now.'

'Low-level stuff over Miteiriya Ridge again, no doubt. Rommel's chaps are well dug in there. Last trip, the flak batteries put on quite a show.'

'It's the same all along the front, from the sea to the Qattara Depression. This is going to be the big one, Kit. There'll be some fireworks when Monty finally lights the blue touchpaper.'

'You're the intelligence wallah, Tom. When is it going to be, do you think?'

'Search me, old boy. When he believes we're ready, I suppose.'

'Is he as good as he seems to think he is?'

'I certainly hope so. Otherwise we're in the mire and Rommel will be in Cairo in a week. The word is, he's already reserved a suite in Shepherd's Hotel.' Keeble pulled on his trousers and battledress jacket, his breath showing in the chill air. 'I'm going in search of a cuppa. Want me to bring you one back?'

'No, thanks. I'm going to check the kites.' It was a small tradition in a Photo Reconnaissance Unit that a flight commander did this personally. 'And then I've got to rustle up the chaps. This will be Porter's first trip.'

'Cause for concern?'

'Not really. He's done a tour on Blenheims, three hundred hours, and appears to have got the hang of Spits. Seems an unflappable type. You know, steady.'

The ground-crews were pulling away the camouflage netting from six of the unit's ten Spitfire IVs. They were painted a uniform pale blue, emphasising the elegance of the design. It lent the machines an unwarlike appearance, as though decorated on the whim of a wealthy and eccentric aviatrix. At first glance, even in the cold dawn light, the PR Spitfires seemed almost frivolous. But then more careful scrutiny took in the matt roundels, dark blue and red, on fuselage and wings, confirming military purpose and steely intent; to pass unseen above the enemy and record his every move.

Some of the other pilots were already there: Kit was pleased to see it. As B Flight commander he had been encouraging them to take an interest in the work of the ground-crews. The work of a PRU was very different from that of an operational fighter squadron: no scrambles; no flying in formation, each man looking out for the other; no sudden and turbulent combat, the sky a confusion of wheeling aircraft, machine-gun bullets and cannon shells, spinning wreckage trailing smoke and fire, with the occasional drifting parachutes but, most often, men trapped in their cockpits, suffering the torment of a long descent enveloped by flames.

Those who had survived another combat sortie chose their own ways to unwind, to release the tension. This did not include, generally, involving themselves in the preparation of their machines. They trusted the airmen who were trained for the task, and anyway – who knew what tomorrow might bring? Life was too short to brood about the complexities of preparing such a machine for flight. A pilot's routine external inspection and cockpit check before take-off were rigorous enough, surely? Why turn yourself into a mechanic? And on readiness, pretending to read the *Daily Mirror*, waiting for the duty corporal to ring the bell that signalled action, you had other things on your mind, more immediate concerns, like whether you had remembered to prop up that envelope by your bed in the billet, where it could be easily seen, or was that rabbit's foot presented to you by the little WAAF driver safely tucked inside the pocket of your Irvin jacket?

For the PR man, as Kit had quickly discovered, there was more time. You had your targets, you devised your own flight plan and dealt with them in whatever order you wished. You flew alone, navigating your way to your objective in silence, sometimes at fifty feet, sometimes at thirty thousand. You did not use your radio-telephone except perhaps when taking off or landing. In distress, away from your base, you stayed silent. To betray your position meant the enemy would be on you in minutes. And there was nothing to be done, no comrade close by to come to your aid. You flew unarmed, your wings stripped of armament. Instead, two cameras were mounted in the belly of your machine, recording shot by shot dispositions of enemy troops, tank movements, runways, oilfields, factories, shipping. The cameras were bulky but still lighter than Brownings so your supercharged Merlin engine could power you through the air 50 mph faster than your combat counterpart. That, and vigilance, was your only defence.

It took a cool and steady head, a different kind of courage, the ability to be methodical, determined, thorough. That was why Kit required his flight to take an interest in the ground-crew's work, not to interfere but to understand, so that when the engine faltered far from home, or the controls grew stiff and unresponsive, or some other fault began to show, and your heart missed a beat or two, poised alone above a hostile land, you had a better chance to do something that might, just might make the difference between life and death. But of course such moments for those whose luck, it was said in the mess, had run out, or whose number, it was agreed over a beer or two, had come up, quickly passed into fading memory with no comrades to witness their fate, and no one to hear any last words they might speak over the R/T.

Now, in the half-light, the airmen were already moving over and round the fighters with a quiet deliberation, working through the list of tasks on the daily inspection form. 'Everything in order, Flight?' said Kit.

Flight Sergeant Matthews nodded. 'We'll have the DIs done in thirty minutes, sir. When's the first take-off?'

'Don't know yet. I'm on my way to the flight tent now.' Kit saw Porter, the Blenheim man, and went across. 'All set?'

'Sure,' said Porter, not looking him in the eye, and Kit felt a flash of irritation. The sergeant pilot was smoking a Woodbine, the tip of the cigarette a tiny red glow in the semi-darkness. He looked calm and undisturbed, older than his years, and Kit reminded himself that here was a man who had come through innumerable gatherings like this, preparing for a sortie on a bleak airfield in the faint light of dawn. No excuse for complacency though.

'Don't forget,' he said, 'to make sure you get plenty of overlap when you press the tit, so the photographic interpreters can get a handle on things. It takes a little patience, making certain, but you don't want to come back without the coverage.'

'Obviously,' said Porter. 'Any idea of targets?'

'Not yet. When you've signed your kite's DI, scoot across to the flight office. Pat Hallam, the ops officer, will have some gen for us by then.'

'Okay. Seems straightforward enough. Bit ruddy parky though, isn't it? Didn't expect that.'

'Colder still if you get a high-altitude trip. Though the Jerries do their best to keep things warm for us.' Kit paused, and rubbed his hands. Porter's cool detachment made him feel uneasy. He wanted to establish at least a vestige of rapport. 'Remind me,' he said, 'where are you from?'

'Chobham.'

'Ah yes.'

'Know it?'

Kit nodded. 'Just down the road from Fairoaks aerodrome. I trained there on Hurricanes for a while.'

Porter took a last drag on his cigarette, threw it down and ground it under the heel of his flying boot. 'We lived a mile away. I used to cycle up to the airfield when I was a kid. That's what got me started, tinkering around with engines. The Flying Club were a right bunch of toffee-nosed snobs, but one way and another I ended up behind the controls. Turned out I was a better ruddy pilot than the lot of them.'

The engine of one of the Spitfires was being run up by the ground-crew, its note hesitant at first before settling into a healthy bellow, the propeller raising a dust cloud that drifted over them, so they raised their hands to shield their faces. Then the engine died.

In the sudden silence Kit said: 'This is a different game to the one you've been used to.'

'Obviously,' said Porter. He seemed to like the word.

'Think you're going to settle to it?'

'Why not? What idiot would moan about flying Spits for a living? Not that I didn't get a bit of leg-pull from my mates when I volunteered. Load of bollocks about PRU meaning Pilots' Rest Unit.'

Kit winced. It was not how he expected a new arrival to talk to his flight commander, particularly an NCO. And so far he had not been addressed as 'sir'. Such things were important to him, not to be overdone but not ignored either. They spoke of discipline, efficiency and respect between the ranks, foundations on which the service was built, qualities that fostered team spirit, high morale and effectiveness in the air. He would tackle it later, and without equivocation, but now was not the time.

'Well,' he said, 'we've all had these nonsenses. You can't let it get to you.'

'I don't.'

'Actually,' said Kit, 'people are beginning to understand what we're up against. It's not everyone's cup of tea.'

'Doesn't worry me,' said Porter. 'They can think what they like.'

'Did someone mention tea?' It was one of the Canadians, his hands in his pockets, shoulders hunched up against the cold.

'Hello, Cocky,' said Kit.

'So what have Wing got lined up for us today?' said Cochrane. 'That damned Miteiriya Ridge again, I'll bet.'

'Signed off your DI?'

'Sure have. The boys have really got their fingers out this morning.' The Canadian's fair moustache showed white against his tan. He had flown low-level sorties over Tobruk when the seaport fell to Axis forces four months earlier, and had returned with pictures of massed Panzers advancing across the desert in miles-wide ranks as Rommel continued his push towards Egypt. He had also landed with flak holes in his machine.

Now he said: 'Keen to get weaving, Sergeant?' Porter had

arrived by road the day before, giving the others no time to remember his name.

'Oh yes,' said Porter. His face was impassive but when he lit another cigarette, his hand trembled very slightly as he flicked his lighter. So, Kit reflected, Sergeant Porter wasn't quite the man of steel he would have them believe. Nothing remarkable there, of course. Even second-tour men got the jitters.

Cochrane had noticed too. 'Piece of cake, old chum,' he said in a kindly tone, but added, 'as long as you don't get Miteiriya Ridge.'

'It's all the same to me,' grunted Porter.

Cochrane looked at Kit and raised his eyebrows. 'Good show, Sergeant. Perhaps we can make sure you get the Ridge every time.'

In the flight tent, by the light of a paraffin lamp, Hallam the operations officer spread out his map on a trestle table. 'Okay, gentlemen, your targets for today.' He traced a wavering line running south from the coast. 'For the new boy, our forward minefields. Concentrations of our forces here.' His finger stabbed the fabric in a dozen places. 'The opposition is gathered all the way from the El Taqa Plateau way down here, to Mersa el Hamza in the north, close enough to the sea for Rommel to go paddling. We've had reports of infantry movements everywhere, from El Wishka to Bab el Qattara, and armour assembled in strength on a broad front. They know we're coming but intelligence reports indicate that they don't think we're ready to mount an attack. They're short on reliable gen because the brown jobs have got radio intercepts buttoned up and the Desert Air Force has been doing its stuff, knocking the Luftwaffe reconnaissance types out of the sky. What info the Jerries have gathered suggests to them, apparently, that Monty will not give the green light until the middle of November at the earliest, a month from now. What I can tell you fellows is that they have never been more wrong. A lot of important people are depending on you characters to come back with the goods, and a lot of lives depend on it. Now here are your objectives.'

Kit took the list of a dozen names and Hallam stepped back out of the light. The pilots leaned in, like gamblers round a croupier's table, as Kit identified the targets on the map and allocated two or three to each man: El Daba, Deir el Dhib, Tel el Eisa, El Mreir, Tel el Makh Khad . . .

'And Miteiriya Ridge?' murmured Cochrane, close to Kit. 'Our new recruit seems keen.'

But Kit did not smile. 'I'll take that. I know the score.'

There was time for a mug of tea and hash beef and eggs. The sun was higher now, a trembling blood-red globe, and the first flies were gathering, blackening the exposed food in the mess tent. Kit sat at the bare wooden table with Tom Keeble, Cochrane, Porter and Johnny Grimshaw, the flight's free spirit, who had once, beating up his fighter base in Kent, shattered the propeller of his Hurricane on the control tower masts and landed, wheels up, on a runway under repair. Jumping from the cockpit he had been confronted by his commanding officer. 'Good afternoon, sir,' Grimshaw had said. 'Meet Mr Grimshaw, ex-RAF.'

At the court martial he had escaped with loss of seniority and a severe reprimand, and had promised to behave. When he volunteered for photo reconnaissance, his squadron leader had endorsed his application with obvious satisfaction saying: 'At least there, the only neck you'll be responsible for breaking is your own.'

Now Grimshaw stretched out a hand to Porter. 'Greetings, old boy. We haven't been properly introduced. Greasy Grimshaw.'

'Greasy?' said Porter.

'The chaps reckon I'm a bit of a scruff-bag, but I say what's the point of sprogging yourself up in this benighted country? I scrub up all right in Cairo.'

'Yeah, we know about you in Cairo,' said Cochrane. He turned to Porter. 'This is the clot who was told the prossies there practised oral sex. "Christ," says our Greasy, "I want to do it, not talk about it".'

'Utter rot, of course,' said Grimshaw. 'I don't need to pay for crumpet. Women flock round me like flies.'

'Correction,' said Cochrane. 'It's flies that flock round you like flies.' He turned to Porter, who was stubbing out a cigarette on his plate. The hot ash fizzed as it burned into the grease. 'So, Blenheims then?'

'Anything wrong with that?'

'Not a thing, brother, not a thing.' A crooked grin. 'Though I've never been much interested in twins myself.'

'Bloody good kites, actually,' said Porter. 'Can't expect a fighter boy to agree, of course.'

'Oh, I agree all right. Keep your shirt on, old sport. Anyway, you're a fighter boy yourself now.'

'Flying a Spit doesn't make me a fighter boy. This is a different game. The aeroplane might be the same, but it seems to me it's no place for tally-ho types. I reckon PR calls for a bit of maturity and commonsense. That's why I chose to get involved.'

'Really?' said Cochrane. 'Well, we're sure as hell glad to have you on board, Sergeant. I know we're all going to benefit from the experience.'

Porter's frown faded. He seemed pleased. 'Of course it works both ways,' he said. 'No doubt there's stuff I need to pick up, but I've got plenty of ideas of my own. I was known for it in my squadron.'

Kit listened in silence, sipping his tea slowly. 'All right, fellows,' he said finally, 'break it up. Time for us to take a look-see at what Jerry's been up to.'

As he walked back to his tent to prepare for the sortie, Tom Keeble fell in beside him. 'Trouble there, do you think?'

'Porter? Yes, a bit of a pain in the neck. I only hope he'll realise he's got to muck in with the rest of us, and do things our way. A few dodgy trips should sort him out. It usually does.'

'Still, be a pity if a member of the awkward squad put his oar in just when you've got the flight as you want it. The way things are, it's very much to your credit.'

'What are you getting at, Tom?'

'The boys look up to you, you know. A reassuring presence. It counts for a lot, you having been through the mill: France, Malta, in the thick of it, and now here. They've all done their bit, of course, but none of them have been in it from the start.'

Kit did not reply, ducking his head to enter the tent.

'The grapevine says they'll be raising PR flights to squadron status at some point in the near future,' said Keeble. 'How does Squadron Leader Curtis sound?'

Kit turned, his flying helmet and goggles in his hand. 'I don't know who you've been talking to, Tom, but I'll take things as they come, thanks. Always have.'

Keeble reddened, aware of the contrast between the man he shared quarters with, somewhat formal and reserved in an old-fashioned way, but always courteous and considerate, and the flight commander – single-minded, uncompromising, with a vitriolic tongue.

'Well,' he said awkwardly, 'I'll see you at take-off.'

Kit did not reply, and was not aware that Keeble had gone. But for a moment he allowed himself to think about A Flight, twenty miles away at Deir el Munassib, operating independently but, on paper at least, part of the same unit. A Flight was led by Percy Briggs, an amiable pre-war regular, his flying skills only average, his navigation fallible, often returning from a trip with a target missed and a thin excuse. To the junior pilots he was No Pix Percy, but he was well regarded by the senior ranks, lulled by his air of authority and reminiscences about the early days of photographic development at Heston. What Keeble did not know, because Kit had not told him, was that he already knew about the rumours of a squadron being formed. He had been alerted by Percy Briggs himself, in the bar of Shepherd's Hotel. There, downing a whisky and signalling for another, Briggs had dropped a hint or two before the Johnnie Walker did its work, and he began to discuss the possibility as though it was accomplished fact.

'How do you know all this?' Kit had asked.

Briggs had tapped his nose, suggesting he enjoyed a confidence with his superiors up the line, and quickly made it plain that he also expected to take command. 'Job for an old hand, my boy. Someone with chums in the right places, when strings need to be pulled. In a squadron's interests, of course.' He had smiled contentedly. 'Ah yes, everything comes in time.' Then he had added: 'And when the time does come, Curtis, I know I can count on you.'

Kit remembered murmuring; 'Of course, of course.' But wondering: count on him for what?

Now, he amazed himself by thinking, even for a moment, about such petty considerations, at this time and place. It was a part of him he did not like, this need to compete, to put himself forward, to suggest, even in some subtle way, that he was better than the next man. But for a squadron to pass, almost by default, into the hands of a man like Percy Briggs would be hard to bear. More, it would be unjust. He wondered who he could talk to, on his next leave. Brewster, perhaps, his old CO in France and Malta, now a wing commander doing something with bombers at Heliopolis, just outside Cairo. Hardly playing the game, of course, but what was the alternative? Stand back, and let it happen, and find himself under the thumb of Percy Briggs, who was known to take credit for all successes and was equally quick to blame others for failures?

Feeling a stab of guilt at wasting time, he picked up the little writing board that, once settled in the cockpit, he would strap to his thigh, and scanned the four targets he had listed there in pencil. They were carefully printed in capitals, with precise directions: map references, topographical features, dispositions of flak positions, concentrations of Luftwaffe squadrons – the *Geschwader*. The entry for Miteiriya Ridge looked no different from the rest.

Down by the improvised runway Kit waved off his pilots, one by one. Another PR custom, for the flight commander to see his men safely in the air before setting off himself. No stirring sight of Spitfires, throttles on take-off boost, lifting away from the runway line abreast and wheeling in finger-four formation, before making a final pass and rising, armed and vigilant, to meet whatever might lie beyond the clouds. Instead, at irregular intervals, the single PR fighters taxied out and turned into wind, before climbing smoothly away, quickly gaining height and following different courses until, blue on blue, they were lost to sight. From that point only one man knew how a sortie went: the pilot who flew alone, isolated at the controls, ears ringing from the engine-roar, eyes flicking from his instruments to the unfriendly sky, checking his position, ticking off his objectives as he completed his photographic runs. He would not be heard from until, much later, he touched down. Though sometimes it did not happen that way. Instead, just silence, the others waiting for the telephone to ring to say their man had put down at a forward base, held up for some reason or another; short on fuel, ropey engine, flak damage to the controls or peppered by a free-hunt Messerschmitt 109. And when the telephone did not ring – well, that was that. Another man had vanished, fate unknown.

The ground-crew had run up the engine of the Spitfire IV Kit was to fly that day. It was shut down now but heat still radiated from beneath the cowlings. It was quite new, shipped out to Gibraltar on a carrier, then flown across the Straits to Egypt, at 30,000 feet to avoid detection. Kit had not taken the controls of this particular machine before. The flight did not believe in assigning pilots their personal aeroplanes.

He laid his parachute on the port wing, then began to walk slowly round the silent fighter with Flight Sergeant Matthews.

The usual routine, but rigorous, as carefully carried out as that first time years ago, at flying training. In the air was not the place to spot or remedy a problem.

Kit checked the alignment of the panel screws, tapped the still-hot exhaust stubs with a knuckle, listening for an off-note that might suggest a crack, ran his hand over the surface of the propeller blades and tugged at them to assess the degree of movement. Wheels and tyres, brakes and undercarriage bay – all okay. Now the wings, the leading and trailing edges, top surface, ailerons, flaps – okay as well. Panels all secured. Tailwheel fine. On to the tailplane. Elevators and rudder moving full and free. He crouched down and looked along the fighter's belly, where the recessed twin F.52 cameras were located, facing vertically but very slightly angled to overlap the target and increase the field of coverage. Each was three foot tall with a magazine of film in place, and it seemed impossible that they should be contained in the slim fuselage of a Spitfire.

'Have the technicians done their stuff, Flight?'

'Cameras loaded and ready, sir.'

'Righty ho. Anything else I need to know?'

'Nothing reported, sir. Flying Officer Grimshaw flew her last. No complaints.'

Kit returned to the port side of his machine, made a small adjustment to the position of his parachute resting on the wing, then turned round and shrugged on the straps. He grunted as Matthews helped him pull them tight. Waddling clumsily now, he jabbed the right toe of his flying boot into the stirrup-step near the wing-root, pulled himself up onto the wing and stepped into the cockpit, wriggling down ready for the Sutton harness to be secured. He pulled on his helmet and goggles, plugging in the oxygen and radio leads, strapped the small writing board to his right thigh and pushed a map into a handy space near the hinged door. In front of him, on top of the instrument panel just behind the windscreen, the usual gunsight had been replaced with the control box for the cameras. It was odd at first, had taken some getting used to. On his early PR trips Kit, like all those with combat experience, had felt naked and exposed.

Matthews leaned in and helped him secure the heavy webbing of the Sutton. Then the NCO nodded, grinned, raised a thumb and jumped down from the wing.

Kit ran through the familiar cockpit procedure: battery check, radiator flap open, trim controls moving freely. He rotated the fuel tank lever to reserve, for starting, to confirm the flow. He would change it to main feed for take-off.

Outside, the airmen were gathered round the Spitfire, staring up. Twin green lights told Kit that the undercarriage was down and locked. He knew that, of course, but it confirmed the system was active. He scanned the flight and engine instruments, dormant now, soon to spring alive. He looked down at the waiting airmen and gave a thumbs-up, then opened the throttle half an inch and set the fuel mixture to weak. Brakes on, ignition switches on. He pressed the starter button. The engine churned and coughed. The propeller began to turn, in fitful bursts of power, flame and blue-white smoke gouting back from the exhaust stubs. He was sweating in the cockpit. He gave the priming pump two or three strokes to make sure the suction and delivery fuel pipes were full. He felt the sudden increase in resistance that told him they were. Then the Merlin caught, the airframe shaking to its song, the propeller a shimmering arc.

Kit jerked his thumb backwards to the ground-crew. Two men ran to the tailplane and perched themselves on the leading edges, legs dangling. He ran the engine up to take-off revs, stick hard back, brakes on, wheels still chocked, the airmen caught in a storm of sand and dirt and grit, arms across their faces, eyes and mouths firm shut. Again his attention focused on the engine instruments, looking for a drop in revs. It was a careful process, laborious even, no detail missed but it had helped to keep him alive through four years of war. Another check of the flying controls, rudder, ailerons, elevator, to ensure they were working to their full extent. He eased the revs and the airmen jumped off the tailplane, running on the crouch, spitting away the filth and wiping their mouths and eyes.

A final look round: cockpit hood locked back, emergency exit door set half-open. You never knew. Mixture rich now. Flaps up. Radiator shutter open. Propeller in fine pitch.

Kit gave the pushing, sideways sign for the ground-crew to remove the chocks and, freed and ready at last, he taxied out and turned into what little wind there was. He increased the throttle, and as the speed picked up there was a bounding lightness to the wheels as they skimmed the ground. He eased the stick forward a little, raising the tailwheel to achieve a level attitude, counteracting the torque of the 1,000-horsepower engine tugging him to the left with a coarse right rudder. He felt the lift beneath the flexing wings, and then the airfield fell away. Undercarriage retracted, he climbed quickly, at 170 mph. The sky was clear, a fathomless, unmarked, pleasing shade of blue, the sky you hoped for on an English summer holiday by the sea, but here lethal, offering no hiding place.

At 19,000 feet he throttled back and set a course for the Miteiriya Ridge. Better to get the tough one in the bag first. No point in snapping softer stuff, and then risk losing the lot to those damned Panzergrenadiers with their towed 37mm guns and heavier 88mm artillery pieces dug in on the Ridge, as deadly to aircraft as tanks. It was the heaviest concentration of batteries on the Front and, as the flight had soon discovered, the gun-crews were damnably good at their jobs, sharp-eyed, alert to the slightest murmur of an aero-engine, quick to pinpoint an intruder's altitude, whatever height it might come in, and adept at loosing rapid salvoes of uncomfortably accurate fire. It had earned a reputation, Miteiriya Ridge. When they had first arrived at the Alam el Halfa forward field its very notoriety had appealed to the bolder, newer members of the flight, keen to make their mark and establish themselves as Miteiryia hands. Pip Elliott lasted less than a week, but at first Roy Bridger had seemed untouchable, following his own mysterious modus operandi – until he too disappeared. That shook the others and Kit, as flight commander, took it on.

Now, he began to gain altitude. He would make two runs across the Ridge, one on a north-easterly course, the other south-east. If he was still alive that would take him neatly towards his next target, a build-up of armour at Deir el Qatami. He already knew from his notes on the writing board what height was required, and what speed, to suit the focal length of the two cameras positioned behind him. Crisp, detailed prints were a matter of pride. When the moment came he would set the time interval on the control box to eight seconds, flying straight and steady, while the cameras recorded what lay below, each lens angled to provide 60 per cent of longitudinal overlap, missing nothing.

He could see the Ridge now, a smudge on the horizon. The dun-grey arid landscape passed slowly beneath his wings. No sign of habitation, a terrain suited only for war, valueless in itself, but its vast expanses the key to victory in North Africa. Soon the Allies and the Axis would be locked in combat on a line of battle that stretched from the waters of the Mediterranean to the immense, dead trough that was the Qattara Depression, the size of Wales, one-third salt marsh and all of it impassable to man, unless he rode a camel.

At 30,000 feet and growing close to his objective, Kit inclined his head to the right and looked back through the teardrop window in the cockpit hood. No sign of a telltale vapour trail that would have the crews of the Junker 88s racing to their positions, or yellow-nosed Messerschmitt Me-109Fs being scrambled from one of the Luftwaffe's Tunisian bases.

But soon enough, he knew, he would be seen, and flak would start to appear, small black puffs of smoke, innocuous-looking with a bright red core, exploding at pre-set heights with a muffled crump, filling the sky with keening shards of metal. That was the time to be steady, not deviate from the course, fight down the impulse to weave or climb or dive, not think, not think of anything but the task in hand.

He gulped in oxygen through his mask and narrowed his eyes against the glare, intense even behind the tinted lenses of his goggles. When he widened his eyes again, red blobs floated across his vision, then cleared. He glanced down at his instruments, the routine minute-by-minute check, almost unconsciously done. But always oil pressure first. And saw, with an intake of breath, that the needle on the vertical gauge showed only forty pounds, twenty less than normal. Instantly he throttled back. Oil was running back from the engine, down the port wing root and whipping off the trailing edge. No chance of Miteiriya Ridge now, or any other target. All he could do was try to reach the nearest friendly base or, failing that, bale out and let the machine destroy itself. To belly-land in the desert was not an option. The Front was fluid and a PR machine could not be allowed to fall into the hands of the enemy.

He pushed forward on the control column, to steepen his angle of descent. The engine was still available to him but he wanted to conserve its power, and use his height to put the Spitfire down. Besides, with oil pressure lower still, down to thirty pounds, and oil temperature climbing, the Merlin, if pressed too hard, could seize and, given his location, that would be the end. He reached out for the map stowed near the exit door. Alam el Halfa was out of the question. He needed to pancake now. The map confirmed what he already knew, that Deir el Munassib, home to A Flight and Percy Briggs, was his only hope. He permitted himself a wry smile, imagining Briggs's reaction, if he made it. 'Bad luck, old boy. But I'll get my lads to look at it. Now they *really* know their stuff.'

He completed a gentle turn on a course for Deir el Munassib. The altimeter needle was unwinding, not fast because he was using all his flying skill to conserve his height, but fast enough. He was down to 28,000 feet, whispering through the air. He fought against the instinct to ease back on the control column and increase the angle of attack. To tyro pilots it seemed like common sense to extend the glide by flattening out, but in fact, nose-high, an aeroplane's descent was steeper, faster, covering fewer miles and risked a stall. Yet still his gloved hand twitched on the stick. He remembered running low on petrol in his Riley Nine, on a Scottish car rally in 1936, the needle of the fuel gauge on reserve, the checkpoint twenty miles away; recalled the inclination to go faster, cover miles more quickly, when the proper course was to idle along in the highest gear. There was the suspense to contend with too; the uncertainty over whether that checkpoint could be reached or, as now, whether you might survive; the same impatience to know the outcome, of wanting it to be over.

At least he seemed to have the sky to himself; there were no distant black dots, growing more distinct, showing finally as a *Schwarm* of Jerry fighters. His airspeed was down to 120 mph. The oil pressure had sunk past twenty-six pounds and the engine temperature was rising fast, although he had opened the radiator shutter for maximum cooling

After fifteen minutes that seemed more like an hour, he made out marks on the desert floor, regular man-made patterns; patterns that, as he drew closer, became a runway, encircling perimeter roads, a scattering of tents, with here and there a few parked fighters, discernible under draped camouflage nets. Deir el Munassib.

No time for formalities. Only one opportunity to put her down. If he opened up to go round again, the engine would probably fail. He would stall, and spin in, powerless to do more than sit back and enjoy the accident, as a certain American pilot had once said.

He turned the machine to line up with the runway. With the engine on tickover the propeller was windmilling, barely under power, rotating in the passage of air. The cockpit hood was locked open, and he could smell burning oil and baked metal. His under-carriage was down, the green indicator lights bright against the dull grey of the instrument panel. He was approaching at 95 mph, controlling his airspeed with minute adjustments to the control column. He lowered the flaps and immediately his speed dropped. He wanted a slow landing, to cut the time it took him to stop and, if something went wrong, to reduce the effects of a crash.

He was closer to the ground now, aware in his peripheral vision of movement to his left, of vehicles setting off from the central knot of tents, trailing swirling clouds of dust. He was flying level, just above the runway, slower, slower with every second, approaching stalling speed, sinking foot by foot. He was holding the stick well back and the aircraft's nose was rising. Stick against his stomach now. Nothing to do but wait. At last the aircraft stalled and dropped the last few feet. He touched down, all three wheels meeting the scrubbed limestone surface simultaneously, a perfect three-point landing.

He allowed the Spitfire to roll some way before gently applying the brakes. The engine was still running, hesitant and uneven, spitting fire from the stub exhausts, and he shut it down quickly, to minimise further damage. Three vehicles had slid to a halt beside him – a fire tender, a battered Morris ambulance and a small Austin saloon. A corporal was quickly on the wing.

'Are you all right, sir?'

'What does it look like?'

'Well, you are and you aren't.'

'That about sums it up.'

'Flight Lieutenant Curtis, isn't it, sir? I recognise you from Helio.'

'What? Oh yes, Heliopolis.'

'Crikey. I can see your problem.' The corporal's feet were slip-ping on green-black oil.

'See if I saved the engine, will you? I did my best to get her down in one piece, but I think it might be cooked. Is Flight Lieutenant Briggs at home?'

'He is, sir. Sent a car.'

Kit undid his harness, unplugged his oxygen and radio leads, placed his hands on the frame of the windscreen and pulled himself upright. He stepped out onto the wing and his feet slid on the oil, but the corporal caught his arm and steadied him. He snatched his arm away. He was consumed with anger, did not want to be touched, felt an unreasoning impulse to lash out.

Men had gathered round the tailplane, where oil was dripping from the fuselage and creating a widening pool in the dirt. 'That's where a lot of it collected, sir,' said a sergeant, 'forced back from the engine.' They had the Spitfire's engine cowling off. An airman shouted: 'Looks like a fractured oil pipe, Sarge.'

'That's no good to me, Sergeant,' said Kit. 'I want a proper report and I want it double quick. Get to it. I need to fly this aeroplane back to Alam el Halfa, with the minimum of delay.' He knew, when he said it, that he was asking for the impossible. But it was the last small influence he could apply to a thorough-going foul-up. 'Now where do I find your flight commander?'

As the Austin squeaked to a halt outside the flight control tent, Percy Briggs looked up from some papers he was signing. 'Hello, Curtis. I thought it was you.'

'Will you tell your radio chaps to let my fellows know I've pancaked? Say I'm otherwise okay, and the kite's in one piece. I'll be in touch again as soon as I've got some up-to-date gen.'

'Done all that, old boy.' Briggs applied a final signature, and laid down his fountain pen. 'Asked myself what I'd expect in your place.' He nodded, smiling. 'Anticipation. Staying one step ahead. Makes for an efficient outfit.'

'Not up then?' said Kit, jerking his head skywards.

'Oh, I do a trip from time to time. But my chaps are pretty keen, you know. They're more than happy to leave old Uncle at home.' Briggs cleared his throat, and added quickly: 'They're well aware, of course, that I wouldn't ask them to do anything I'm not prepared to do myself. But you have to let the young bloods have their head. Besides,' he indicated the papers on his desk, 'I have certain requests from on high to deal with.'

'Really?' said Kit. 'Such as?'

'Can't tell you that, old boy.' Briggs turned the top page face down. 'Cup of tea?'

'You read my mind,' said Kit. 'Anticipation again, I suppose.'

Briggs looked at him doubtfully, but Kit was staring out through the tent flap. On the other side of the airfield men were busy about his machine. Minutes passed, as they drank their tea from tin mugs, and Briggs rearranged his documents. Kit allowed the silence to hang between them.

Finally, Briggs said: 'No more news about this squadron business?' It was less a statement, more a question, probing.

'I wouldn't know,' said Kit. 'The high-ups don't confide in me.'

'No,' said Briggs, recovering himself. 'I mean, there *is* no more news. And not likely to be until after Monty's big push.'

'So you have heard something,' said Kit innocently.

'Stands to sense.' Briggs paused, and changed the subject. 'It's funny, you know. I never thought I'd find myself in a shooting-war.'

'It's what one joins for, surely?'

'Of course.'

'Tell me,' said Kit. 'I'd like your opinion. Do you think our cause is just?'

'Odd question, Curtis, but yes, absolutely.'

'So how do you view our Bolshie chums? Gallant allies now, of course, but they'd still be at our throats, if Hitler hadn't done the dirty on them. What would we have been calling them then?'

'Not quite sure I get your drift, old boy.'

'Let's face it, everybody knows the Russians are doing frightful things to their own people. It's just as much a totalitarian state as Germany, but now we're required to turn a blind eye. It all seems rather different to how we started out, after France fell, alone, with the odds against us, and the slimmest chance of victory. Simple then. A very English war, with right unquestionably on our side. I think it suited us extremely well. But now, strange bedfellows, wouldn't you say? At the stroke of someone's pen, an enemy becomes a friend. For the moment at least.'

'You can't afford to be choosy if you want to win.'

'Ah, the pragmatic view. So you'd say God is still with us?'

'Why wouldn't He be? He understands. The greater good, and all that sort of thing.' Briggs shook his head, like a schoolmaster confronted with an ignoramus. 'You've got to be realistic, Curtis. Without the Soviets and Americans on our side, I reckon we'd have been for the high jump, whatever Winston said.' Briggs always used Churchill's Christian name, as though he had a direct line to Downing Street.

'Oh, I'm sure the Allies will prevail,' said Kit. 'Sheer weight of resources dictates that, although the cost is going to be very great. But who knows if it will be for the greater good, in the longer term? The Fascists must be beaten, no doubt of that. But what then? Who will win the peace, if there is a peace? The eagle or the bear? It won't be the lion, that's for sure.'

'You've lost me, old man. I don't concern myself with politics. I just do my duty. Quite honestly, I think you'd be well advised to do the same. No offence intended.' He leaned forward. 'Incidentally, talking of our Yankee brethren, I hear your chum Wolf is in hot water again.'

'Not exactly a chum.'

'Rum sort of cove, if you ask me. Rummer still when you hear what he's been up to. Upset a load of bigwigs on some sort of American junket to help the war effort. Apparently put the fear of God into a bunch of trainee pilots, just when they were about to sign on the dotted. Went down very badly with the powers-that-be.'

'Ah, them again,' said Kit.

The thickset figure of the sergeant had detached itself from the group of airmen and was hurrying across the runway towards them. He came into the tent, his face streaked with grime, breathing hard, and saw Kit seated by Briggs's desk. 'It's as we suspected, sir . . .'

'*I'll* take your report, Sergeant,' said Briggs.

The sergeant swivelled on his heels. 'Yes, sir. As we suspected. Fractured oil pipe, tank virtually empty, fourteen gallons gone.' He glanced at Kit. 'Me and the lads reckon that was quite a show of airmanship, sir, you getting her down like that.'

'Thank you,' said Kit.

'I'm sure Flight Lieutenant Curtis doesn't require your opinion about his flying skills,' said Briggs.

'No, sir,' said the sergeant. 'Sorry, sir.'

'So what's the verdict, Sergeant? Did I save the engine?'

''Fraid not, sir. Metal in the filters.'

'Damn.'

'I'll get one of our chaps to fly you over to Alam el Halfa in the Proctor,' said Briggs, when the sergeant had gone.

'Thanks awfully.' Kit wondered, briefly, if he had treated Briggs quite fairly. 'Pity about that engine,' he said. 'Blasted oil pipe fracturing like that. Nobody's fault, of course.'

'Perhaps you're right,' said Briggs.

'There's no perhaps about it.'

'Still,' said Briggs, 'it might be worth checking out your other engines, when you get back, for signs of fatigue. It's what I'd do.' He patted Kit on the back. 'Just a piece of friendly advice, old man.'

When the Proctor landed at Alam el Halfa, Kit was met by Tom Keeble.

'Glad to see you back, Kit,' the intelligence officer said. 'Thought you were a goner.'

'The engine is, but at least the kite's in one piece. Percy Briggs swears he'll have it back in commission in a matter of days.'

'He's got some good ground-crew boys over there.'

'Don't you start.'

'Some bad news, I'm afraid. One of the chaps hasn't turned up.'

'Who?'

'Sergeant Porter.'

'Christ, on his first trip?'

'Well, it happens.'

'No reports? Nothing spotted?'

'No, we've drawn a blank. Let's hope he's in the bag.'

'Fat lot of good to me. Not worth his ticket out here. I thought he was taking things too damned casually.'

Kit remembered Porter's easy assurance, smoking a Woodbine as the dawn came up, preparing for the sortie. 'This is a different game from the one you've been used to, Porter,' he'd said, and Porter, shrugging; had replied: 'Obviously.' What else might he have said to the man? 'For God's sake, Porter, don't be so damned complacent. Okay, so this is your first trip. But, for some chaps, it's been their last.' Now he said: 'What about the rest of them, Tom? Did they deliver the goods?'

'The magazines went into the dispatch rider's pouches fifteen minutes ago. They should be at processing already.'

'Without Miteiriya Ridge.'

'No, no, young Finlay was on standby. He covered that, when we heard you were on the deck. Landed full of himself, of course. Pretty good show though, you have to admit.'

'I'll tell him so,' said Kit.

'Another thing,' Keeble added. 'No ops until further notice. Wing says the mosaic's pretty well complete. We've covered every blasted foot of Rommel's territory.'

'Doesn't sound like Wing. They always ask for more.'

'Maybe it's significant.'

'Maybe,' said Kit.

On his way back to the flight tent, he thought about Ossie Wolf. 'Went down very badly with the powers-that-be.' Yes, that sounded like Wolf. He marvelled that someone had thought it wise to involve him in some kind of stunt. Call it a morale-booster, call it helping the war effort, call it what you want. Stunt it clearly was, and the only stunts Ossie Wolf could be trusted with were at the controls of a fighter plane.

He also seemed to hear a thin voice in the great void that lay beyond the boundaries of the airfield. A voice from the morning, only hours ago: 'Seems to me this is no place for tally-ho types. I reckon it calls for a bit of maturity and common sense.' Sergeant Porter had not been given the chance to prove his point. Obviously . . .

In the flight tent Pat Hallam was reading a transcript of a radio message. He looked up and, without a word, passed it to Kit, who scanned it quickly. 'When did this come in?'

'A few minutes ago. The show's on the road, or will be tonight. They're calling it Operation Lightfoot.'

'Appropriate, considering the number of minefields the brown jobs are going to have to pick their way through.'

'They've chosen their time well – one day before a full moon. Gives the sappers a chance.'

'Thank God I didn't join the Army.'

'Absolutely,' said Kit. 'Have you caught up with Montgomery's Order of the Day? Turning point of the war, one of the decisive battles of history, watched by the eyes of the whole world, every officer and man to fight and to kill, and hit the enemy for six, right out of Africa.'

'Stirring stuff.'

'Touch facile, though, wouldn't you say? That cricket analogy?'

'Oh, I think you're rather hard on the little man,' said Hallam. 'He may be prone to a touch of bullshit, but he makes no bones about what's involved. In fact, he's been accused of whipping up bloodlust among the men, so they go into battle wanting nothing more than to kill Germans. After all,' added Hallam, 'that's what we're here for.'

'Yes,' said Kit. 'Killing Germans. That's the game.' The game that Ossie Wolf had understood from the start, before the others had begun to realise that these were the rules you played by; when Kit had thought of deeds of arms, acquitting himself well, earning the respect of his comrades, proving his valour against a worthy foe; detesting the regime for which his opponent stood, but respecting a fellow pilot. He remembered a time in France in November 1939, when the squadron was sitting out the Phoney War on its makeshift airfield at Revigncourt, near Metz, not far from the Franco-German border, waiting for Hitler to make his move. A time when Wolf, still a sergeant pilot and with no kills to his name, had raged: 'While guys like you are flying round the fucking clouds like Sir Lancelot looking for the Holy Grail, down below the Krauts will be destroying civilisation. Wise up, buster. There's only one rule you need to remember: do it to him before the sonofabitch does it to you.' But then the American had the advantage on them all. He had fought for the Republicans in Spain and knew the score, before he had escaped to Britain and volunteered to fly for the RAF and continue his fight against the Fascists.

Now men were wiser, tempered by three years of war, and Kit reflected that, while Montgomery might not have approved of Ossie Wolf's language, he would certainly have supported the sentiment.

He remembered the last time he had seen Wolf, stalking down a corridor in the Air Ministry, his crumpled service cap set low over his eyes, his hands deep in his trouser pockets, seeming not to listen to the man at his shoulder, a major in the US Army Air Corps, who appeared to be cajoling him in some way. Ossie had barely paused.

'Hey, Curtis, how you doing?'

'Okay, thanks. Just finished PR training.'

'Photo reconnaissance? What in hell for?'

'I'll tell you some time.'

'Know where they're posting you?'

'Oh, yes. And you?'

'I'll tell you some time. Well, see you around.'

'Yes, as you say, see you around.'

That had been months ago. Now Kit looked at the Order of the Day, held lightly in his hand. It was dated 23 October 1942. Friday, he saw with some surprise. Autumn light would be washing over the green folds of Lynch Down, below the big house on the rim of its valley near Midhurst. His father, despite his stroke, would be with Ben, the Airedale, both of them aged and moving slowly, step for step. The weekend lay ahead, with its small traditions, the old man too frail in this busy season to more than watch a hired man clear the leaves or give the lawn a final cut; then a browse through the magazines and newspapers that had accumulated in the hall, unread; perhaps an English roast, a parody now with the joint no bigger than a child's ball, but the beef aroma redolent of times past and, perhaps, of better times to come. So the routine went, the weekend preserved like some perpetual holiday, to be anticipated, planned for, a special time although, in reality, for Farve each day passed much as another. It was an illusion made real by custom, that suggested England had not changed so very much.

Pat Hallam was still extolling the fighting spirit of the Commander of the Eighth Army. 'It's even been reported that Monty told an officers' meeting that padres should kill Germans too. One on weekdays, two on Sundays. Everybody hooted, I understand.'

Kit could not laugh, or smile. Death was stalking in the growing shadows of the desert, waiting for the killing game to start.

TWO

Ossie Wolf watched London pass by his taxi window. It was a month since he had shipped out from Malta. His stay in hospital had been short. It was ironic. After surviving a hundred battles in the air, unmarked, he had fallen to an attacker's knife in an alley running off 'The Gut', where Valletta's whores called after any uniform: 'Hey, you want nice time?'

The guys who had flown the *Ohio* patrol, and helped to escort the stricken oil tanker safely into port, had hit the town to celebrate. They didn't want a nice time – not that kind, at least. They wanted to savour being alive, immerse themselves in the city's *festa* spirit, walk the streets with thousands of Vallettans, drinking beer and *ambete*, the dangerous red wine dubbed 'Stuka juice', celebrating the Feast of the Assumption, 15 August, 1942, when the last vessels of Operation Pedestal had crawled into Grand Harbour with their cargoes of fuel and ammunition, mechanical spares and medical supplies; cargoes that enabled the garrison to fight on. They did not know it had saved the island. No one did, not then. But it was a happy time, after so much sorrow.

For Ossie, however, it had not been a happy time. The night had started badly, and ended worse. His head had been spinning, from the booze he had taken in to blank stuff out, and Malta Dog, the dysentery that left a lingering bite. He had seen, through eyes that barely focused, the figure of a man, a man who hollered

36

his name, coming towards him down the cobbled alley, silhouetted against the light from the main drag. And then he had been spun around, and something hit him in the ribs, a kind of punch but different, and there was a sticky wetness when his hands went to the spot. And going down, in the yellow wash of a street lamp, he had made out the face of a man he knew.

He did not tell the name, in hospital or later. He guessed, in a vague, unreasoning way, that maybe he'd had it coming, something of the sort. It kind of squared things up. He remembered that stuffed shirt Curtis, when they landed after he'd laced the German bomber crew in their dinghy off Mgarr harbour: 'You bastard, you murdering bastard.' Him pulling away. 'Oh, go to hell.' And Curtis catching him by the arm. 'You bloody butcher. I'm going to have you grounded.'

But before that could happen, he had wound up in Imtarfa military hospital with a nice, neat wound to his thoracic cavity – a hunter's knife, in and out. Minor laceration of the lung, no damage to the liver. A merciful escape, that hadn't been planned that way. Still, it was enough to put him in a bed and give him time to think about what, that *festa* night, he had tried so hard to forget. The girl, Claudia Farinacci, dead outside the Mellieha church, her blue-black hair tangled and spread out in the dust; Goofy Gates swinging under the canopy of his 'chute, above Dahlet ix-Xilep, but safe, until the yellow-nosed Messerschmitt 109 snapped off a burst and ripped the silk and Goofy fell two hundred feet to the rocks below the cliffs; and how, a little while later, he had dived his Spit, yelling Christ knew what, and thumbed his gun-button and watched as the crew of the downed Junkers 88, their dinghy rising and falling on the swell, safe too, had raised their arms to shield themselves from his cannon shells as they rushed towards them in two neat lines.

Now his taxi put him down in the Aldwych, close to the Strand Theatre. The posters told him about the current show, *Arsenic and Old Lace*, a comedy about murder. 'Packing 'em in,' his cabbie said. In a city where people died every night, it seemed kind of odd.

He walked slowly, virtually restored, Malta Dog subdued by drugs and a decent diet, his wound no more than a dull sensation, like a bruise. He turned into Kingsway and saw, across the street, behind the rush of traffic, Adastral House. It was three years since he had last been here, to volunteer as a pilot. He had been drinking too much and eating not enough, mixing with a crowd of spivs, chisellers and easy women in a clutch of dives off Piccadilly. Their small-time misdemeanours took his mind off what was happening big-time in Spain. Then he had been quite alone, living in a cheap hotel in Paddington, denounced by his own government for fighting for the Republican cause, a premature anti-fascist they said, and likely to forfeit his citizenship, although it did not come to that. He had not wanted to remember Spain, how Barcelona had fallen to the Nationalists without a fight, the leadership of the Left destroyed from within by squabbling factions. He had not read the British newspapers that told of the final fascist onslaught, supported by the forces of the Reich, as the world looked on, mute. Then, finally, through the fug of booze, he had begun to think about flying again, knowing that it was all caught up with Spain, and what had happened there, and wanting to stop it happening here. And so he had presented himself at the RAF recruiting office in Kingsway with impressive credentials as a flier, but a flier with a battered and neglected body, skeletal, marked with fresh bruises and abrasions from fist fights with Mosley's fascists.

But they took him, because the time was right to accept men with such skills, straight into intensive service training, and he gained his wings. He also gained two stone, eating regularly if not well, and acquired a taste for tea. Six weeks of operational training and he was assigned to Hurricanes, and found himself in France during the Phoney War, the *Drôle de Guerre*, waiting for Hitler to make his move.

Now, he crossed the road to Adastral House, presented his papers at reception and was directed to the third floor. He shared the lift with a WAAF flying officer and tried to start a conversation, but she gave him the brush-off in that raised-eyebrow way that English dames did so well. Besides, he guessed she had heard every angle, and everyone knew that Ministry dolls with rank only went for big shots with scrambled egg on their peaks. He stood back to let her leave the lift first, giving her his lopsided smile, but nothing doing. She avoided his eye and hurried away. He watched her go, appreciating the sway of her hips, the way her tunic pinched in around her narrow waist, then turned and headed along the bare corridor. Occasionally, doors opened, revealing interiors wreathed in tobacco smoke through which he glimpsed figures in blue uniforms bent over unknown tasks.

He stopped outside an office marked AMI(HOF), and could hear voices inside. He rapped on the door with his knuckles, once, twice. The voices broke off for a moment, and then resumed, so he went on in. Two men were there, one a wing commander, the other in the uniform of a major in the US Army Air Corps. There were two wall maps, one of Britain, one of North America, each dotted with coloured pins and crayonned dates. Some might have thought it impressive. To Ossie Wolf it looked like bullshit. He had an instinctive distrust of men in offices who stuck pins in maps.

'Flight Lieutenant Wolf,' he said, his salute a vague raising of the hand, like a man brushing away a fly.

Behind the wing commander's desk, through the sash window, criss-crossed with white bomb-blast tape, he could see, above the distant rooftops, barrage balloons, silver against a dull grey sky, nodding like Barnum circus beasts beyond the river, which coursed in flood between granite-faced banks. The wing commander swivelled in his chair, laid down a smoking pipe and eased himself to his feet with a grunt. 'For future reference, Wolf, we'd prefer it if you waited until we're quite ready for you. This is an intelligence operation, you know.'

'I reckoned you hadn't heard me.'

'Oh, we heard you all right. We were in conference.' The wing commander was fat and out of shape, with the pallor and bulk of a man who dined well and often. By the window, the American major looked Ossie up and down, then turned and stared out at the lugubrious balloons.

'I'm Booth,' said the wing commander. He indicated a tent-card on his desk, gold letters over black that said: *Wing Commander B.T. Booth*.

'Yeah,' said Ossie. 'I guess that's your desk all right.'

'I'm Winthrop,' said the major, without turning round.

'So,' said Ossie, 'what in hell is amihof?'

'Amihof? Oh, AMIHOF.' Booth looked mysterious. 'All will be revealed, in time.'

'How much time?' said Ossie. 'See, I got things to do.'

The major left the window and perched himself on the corner of the desk. He was chewing gum very slowly, parking it in his cheek when he talked. 'We know that, son. That's why you're here. You're going to be doing things for us.' He shook out a cigarette from a pack of Lucky Strike. Ossie took one and leaned forward for a light.

'So, Malta,' said the major. 'Quite a show.' Ossie said nothing, looking at him steadily. 'You did pretty well there. An all-American ace. Added to your score. How many victories is it now?'

Ossie shook his head. 'I kinda lost count.' In truth, it did not interest him. He looked to future kills.

'Twenty-one. Some going.'

'History,' Ossie said.

The major shrugged, and narrowed his eyes. 'By all means play the aw-shucks hero, Wolf. That's fine with us. Isn't it, Bernard?'

'Absolutely,' said the wing commander.

Ossie fixed his eyes on the medal ribbon above the left breast pocket of Booth's tunic, the blue, maroon and white that marked long service and good conduct. That was all. No wings. Booth knew that look, flashed quickly at those who did not fly by those who did. Nothing was ever said, but no pilot understood why, in an Air Force, there were men content to remain firmly on the ground, when hangars were full of aeroplanes waiting to be taken up.

'We fight a different kind of war here, Wolf,' said Booth. 'You'll find it's not without its value.'

'So, intelligence. Hush-hush, huh?'

'Not exactly, no. Quite the reverse, you might say. Our object-ive is to obtain as much publicity as possible. You're talking to Air Ministry Intelligence, Wolf. The Hand of Friendship Bureau.'

'Amihof.'

'That's it. Our aim is to promote the special relationship that exists between Britain and the United States, by talking to audi-ences on both sides of the Atlantic. The aims of the war, the nature of patriotism and duty, where and how they can do their bit, that kind of thing, coming from people they can respect. Men who have fought with distinction, like you. Opinion-formers, of course, minor royalty, politicians, the odd journalist.' He broke off, chuckling. 'What other sort is there? And faces they'd recog-nise from stage and screen.'

'Jesus. Actors?'

'You'd be amazed at the impact someone like Olivier has. Extremely rousing stuff. Besides,' Booth added, 'he is a serving officer in the Fleet Air Arm, so we are doubly blessed.' He drew on his pipe. 'Every pin you see marks the progress of one of our goodwill lecture tours. Factories, offices, universities, military bases. Anywhere we can raise morale. As I say, it's a two-way thing. Our people in the States, theirs over here. See this pin in Stockport? That's Tyrone Power.'

'In your case, son,' said Winthrop, 'you kind of fall in between. An American in the RAF. So you can present a pretty unique perspective.'

'Unique perspective, hell,' said Ossie. 'I don't want any part of this. Leave it to the goddamned politicos who got us into this mess, the pen-pushers feeding folk propaganda, chorus boys willing to spout whatever crap you guys can dream up.'

'Whoah, son,' said Winthrop. 'Easy now. If you're going to be an ambassador for the war effort, you're going to have to curb your language.'

'I'm no goddamned ambassador. The CME has passed me A1.B, operational for fighters.'

'We're well aware of the deliberations of the Central Medical Establishment,' said Booth. 'No doubt, in time, you'll find yourself back in action. Meanwhile, you've been assigned to us. The supply of pilots isn't as critical as it was in the early days. Even those of your ability can be spared, for a month or so at least.' He pointed at Ossie with the stem of his pipe. 'You have seen war. The victories, the defeats, the heroism, the hardships. You know what it takes to win. That,' another jab with the pipe stem, 'will be your message.'

'Do I have a goddamned say in this thing?' said Ossie.

'No,' said Booth. 'Well, perhaps that's not entirely true. But to refuse to cooperate would go down very badly, I'm afraid. Smacks of a want of patriotism, wouldn't you say – devotion to the cause? Bound to be chalked up as another black mark.'

'Another?'

Booth slid back a drawer in his desk and removed a file. He opened it and began to flick through papers, looking thoughtful. From time to time he glanced at Ossie, who smoked his Lucky Strike and puffed smoke towards the ceiling.

'You've led a colourful career, Flight Lieutenant. We've built up quite a dossier. December 1939, Revigncourt, Franco-German border. Suspected of disobeying orders and attacking an enemy base near Freudenstadt, risking the loss of two valuable Hurricane fighters, something we were rather short of at the time.' He scanned down the pages. 'Numerous examples of insubordination. Refusal to accept a commission. Rumpus in a London drinking den that left civilians injured. More recently the little matter of a Luftwaffe bomber crew machine-gunned in their dinghy north of Malta. No actual proof, so nothing taken further. But skating on very thin ice, I'd say. Yes, colourful, distinctly.'

Booth took up his pipe, tamped down the tobacco, and turned to another section in the file. 'Let's see. Privileged background, family wealthy brewers, St Louis, Missouri. Fluent German. Well, that came through the family, so it doesn't count. Otherwise a patchy academic record. Keen on flying, proved a natural pilot. Then, in 1936, you left for Europe on the *Bremen*, travelling first class no less, and made your way to Spain.' A pause. 'Where you flew with the Condor Legion, for the fascists.' He looked at Ossie reflectively. 'You didn't know we were aware of that, I imagine?'

Ossie's jaw began to work. 'I was just a naive punk getting mixed up with the wrong bunch, thanks to my old man. I got the picture soon enough.'

'Nonetheless . . .'

'One goddamned flight. They took me along as an observer, blasting the hell out of women and kids. I lit out of Burgos as soon as we landed from the Guernica trip.' He was fighting to contain his anger, his mind confused. Jesus, he was thinking, so Kit Curtis, the only man who knew all this, had spilled the beans. 'I reckon I know where this has come from,' he said.

'Not unless you have contacts in Berlin,' said Booth. 'Please don't tell me that. Otherwise, instead of standing up on your hind legs in front of a bunch of factory girls, you'll find yourself facing a firing squad. And we wouldn't want that, Wolf, would we, square peg though you be?' He and Winthrop exchanged a wry glance. 'No, whoever you suspect, and I advise you to be more careful with your friends, the truth is relatively mundane. You've achieved a small fame, with your face on the cover of *Picture Post*, reports of your exploits in the popular press, interviews on CBS and so forth. Inevitably it jogged some memories amongst our opposite numbers in the *Abwehr*, and naturally they were more than happy to enlighten us.' Booth turned a page. 'Let's see, after your sojourn in Burgos, you chose to support the Republican cause.'

Winthrop stopped chewing for a moment. 'Fascists, Communists. You seem to have covered the field, son.'

'I was no fascist,' said Ossie. 'I was for the people.'

'Ah, the people,' said Booth.

'Meaning?'

'No matter. And then you turned up here, somewhat the worse for wear, and the rest we know.' Booth closed the file. 'Why didn't you tell us all this when you volunteered?'

'Would you have taken me on?'

'Perhaps. Perhaps not.' The pipe was lit. 'Your father, Wolf, a real old *Volksdeutscher*, convinced that all true Aryans should answer the call.'

'Yeah,' said Ossie. 'Me in particular. If that sonofabitch was selling his beer in the Reich, he'd have a swastika on every bottle.'

'It would seem sensible,' said Booth to Winthrop, 'to omit St Louis from Wolf's schedule.'

'I don't want any goddamned schedule,' said Ossie. He saw a sudden spark of hope. 'Anyway, what about these *Abwehr* guys? They'll be on my case the moment I hit the road. They're not going to let this thing go.'

'Oh, I think they will,' said Booth. 'The world moves on. They have other considerations on their plate by now. Tipping us off was just a little low-grade mischief-making, not at all significant in the great scheme of things.'

'Look, son,' said Winthrop, like a reasoning parent with a recalcitrant child, 'you should take this opportunity in the spirit in which it's offered. It's an accolade, of a kind, and one that provides plenty of opportunity for a young feller like you to unwind a little, along the way. For example, we'll be shipping you out to the States on the *Queen Elizabeth*.'

'Uh-huh?' said Ossie. 'And when I get there, what the hell am I expected to say?'

'Leave that to us,' said Booth. 'We're the experts. You just read what we write for you, and press the flesh. To be candid, your countrymen are a getting a bit fed up with a parade of Britishers. They want some heroes of their own. You fit the bill.' His jowls trembled, and his small mouth formed itself into a slight smirk. 'Why, old man, you'll find they'll hang on your every word.'

'*Your* every word.'

Yet Ossie was beginning to feel resigned. So maybe it wasn't such a crazy idea after all. He still felt fatigued after the Malta tour, despite his CME rating. Even now his guts played up from time to time. And when he got back behind the controls, he needed to feel sharp and ready. He knew the penalty for dull reactions, the slightest decline in coordination between hand and eye, a split second of hesitation in thumbing the gun-button. He could find himself reduced, at first, to being an ordinary pilot, and ordinary pilots did not live too long. He was not afraid of dying, in fact expected it, but he wanted to live for a while yet, so he could be what he had been before, in fighting shape. So maybe, he thought, a month of R&R wouldn't be so bad, help get him back in fighting shape. And what had Winthrop said? Plenty of opportunities to unwind. Well, maybe Winthrop had a different understanding of the phrase. Ossie knew what it meant to him.

'Okay,' he said. 'Tell me what you got in mind.'

Later, in the corridor, Winthrop said: 'Go easy on our friend. Not everyone can be a hero.' He paused, waiting for Ossie to reply, but nothing came. 'I flew transports before the war, but my eyesight was always marginal. Then the medical got tougher. I didn't want to be around airplanes any more, not on the ground. Then this came up. Like Booth said, it's a different kind of war, but it has its place.' Still Ossie remained silent, as they moved slowly towards the lift. Winthrop chewed his gum for a while, then parked it. 'I realise you're not too tickled by all of this. That's understandable, for a feller like you, who likes to call the shots. On the q.t, son, as one American to another, there is another outfit where you'd have a bit more pull, though don't let on to Booth I told you so.'

'Oh, yeah?'

'You could always transfer from the RAF to the US Army Air Corps. We'd be proud to have you on board.'

'What?' said Ossie. 'Just when I've mastered the accent?'

As he neared the lift, with Winthrop hovering uncertainly at his shoulder, he saw Kit Curtis emerging from another office.

'Hey, Curtis, how you doing?'

'Okay, thanks. Just finished PR training.'

'Photo reconnaissance? What in hell for?'

'I'll tell you some time.'

'Know where they're posting you?'

'Oh, yes. And you?'

'I'll tell you some time. Well, see you around.'

The Englishman hesitated for a moment. 'Cheerio,' came more easily. Then he said: 'Yes, as you say, see you around.'

In the lift Winthrop began to chew his gum again, looking at his well-manicured fingernails. 'So, who's the swell?'

'Guy I know. He's okay.'

Winthrop stowed his gum. 'Well, it seems to me we've got ourselves a deal – the Stateside tour, I mean.'

'Seems that way.'

'I'll be tagging along.'

'To keep me in line, huh?'

'Oh, I'm just there to liaise, help us stick to the schedule, over-come any little problems that might arise, that kind of thing. But you won't be saddled with me all the while. I'm planning time out to visit my wife and kids in West Virginia. One of the perks when you're in this kind of business. When I'm not there, though,

46

you'll find plenty of folk on hand to make sure everything's running smoothly.'

'Sounds like you'll have me pinned down good.'

'Oh, you'll find we give you sufficient rope to have yourself some fun. But understand this. That doesn't mean a licence to raise hell. No feeling up the mayor's wife, no cussing in mixed company, no sinking so much juice you throw up over the Daughters of America. Don't let us down, Wolf. It's part of the deal. Remember, the honour of two countries is at stake.'

'I reckon I've got the objective pretty clear,' said Ossie. 'It's like the wing-co said.' He dropped into a bad approximation of Booth's fruity tones. 'I have seen the war. The victories, the defeats, the heroism, the hardships. I know what it takes to win. That will be my message.'

'Remember that, son,' said Winthrop, 'and everything will turn out swell.'

Later, in his club, Wing Commander Booth came across Rupert Pringle.

'Hello, Pringle. How are things in the War Office?'

'Hello, Grunter. Much as usual. Lots of war.'

'Had a chap in today I think you know. Yankee fellow. Oswald Wolf.'

'Good God. What do you want with him?'

'May wheel him out across the Pond. You knew him in Paris, I gather, during the Phoney War. Bit of a loose cannon, of course, but a wonderful war record. And he's perfect for Hand of Friendship, as an American volunteer. They're desperate over there for Yankee heroes. He's got the common touch as well.'

'That is certainly true,' said Pringle. 'In Paris he gave the phrase new meaning.' He moved towards the dining room. 'Well, no doubt you chaps know what you're doing. Wolf was a sergeant pilot when I encountered him in France. Perhaps the King's commission has had the desired effect. If not, Grunter, well, while the man is unquestionably deadly in the air, you may find he's even deadlier on the ground.'

'Oh Lord,' said Booth. 'I hope we haven't picked a wrong 'un.'

The Hand of Friendship tour began in Washington, where Ossie addressed a motley assemblage of senators of various persuasions, not merely Democrat and Republican. A few responded to his 'I have seen the war, I know what it takes to win' routine, rehearsed for many hours with Winthrop in hotel bedrooms, where the major wiped his brow and muttered: 'For crying out loud, Wolf, you may be a natural flier, but if oratory was flying they wouldn't let you near the darned hangar.'

Generally, though, the reception was, to say the least, mixed. In one of the more remote meeting rooms in the north wing of the Capitol building Ossie encountered not only his first attack of stage fright, but also isolationists, pro-Germans, anti-Communists and those who considered him a traitor to the flag, a left-wing mercenary who had sworn allegiance to a foreign king. He stumbled his way through his lines, answered questions that frequently resembled accusations in mumbled monosyllables, and left the podium to the merest smatter of applause.

'What's with those guys?' said Ossie. 'Not one goddamned question about flying.'

'Tough audience,' said Major Winthrop. 'It can only get better. Tomorrow it's Rosie the Riveter and her pals in a Philly ship-yard.'

'Jesus,' said Ossie. 'They sound plenty tough to me.'

Next day, delayed by fog that persisted throughout the bumpy flight, they were flown by Dakota to a military base near League Island, landing heavily on a runway lit by flares, where a Dodge sedan, decked out in warlike camouflage like the DC-3, took them the final mile or so to a naval shipyard, spread across a thousand acres on the banks of the Delaware River.

A US Navy lieutenant commander stepped forward, looking anxious. 'So you made it at last. Let's get you down to the canteen PDQ.' He hurried them past dry docks ringed by cranes, where ships were being constructed or repaired. 'Cruiser, destroyer, frigate. You'll see every kind of vessel here. We build 'em up to 45,000 tons. Got moorings for babies 800 feet overall.' He ran through a list of facts and figures, like a child reciting by rote, his commentary lifeless and stale from repetition. To Ossie he was a warning. Here was a guy, he thought, who might have seen himself on the bridge of a destroyer, hunting subs in mid-Atlantic. Yet, somehow, he had wound up here, acting like a tourist guide, delivering the same tired spiel. What wrong turn had he taken, to find himself in this literal backwater? Had *he* taken a wrong turn himself?

As they picked their way through the apparent muddle of machinery and men, the noise of construction swelled all around them. Workers were busy everywhere, full of purpose, swarming over the looming hulls, dark, small shapes, bug-like, scarcely human.

'The joint's sure jumping,' Ossie said.

'Forty thousand people with one intent,' said the lieutenant commander. 'To win the war.'

Ossie and Winthrop exchanged a glance. 'Booth could have written that,' said Ossie.

In the canteen, it seemed the entire workforce was female, garbed in overalls, with bright bandannas tied around their heads. The sound was as of a great gathering of birds, a multitude of voices, high and lively, ringing round the steel girders of the roof.

One shift was finishing its meal, another was about to start. The first was piling dirty crocks and cutlery on trays, and scraping back metal chairs. The second was gathered by the serving hatches, shouting out its orders, then moving through the hall and banging down its plates and knives and forks. Few took any notice of the small group gathering on the stage.

'The thing of it is, your ETA was way off,' said the Navy man. 'If you'd been on time, I can assure you, you would have had their full attention.'

'They *are* expecting us?' said Winthrop.

'Oh sure. They've been thoroughly briefed. Red shift, that is.'

'Which are Red shift?'

'The ones starting to leave. Blue shift are the ones arriving. It's kind of unfortunate, but I guess you'll have to do the best you can. I'll announce you anyway.' He walked over to a microphone, flicked a switch, got a burst of static and began to speak. Some of the departing workers looked back at him over their shoulders, as the newcomers slid into seats and began to bend over their food. As Ossie stepped forward he noticed that the last few stragglers of Red shift were sidling out of the doors at the back of the hall. He had not listened to his introduction. He knew how it would go, and spared himself the pain. And so he stood there on the creaking platform, an emissary from a distant, unreal war, in his unfamiliar RAF uniform, reading haltingly from his script, Booth's facile exhortations drifting into the void that hung above the crowded tables. Some of the women fixed him with an apprehensive gaze, thinking, maybe, of the fearful, unknown world that might await their menfolk. Others listened, suspicious of his message and his motives, much as they might regard the doorstep salesman from Fuller Brush.

There were a few questions. 'When do you reckon this war will end?'

'Hard to say, ma'am. It's got a ways to run, that's for sure.'

'Why are we fighting the Germans? Isn't our beef with the Japs?'

'That's a big question that takes a big answer. You'd better ask the President – I'm just a pilot. But it seems to me that if someone comes knocking on your door with a rifle butt, you don't ask him in for tea. Maybe they haven't got around to your neighbourhood yet, sister, but if we don't stop 'em now, you can bet they will.'

'Have you met the King of England?'

'Some of my buddies have, collecting medals at the Palace.'

'Why are you serving with the British Air Force?'

'Well, they got stuck into the Nazis first. I'd wound up in England, a swell country by the way, and I had the flying experience they were looking for, so they took me on. Besides, I love to fly Spitfires, one hell of a machine.'

'Say, honey, have you got a date tonight?'

'No, ma'am, but they're putting us up at the Bellevue-Stratford in Philly. Be glad to buy you a cocktail.'

Later, the same camouflaged Dodge sedan took them to the hotel, where a gathering of Philadelphian notables had organised a Bond Blitz. Ossie was in his room when Winthrop knocked and came in. His eyes took in the opened bottle of Jack Daniel's whiskey by the bed.

'Hey, Wolf, go easy on that stuff. Showtime's not over yet.'

'I drink when I can. When I'm flying I can't.'

'This is a mission, son, like any other. Respect that.'

'Loosen up, Winthrop. Treat yourself to a slug or two before we go down.' He found the major a glass, and Winthrop removed his Dentyne gum and sipped at the bourbon reluctantly.

'There's no denying it's been one heck of a day,' he said. 'I'm not sure how many of those shipyard gals knew who the heck we were. And putting down in the fog in that darned Dakota, with a gorilla at the controls, was a real bonus.'

'Like they say, a good landing is one you walk away from.' Ossie topped up their glasses. 'Anyway, things are on the up-and-up. This is quite a joint.'

'Philly's finest. Haunted, so they say. Some society princess tried to slide down that fancy staircase with the curving balustrades. Fell forty feet. Now they say she prowls the corridors.'

Ossie waved the bourbon bottle. 'Here's the only spirit that's got my attention.'

In the ballroom, banners had been strung up, proclaiming *Buy War Bonds*. Dining tables had been set out around the dance floor and on the stage was gathered a throng of tycoons, politicians, senior members of the military, church leaders and middle-aged women in high-life outfits. Ossie was told he was a guest of honour, along with a bored blonde with a familiar face, who he recognised from B-movies. They were to sell kisses to purchasers of $25,000 bonds. He thought maybe he should have cleaned his teeth.

The evening wore its course. Few women claimed a kiss from Ossie, a handful of snickering matrons only, prompted by husbands who sat back and seemed to enjoy the spectacle. The matrons smelled of lavender and martini, and offered themselves, eyes closed, noses wrinkled, like kids about to have their faces scrubbed. But numbers of men of means, flushed and breathing heavily, ran their lips across the unyielding mouth of the blonde with the familiar face, who was halfway through a tour of three hundred towns and cities, working eighteen hours a day. She spoke to Ossie once, when he asked if she knew Howard Hughes. 'Get lost,' was all she said.

The auction finished, the tables were pushed back and the floor was quickly filled with a press of couples shuffling to the music of a small dance combo. But the alcohol had done its work on ageing constitutions and finally, near midnight, the Bond Blitz began to wind down. Formality had dropped away. Folk reeled up and shook Ossie's hand or slapped him on the back, saying they were real proud of him, a good American boy who'd shown the Limeys a thing or two, not to mention Adolf Hitler.

'If there's anything you want while you're in Philly, son, you've only got to name it.' But there was only one thing Ossie wanted at that moment, and the Hollywood blonde was no longer to be seen.

Finally, unwilling to enter the crowded lift, he mounted the yellow marble staircase with the fancy balustrade, running his hand along the bronzed banister from which the dumb society chick had toppled, to become the stuff of ghostly legend. Major Winthrop was poised to stop it happening again.

At the door of Ossie's room, Winthrop said: 'Well, I guess it didn't turn out too bad, at that.'

'Wanna snifter?'

'Are you kidding? Get your head down. That's an order.'

'This baloney that Booth dreamed up, it's one load of shit.'

'It's worthy shit and usually it works.'

'You saying I ain't doing a good job?'

'Let's face it, you're no John Barrymore.'

'I need different material.'

'Don't get temperamental on me, son. Now lay off the booze, and lights out. Tomorrow, it's Cleveland.'

But very soon Ossie was woken by a soft knocking on his door. He was stretched out on his bed, still in his uniform. The empty Jack Daniel's bottle rested between his legs. He stared up at the ceiling and it began to revolve, as though he was in the cockpit of an airplane in a flat spin, blurring, spinning, faster, faster. He leaned over the side of the bed and threw up on the carpet. The gentle knocking began again. 'Yeah?' he croaked, wiping his mouth with his sleeve.

'Your soirée's over, honey. Now the fun begins.'

'Says who?'

'I've been waiting, honey. You promised you'd buy me a cocktail.'

'Sister, I'm busy right now.'

'C'mon, honey, be a sport. I come out here special.'

'No can do.' How right that was, thought Ossie. Shoot. If he'd known it would be this easy, maybe he'd have laid off the liquor. But now, well, there was no point in opening the goddamned door. Besides, he had a vague memory of a thick-set dame with big shoulders and heavy eyebrows.

'Oh, c'mon, honey, I do it with all the guys who bullshit us at the yard. I ain't never been turned down yet.'

'I'm about to spoil your record.'

'But, hon, you ain't even seen me. I'm all fixed up.'

'Okay. Tell me this. Have you got twenty-five thousand dollars?'

'Twenty-five thousand dollars? You crazy?'

'Well, then, you can't afford me. Now haul your little ass out of there.'

The woman rattled the latch, then kicked the door. It was a substantial impact. 'Then you go right to hell, you miserable sonofabitch.'

'I'm on my way,' Ossie said, and was sick again.

It seemed that only minutes had passed when the knocking started again. 'For crying out loud,' shouted Ossie. 'On your horse, sister, before I call the goddamned manager.'

A man's voice said: 'This is First Lieutenant Robert Mulalley, sir. It's eight o'clock and we're due at the field in an hour.'

Ossie rolled himself off the bed and opened the door. A young Army Air Corps man stood there, bright-eyed, intelligent-looking, his service cap tucked smartly under his arm.

'Who the hell are you? Where's Winthrop?'

'Major Winthrop has designated me to escort you to your engagement at the air cadet school in Cleveland, sir. He will join us there.'

'Lit out to see his wife and kids in Charleston, I'll bet.'

'I was not appraised of the reason for his absence, sir. Merely received the order.' Mulalley cleared his throat. 'Incidentally, sir, the hotel has received a complaint. Are you familiar with a woman named Bernice Kolb? She claims she was invited to your room, where you subjected her to verbal abuse.'

'Can you beat that?' said Ossie. 'The dame never made it past my door. You'll find her footmarks on the panels. I told her to haul her ass out of the hotel.'

Mulalley nodded, then wrinkled his nose. 'Gee whizz, has something died in here?'

'Yeah, my will to live,' said Ossie.

'I'll see you in the lobby, sir,' said Mulalley.

Ossie collected his few belongings and went down. At the checkout desk, the manager came forward. 'The lieutenant has explained the situation, sir. You understand, of course, that we have to treat every complaint in an even-handed manner. However, Miss Kolb, or rather Mrs Kolb, is known to us and you can rely on us not to take the matter further.'

'Has the dumb broad ever scored?' said Ossie.

'Not to my knowledge, sir,' said the manager, straight-faced. 'I do hope you've enjoyed your stay.'

There was no fog. The DC-3 lifted off from the airbase into a clear, cold sky and turned north-west for Cleveland. It was a short flight. Soon they were banking over the glittering waters of Lake Erie. Ossie had once gone fishing there with his Cousin Boyd and some other guys in their rich-kid Riva speedboat, catching few fish, intent on landing prey of a different sort. He remembered putting into remote beaches, barbecuing rainbow trout and acting goofy to Benny Goodman on the gramophone, making the chicks laugh. Through the Dakota window he could see the shape of South Bass Island, rotating slowly five hundred feet below. For a second, it had the look of Malta, and he felt a primal need to be back again, in the cockpit of a fighter plane, breathing in the heady fumes of aviation fuel, glycol, hot oil and metal, his body shaking with the power of a thousand horse-power, the mastery of stick and rudder controlling countless tiny shifts of altitude, the machine alive, responsive, his to fly, to wield, as lethal as any weapon yet invented.

'Hey, Mulalley,' Ossie said abruptly. 'How come you're a penguin?'

'Penguin, sir?'

'Got wings, don't fly.'

Mulalley grinned good-naturedly. 'Well, yes, I've got my wings up, sir, sure enough. But I'm no fighter jock. And who wants to be a cab-driver in a DC-3? I was a reporter on the *Boston Globe* before Pearl, so when a vacancy in the publicity bureau came up, it seemed like a swell idea.'

The air, when they swung back the door of the Dakota, was fresh and pure, blowing clear across the lake from Canada. It hit Ossie on the chest and he began to cough.

'How're you feeling, sir?' said Mulalley.

'How do I look?'

'Somewhat rocky, sir.'

'That's how I feel.'

A khaki Chevrolet sedan with a circled white star on its hood was ticking over by the airplane steps. Soon they were in another hotel lobby, the Fenway Hall, on East 107th and Euclid, not far from the university, and close to the air cadet school.

Signed in, Ossie told the baggage porter to take his case to his room.

'I could use me a coffee and a smoke, Mulalley.'

'Sure thing.'

They settled themselves in the lounge. Ossie took a deep drag on one of Mulalley's Chesterfields, tapped off the ash and said abruptly: 'I've been thinking of using my own material.'

'What?'

'Yeah, starting with tonight. I'm kind of uncomfortable with the sales pitch I've been issued with. It just don't ring natural.'

'Want me to give you a hand at writing some new stuff?'

'Hell no. I reckon I can do it better off the cuff.'

'I think Major Winthrop might have a view on that.'

'He already knows my opinion, and anyway, the guy's not here.' Ossie rested a heavy hand on Mulalley's shoulder. 'Relax, kid, I know the kind of thing they're after. You forget, I was thoroughly briefed in London.' He dropped into his Wing Commander Booth voice. 'I have seen the war. The victories, the defeats, the heroism, the hardships. I know what it takes to win. That will be my message.'

'Well,' said Lieutenant Mulalley doubtfully, 'that's the nub of it, all right.'

'Trust me. It'll be a breeze. But here's a chance to wise them up some.'

'With respect, sir, these young fellows are still in ground training. Some of them are hardly started on their courses. If they wind up as fliers I believe they'll discover the reality of their situation, and what they've volunteered for, fast enough. Right now, I guess their thoughts are all of learning their jobs, doing their duty, and maybe one day hoping to garner a little glory along the way.'

'You think I should go easy on them, huh?'

'I'd say keeping it general is the way to go. Nothing wrong with a platitude or two, at this stage in their careers. No point in putting the fear of God into them, if that's what you've got in mind.'

Ossie stubbed out his cigarette. 'Like you say, Lieutenant, one way or another a lot of these kids are going to wind up in a combat situation. I reckon I can help prepare them for that moment.'

The air cadet faculty seemed to be linked to the university in some way. Mulalley explained it all to Ossie in the Chevrolet, on the way over after an early and alcohol-free supper in the hotel, but Ossie paid little heed. He contemplated the weeks to come, shepherded from city to city and state to state, squirming in the unwelcome spotlight of transient fame, resenting the attention, the need to talk about matters that did not lend themselves to words, except in the broad, bland terms of Winthrop's windbag verbiage. His impulse to provide the cadets with an insight into the reality of conflict, or as he put it 'to wise 'em up', had apparently been abandoned, influenced by Mulalley's subtle counsel. 'Take it from me, sir, just stick to the script. Otherwise you could wind up looking a mug. I've seen it a dozen times, men who've tried to wing it, men with medals on their chests, frozen centre stage like deer in headlights, with nary a thought about what they were planning to say.'

At the school a fledgling flier, his small face ardent and intense under the visor of his cadet-style hot-pilot cap, escorted them to the office of the commanding officer. The walls were decorated with the American flag, crossed with the banner of the faculty, pictures of assorted airplanes and photographs of a large man shaking hands with various dignitaries including President Roosevelt. The large man now rose from behind his desk and held out his hand to Ossie. 'Colonel Emmett. You're mighty welcome, young man. Your reputation precedes you.'

'Uh-oh,' said Ossie.

Emmett laughed. 'I see you've picked up the British sense of humour.'

'That's about all I've picked up lately, Colonel,' said Ossie.

On their way to the assembly hall Emmett talked about the work they did, how they identified the best recruits and prepared them to be pilots, navigators, bombardiers.

'And what about the rest?' asked Ossie.

'Oh, we wash 'em out and they wind up toting a rifle in an infantry platoon,' said Emmett. 'We're in the business of honing the finest fighting Air Force in the world. No room for those who don't shape up. We ship 'em out at the earliest opportunity. Yes, sir. At this facility, we aim for the best of the very best.'

'That's good,' said Ossie. 'That's very good. Say, do you know a feller name of Booth?'

In the hall, the cadets were seated, row on row, seemingly identical, crop-headed, smart in their service jackets, an expanse of brown, resembling a muddy lake.

'Jesus,' said Ossie out of the side of his mouth to Lieutenant Mulalley, 'there's hundreds of the bastards.'

The cadets fell silent as Colonel Emmett led his guests onto the platform. Then they rose to their feet and began to applaud. To this audience, at least, Ossie seemed to mean something; a pilot with a pilot's tale to tell.

He felt a sudden warmth towards these unknown ranks, and

a sensation he had not known for a very long time: a sense of being an American. It came to him, as a slight surprise, that he had not been in the country of his birth for five years. He had gotten used to Britain, where matters were ordered differently; where emotions were held in check, where much was left unsaid, where irony and diffidence deflected too much interest in what might be felt within, where an instinctive politeness often masked what folk really thought; sure, it held them back from gush but it also suppressed plain speaking, saying what was on their mind. No British audience would have greeted him this way. He remembered his reception at the Capitol, those shrewd and doubting faces, well-fed and reactionary, regarding him like a messenger from hell. And the shipyard gals, doing their bit for Uncle Sam, reluctant to hear what he had to say, because it meant the world they knew was passing, without them really understanding why, as they stood at their machines and contemplated the loss of fathers, brothers, husbands, sons. They'd made no attempt to cover up what they thought, to spare him awkwardness, embarrassment, ease his task. At first he had felt like a stranger in his own land, wondering what America was, whether it was even possible to say. But now he could see that he was part of it still, much more than he had realised, for a long, long time. He thought about the words of Major Winthrop, back in London. 'You could always transfer to the US Army Air Corps. We'd be proud to have you on board.'

He took from the pocket of his tunic the cards on which were typed the words of Bernard Booth, soft and empty banalities that rang hollow, even to the most credulous ear. They swam before his eyes, the individual letters just shapes and patterns, meaningless, unreadable. No wonder that in Washington and Philly he had been given the bum's rush. He pushed the cards back in his pocket and moved towards the lectern . . .

*   *   *

Major Winthrop, fresh from West Virginia, sensed a commotion as soon as he stepped from the pool car outside the assembly hall. Groups of cadets were gathered in close-mouthed discussion about something that seemed to have caught them unprepared. They appeared disturbed, unsettled. There was almost palpable agitation in the air. He came across Colonel Emmett in the lobby.

'Winthrop, where the hell have you been?'

'Special assignment, sir. What have I missed?'

Emmett turned away. 'See me in my office.'

In the main hall Winthrop saw Ossie Wolf in a corner with half a dozen cadets. He was using his hands as airplanes and demonstrating methods of attack. The cadets around him looked tougher and older than the rest, like crop-spray cowboys who had signed up for a ready meal and a dry place to sleep, or propilots who flew commercial lines down Mexico way, seat-of-the-pants aviators without a licence to their name, or barnstormers who had once pulled stunts at county fairs in Government surplus string-backs from World War One. Lieutenant Mulalley was leaning against a wall nearby, staring into space. He saw Winthrop and came across.

'What gives, Mulalley? It looks like everyone's heard their mothers have died, apart from the roughnecks boning up on dogfights.'

'It was okay at first,' said Mulalley. 'It was even quite good. Wolf gave the guys something of an insight into what's gone on in Europe, what they're fighting for and how; the way it goes in the Royal Air Force, how they organise themselves, what it means to serve with the Brits, the machines they fly, particularly the Spitfire. He was a whole lot easier without the cards.'

'For crying out loud, *without* the cards?'

'He promised he'd stick to the script, sir, but well, he didn't, although for a while it seemed to be going swell. But then it kind of got out of hand.'

'How out of hand?'

'He'd told me he wanted to wise 'em up, about how it really was out there.'

'What happened?

'He did.'

Ossie Wolf had begun straightforwardly enough by taking them, in his mumbling way, to Revigncourt in May 1940, waiting in the cockpit of a Hurricane on a bare grass airfield close to Bar-le-Duc, not far from the Franco-German border; waiting for the sky to darken with the massed Luftwaffe fleets that, together with the Panzers on the ground, would mark the end of the Phoney War and herald the fall of France. How, outnumbered twenty to one, he and a handful of others had lifted away to join the fight, to tangle with the formidable Heinkel 111s and Junkers Ju 88s, the howling Ju 87 Stukas, and, most lethal, the yellow-nosed boys, the Messerschmitt 109s. And later, how the battle for France, hopeless from the first, became the battle for Britain and Hitler made his first mistakes, believing Goering's bombast, allowing the Royal Air Force to prevail against a mighty force, superior in numbers but not in spirit and leadership; the close-run combats joined above the verdant English landscape, specked with ancient villages and towns, free from invasion for nearly a thousand years, or wheeling over the numbing waters of the Channel, the final bulwark against the Wehrmacht's barges gathered on the Pas de Calais coast. He talked of Malta, in 1941, another small island besieged by Axis might, the key to Suez, North Africa and the East, that earned a reputation as the most bombed place on earth, and also a British medal for the fortitude of its people. How by air and sea, poorly supplied and armed, the garrison resisted the aggressors who, believing no population, military or civilian, could resist so many tons of high explosive, grew complacent but found that they were wrong, and began to find the cost too great. How he and other fliers, in Mediterranean skies that some thought fighter pilots' paradise, but others hell, won against all the odds, downing a thousand German and Italian aircraft, killing four times as many men.

This was the framework of what he had to say, conveyed in plainer terms, but interlaced with this narrative he recounted events more personal, immediate, brutal, made more shocking by his matter-of-fact delivery, as though the horrors of which he spoke were routine, to be expected. Which, as he knew but the cadets did not, they were.

He told them how men had died, pinned screaming in a ball of flame, taking an eternity to hit the ground, or blown to fragments without a moment to say a word or feel a thing; how others had survived, though dipped in saline baths, their skin burned clear away to show white bone, or missing limbs or losing sight. He told them of the ground-crews, strafed and bombed yet working on and fighting back, keeping their pilots in the air, marking the squadron's retreat to Brittany with men roasted at the wheels of machine-gunned trucks or torn in pieces by random bursts of fire and bundled into hasty roadside graves. He told of a crashed Luftwaffe crew butchered by French colonial troops, their heads driven onto stakes; of shooting two Fifth Columnists on a country road near Verdun, and leaving their bodies in a ditch; of a particular pal who chose to belly-land his Hurricane instead of baling, when he had the chance, and had been seen to move for many minutes in the inferno of his cockpit, until they wondered if they should shoot him; of how the medics needed three stretchers to take away the remains, and how Ossie could smell his particular pal for three days afterwards; of how men you had known for months and even years, who seemed invulnerable, the best, certain to survive, did not return, often untraced, leaving a locker full of bits and pieces of little value, like items from a kid's pants pockets, photos of a girl or Mom and Dad, a favourite book, a watch, a pen, an old scratched record that had reminded them of before the war. Just went to show, said Ossie, that you never could tell when you might buy the farm.

Listening to all this, the air cadets had been silent. Colonel Emmett, in a pause, smacked his hands together and stood up. 'Well, I guess that about wraps it up, gentlemen.'

It was then that the voice from the body of the hall said: 'I'd like to ask the flight lieutenant what combat tips he's got.'

Ossie grunted, ran through the gospel according to the Holy Fighter Pilot. See the whites of his eyes and fire in two-second bursts. Think of nothing else while shooting; when not, keep your eyes peeled for the enemy. Always go for height, for that is where security lies – altitude is life. If attacked, turn and face them. Be decisive – better to risk the wrong decision than make none at all. Never fly straight and level for more than thirty seconds at a time. Post guys upstairs to act as cover. Go in fast, hit hard, get the hell out.

'All good combat pilots live by these rules,' said Ossie. 'It's when they forget them that they die.'

The hall was quiet now. Ossie was looking from face to face, to gauge the impact he was making. He wanted these youngsters to listen, learn, survive. That was why he was here, not to beat the patriot drum. 'I guess you characters know all about deflection shooting?'

Colonel Emmett eased forward in his chair. 'These men are in ground training, Wolf. This is not the time or place.'

Ossie ignored him. 'It's an art, boys. Matching the arc of your fire with the speed of your target, working out where he's going to be so your bullets arrive at the same time he does. You can be born with this gift, which I guess I was, or acquire it if you live long enough. But while you're learning, and want to make sure you don't waste ammo, get in close, real close. And just when you think you're close enough, then get in closer. Fill your goddamned gunsight. And give it to him good.' He seized an invisible control column and pressed the gun button. 'In Malta

I had the guns on my Hurry synchronised on one hundred and fifty yards.'

Ossie was confident now, thinking what a crackerjack job he was doing. Who said you needed to sugar-coat the spiel? These kids were wising up, just like he wanted. Their expressions seemed to tell him that, their eyes focused on him, kind of solemn, thoughtful, taking it all in. After a moment, another question. Ossie, was scornful; replied. 'Do I think of the machine not the man, when I nail a Hun? Bullshit. I know it's a man all right. I always think about the bastard who's going down. I recall one time with a 109 over St Nazaire. I blew this sonofabitch's head clean off, brains running back inside his canopy. And the funny thing was, that what was left of him was still flying the goddamned plane. Damnedest thing I ever saw.'

He looked out at the rows of rookie aircrew. For a moment it was like staring at ghosts. He knew that, once in squadrons, their lives could be counted in weeks. They did not know this yet. He felt they should, so they could put the fear of dying behind them. Should he tell them that as well? But he noticed they were looking at him, very quiet, as though he had said something out of line. He felt a hand on his elbow. It was Lieutenant Mulalley.

'Okay, sir, okay. I think the poor mugs have got the message.'

'Huh?' said Ossie.

Colonel Emmett was quickly on his feet, before Ossie had a chance to suggest to his cadets that their futures might be easier if they considered themselves already dead. He thanked Ossie in the briefest terms. He did not look at him as he spoke. When he finished, the hall once more reverberated to the rumble of the air cadets rising from their seats, the applause more muted this time. Emmett was quickly gone.

Filing out, the cadets began to talk about what they had been told. Many of their faces showed that they were wondering if this was truly what awaited them, this unknown world of war that, in fifteen minutes, had changed from a great adventure, a chance to assert their manhood, to test themselves against hardship and some danger, most of all perhaps simply to learn to fly, to what now seemed like a one-way ticket to oblivion. Except, for some, it was as though Ossie had thrown open a window in a darkened room and let in the light. And so he had found himself the centre of a handful of seasoned aviators who recognised the environment he had described, understood and accepted the imminence of death in everything they did, found refreshing his turn of phrase after the euphemistic jargon of the service, pressed him for tips on how to live a little longer. But then Major Winthrop had pushed his way through the group, tracked by a small man in a snap-brimmed grey fedora.

'So tell me, Wolf, what have I missed?'

'Plenty,' said the man in the fedora. 'He's been laying it on the line.'

'Who the hell are you?' said Winthrop.

'Press,' said the small man. He tapped a notebook in his left hand. 'I got it all in here. Want a transcript?'

'Get lost,' said Winthrop. 'Someone get this bum out of here.'

'Sure,' said Ossie. He pulled the newsman's fedora down over his eyes, spun him round and propelled him towards the door with his foot.

Later, pacing around his office, head down, his hands clasped behind his back, Colonel Emmett experienced difficulty marshalling his thoughts. He looked at Ossie the way that George Washington might have regarded Benedict Arnold, with a blend of anger and disbelief. Finally, he said: 'I imagine you think you've done one helluva job?'

Ossie shrugged. 'It seemed to get their attention.'

'Good grief, Winthrop, this wise guy as good as told those kids they're dead meat. There are penalties for spreading alarm and despondency, you know. I've a mind to take this matter further.' He paused, breathing heavily. 'And anyway, where the hell were you? I thought this junket was your responsibility?'

'Slightly delayed, Colonel. As I told you, special assignment.'

'Special assignment, baloney. I'm having you checked you out, Winthrop. If my suspicions turn out to be true, I reckon I'll be taking that further too. How the hell you people think this is helping the war effort sure beats me. You're dismissed. All of you, dismissed. That's Army Corps speak for telling you to get the hell off this establishment.'

On their way to the car Ossie slowed for a moment. 'I've got an awful strong urge to give that feller a fat lip.'

'Terrific,' said Major Winthrop. 'We'll just wait here, while you work the Colonel over. Mulalley and I can discuss our futures.' He gave Ossie a not-so-gentle shove. 'Get in that goddamned automobile and don't say another word.'

Next morning, at the Fenway Hall Hotel, a copy of the *Cincinnati Enquirer* was delivered to Ossie's room, along with his breakfast tray. On the front page was a report, small but prominent, headlined *ROOKIE FLIERS HEAR GRIM TALES OF WAR. A first-hand account of dogfights against the Nazis in the skies of Europe was delivered to an audience of fresher aviators by a St Louis-born fighter ace serving with the British Royal Air Force. Flight Lieutenant Oswald Wolf, with twenty-two kills to his credit, pulled no punches in describing the ferocity of war in the air. One cadet opined: 'If we were in any doubt about what lies ahead for those of us who qualify for air-crew, now there are no illusions.' Asked to comment on whether the fighter ace's lecture was too rugged for trainee fliers, the faculty's commanding officer, Colonel Roland K. Emmett, was unavailable for comment.'*

Next to the newspaper was an envelope with a message from a local radio station wanting to interview Ossie live on air that morning. When Major Winthrop came into his room, Ossie waved the invitation. 'Looks like some folk don't reckon I was talking horse-shit. Maybe I should do this.'

'Like fun you should,' said Winthrop.

'Where's Mulalley?'

'He's been recalled.'

'So, it's just you and me to hit Chicago.'

'Negative. Chicago's off. The whole tour's been aborted. You're shipping out to Europe on the first available B-17. The top brass reckon you're a liability, Wolf.'

'Sonofabitch,' said Ossie. 'How about you?'

'I tend to share that opinion.'

'I mean, where does that leave you?'

'There's a high mortality rate among transport pilots, they tell me. The medical requirements have been relaxed. They say, with any luck, this time I'll make the grade.'

'Well,' said Ossie, 'at least there's a little good news around here.' He rummaged under a pillow and pulled out a bottle of bourbon.

Winthrop took it, and gulped the liquor down. 'Happy landings, Wolf.'

'Sure,' said Ossie. 'Break a leg.'

Winthrop sat down heavily on the bed. He had not eaten breakfast, and the alcohol hit him fast. 'I think you should know,' he said, speaking very carefully, 'that my fate did not entirely rest in your hands. I have brought some of this on myself.'

'That special assignment, huh? How was your old lady?'

'Ironically, Wolf, it was a wasted journey. She's left me, gone back to San Francisco with the kids, to be with some damned Navy man.'

'One less worry,' said Ossie consolingly.

'You could look at it like that,' said Winthrop, falling slowly sideways onto the bed.

A few days later, in the Club in London, Rupert Pringle came across Bernard Booth.

'Hello, Grunter. What news of Hand of Friendship?'

The wing commander groaned. 'Something of a shemozzle with your friend Wolf.'

'No friend of mine.'

'Pretty much a balls-up, I'm afraid. The Yanks are in a terrific bate. And Glenn Winthrop's got the chop. I'm speaking metaphorically, of course, but where he's gone I wouldn't be at all surprised if it turns out to be true.'

'I told you Wolf was deadly.'

'Hasn't gone down too well with the high-ups over here either, I'm afraid. AMIHOF is currently on a complete as-you-were.'

'And where's Wolf now?'

'Where he can do the least harm, or the most, depending on which side you're on.'

'Have a drink, old man.'

'Thanks most awfully. This dratted war. Throws up the rummest types. Can't rely on anybody.'

Some weeks later Ossie Wolf sailed from Liverpool in a converted cattle boat. The vessel, unescorted, headed north at first, to throw off any U-boats, the Scottish mainland visible to starboard, but then looped back, crossing the Atlantic and following the American coast until it dog-legged east to make landfall at Gibraltar. A day or so in port, to purge the ship of rats that scurried along the girders above the hammocks, and the voyage continued south, slowly moving down the coast of Africa, close enough for pungent unknown smells to carry across the sea, putting in at last at Takoradi on the Gold Coast, for centuries known as 'the white man's grave', where malaria, yellow and blackwater fevers, pneumonia and countless variations ruled as surely as any local chief.

When, with his fellow passengers, some Army but mostly RAF, Ossie came ashore he learned that nearly four thousand miles to the north, things were building up on the Egyptian Front, where two great armies were battling for advantage in an arena of sand

and stone, devoid of population and perfectly suited for war; where their successive attacks and counter-attacks ebbed and flowed across the empty desert like a bloody tide. Now, if the grapevine was to be believed, fortunes seemed to have moved the Allies, way. Hell, thought Ossie, that was where the action was, not this lousy sink-hole, and he ached to be there.

Three

It was the scar tissue between the thumb and forefinger of his right hand that had made Kit Curtis begin to question his role as flight commander of a Spitfire squadron in constant action in the skies of Malta. The burnt skin had healed in an awkward way, stiff like leather, although he tried to soften it by massaging it with olive oil, and clenching and unclenching his fist, unseen, to restore its flexibility. In the air his touch on the controls, so natural, barely thought of, grew clumsy and constrained. More than once, in combat, a momentary delay in pressing down the gun button left an enemy untouched, though perfectly in his sights. Then, near the end of his Malta tour, his flight had been ordered to patrol north of Zonqor Point. Radar had picked up sixteen Junkers Ju 88s, each carrying 4,000 lbs of bombs, bound for Luqa airfield. His hand was particularly bad that day, the skin cracked and raw and seeping blood, either through infection or because he had worked at it so hard.

At least there was no shortage of Spitfires now, the time long past when the island's air strength comprised a handful of out-classed, oil-stained Hurricane Mark 1s, short on spares and fuel and ammunition. During the hot, high summer of 1942 the convoys had started getting through, despite the cost, bringing supplies and reinforcements. And week by week more Spitfires arrived from carriers that had taken them to the fly-off point, three hundred miles due east of Gibraltar, leaving them to cover seven hundred miles of open sea before crossing Malta's south-western coast, above the scrub-covered Dingli Cliffs, and landing at Takali.

The battle had entered another phase, less defence and more attack. Attrition was costing the Luftwaffe men it could not afford to lose – crack aircrew, as many as two hundred in a week – as well as costly aircraft, hard to replace with demand for new machines so high on the faltering Russian Front.

Now nearly thirty Spitfires wheeled above the small port of Marascala, where fishing fleets of *luzzu* boats, daubed in bright greens and blues and yellows, appeared suspended on the transparent sapphire sea. And yet, despite their numbers, the fighters somehow failed at first to intercept the raiders until they were spotted at 19,000 feet near the island's most south-easterly point, Kalafrana Bay, only minutes from their objective. And with them, a thousand feet above, an escort waited, twenty Messerschmitt 109s, poised to drop down at the first sign of an assault.

Over his RT, Barrett, the squadron leader, called the operations room in Valletta. 'Red Leader to Control. Red Leader to Control. Bogeys sighted. Bogeys sighted. Preparing to engage.'

'Control to Red Leader. Okay, Tim. Advise when the party's over.'

Barrett went in first, leading his section down from 22,000 feet, the sun behind them, in a quarter head-on attack, loosing machine-gun and cannon fire on the Ju 88s from less than four hundred yards. Black smoke began to stream from the starboard Jumo engine of the *Staffel* leader who turned away towards the sea and jettisoned his bombs, quickly losing height. Another, with no visible signs of damage, began to climb, then stalled, rolled on its back and dived vertically into open fields. No parachutes.

Next, Kit: 'Blue section, line astern, line astern. Going down. Now!' He had set his gun switch to its third position, wing-mounted Browning .303 machine guns and twin 20mm cannon unleashed as one. In seconds he was in among the bombers, those not damaged stolidly holding course in their usual *Kette* v-formation, three by three. At first he could not fix upon a target but when he did, a Junkers with a broad white stripe encircling its drab olive fuselage, just behind the big black Nazi cross, outlined in white, he found that his hand, fixed round the oval spade grip of the control column like a claw, was momentarily rigid and, for that vital instant, it refused to move. Now it was too late and, unwilling to waste ammunition by chancing a fleeting shot or two, the mark of a beginner that never worked, he pushed forward on the stick and continued down, at 400 mph, levelling out at 15,000 feet, then climbing back towards the running battle.

He cursed, but nothing was lost. Plenty more chances yet. He was closing quickly when his Spitfire was shaken by a sudden force, engulfed in shock waves from an explosion of great violence. He saw, above and to his right, a rapidly rotating ball of yellow and crimson flame with, at its heart, the shadowy outline of a Ju 88. Then it lost its shape and burst apart, scattering a deadly rain of red-hot fragments. Holes appeared in his starboard wing and something struck the windscreen a glancing blow, but not a bullet or a shell; it was heavier, not fired but falling, still striking with power enough to gouge a sizeable indentation in the armoured glass. Behind his tinted goggles, Kit's eyes were wide and focused on the splintered screen, thinking that if his speed had been a fraction faster, or the object's trajectory a few inches to the left, he might be dead. Such reflections came in a nanosecond and were gone again as quickly, not to be remembered until later on the ground, if then.

His machine was still shaking from the turbulence of the Ju 88's destruction when another Spitfire passed across in front of him, left to right, in a steep climbing turn with tracer licking past its tailplane in vivid streams. He knew the pilot from the fighter's markings: it was Sam Rosenstein, four weeks with the squadron, frustrated at not securing his first kill, determined to avenge his grandparents taken from their home in Munich and murdered in the camps. He had talked to Kit of this, in the *palazzo* in Mdina, the ancient palace commandeered for pilots' quarters, overlooking the plain where Takali airfield lay; Mdina, safe from Axis bombs because, it was said, the Pope had pronounced it a holy city. 'Respect for one religion,' Rosenstein had said. 'Persecution for another. I'm going to make these Nazi swine pay.' But when the victories did not come, his flying grew erratic, his eagerness a liability to the flight. And now he had a Messerschmitt on his tail.

The covering *Schwarm* of 109s had dispatched three *Rotten* – two aircraft, a leader and his wingman – to protect the remaining Ju 88s. The sky around the bombers was a confusion of wheeling aircraft. From below it was like a whirlpool, as if the machines were caught by an invisible force and sucked in towards the core, where extinction awaited the greenhorn short on combat time, the time-served man who had never been quite good enough, at last found out, the plain unlucky, wrong time, wrong place, no chance to prove his worth, the ace whose number had come up, as it usually did, however many battles and tours he had survived. And as a backdrop to this deadly game, the blue expanse criss-crossed with tracer and cannon fire, trails of white-black smoke tracking the last moments of those about to die who, only a little while before, had known they were immortal but now slammed, mostly conscious, into Maltese limestone, to be buried ten feet deep.

The sounds of battle hung above the island, the low growl of bombers on constant throttle, the whistle of descending sticks of bombs, the variable scream of high-stressed fighter engines, the rattle of guns like hailstones on a metal roof, occasionally a deafening burst of sound, as bomb-loads conflagrated and filled the air like thunder, but from a different kind of passing summer storm, and fragments of the conflict drifted down, resembling just-spent fireworks, blackened but still glowing red.

Kit knew this world, where everything happened fast, so fast that afterwards your actions had gone beyond recall; where instinctive and spontaneous reactions, honed by years of combat, kept you in the air and seeing, in this maelstrom of machines, the pattern of the engagement, coldly aware of where and how to kill; where, in those moments of curious calm, details of the action passed in front of him like a slowed-up film. As now, with the Messerschmitt 109 on Rosenstein's tail, seeming to drift across in front of him, black spinner, fuselage mottled grey, the pilot leaning forward, hunched, intent on bringing down his quarry, unaware of another Spitfire closing on his right. Kit kicked the rudder to the left, placing the 109 at right angles to his approach, ready for a four-second burst with full deflection. The Messerschmitt came, lazily almost, right through his gunsight. His muscles tensed, he felt the impulse rush down his forearm to his hand. His thumb was resting on the gun-button. It wavered, trembling, as though hooked on an invisible wire, holding it back, unable to press down. Then, after a fractional delay, he opened fire but already the 109 had vanished.

The raid dispersed, many of its bombs dropped in Marascala Bay where fishermen put out in their *luzzu* boats and enjoyed a providential catch.

Kit touched down at Takali and, with two airmen on his wings, taxied towards his glinting blast pen built from unpainted fuel cans filled with concrete. He cut his engine and his ground-crew pushed his Spitfire round and rolled it backwards into the pen. He snapped loose his Sutton harness, tugged off his leather helmet and hung it on his gunsight, oxygen and R/T leads connected. He stood up on the seat. Flight Sergeant Myers was on the wing beside him.

'Everything all right, sir? She looks a bit knocked about.'

'Yes, Flight. Not my day. Drew a blank as well.'

'Blimey, sir, your hand's a mess.'

'Worse than it looks. Have you heard about the others? What's the score?'

'Bit early to say, sir, but they reckon five Ju 88s and four 109s.'

'Good show. Everyone make it back?'

'Squadron Leader Barrett bought it, I'm afraid. Collided with a 109.'

'Tim Barrett? Are you sure?'

'Yes, all the blokes feel bad about it. Never thought he'd get the chop. Oh, Luqa phoned. Sergeant Tempest did a wheels-up there. He's okay but his Spit's a bit the worse for wear. Do for spares, they reckon. Pilot Officer Crocker had to jump. Got a cannon shell in his engine. Managed to direct the kite out to sea. He came down on dry land near Marsaxlokk. Bust an ankle landing so he'll be out of things for a while. And Flying Officer Rosenstein's overdue.'

'Rosenstein? Are you sure?' Stupid question. Automatic. Hoping, he supposed, that he had misheard.

'Yes, sir. Not a word.'

Kit delivered his report to Threlfall, the intelligence officer, in his usual manner; matter-of-fact, the bare essentials, no opinions ventured, on this occasion nothing claimed. 'Anything new on Sam Rosenstein, Spy?'

Threlfall shook his head. 'Doesn't sound too rosy. Crocker saw him nailed by a 109. Chopped his port wing off. When that happens it's hard to get out.'

'I don't need you to tell me that.'

'Sorry, old boy. I'll let you know if there's any news.'

Later, much later, when it was growing dark Kit sat in a corner of the mess alone. He wanted to get slightly drunk and was making decent progress. He needed to blur the image of the 109, hanging in his sights, to wipe away that moment when his hand seemed frozen, unable to respond – a moment that had cost Sam Rosenstein his life. Again, he heard Spy Threlfall: 'Crocker saw him nailed by a 109. Chopped his port wing off.

When that happens it's hard to get out.' He knew that well, had seen it many times. The rapid, violent rolls that left a pilot disorientated, confused, fixed by gravity in his cockpit, with no time left to brolly-hop, just moments to watch the ground come up, counted lucky if he blacked out.

A nausea overcame him. Why had this loss hit him so hard? He hardly knew Sam Rosenstein, a decent enough young chap, but no different from the rest; the cavalcade of spectres who gathered round the living when there was a chance to brood, barely remembered faces, nameless often, who died at times and places now forgotten. No, not forgotten, but pushed away, suppressed, because it made you think about the road you had already trodden, a journey three years long, from 1939, from another world to here, where it was hard to see the way ahead, the route unknown, unknowable.

He knew, of course, that Rosenstein was different from the rest because he had failed to stop him dying when, with things as normal, he might have stopped him being nailed. Rotten luck, things working out like that, the youngster getting bounced by that bloody 109. But he should have expected such a situation. That was his job, as flight commander.

He went up to the room he shared with Threlfall and Tim Barrett. Already the squadron leader's locker had been cleared, his bed stripped clean. He closed the door. A racking sob rose in his throat. He gulped for air, horrified by an emotion he did not understand, could not control. His eyes were stinging, wet. He rubbed them with his hands and when his fingers touched his lips they tasted salt. A fierce pain ran through his wound as the saline moisture seeped into the excoriated flesh. Small punishment, he thought.

The door banged open. 'I say,' said Threlfall, 'are you okay?'

'Yes,' said Kit. 'My eyes are playing up. Must have picked up some bits of muck when I was hit by chunks of that Ju 88. I'll see if the Doc can fix me up.'

'Should have done it sooner. And what about that paw? That needs a once-over too, I'd say. Anyway, good news.'

'Oh, yes?'

'Rosenstein's been picked up. Down in the drink off Delimara Point. Four hours in the water, but some Malties after those *lampuki* dolphin the Jerries killed spotted him at dusk. Not quite the catch they had in mind but the rescue fleet chaps at Marsaxlokk made it worth their while. A very lucky lad.'

'Yes,' said Kit. 'He is.'

Two weeks later, Kit's tour in Malta ended. He had not flown again, grounded by the open wound that would not heal. He had experienced no further trouble with his eyes.

Back in England, Kit was granted leave. There was talk of a posting to a fighter squadron in the north, as a supernumerary instructor after a medical review. He did not travel home to Midhurst but took a room at the Connaught, savouring the luxury and its ambiance of an English private house. It was convenient, too, for his visits to the nondescript two-storey building in the grounds of Middlesex Hospital where he was appraised by the specialists of the RAF medical board. The physical examinations of the Central Medical Establishment were notorious for their rigour, and flying careers hung in the balance until verdicts were delivered.

Kit had caused concern at first, being malnourished, skeletal almost, like many of the Malta pilots, reduced by dysentery and the stress of constant battle. But soon he regained weight and, no longer under strain, his hand, his weakest spot, began to mend. Finally, he faced the president of the board. The air commodore leafed through Kit's file, scanning the reports.

'You've bounced back very well. You picked up your burns in that Hudson crash at Hendon in forty-one, I see, trying to get the other fellows out.'

'That's right.'

'A decent show. And everything nicely healed, apart from your little setback with that hand. Made it tricky, I imagine, in certain situations.'

He looked at Kit, his eyes shrewd, expecting a reply but Kit remained silent, his emotions mixed. He did not want to fail, to be downgraded to non-operational flying, but he remembered the moment when he thought he had got Sam Rosenstein killed. If he walked out of the CME with an A1.B, the highest flying category, there was no reason why, after a period in a less demanding role, he would not find himself in command once more, responsible for men's lives. He questioned if he was worthy, deserved another chance. He stared at the air commodore, his face expressionless. His bodily health had been appraised, and soon he would know the verdict. The state of his mind, clouded with doubt and disorder, remained hidden behind a steady gaze that betrayed no hint of inner turmoil. He wondered if, having come so far, at last he was cracking up. Should he request a downgrade himself, admit his apprehensions, his fear of letting others down?

'This mitt,' he said. 'It's been a blasted nuisance, that's for sure. What chance of it giving trouble again?'

'Treated sensibly,' said the air commodore, 'there's no reason why it shouldn't see you through. The Med didn't help, extremes of heat, the rampant bugs, your sweat, the dirt and dust, and what it had to cope with. On top of that, you couldn't let it be, didn't give it a chance to mend properly. No good trying to outdo nature, Curtis. It can't be done. These things take their course and can't be hurried.' He paused, and tapped a document. 'Anyway, congratulations are in order. You've been judged A1.B all right, operational for fighters. I hope you're pleased.'

It seemed an odd remark. Kit forced a grin. 'Of course.'

Within a week he had joined a squadron flying from a comfortless and windswept airfield a few miles from Aberdeen, briefed to impart his combat knowledge to flights of mostly untried pilots.

They treated him as boisterous nephews might treat a favourite uncle, but also with something close to awe, aware of his record in the air. The commanding officer was known to him from France, Jack Tucker; he had flown a Hurricane stationed at Rouvres, quite close to Revigncourt. Like Kit he had escaped to Britain in the chaos of retreat, to be shot down near Ashford within a fortnight. That way he had picked up a tin leg – Bader's understudy, as he put it – and now found himself leading a force of Spitfires charged with countering enemy raids from Norway. These were infrequent, usually a lone reconnaissance machine, subjected to a copybook attack with minimal resistance, and quickly dispatched forty miles out to sea. It had become routine: no expected losses, if care was taken, as it could be, because there was no fighter cover. Kit found his tactical advice untested and untried, effectively superfluous.

But he did not stay with Tucker long. A signal was received requesting second-and third-tour men with experience of Spitfires to volunteer for a branch of the service that seemed intriguing and mysterious: photographic reconnaissance, or PR. Immediately Kit knew this was the answer, to continue flying the aeroplane he had come to love, part of a team and yet, once in the air, accountable only to himself. Later, who could tell? He put in his application, and was accepted.

Tucker took it badly. 'For Pete's sake, Kit, I rather hoped you'd become a fixture here. Perhaps take over the reins, when they move me on. I'd have been happy to recommend you. Don't you want command?'

Kit was unwilling to explain. His emotions were too complex to express in words. As it was, he felt the chance to join PR was providential. It gave him time to work things out, to devote himself to a new and unknown line of work that required different qualities, made fresh demands; a test of skill and nerve and guts. He knew he retained those unimpaired. Now they could be put to use, without the burden of responsibility for others.

*   *   *

He trained at the PR unit's base at Benson, on the flatlands bordering the Thames north-west of Henley. In Henley town the surroundings were familiar: the regatta course where he stroked a Trinity lightweight crew in 1937 but lost to Princeton; the garage on Remenham Hill where Adrian Squire built Buster Brown one of his fast and fragile cars to race at Brooklands; the Angel on the Bridge pub, that once rang to the laughter of the Oxford crowd, cloaked in a fug of cheap tobacco and the sweet-sour smell, not unpleasant, of Brakspear bitter beer; upstream and down, the river locks where the trickling water echoed off the walls of slimy brick, empty now of skiffs and punts and slipper launches, bearing picnickers to some willow-shaded bank.

In a break from flying, he walked from the clubhouse of Leander, close by Henley Bridge, to the Flower Pot at Aston with Alec Finch. The Quaker told Kit of his beliefs: that in what the movement described as an ocean of death and darkness there was also light and love; that good and evil were latent in every living soul, and so demanded understanding and awareness. 'It's a difficult path. I feel an obligation to resist what Hitler stands for but I detest what he forces us to do. That's why I've chosen to be a PR pilot. At least I won't be faced with killing someone.'

'Not directly, no,' said Kit. He glanced at his companion but Finch had apparently missed his point. His beak-nosed face appeared serene and certain, seemingly content in his chosen role, believing that this way he would not contravene his faith, that he would not be the cause of harm. Had he considered that it was only a step away, would lead to others carrying out the slaughter? Certainly PR was a specialised line of work, where the evidence of conflict was viewed with a detached and dispassionate eye, in some sense that of a non-protagonist, a being once removed, recording man's folly through the unblinking focus of a camera lens. However, it was still a means of waging war, and war was killing. He felt a spark of irritation.

They had passed, on their right, the square flint tower of

Remenham church. Ahead lay Temple Island, unchanged, with at its centre the little folly that gave the place its name, decked out Etruscan-style, its green-roofed cupola supported by slim white columns, now wreathed in rising mist, an insubstantial fancy. Close by, Kit knew, lay the regatta's invisible startline.

'Alec, do you row?' Kit asked.

Finch compressed his lower lip so his mouth curved down and shook his head, as though the possibility of such a thing had never occurred to him. Kit felt an urge to reminisce, so close to the spot that prompted so many memories, but dismissed the impulse quickly. It was just an excuse to line-shoot. What possible interest could it hold for Finch? Such frivolous pastimes seemed to have no place in the Quaker's austere and pious world. They walked on, silent, following the river's curve.

At Hambleden Kit took Finch on a short diversion, across the lock and past the keeper's cottage to where the weir ran across to the Marlow bank. Enveloped in fine spray, they stood on the raised walkway above the water, watching it rush over the barrier's rim and course down the expanse of sloping concrete on the other side, churning itself to a yellow froth.

'There's always something sinister about these places,' said Kit. 'You imagine bodies tumbling and turning in the weir-pool, caught in the currents, trapped.'

'We're trapped,' said Finch. He turned away and began to walk back towards the lock. Over his shoulder he said suddenly, 'I imagine you think I'm pretty naive.'

'Naive?'

'Playing the pacifist pilot.'

'Nothing to do with me. Why should my opinion count?'

'You made your meaning rather plain.'

'Did I? Sorry.'

'I suppose you think I'm ducking the issue, fooling myself that I'm not really involved.'

'Something like that, I suppose. I wouldn't have the nerve to blame you though. Everything's gone to blazes. Old rules don't apply. Little wonder that beliefs get shaken, or eroded, don't fit some neat box with "morality" written on the lid. In this rotten business good men are continually compromised. It's the nature of the beast. They find themselves doing evil things for reasons they tell themselves are just. Sometimes they can almost make themselves believe it. It's probably the same on the other side. They follow a distorted creed but they're not all monsters.' Kit paused. 'You say Hitler forced this upon us and obviously you're right. But was he alone? Russia desired it, and Italy, and Japan. The Allies as well, once they'd gone beyond the point of no return. Everyone was swept along, like fragments on the current there. It was like a death wish, as though there was a will for war, as though everyone had tired of words, and decided to settle things with force to achieve their different aims, to dominate and enslave and shape the future world, or take a moral stand against dictatorship, or simply to assert themselves as men, concerned with private honour and seeing the chance to defend one's country, to fight for what one thinks is right, a privilege granted to very few generations, despite everything that's gone before.' Kit stepped back to let Finch through a wooden gate. 'Would you believe that in 1939 I was just such a bloody fool?' Somewhere, a good way off, a dog began to bark. The distant sound of voices was carried on the breeze.

'What was the alternative, do you think?' said Finch.

'None, that I can see,' said Kit. 'Come on. Step out. Let's find that pub and get ourselves a pint.'

In six weeks the training course was over. Kit had completed his practice trips successfully, climbing above the silver river that curved below the ramparts of Wallingford Castle, and navigating his way to his various objectives. He found he had an aptitude for the task, enjoying the routine of switching on his cameras, using the control box where the gunsight used to be, matching timings and focal length to suit his height and airspeed. He had a knack of knowing when he had reached the critical moment to turn towards the target, keeping it below his wing, flying with great accuracy so the twin shutters could operate eight seconds apart, giving him his overlap, his pictures blending in the middle and ensuring that every piece of ground was covered twice. Another pass, from a fresh direction. Then off to the next location on his map.

He passed out well, blending his flying skill with meticulous attention to detail when planning what, in PR slang, were always referred to as trips; a gentle euphemism that seemed appropriate now but promised to prove more like a hollow joke on operations, for the graduates had learned that there were other terms in PR's sardonic jargon, like 'dicing' for low-level sorties on targets such as German naval bases and the Channel ports, bristling with defensive flak.

Like the others Kit had learned many things that might prolong his life and usefulness; the critical importance of the pre-operation briefing, building a mental picture of the first and second priority targets, because they could not be shown on maps; knowing the likely enemy opposition, the fighters, radar, flak positions; planning the direction of his runs before he was in the air; studying the weather reports, wind speed and direction, cloud cover, icing, possible in cumulus even in the Med; the danger of leaving vapour trails, particularly near the base of high cirrus accumulations, but also watching for other trails that might give away the positions of prowling Messerschmitt 109s and Focke-Wulf 190s; the need to monitor his fuel against the duration of his flight, plotting his arrival time at various points en route, and even turning back if missing his ETA or going significantly off-course: 'Better a live pilot without the pix than landing in the drink or in Hunland because you ran out of juice,' as the instructors put it; the routine of checking his equipment, the flying helmet that should stay comfortable during a flight of many hours, the parachute and rubber dinghy primed for use, the cameras to be turned over before take-off, making sure the ammeter above the camera box showed a charge.

Once in the air, unarmed of course, a knowledge of tactics to outwit attackers. There was no chance to aerobat, because cameras would become dislodged from their mountings, at best disturbing the trim, at worst destroying the fuselage. So two words only applied: *keep weaving*. There was scant sympathy from the instructors here. 'If you're bounced you've nobody to blame but yourself. It means you damned well didn't keep 'em skinned. The blister in your canopy isn't there for decoration.' And last, the overarching purpose, to watch for every kind of enemy movement: shipping, aircraft, tanks, military transport, anything of significance that might be spotted on the way to targets and returning home, always logging position, direction of movement, number. 'And remember, chaps, *always take the ruddy photographs*. It's your job.'

His overseas posting came through quickly. Before he left he drove down to Midhurst in his little Lea-Francis Hyper. His father met him on the porch of the big, old house above Lynch Down. His stroke had left him with a drooping jowl, giving him a scowling, desperate look, his eyes distended, rimmed with red, and moist. Panting at his side was Ben, the dog unsteady on his feet, as decrepit as his master.

'Hello, Farve.'

'My boy.' His father's speech was slurred; a trickle of drool ran from the corner of his mouth. Kit was startled by his appearance, a shadow no longer entirely of this world, as though he was already in transition to the next. And yet, ironic as it seemed, it struck him, this pilot fresh from training, bristling with energy and health, freshly graded A1.B and operational for fighters, that even so he might get there first.

They shook hands briefly, the old man's fingers feeling bone-like, brittle, devoid of strength, under Kit's firm grasp.

They ate together in the conservatory, scrambled egg on toast prepared by Agnes Hobbes, alone in the cavernous kitchen, ranks of pots and pans unused, ovens cold. Cracking the eggs into a bowl, she had been apologetic, taken unawares and short of stores, grumbling that things had come to a pretty pass when this was all you could offer a young man fresh from fighting for his country. Kit laid a consoling hand upon her shoulder and, abruptly, she began to cry. 'Your father takes it bravely, Mr Kit, but it's awful to see him laid so low. I do my best to keep his spirits up, but I can't be here continually. I've got my own family to attend to.'

In the conservatory, peering across the valley lit by a lowering sun, Farve left his food untouched. 'No appetite to speak of. Can't think why. Need to put on a little weight. Weak as a blessed kitten.'

'You should get someone in to help. I know Agnes does her best, but honestly, Farve, you really ought have someone here full-time.'

'I don't need a nursemaid yet. Perfectly able to cope, with Agnes to lend a hand. Besides, I don't want a stranger in the house.' Farve hesitated. 'Of course it does seem confoundedly empty since Louis went away.'

'How is the boy?'

'He prospers. He has a way with him, that little fellow. His English is nigh on perfect now. But it was the right decision, to board him. Not our original intention, of course, but since I got struck down . . .' He shrugged. 'It's not much fun being stuck with a doddering relic.'

'Where did you send him, Farve?'

'The Grange, of course.'

'Of course,' said Kit. 'And Juliette?'

'No news, my boy. I've delved, as far as one can these days. We know she went to France, and we can suspect what took her there. But that's about the sum of it. She hasn't returned, that's all.'

'And Louis? What does he make of this?'

'You know him, Christopher. Tight-lipped, keeps it all inside. I think he hopes.'

'We all do that,' said Kit. He thought back to the cool *salon* of the *maison du maître* with the garden that ran down to the river at Boulay-sur-Sarthe where, two years ago, in that hot and deadly summer of 1940, the squadron had billeted itself in a barn across the courtyard. There, in between snatched hours of troubled sleep, they had patrolled the skies in their Hurricanes above the ports of Brittany, covering the embarking rearguard of the BEF, thrown back by the advancing forces of the Reich. Then the time arrived for them to get out too. And there, come to say goodbye, ill-timed, astonishing, he had held Juliette Garencières in his arms, leaving much unsaid, except a request for her to come to England with her small son, to another house above another valley.

And so, in time, they came – Juliette and Louis, their home abandoned, her husband, the boy's father, dead in his Char B1 tank, overwhelmed by Panzers near Sedan. They came safely to Lynch Down with its milieu of a world unchanged, before Juliette turned away from such illusions and chose to follow a perilous but, to her, a necessary path. And Louis was left to continue his education into English ways.

When, after another day during which time moved slowly, filled with reminiscences on his father's part, but no talk of the uncertain future, Kit finally said goodbye. He was conscious that he might not see this frail old man again, that for whatever reason, this might be their last farewell. They both stood in the shadow of extinction, yet parted with feigned light-heartedness, exchanging easy, empty phrases of reassurance, jocular and hopeful, as though they might live for ever, always remain like this. But as he drove away and glanced back over his shoulder, waving, waving, his father's face began to sag, his features becoming ghastly, filled with grief.

Kit did not immediately drive to Hendon, where a transport was to fly him to the Middle East. Instead he took the little sports car along the familiar route through Petworth, Wisborough Green and Horsham, the road he had followed as a child, deep in the soft hide back seat of the Rolls, heading for the Grange and another term, then as now breathing in the rich country smell of earth and grass and beasts, that mingled with the pleasant stench of petrol fumes and hot exhausts and singing tyres. He turned into the driveway of the school, redbrick and monstrous in the Victorian way, everything the same but himself much changed. In the hallway he heard the sound of children's voices, shrill behind the various classroom doors. He was taken up the curving stairs to Colonel Villiers's study by a woman he did not know. At her knock the headmaster looked up from a scatter of exercise books. By his hand lay Kennedy's *Shorter Latin Primer*.

'Hello, sir,' said Kit. '*Shortbread Eating Primer* still in vogue, I see.' He removed his service cap. 'Sorry to butt in unannounced.'

'Good heavens,' said Villiers, 'it's Curtis, isn't it? Just marking prep.' He stood up. 'We hear great things of you.' His tone was warm. Kit had brought credit to the school. But their talk was brief, inconsequential. Kit had neither time nor patience to dwell on more remembrances.

'The boys would love a word or two from you,' said Villiers. 'It's the matter of a moment to round them up.'

Kit shook his head. 'I'm rather pressed, sir, sorry.'

'I understand. Perhaps another time. You want to see Garencières, of course. Mrs Latimer, will you fetch the boy?' He waved Kit to sit down in one of the worn armchairs beside the empty fireplace. 'He's doing well, you'll be pleased to hear. A bright little fellow, industrious and quick to learn. Popular too. His classmates call him Boney.'

'Boney?'

'After Bonaparte.'

'He won't mind that.'

Villiers left Kit and Louis Garencières together, closing the study door behind him. Kit picked up the Latin primer. 'I was never any good at this. How do you get on?'

'Not bad.'

'And English too?'

'Not bad.'

'Everything not bad?'

Louis smiled reluctantly. 'Have you shot down many Germans?'

'Not recently, no. I'm starting a different line of work.'

The boy did not ask what that might be. He fidgeted by the desk, as though he wanted to get away.

'I hear they call you Boney.'

'Yes.'

'No news from your mother, I'm afraid.'

'I believe she must be dead.'

'Oh no, no reason to think that.'

'She is dead, I am sure of it. Otherwise she would not leave me here alone, without a word.'

'Louis, you're not alone.'

'I wish we had never come to England. I hate it here.'

'Believe me, you would hate it more in France.'

'If we had stayed,' said the boy, '*Maman* would not be dead.'

'If you had stayed,' said Kit, 'things would have been the same. Your mother is not the type to stand by and let things happen, bad things that harm your country.'

Louis chewed his lip. 'I think I should be going now.'

'My father sends his love. He has been very ill.'

'I know. Soon he will also die, I think.' The boy said it with a subtle emphasis, as though he wanted it to hurt. Kit looked at him, small in his purple blazer and grey short trousers, defiant, troubled, his knees stuck about with plasters from schoolboy tumbles.

'I don't know when we'll meet again,' said Kit.

'Never, perhaps,' said Louis, with the same little twist of bitterness in his tone.

Kit was amused by his insouciance. 'You could be right. If so, we've made provisions. You understand provisions?'

'*Provisions de bouche?*'

Kit grinned. 'More than victuals. Your future, and your mother's. She will come back: she is not dead. Believe that, as I do, and in time you will find it to be true.' He held out his hand. 'Don't write me off too soon, old chap. I've got a way of bouncing back.' He could see that the boy had failed to understand, but did not bother to explain, and added finally: '*Louis, au revoir. Nous nous reverrons.*'

'*Oui, Monsieur,*' said Louis gravely. '*Au revoir.*' Then, at the door, he paused and nodded, his mouth in the faintest curve. '*Bonne chance.*'

Kit left the Lea-Francis in a Kensington mews garage owned by a friend from his Oxford days. He took an underground train to Holborn and walked down Kingsway to York House, where he received a desultory briefing on the situation in North Africa by a professorial squadron leader and collected his travel orders. As he stepped into the corridor he saw, advancing, Ossie Wolf with a US Army Air Corps major. They exchanged a few words, and then he found the pool car that was to take him and two others to Hendon. The men were sergeant pilots bound for Malta, to join a Bristol Beaufighter squadron. He told them something of what they could expect, but not too much.

He stared out at the passing scene as they crossed the Euston Road and headed north through Camden Town. Bombs had damaged many of the shops, and whole interiors were revealed with, propped up on the pavement, the predictable *Business As Usual* and *We Can Take It* signs. In terraces great gaps yawned, modest villas reduced to piles of bricks and burnt-black timbers. In places pictures still hung on the walls of bedrooms without floors or ceilings.

At Hendon the Austin stopped beside a hangar. Inside, airmen were busy loading cargo into a Lockheed Hudson. Kit felt an instant rush of apprehension. He knew it made no sense, that the Hudson did not have an inherent fault. By contrast it was valued by its crews as a tough old workhorse that would always get them home. It had just been rotten luck, he told himself, that day in October 1941 – the sort of thing that could happen at any moment, any time, to any type who logged the hours. That was flying. Some drew the short straw, some did not. There were no illusions among those whose business was conducted in the skies. If the equipment failed, and it could, they all knew that, it was a long way down and the God of gravity was unforgiving.

They had been over the Thames Valley somewhere when he and Pop Penrose had heard the engine note of the starboard Pratt & Whitney of that other Hudson begin to rise and fall, to falter – and saw black smoke. Damn, he had thought. This could be it. No fresh assignment, then, briefly back in England before embarking on a carrier and leading a fly-off of Hurricanes to re-inforce the Malta strength. He had prepared himself to die, curiously resigned, feeling the Hudson, on approach, drop towards the Hendon runway, starboard engine feathered, port engine screaming, port wing too high, yes, far too high; the thump beneath them as the undercarriage was retracted; a belly-landing then – the last resort. A sense of lightness, then his body pressing down, as the Hudson porpoised. The runway streaming past the wing; grass, tarmac, in the distance buildings. Finally, the stall at forty feet, the dive, the ground coming up very fast. As it was, he did not draw the shortest straw that day. That went to Penrose, screaming, pinned in his seat with his hair alight; Kit, thrown clear but staggering back towards the shattered fuselage, already dazed and scorched, unable to get him out.

Now he climbed on board the loaded Hudson ahead of the two Beaufighter men and settled himself in a single seat towards the tail, ready to meet any lingering unease alone.

They followed the usual route, the long Atlantic detour to take them clear of Brest, flying low beneath the enemy radar cover, careful not to alert the free-hunt Messerschmitt 109s that scoured those seas. Three hours later, heading south across the Bay of Biscay, the threat was Bordeaux's long-range Junkers Ju 88s. But nothing was encountered and at the end of a ten-hour flight they landed in Gibraltar with its blaze of lights and disarming air of normal life. A beer or two and then, the Hudson also fuelled, they set course for Malta to drop the bomber boys and fresh supplies. No time to visit the squadron and old friends. Refuelled again at Luqa, the Hudson took off on its final leg, cloaked by darkness, and touched down in Heliopolis, with relics of the ancient world, pyramids and evidence of settlements in the sand, their shadow outlines picked out by a rising, burnished sun.

It was already hot, the air still and oppressive and smelling of dust. Descending from the cool and dim interior of the Hudson the world outside seemed savage, blinding. As Kit's eyes grew used to the light they took in the arching purple skies that shaded into a boundless landscape of saffron and gold and tawny reddish-brown. This prospect had been known to Alexander more than two thousand years ago. Here he had paused on his march from Pelusium to Memphis to offer sacrifices in the temple of Ra. Here he had been named Pharaoh, the Macedonian one of a host of invaders to use Egypt as a pawn in a greater game.

Now, in the middle distance, men were assembling on the parade ground. The day's drill was about to begin. Beyond the square, others were working on blast walls surrounding an underground facility, and still further back were hangars, one with its doors slid open, revealing four high-winged Bristol Bombay transports, noses tilted, ungainly as new-hatched dragonflies on their primitive-looking fixed landing gear.

Kit reported to the adjutant's office. A squadron leader whose tunic was already blackened with sweat checked him in. 'Welcome to Helio, old boy. Not that you'll be here long.'

'Something special brewing?'

'You could say that. You PR chaps are in high demand. The eyes of the Eighth Army and all that. I should pop over to the Mess while you've got the chance. But make sure I know where you are, if you feel like going further afield. Your orders should come through pretty sharpish.'

The officers' mess, a solid two-storey block, resembled a smart hotel. It was set in well-ordered gardens with neat paths edged by low brick walls that passed between beds of oleanders, roses, carnations and geraniums. Water trickled from a fountain in the centre of a pond and, nearby, doves fussed and fluttered round a dovecote. Date and dum palms spread their shade and, here and there, the fruit of orange and lemon trees stood out bright against the green of common olive, tamarisk and sycamore. It had a look of permanence, worked on since the service was first established at Heliopolis more than twenty years before.

Kit signed himself in and was given a temporary room with slatted doors that opened onto a roofed-in terrace with a prospect of the garden. A fan rotated lazily from the ceiling, stirring the hot air.

Downstairs, a native servant in an ankle-length white *djellabah* brought him a glass of fresh-crushed orange juice with soda. By the window, leaning back in a Lloyd Loom chair, a portly flight lieutenant was scanning *Punch*.

'What ho,' he said, 'just dropped in?'

'That's right.'

'Not PR by any chance?'

'As it happens, yes.'

'We heard we could expect a few replacements.' The man stood up. 'I'm Briggs. Based over Deir el Munassib way.'

'I'm Curtis.'

'Ah, the Malta hand. Know where you'll be stationed yet?'

'Not yet.'

'Be glad to have you on my strength. Perhaps you'd like me to put in a word.'

'I'll take what comes, thanks all the same.'

'Up to you, of course.' Briggs snapped his fingers at the servant and pointed at his coffee cup. 'Wangled a bit of leave. Last day today. I'm popping into Cairo later. Perhaps you'd like to join me? Lots to see. The jolly old Pyramids, of course, Shepherd's Hotel, the El Gezira Sporting Club, just across the Nile from the military hospital at Guava. Green grass, would you believe, and cricket. I've seen county players in action there – Wally Hammond, Freddie Brown. Just like being at Lord's, apart from the dratted heat.' He tapped his nose. 'Also plenty of fruity stuff, if you understand me. Anything that takes your fancy, providing you know where to look.'

'Which you do, I suppose,' said Kit.

'Common knowledge, old boy,' said Briggs. 'Common knowledge.'

That afternoon, they joined some others in a truck that dropped them in the centre of the city, close to Ezbekieh Place. From there Briggs led Kit to Muski Street and the narrow alleys of the bazaar. In tiny open-fronted shops craftsmen sat cross-legged tooling leather, weaving rugs or working metal. The sounds of their industry rang back from the walls, mixed with the cries of pedlars selling sweets and souvenirs and the entreaties of the beggars; the crippled, the blind, the poor.

'Bit of local colour, old boy,' said Briggs, pushing his way past, 'before we go to Groppi's.'

In the cafe's shady garden they found a table and ordered tea and prettily coloured ice-creams served in shallow coupes. Briggs devoured his like a schoolboy, crunching the wafer loudly, his small eyes darting here and there, as though he feared that the unaccustomed treat might be snatched away.

It was later, in the Long Bar at Shepherd's Hotel, that Briggs passed on the rumours he had heard of a PR squadron being formed; speculated on the question of command, the need for the powers-that-be to choose an old hand; his belief that everything came in time; his optimism that he would be favoured for the job, confident enough to venture that, 'When the time comes, Curtis, I know I can count on you.'

Within days Kit's orders were received, but not to join Briggs's flight. Instead, he had to report to Alam el Halfa, separated by twenty miles of scrub desert from Deir el Munassib.

A brisk wind was whipping across the forward airfield when he jumped down from a Bristol Bombay bringing in supplies and, covering his face with his hands against the dust, he followed an airman towards the flight commander's tent. More tents were ranged around the landing strip scraped flat and clear on the grit-grey desert floor. Outside the nearest, its guy ropes quivering, a sign said *Pilots' Mess* and, sheltered by the tent flap, a sergeant pilot was sleeping soundly in a deckchair. So, Kit thought, no distinctions here.

He heard the rumble of a Merlin and paused to watch an all-over blue Spitfire touch down for a perfect landing and taxi towards an area where half a dozen more were parked. The airman he was following had stopped and turned, his face caked white. When he licked his lips, his tongue was red. He snorted and expelled a gob of spit. 'That's one of Flying Officer Grimshaw's better ones.'

Kit's expression hardened. 'I don't appreciate ground-crew commenting on flying matters.'

'Sorry, sir. No offence.'

'I'll be the judge of that. Now get your finger out and show me to the CO's tent.'

They passed a scatter of vehicles: a battered civilian car of indeterminate make, assorted light and heavy trucks, bowsers of aviation fuel. Close by, stores were neatly stacked and covered with roped-down tarpaulins. The contrast with the comforts of

Heliopolis was extreme, but everything was businesslike and neatly ordered.

The flight commander was a short, gruff Scotsman with a beady eye. He brushed away a cloud of flies. 'I'm Mackintosh. Part of Sid Cotton's merry band back in 1939. Did you ever meet the Wingco?'

Kit shook his head. He knew of the man who, as a civilian, had championed the cause of aerial reconnaissance before the war; had demonstrated its value with flights in Lockheeds testing cameras, to prove that clear pictures could be captured at high speed and at heights above 20,000 feet. Commissioned, Cotton had created the RAF's newest unit, the Heston flight, that quickly moved from experimental stage to being operational. But its creator, mercurial, impatient and energetic, inclined to disregard orders he considered misguided, had like many visionaries alienated others along the way. Abruptly the Air Staff replaced him with a regular officer they thought more suited to day-to-day command, to the chagrin of Cotton's fellow PR pioneers who, even now, more than two years on, were still inclined to count themselves as members of Sidney Cotton's private air force.

Now Mackintosh growled, 'Damned disgrace, the way their Airships dumped the old man. Gave him a minor gong and chucked him back into civvy street. Poor bloody reward, I say. If it hadn't been for him, our forces wouldn't have a clue about what lies on the other side of the hill. As it is, the Eighth Army has a mosaic of every bit of ground between Cairo and Cape Bon. Without the Wingco, PR would have been years behind.'

For two weeks Kit flew daily sorties, getting to know the flight's machines and men. Mackintosh was satisfied with his progress; his quiet, calm manner, his readiness to work with ground-crews to help make sure the unit's Spitfires and their cameras were protected against the all-pervading dust and sand; his interest in the complexities of photo-interpretation, even finding time to visit the mobile trailers where the specialists developed and studied film; the way he tempered his obvious flying skills to suit the precise and different needs of aerial photography.

The word passed up the line that Curtis was, in Mackintosh's estimation, 'an experienced and efficient officer with obvious potential for our branch of the service' and, more informally, 'a first-class type'.

Then Mackintosh did not come back from a long-range flight to Crete, now in German hands. There, Messerschmitt 109s, it was later learned, had been vectored by the island's triple radar stations to intercept a prowling Spitfire. That was all, a fragment of information received by intelligence from an unknown source. Nothing to be done, of course. Too late to mount a search. All that was certain was that Mackintosh was dead. Within hours Kit was confirmed as flight commander. He felt sick at Mackintosh's passing, barely given time to know the man, but also proud.

Four

The tropical storm was sudden and fierce, sweeping out of the tangled jungle that lay inland and assaulting the sleeping settlement of Takoradi like some wrathful spirit. Rain pounded on the roofs of the little huts that clustered on a slight incline within sight of the Atlantic, the racket of the downpour on the corrugated iron blending with the lower rumble of the distant surf that broke on the yellow beaches where the fronds of palm trees flailed and twisted in the wind.

In the hut closest to the nine-hole golf course with its greens of sand, Ossie Wolf pushed aside his mosquito net and walked over to the open window where water was rushing off the roof and splattering the reddish earth. At least the storm would cool things down some, provide a little relief from the goddamned insects that didn't seem to fancy flying when the met report was lousy. They were not alone. He wondered if that morning's trip was on, the two-and-a-half-hour flight from this Gold Coast outpost of the RAF, across the Bight of Benin to Lagos, first stage of the 3,600-mile Takoradi route that would take them all the way Cairo.

Buckeridge read his mind. 'Worth getting up, do you reckon?'

'Are you kidding, Buck?' said Ossie. 'It's already passing over.'

He was right. It was growing lighter by the moment, shadows vanishing as the sun broke through the scudding haze. The torrents of water from the roof had eased to trickles now, everything dripping wet and steaming, indoors too, the humidity almost tangible, as though it could be rubbed like silk between the fingers. Suspended on wire hangers, the pilots' uniforms were already damp, and furry mould, a bilious bluish-green, flourished on their shoes and leather belts and flying jackets.

Still, as quarters went, these were not uncomfortable, built before the war as rest houses for the whites who ran the gold mine 100 miles up-country. They had done as well for themselves as could be expected, Ossie thought, in this stinking climate, creating a semblance of home around the artificial harbour where there was depth enough for big vessels to berth alongside. At most other ports along that coast, seafarers still had to trust their cargoes to small boats fighting through the breaking surf.

At Takoradi life followed an orderly thought-through routine, of sensible solutions to anticipated problems, of opportunities seen and grasped, of constant improvement to man's lot – any man, white or black – a legacy of Empire, so different to the African way of following tradition, not adapting, muddling along as they always had, going nowhere, biddable but chaotic. At least, that was what the British said; the British preoccupied with a conflict of which the local people had little understanding, or wished to, apart from the dockers who helped to unload the aeroplanes in their crates or the labourers at the airfield constructing still more buildings and clearing additional runways from the scrub. And even they remained incurious when the flying men died in accidents or from disease, waging a war that seemed to have spread across a world of which they, the Ashanti, knew so very little. They would shrug in the face of death, perhaps when something failed on a Hurricane on a proving flight and it struck the ground and burned. An Ashanti proverb was often on their lips: 'What is bad luck for one man is good for another.' And they would resume their welcome tasks as the bells of the ambulance and fire engine began to sound.

From this distant enclave a defence flight patrolled the maritime lanes of the West African coast, protecting Allied shipping from U-boats and those Vichy French who might venture out, by sea or air, from their territories in the neighbouring Ivory Coast, Togo and Dahomey. From here too, convoys of bombers and fighter planes, shipped from Britain and the United States, reassembled and freshly tested, were dispatched across the wastes of central Africa to make good the losses of the Desert Air Force. It had to be that way. The long sea route, around the Cape to Suez, was slower by weeks, as well as exposing soft targets to German wolf-packs. And the cauldron of the Mediterranean, ringed by hostile Axis bases, was still more hazardous.

Ossie Wolf had flown the Takoradi route three times now. This trip, Buckeridge would lead as usual, in a long-nosed Blenheim Mark IV, a pig to fly, heavy with armour-plate and guns, tough to keep in the air if one of its twin Mercury engines failed. The only reassurance for Buckeridge and his crew was that, on the course they followed, they were separated from the attentions of the Luftwaffe by the immensity of the Sahara and so unlikely to encounter the enemies, at least an enemy with a swastika on its flank. The only enemies they faced, like the rest who did the trip, were the weather, the land that lay below and the machine itself. That is, until they neared the Nile.

Ossie had pulled on vest and khaki shorts, ready to go down to the wash-house, but first he lit up a Woodbine, coughing and spitting tobacco fragments through the window. 'Jesus, what wouldn't I give for a Lucky Strike.'

'Put 'em on your shopping list,' said Puss Catt, 'in Cairo.'

Ossie squinted at the navigator through a haze of smoke. 'What's on your list, Puss? Going to buy yourself a dose of clap?'

'For God's sake, chaps,' said Buckeridge, 'not this early in the morning.'

'Actually,' said Catt, 'I'm selling. Picking up more snake-skins from old Obdulu when we get to Kano.'

Buckeridge snorted. 'You'll land yourself in trouble, dealing with your dodgy witch-doctor chum. Strictly against the regs, you know. I'm not at all sure I shouldn't report you. Just make sure you keep me in the dark.'

'Hell, Buck,' said Ossie, 'this is chicken-feed compared with the racket those Polish guys were running, smuggling Lagos gold to Cairo in the axles of their Blenheims.'

'That's right,' said Catt. 'This is strictly pocket money, nothing serious. God knows, on what we're paid you need a ruddy side-line. Besides, it keeps the local economy oiled. I'm doing old Obdulu a favour.' He grinned. 'Doing us both a favour. Those skins fetch decent money. You'd be surprised.'

'Beats me what the wogs want with the stuff,' said Buckeridge.

'Wise up, brother,' said Ossie. 'They make it into handbags for the whores who're going to give Puss here his dose of clap.' He picked up a shoe but quickly threw it down again. 'Holy Christ.' A scorpion scuttled from the shoe into a corner, then turned and faced him, crouching, quivering, erectile tail poised to strike. For a second, Ossie admired its spirit. Then he seized the discarded shoe and hammered the scorpion flat and went to shave.

He did not dislike Takoradi, despite the climate. The joke of a golf course boasted what the British called the Clubhouse, where they tried to imagine themselves on the links of Royal St Georges; no soft, emerald turf, no skylarks rising from the bunkers, no distant cliffs, no Pegwell Bay – only sea and sand hills – but it was enough to make men thoughtful as they nursed their whiskies. Ossie had no time for golf, 'a sucker play', but he was good at sinking a Scotch in one.

The officers' mess provided some variety, cheap alcohol and local beer that hit the spot, where even slight excuses led to cele-brations – birthdays, promotions, survival from a crash or one more Takoradi run completed, back safe from a round trip of 7,000 miles.

There was English cricket, 'crazy goddamned game', football despite the heat, and boxing bouts, officers versus men, which Ossie thought less crazy, a chance to even a score or two. He took on Sergeant Nesbit, some kind of pre-war champ at welterweight, and knocked him cold; Nesbit, who he had overheard describing him as 'that cocky bleeding Yank'. 'Now who's bleeding, you sonofabitch?' Ossie had said, squatting by Nesbit's spreadeagled body as he was counted out; saying it quietly so he wouldn't lose the win. The spectators thought he was worried for the man.

Then, for those who dreamed of Africa, an Africa of Burton, Speke and Livingstone, of jungle kingdoms and lost tribes, a maze of dirt roads led inland, winding through the forest where the rasping chorus of unseen creatures filled the bug-infested air; where vividly coloured parrots flew between trunks of close-growing silk cotton trees and monkeys swung from branch to branch like Johnny Weissmuller; where for pence you could take a hollowed-out wood canoe and be paddled up to some mud-hut village to be greeted by the chief. Ossie took the trails just once. He had no stomach for the deference of the natives, who bowed and scraped and all but laid themselves out on the dirt floors of their compounds, and put too much damned starch in the collars of Ossie's companions. Treated like regular white bwanas he saw them swell, but they soon changed back to no-account sweating airmen scourged by prickly heat, and worse, when they straggled back to camp.

But still, for Ossie, Takoradi was somewhere to escape from, not just a place from which to ferry fighter planes to where the action was and then come back. He had tackled Squadron Leader Fletcher about a posting. The CO had checked his file.

'You've been a considerable nuisance, Wolf, one way or another. This is your chance to make amends.'

'So who was the guy who reckoned I should be taught a lesson?'

'A need arose for pilots who knew their stuff. Your name came up. This isn't a penal colony, you know. We're doing vital work.'

'Yeah, sure. But this kind of duty's not my style. I mean, of course it has its place. But I'm a fighter pilot, sir, and I've got the score to prove it. Gee whizz, what about my flying record? Doesn't that count for something?'

'Of course. Nobody questions your ability in the air. But the service demands more than that. Take my advice, Wolf. Keep your head down and do what's required of you here. Don't make waves. Do that and I'll make sure the word gets round. I can't do more.'

But still Ossie brooded about who had fingered him, dumping him in this superheated sideshow to do a delivery job that any greenhorn straight from flying training could do as well.

One time, it seemed his prayers for action had been answered. A single Martin Maryland of the Vichy French carried out a low-level hit-and-run attack, dropping bombs at random but causing little damage, before fleeing back to its Dahomey base. Ossie had scrambled into the cockpit of the nearest armed-and-ready Hurricane and taken off crosswind, not bothering to secure his Sutton harness or even wear a helmet. A Maryland was a slow old crate. No need for fancy flying. Keep it straight and level, and wax the sucker's tailplane from below: he wouldn't know what hit him. His thumb was already trembling on the gun-button. Except he lost the bomber against the green confusion of the forest and rising, humid swathes of mist. He landed, cursing, floating in his seat unsecured by belts, finding it hard to keep his feet pressed firm against the rudder pedals, only a tight grip on the control column, and his flying skill, holding him in place.

Fletcher was incensed. 'Step out of line once more,' he said, his scalp stretched tight with anger, 'and I'll have you grounded. Men risked their lives to deliver that aircraft here and you, you bloody fool, decide it's a good idea to chase some panicky Johnny Frenchman who bombs a couple of palm trees. I'll give you one more chance. Remember what I said. Keep your head down and don't make waves. Otherwise I'll make sure you stay here for the duration, whether you reckon yourself an ace or not. Is that clearly understood?'

'Yes, sir. Understood.'

'I hope so, Wolf, for your sake. Life's difficult enough here, God knows. To do our job we must rely on teamwork. I've no time for egocentrics waging a private war.'

'You saying that's what I am, sir?'

'Prove you're not. That's all.'

Later, in the mess, Fletcher took Ossie Wolf aside. 'Look, old man, I gave you a bit of a dressing down back there. I'm not saying you didn't deserve it, but I'd hate to see a chap like you fail to make the grade after all you've done. You're an exceptional pilot, Wolf, we all know that but sometimes you're your own worst enemy. Believe me, you won't get where you want to by causing trouble. Quite the reverse. I thought that would have clicked by now. So pull your finger out, there's a good chap, so I can recommend you, in all good conscience, when something suitable comes up. Nuff said, I think. Now, what'll you have?'

'A beer,' said Ossie, 'and maybe I'll try me a slice of humble pie.' He'd taste a crumb or two, to get old Fletcher off his back, if it meant he might get back to business.

Now, a month later, with Buckeridge and the others, Ossie studied the meteorological report covering the five-day flight ahead. The forecast was favourable; no storms of any kind predicted along the route, no adverse winds, the cloud cover thin, so they could stay within sight of ground even at 10,000 feet. Nothing to stop them going.

They checked their route: east past the Volta estuary, keeping out to sea, well clear of Togo's curious Vichy French who might send up an interceptor or, more likely, count the aircraft in the flight and pass the information to the Germans. Touchdown at

Lagos to refuel, after nearly three hours in the air, then north to Oshogbo, three hours more, passing over a forest canopy so densely packed it resembled a boundless lake, disturbed by the downdraft of propellers, landing with the night. Next day, destination Kano, where the Trans-Saharan highway began or ended, depending on the direction of your journey, hotter than the humid coast but, higher by 1,500 feet, its climate dry and oddly pleasant; Kano, where Puss Catt would collect his snake-skins from his shady partner, old Obdulu. Next, the third leg, east across the heart of Africa to El Geneina, close to the Marra Mountains whose peaks rose 10,000 feet above the arid plain. Day four, 800 miles more, and now the blue-green waters of the Nile in sight, something like a miracle after days of passing over dry, brown grassland; touchdown in Khartoum, or rather Wadi Sidina, a few miles down the river. Fifth day, a final midway refuelling stop at Wadi Halfa, then on to Cairo, the landing ground in Fayoum Road within sight of Giza, where the three Great Pyramids – Menkaure, Khafre and Khufu – rose from the desert floor. Five days, 3,600 miles. If all went well, nine fresh aircraft delivered safe, ready to join the fight.

Twenty-four hours' notice had been given by Takoradi to the staging posts along the way that another ferrying flight would be setting off that morning. The nine machines took off individually and circled until the formation was complete, assembling in a shallow vic led by Buckeridge's Blenheim, the top of its broad perspex canopy daubed with whitewash to shield its three-man crew from the unrelenting sun. They made a final pass across the airfield, and on the ground, men paused in their work to see them go, waving, giving thumbs-up and v-for-victory signs.

Standing by the runway, Squadron Leader Fletcher watched until they were out of sight, then turned and went back to his office. There, day by day, news would filter through of the convoy's progress: distance covered, problems encountered, any losses of machines and men, rescue plans launched if enough was known about where a pilot had come down and if there was any hope.

In the cockpit of his Hurricane Mark II, Ossie shifted his body to make himself more comfortable and looked across at Buckeridge 200 feet to starboard. The Blenheim was flanked by Hurricanes, four on each side, keeping visual contact only, no wireless communication between machines, strict radio silence imposed in case the convoy might be detected and an unwelcome welcoming committee arranged, probably near the Libyan border where, at last, they would come within range of the bolder German fighters. And there was only infrequent wireless contact with the bases on the ground, the briefest of exchanges in the tap-tap-tap of Morse; no measured, reassuring voice to guide them on their way or talk them down. Most outposts lacked the right equipment, what they had being low-powered, short-range and unreliable, subject to central Africa's atmospheric quirks, where reception was always bad except, confoundedly, at night, when nothing flew. So convoy pilots had grown adept at sharing information through simple signs and mouthing words and phrases. They flew close enough for that, but not so close that their passage through the air would be affected by the turbulence created by their machines. That would lead to constant, tiring adjustments to the throttle to hold position and, more important, the fluctuating engine revs consuming and wasting extra fuel.

They had been in the air for forty minutes, following the coastline but keeping out to sea. Slowly the smudge that was Accra fell away to port. A single anonymous vessel crawled west below, leaving a wake of brilliant white against deep blue. Surf was breaking on beaches fringed with palm, mile on mile, with here and there a native village marked by huts and a scatter of fishing craft or an occasional stark white fort built by traders in human flesh.

At first, like always, Ossie relished the power of the Merlin engine coursing through his body, the way it shook the Hurricane's airframe as he climbed to 8,000 feet, then settled to a steady cruising speed of 160 mph, the bellowing of the stub-exhausts seeming to fill his head, banishing thoughts of anything but flying. The sensation was as potent as a shot of rye but also, like a shot of rye, wore off. This was not his trade, guiding a fighter plane through skies empty of a tangible foe. It was like holding an axe without a tree to fell. Hell, all he was required to do was hold position, fly right and tight. Even route-finding he could safely leave to Buckeridge. Not that there was much to leave, just basic navigation, knowing the compass bearing and trying to make the details on the map fit the details on the ground. Tough enough when visibility was good; few signs of habitation, no railway lines, roads mere tracks, most rivers only rivers for a week or so, other-wise dry scratches on the surface. But when visibility was bad, just glimpses of the ground through dense cloud; or when you buffeted your way through tropical storms, caught by rough air that dropped you 100 feet or more, reminding Ossie of the Cyclone ride on Coney Island, then red-eyed pilots would look to their leader like chicks to a mother hen, crowding in a little, not wanting to find themselves alone and seeing the needle on the fuel gauge nudging empty, thinking about that close-packed forest canopy said to be dense enough to land on, and survive, though no one knew a flier who had tried it and told the tale. Thinking how it might be to put it down wheels-up on iron-hard scrub savannah, wondering if you would live to survive the landing and, if you did, how long you would last alone, with no food, no water, no way of knowing where you were, or telling someone else, unless you were in luck and got picked up by a nomad camel train that would take weeks to cover ground you had flown across in minutes. Okay, such rescues had been known, but they were rare.

Now, after sixty minutes in the air, Ossie caught himself musing on these things. He shook his head to clear his brain, rapidly opened and closed his eyes to refresh his vision, breathed very deeply and began to sing, 'You are my sunshine, my only sunshine.' Sunshine. Jesus, that was rich. Who needed reminding? Who could forget? Still, anything to stay alert, maintain sharp focus on every routine task that kept him in the air, anything to fend off fatigue, that drowsy pleasant feeling that could make him lose touch with that mother hen Blenheim, that could get him killed as surely as any bum move in a dogfight.

At Lagos, their first refuelling stop, they followed the old routine. Five miles out, Buckeridge waggled the Blenheim's wings and overflew the airfield at circuit height, followed by the fighters in line-astern, before they landed one by one and taxied in towards the area where airmen waited by the stacks of four-gallon petrol cans. Then, fuel tanks full, they took off for Oshogbo, where a few plain Air Force buildings were clustered incongruously on the outskirts of the little township of mud-walled huts with deep-thatched roofs. There, under canvas, they drank warm beer and chewed on rounds of stale bread and bully beef not-so-fresh from the Takoradi cookhouse, or strolled about Oshogbo, buying snacks from the roadside stalls: bowls of peppery stew and fried yams, washed down with sweet palm wine.

The next night's stop, in Kano, Catt met up with old Obdulu somewhere off the station and, with the help of Sergeant Sewell, the Blenheim's radio operator/gunner, stowed ill-wrapped bundles of snakeskin in the hold, careful to keep them out of Buckeridge's sight. Catt rubbed his hands with glee. 'A wizard trip. Old Obby's done us proud. Rattlers, spitting cobra, carpet vipers. We'll make a tidy profit, that's for sure.'

'Feller, nothing's sure,' said Ossie. 'We got three days to go.'

'Relax, old boy,' said Catt. 'This one's a bloody milk run. You just see.'

But not everything was proceeding smoothly. The Hurricanes were running on internal fuel, without the forty-gallon wing-borne drop tanks sometimes fitted, so their range was short and refuelling stops more frequent. That, of course, had been allowed for but it was an irritation, breaking up the rhythm of the flight. It meant that after leaving Kano for El Geneina they not only had to land at Maiduguri but also Fort Lamy to top up the fighters' tanks, because that day's final stage covered 550 miles. Again, a factor known to those who planned the flight but compounded now by one of the Hurricane pilots, Stafford-Smith, who reported that his Hurricane's fuel consumption was running high.

'All right, Hyphen,' Buckeridge said, before they took off from Kano. 'It's only three hundred miles to Maiduguri and the hop to Fort Lamy is even shorter, less than one hundred and fifty. The ground-crew chaps have checked things over and drawn a blank. Most likely you've been a bit heavy-handed on the throttle, trying to keep formation. I say press on, lacking any evidence of gremlins. Be a pity to lose a kite so soon.'

'Okay, Buck,' said Stafford-Smith, 'but if I hit the deck, you pay the taxi fare.'

The payment was not required. In less than two hours they reached Maiduguri, the flight intact, and within another hour had crossed from Nigeria into Chad, landing on the red-stone runway of Fort Lamy, where the Free French ruled.

The colony had been established for forty years, under the light hand of French administration, a source of willing labour and raw cotton. After the Fall of France in 1940, Chad had been the first French province to declare itself with the Allies, and had remained undisturbed by war, except for a small garrison of soldiers and a detachment of the Free French Air Force, equipped with Potez and Bloch heavy fighters. It also acted as host to a party of RAF personnel who lived out at the airport, and tended the needs of ferry-crews and their machines. It was a popular posting, the way of life relaxed and multicultural with a Gallic twist, the food and drink a revelation, the local women practised in European ways; a favourite stop-off point for senior ranks in transit.

The convoy flight was lined up beside a hangar, wing to wing, tidily arranged, quickly worked on by the teams of fitters and mechanics. A fuel bowser here, no refuelling from metal cans. But Stafford-Smith was still concerned. He sought out the nearest NCO. 'Make sure your chaps check those fuel lines, Flight. I'm sure there's muck in the system somewhere.'

The flight sergeant grunted. 'If it's there, we'll find it, sir.'

Buckeridge came across. 'Still fretting, Hyphen?'

'She's just sucking up the juice. Got to be more than my ham-fist.'

'Bugger. Sounds as though we'll have to dump you here. Sure it's not a put-up job?'

'Meaning?'

'I can think of worse places to be marooned.'

Stafford-Smith smiled wryly. 'Normally, I'd agree. Except I've got a burning date with a Canadian nurse in Cairo. Bugger squared.'

A hundred yards away, Catt jumped down from the Blenheim.

'I say, Puss,' said Buckeridge, 'what's keeping you? The others are heading for the mess.'

Catt looked evasive. 'Just checking.'

'Checking what?'

'Oh, making sure I've got a fix on El Geneina. Bit of a head-wind blowing up, I'm told.'

'Good show, Puss,' said Buckeridge, pleased. 'Good show.'

The mess was large and comfortable; cane furniture with cush-ions, plenty of week-old newspapers and well-thumbed English magazines. Native art was mixed in with various pinned-up posters: a Fougasse warning against careless talk, with Hitler and Goering seated behind two gossipping women on a London bus; the idiot-pilot Prune looking smug with, underneath, the legend: *P.O. Prune simply never has accidents*; a Great Western locomotive pulling a holiday train under the slogan *Speed to the West*. At the windows of the Mess were Venetian blinds, on the ceiling revolving fans. On the tables, quickly, cups of strong, sugared tea. In the chairs, also without delay, the aircrew of the convoy.

A group captain came over from the bar. He was in a mood to talk, to show he was at ease with lower ranks, particularly if they flew. He was conscious of his wings. He hoped it gave him status with these youngsters. He wanted them to ask about his flying, so he could reminisce about an earlier show, offensive patrols perhaps, over the trenches near Douai, dodging Archie in the SE5, looking for Hun scouts. He had an impulse to prove he understood, still had a young man's heart.

'Hello, gentlemen,' he said. 'Just dropped in?'

'That's right,' said Ossie Wolf. He did not get up, but hung a leg across the arm of his wicker chair. The others nodded, smiled a little but did not say a word.

The group captain sipped his gin and tonic. He studied the men's faces. They shared the otherworldly look of those whose thoughts were still aloft, their element the air, the earth below inconsequential. To them, he ruefully acknowledged, his presence was unimportant, irrelevant to their mission. He had felt the same, confronted by a bore of an RFC brigadier general curious to learn about matters that did not concern him, or experiences a pilot wanted to forget. He turned away and almost bumped into a flight lieutenant, older than the rest, who had just come in.

'Hello, sir,' said Buckeridge. 'Hope the chaps are behaving themselves.'

The group captain nodded at Ossie Wolf. 'That young man's attitude leaves a lot to be desired. However, I gave him the benefit of the doubt. Not the time or place to haul him over the coals. No doubt he's a bit done up, like the rest. Does he report to you?'

'Only because I'm leading the flight. Otherwise we're of equal rank.'

'Strikes me as a bolshie type. What's his background?'

'He's an American, sir.'

'Ah, well, that explains it.' The group captain looked across at the pilots, who were mostly sipping their drinks and staring into space, not talking.

'Cool bunch, aren't they?'

'They have their moments.'

'Different in my day, I can tell you,' said the group captain, hoping to open a door to his venturesome past. 'We were apt to raise a rumpus.'

Buckeridge only laughed. 'Trouble is, sir, we've only reached halfway. These fellows know what lies ahead. When we get to Cairo, things will liven up.' His cup of tea arrived. 'I say, are you based here?'

'Good God, no. Dropped in for a spot of liaison work with the French and then it's back to Blighty. Just completed a tour in Heliopolis, sorting out air-transport procedures. Flying a blasted desk, to my regret. The service doesn't need old buffers like me, not in aeroplanes at least.' He paused, and sipped his drink. 'What do you fly – fighters? You look like a fighter boy to me.'

''Fraid not, sir. Blenheims, decent crates, particularly the Mark I. That was quite a handy little beast, but easy meat for 109s, so the powers-that-be decided to add some armour plate and extra guns. End result, of course, with all that weight . . . well, it just made the performance worse. Even easier meat. Luckily for me, someone thought I was the perfect type for the Takoradi route. Just deliver the things to chaps who do the fighting.'

The group captain glanced at the DFM medal ribbon on Buckeridge's tunic. 'But you've done your share, I see.'

'Picked it up before I was commissioned, bouncing Jerry convoys in the Channel. A few narrow squeaks. Probably shouldn't say it, sir, but this ferrying business suits me fine. I'm not exactly eager to get back in the thick of things, at least not in a Blenheim IV.'

'Not much chance of that – at least, not here. Now, let's get you something stronger.' The group captain banged the round brass bell on the corner of the bar. 'Actually, if you think the Blenheim takes the biscuit, let me tell you about the Maurice Farman Longhorn I trained on at Brooklands in 1916 . . .'

'Heard about my snake-skins, chaps?' Puss Catt was saying. 'One of the bundles worked itself loose. Bouncing round inside the fuselage like a bloody football. Some of the skins are absolutely ruined.'

'When your pard with the bone through his nose finds out,' said Ossie, 'he's gonna be sticking pins in that little effigy of you he keeps in his mud hut.'

'I managed to get the stuff stowed again without Buck seeing,' said Catt. 'I'm depending on you blokes not to let on.'

'How much is it worth?' said Stafford-Smith. 'I need some extra cash if I'm going to be stuck here for a bit.'

'Have a heart, Hyphen,' said Catt. 'I'm still counting my losses.'

'If you spent more time figuring out our course,' said Ossie, 'and less keeping the Cairo tarts in handbags, maybe I'd sleep at nights. I've heard of some small-potatoes rackets in my time . . .' He broke off. Quickly he was on his feet. His head was tilted, his body tensed, his senses roused, instinctively aware of an approaching threat, something as yet unseen, but heard. The others could hear nothing, but he had picked up the far-off *woo-woo-woo* of oscillating aero-engines. 'Jesus,' said Ossie, 'that sounds like a goddamned Heinkel 111.'

Over by the bar, the group captain snorted. 'Don't be ridiculous, man. There isn't a Hun within two thousand miles.'

'Oh yeah?' Ossie went outside, followed by the others. Over by the hangar, the ground-crews were still working on their machines. The sun was high and the shadows short. Everything had a pin-sharp, pristine look, the sharpness of a photograph taken with a Leica, perfectly in focus. And yet there was something wrong.

Ossie shielded his eyes. Looking north, the sky was filling with a yellowish mist. 'What in hell is that?'

Two officers of the permanent staff had joined the group. One muttered, 'It's the harmattan haze, old man, a load of dust and sand blowing down from the Sahara. Infernal nuisance, but at least it cools things down. It's called "the doctor" by the locals, because it brings us some relief from this dratted heat.'

The group captain looked at Ossie with a satisfied smile. 'You see? That's obviously what you heard.' He turned to go inside.

'I'm telling you,' persisted Ossie, 'there's something more than a goddamned sandstorm heading this way.'

And now, at last, they all began to hear it, the unmistakable growl of engines, growing louder, but still its source unseen, cloaked by the Harmattan haze. The sound was menacing and full of purpose.

One of the permanent officers frowned. 'There's certainly something there. Winfield, you're air-traffic control. Have we or the Frenchies got anything up?'

His companion shook his head. 'Not that I know of. And we haven't been notified about more visitors either. These chaps were the last today. Damned odd. I'll have a word with the duty staff.'

'Ask if they're expecting a Heinkel 111,' said Ossie. 'I'd know those Jumos anywhere.'

Winfield stared at him for a moment, his mouth slightly open, and gave an unamused laugh. 'A Heinkel, you say? You mean we're under attack?'

The group captain was quick to join the ripple of laughter. But still, when the air-traffic-control man set off down the cinder track that led to the square, white control tower a few hundred yards away there was an urgency in his step.

Now, in the far distance, emerging from the yellow haze, it

was possible to see the slowly moving dot that was an aeroplane. It appeared to be following a course that would take it east of them, at a height of about eight thousand feet, passing over the conjunction of the Logone and Chari Rivers where many vessels plied their trade in livestock, fruit and cotton, salt and dates and grain. 'Whatever it is,' said the permanent officer, 'it doesn't seem much interested in us.'

'That's a goddamned Heinkel,' said Ossie, 'and those guys haven't come all this way to check out the shipping. If you've got an air-raid siren, I should trigger it pronto.'

The permanent officer sighed. 'Give it a rest, there's a good chap. Let's wait and see what Winfield's got to say.'

The engine notes of the distant machine had changed, were deeper now, under stress. 'Sonofabitch,' said Ossie, 'it's banking – turning back this way. That bastard's on a bombing run.'

'Bombing run be damned. It's probably just a Frog Potez that's got itself lost, or forgotten to file a flight plan. They do it all the time.'

Buckeridge and the rest had listened to the back-and-forth exchange in silence, crowding round, uncertain. The group captain remained a little apart, but had not gone inside. 'Well,' said Ossie, 'you mugs can stand here all you like. I'm going up. Then we'll find out whether it's a lousy Potez or not.' He began to run towards the line of aircraft by the big grey hangar, and grinned when he heard the others pounding along behind. On the way, he noticed Winfield hurrying back from the control tower. 'So what's the story, smart guy?'

'Nothing,' shouted the air-traffic control officer. 'Bit of a mystery. We're waiting for some gen from Takoradi.'

Ossie continued running. His Hurricane was 200 yards away. As he ran, his blood pumping through his veins, he seemed to hear the voice of Fletcher. 'Men risked their lives to deliver that aircraft, and you, you bloody fool, decide it's a good idea to chase some panicky Johnny Frenchman. Step out of line again and I'll have you grounded.' Well, here he was again, stepping out of line. Like always, he could see no other way.

Behind him, Stafford-Smith was panting: 'I hope you're right about this, you bloody Yank. Otherwise we'll never live it down.'

'Hyphen, trust me, it's a goddamned Heinkel. Now scramble that bloody kite before we get a stick of fifty-kilo mothers on our heads.'

He had reached his Hurricane. The ground-crew had not heard him coming, or noticed the presence of the unknown aircraft; they were absorbed in their various tasks, one airman low down in the cockpit checking the controls, the elevators, ailerons and rudder clacking back and forth with a dull, dead, wooden sound. Another was on a steel ladder, securing the panel screws of the engine cowling and, refuelling done, a small Bedford truck was starting to tow away a four-wheel bowser. The noise of the approaching plane was quite loud now and still they took no heed. But in Ossie's mind, what little doubt there might have been had gone. He had heard the rise-and-fall reverberation of Jumo twelve-cylinder engines too often to be wrong: in France, England, Malta and now here, in Chad, where everyone said it was impossible, except for him.

'Hey, brother,' Ossie shouted at the fitter on the ladder, 'get that goddamned accumulator plugged in. I'm taking this baby up.' Then he was on the port wing, jerking his thumb at the startled rigger. 'Okay feller, out of there. Help me with my belts.'

'Blimey, sir, what's up?' Ossie was already in his seat, the airman leaning in to fumble with the fastenings of the Sutton harness, clumsy in his haste.

'Get the lead out, for Chrissake. We got Jerries coming in.'

'Jerries? Are you kidding?'

'What am I? Bob Hope? Jesus, get the hell off my goddamned wing and give your buddy a hand to pull away those chocks.'

Ossie switched on the ignition and magneto and pressed the starter button. The engine spluttered alive, blue smoke gouting from the stub exhausts, the propeller starting to spin. He was working hard at the priming pump, making sure the fuel was getting through. The Merlin settled to an even roar. He waved away the chocks and started to taxi out, checking the windsock on the far side of the field. The wind was still coming from the north, where the sky was ochre-coloured, heavy with the approaching sandstorm. To his right, two Hurricanes were also moving. He recognised Stafford-Smith, circled the finger and thumb of his right hand, then pointed up and mouthed: 'Let's get the sonofabitch.' Stafford-Smith only grinned and shook his head, not understanding.

Then, moving at no more than 20 mph, starting to gather speed along the runway, Ossie heard the bombs – the familiar, distant whistle that became a shriek, filling the air and pressing on the ears, even before the detonations came. Looking up, he saw a Heinkel passing overhead, on a steady course, unhurried and untroubled. No anti-aircraft fire and still no warning siren. The bomber looked rugged and well prepared, smart in its desert camouflage of sand-yellow blotched with black, its undersides pale blue. The stark black crosses showed up well beneath the wings and on its flanks. As the stick of bombs came down, the gunners in the nose and ventral gun positions strafed the ground with their cannon and machine guns. Then the explosions came, shaking the ground at intervals too small to measure, shock waves throwing out a lethal spray of shrapnel, rock and debris, perforating anything in its path.

Slightly ahead of Ossie, Stafford-Smith's Hurricane wavered, lifted by the blast. Left wing raised, it sank back down, engine roaring, the starboard elevator and wing tip striking the ground together. Under stress, the starboard wheel collapsed. The fighter tilted to the left, as the other wheel gave way, spinning to a halt, the propeller blades bent back, smoke rising from the engine.

Further down the runway, another Hurricane was rolling to a stop engulfed in flames. The tyres were still turning, the rubber alight, small circles of wind-fanned fire. The canopy was open and a burning figure climbed slowly from the cockpit, slipped down the wing and began to writhe and struggle in the dirt. All this Ossie saw in moments and then, in his peripheral vision, he caught a flash of something coming towards him fast across the runway to his left, a truck wheel, rolling loose and bouncing high. It reached him at the bottom of a bounce and struck the fuselage between the wing root and the roundel with a sound like tearing paper. His Hurricane abruptly tilted upwards and, although his harness was secure, he was flattened back against his seat. In his rearview mirror, mounted above the windscreen, he saw the reddish surface of the runway rushing past. The tailplane had gone, sheered off, and suddenly light, the rudder-less machine began to veer from side to side, its wheels still down, the stub of fuselage scraping along the runway, the long nose lifting with the thrust of the propeller, pointing to the sky.

Ossie's left hand was on the throttle, trembling with the strain, trying to pull it back and shut the engine down. At last the engine revs of the Merlin died and, devoid of thrust, the Hurricane dropped into an instant dive from fifty feet. The spinner and propeller pierced the runway with a scream of rending metal, spinning the upright fuselage like a top, while Ossie, thrown forward by the impact but held securely by his belts, could only wait for it to end, powerless, a passenger. Then the tail began to fall and the wreck sank down but the right way up. Ossie, conscious and alert throughout the wild ride, quickly pulled the release pin of his harness straps and stepped out of the cockpit, walking across the shattered wing and onto the churned-up dirt beside the runway. The smell of escaping fuel was strong. Beneath its cowling, knocked askew, the engine with all its arteries ruptured, hissed and groaned and ticked, like a boiler about to burst.

Ossie did not run. He headed at an even pace across the runway towards the hangar, or where the hangar used to be, for it was largely gone, just twisted framework like he'd seen in newsreels of the *Hindenburg* disaster at Lakeland field. All around, the sky was stained with rolling clouds of oil-black smoke. Behind him, his Hurricane ignited with a *woomph*. He did not to turn to look. He was clear, untouched. That was all that counted. For sure, he was a little bruised around the shoulders, with maybe the beginnings of a stiff neck. But hell, he'd walked away from worse than that.

Not every poor sucker had. Men were gathered round the pilot who had struggled, burning, on the ground. The flames were out but in between the bending figures Ossie could see a blackened shape, screaming out as it was lifted onto a stretcher. Nothing he could do. He continued walking, brushing himself down, coming up on Stafford-Smith who was limping, wincing, holding his left arm across his chest, right hand held tight around left wrist. He did not ask about it, but Stafford-Smith told him anyway. 'Busted a bloody collarbone, I think. Are you okay?'

'Yeah,' said Ossie. He jerked his head. 'One thing's sure. We're luckier than the guy who fried.'

Stafford-Smith winced, but this time not with pain. 'Sensitive bloody bastard, aren't you?' He looked across to where the ambulance doors were closing. 'Poor old Tony Page. This was his last trip. He'd wangled a posting back to Biggin. Had a girl . . .' His voice tailed off.

'Tough break,' said Ossie.

They could hear the engines of the Heinkel far away, receding. 'The murdering sods,' said Stafford-Smith.

Ossie shrugged. 'One hell of a trick to pull.' He glanced at his watch. 'The distance they've got to cover, they'll never make it. Sundown in a couple of hours. They'll have to put down while there's light enough to land. They'll be low on fuel as well. I wouldn't bet on any of those guys collecting his Iron Cross.'

The airfield was alive with running figures, speeding vehicles, the shouts and cries of rescuers, the injured and the dying. The dead were spread about, killed by blast, lying startled and intact

118

or, closer to the points of the explosions, dismembered. And still it was not over. Without warning the air was torn by a vast concussion and, a mile away, a tower of flame and debris rose into the sky.

'Christ,' said Stafford-Smith. 'Another raid.'

Ossie shook his head. 'No, that sonofabitch was on his own. I reckon that's the Free Frogs' ammo dump gone up. The crazy bastards put it next to their store of fuel, which took a hit.'

They had reached the ruined hangar where, a little while before, the convoy machines had been neatly parked, ready to resume the flight. Only two remained intact, both Hurricanes, a little apart as though they had been pushed away. The rest were scattered about in piled-up, smouldering concentrations of aviation junk, remains of wings, cooked engines, twisted props, a bucket seat, a wheel; a breaker's yard for aeroplanes, the wood and fabric consumed by fire, the tubular metal framework heated white, exposed, as startling as skeletons stripped of flesh. In the centre of the devastation lay Buckeridge's Blenheim, spreadeagled on its belly, torn in two, the forward section quite unharmed, the rear a burned-out husk, its squadron markings baked away by the inferno that had raged inside. Near the surviving Hurricanes, two men stood, their uniforms filthy, their faces black.

'Oh brother,' Ossie said. 'Amos 'n' Andy.'

'Cut that out,' said Buckeridge quietly. 'Groupie's done a sterling job.'

The group captain cupped an ear. 'You'll have to speak up. We had a narrow squeak, helping to manhandle these kites. One of those damned bombs came down too close for comfort. Can't hear a blessed thing. However, you were bang on about that Heinkel, I must admit. I won't make the same mistake again.' He cleared his throat. 'Incidentally, that was a damned good show, you fellows scrambling like that.'

'Tell my CO back in Takoradi,' Ossie said. 'Last time I did that, he said I was a psycho fighting a private war.'

'Come again?'

'Actually, sir,' said Stafford-Smith, 'we could have saved ourselves the trouble. Three Hurrys written off, not to mention one of our most experienced blokes.'

Buckeridge groaned. 'Who copped it, Hyphen?'

'Tony Page.'

'Oh hell. What shape's he in?'

'The worst,' said Stafford-Smith. 'And McIndoe three thousand miles away.' He was shivering, his left hand clasping and unclasping, flinching with the pain. 'Sorry, Buck. It's nothing much.'

'Come on,' said Buckeridge. 'Let's get that seen to by the medics. A few of the boys are over at the hospital already. None of them too bad, thank God.' He glanced at Ossie. 'How about you?'

'Oh, hunky-dory.'

'Good,' said Buckeridge. 'Then be a good chap and rustle up some transport.'

At the hospital the medics had no time for Stafford-Smith. Men died while he waited on a bench, with the other walking wounded. The bare wood floor was slippery with blood, the corridors busy with staff in stained white coats. The noises that rang out from the theatre and the wards reminded Ossie of the Takoradi forest, after dark, where agonies were heard, not seen, and creatures cried out in torment, alone in pain. He did not know why he waited with Stafford-Smith. He offered him no comfort; his injuries were trivial. But anyway, he stayed awhile, leaning against a wall and thinking of something else: that bouncing wheel that took his tailplane off. Thinking of how it might have turned out differently, how it would have been to get that lousy Heinkel lined up in his sights. Someone said his name. He looked up. Puss Catt was coming along the corridor, with Buckeridge and the group captain. He was holding on to Buckeridge's arm, and weirdly changed. His hands were bandaged, his hair and eyebrows had been burned off. His singed scalp was purple with gentian violet. So was his nose.

'I'm in something of a mess,' he said.

'I've seen you looking better,' Ossie said.

'That's not what I mean.'

Buckeridge looked solemn. 'This is the man of the moment.'

'Bravest thing I ever saw,' said the group captain. 'When the Blenheim caught it, this young fellow went off like a greyhound. We yelled to him that everyone was out but, no, he disregarded every warning. Disappeared inside, with all that smoke and flame. Seemed like an eternity. He must have scoured every inch of that fuselage before he was driven out. Quite magnificent. God knows what possessed him.'

'God knows,' said Ossie quietly, looking hard at Catt who did not meet his eye.

'I'm putting in a recommendation,' said the group captain.

'This is the nature of my mess,' Catt muttered under his breath.

The group captain rubbed his hands enthusiastically. 'I mean, good Lord, if a deed like that doesn't deserve a gong, what does?'

'Well,' said Ossie, 'I know one guy who wouldn't agree.' The group captain did not hear, but Buckeridge did. He looked at Ossie sharply.

'Who's that?'

'Old Obdulu.'

'Ah.'

Catt looked oddly grateful. Then somewhere, somewhere close, they heard a high, thin screaming, the thrashing of a body, medics' voices, panicky, but trying to stay professional and calm. Suddenly, what should have been funny wasn't funny any more.

Buckeridge said: 'Oh, by the way, Tony didn't make it. I hate to say it, but it's probably just as well.'

Outside, driven in by a rising wind, the harmattan haze, a tempest of sand and dust, gusted round the burned-out wrecks of aeroplanes, vehicles and buildings, scouring the faces of the rescue teams, still searching for the dead and injured, piling up little drifts against undiscovered bodies. The hospital doors and windows were closed against the onslaught, and trapped flies ricocheted from the glass, whirling in clouds, filling the dense air with the thrum of wings before settling on bloody bandages and open wounds. Very soon the temperature was not to be endured. When Ossie slipped outside it was like stepping from an oven. He looked about, to see what he might do. Only dim shapes were visible in the yellow-brown haze that mingled with the red and black of guttering flames and oily smoke. It was the very picture, Ossie thought, of holy hell.

A Blenheim IV was found for Buckeridge to take on. The engine fault that had rendered it unserviceable, halfway through an earlier trip, had been corrected. It was wheeled out of a hangar that had escaped the raid, watched by Buckeridge and his replacement navigator, Goodall, laid up at Fort-Lamy with a malarial attack but suddenly considered fit to fly.

'Bit marginal, I'll grant you,' a doctor had confided to Buckeridge, 'but he'll see you through, I'm sure. Besides, we're devilishly short of beds.'

The Blenheim's wireless operator/gunner, Sergeant Hirst, stood with the bandaged Catt. 'Well, bad luck, Puss. See you back in Tako.'

'Unless they've shipped me back to Blighty first. These mitts will take some sorting.'

Ossie Wolf came over, sweating in flying kit, ready to pilot one of the two surviving fighters. 'So long, Puss. I guess I landed you in the shit about the gong. No hard feelings, huh?'

'Why should there be? You got me off the hook. Big bollocking from the skipper, of course, but somehow he prevailed on Groupie to drop the whole idea, without the old boy knowing why. But bang goes my chance of seeing inside Buck House.'

'Glasshouse, more likely,' Ossie said. 'Hey, you want me to

look up old Obdulu when I'm next in Kano? Check out his little voodoo doll? He's going to be sharpening up his pins, one of his shipments going up in smoke.'

'Bugger old Obdulu,' said Catt.

The three aircraft reached El Geneina that night. The weather had cleared and, before they landed, the Marra Mountains stood out sharp and blue, rising from green foothills, surrounded by the semi-arid plain of west Sudan. Next day, they reached Khartoum, and then completed the final leg to Cairo and the landing ground at Fayoum Road, 1,800 miles of uneventful, steady flying. The bombing of Fort-Lamy seemed like some wild imagining, unreal, in contrast to the lazily flowing waters of the Nile, moving as they had always moved, impassive and unchanging. And on the further bank the sprawl of Cairo gathered under a lilac sky, its minarets catching the fading light, clatters of pigeons wheeling above the twists and turns of the streets and alleys thronged with uniforms and white-robed figures.

Three aircraft delivered for nine despatched seemed a meagre outcome. The squadron leader at Fayoum Road was of that opinion. 'Of course Fort-Lamy's advised us of what occurred. But, good God, how could a single Heinkel catch everyone with their trousers down like that? I mean, six aircraft lost, not to mention substantial damage to the airfield.' He sniffed. 'It's gone down badly with our lords and masters, I can tell you.'

'I suggest you convey their feelings to our Gallic chums,' said Buckeridge evenly. 'There was no air raid warning and absolutely no defence. Wolf here was the only one who twigged we had a Jerry coming in.'

'A pity it wasn't picked up sooner,' said the squadron leader. 'Do you fellows have any idea how much those aeroplanes cost?'

'I know exactly how much they cost,' said Ossie. 'The life of a guy called Tony Page.'

*   *   *

A driver was found to take them to the *Dahabieh* houseboats at Gezira Island. Two had been leased from rich Cairenes for the use of ferry crews: the *Egypt* for the officers, the *Nile* for NCOs. Ossie was shown his quarters, a neat, small cabin with two beds, some chairs, a washbasin, water jug, crisp, clean towels and a double slatted door that opened onto a balcony fronted by an ornate carved balustrade. Outside, dhows slipped past with sagging sails, and pedlars moved along the line of *dahabeeyahs* hollering their patter from rowing boats and rickety *feluccas*.

Ossie had the cabin to himself. He stretched out on a bed and thought about what to do. He had a need to see whole, healthy women's bodies. The prospect of it stirred his groin. He knew that, among the houseboats, there were some that offered the necessary distractions to men who, even briefly, had escaped from war: bordellos, nightclubs, gambling and drinking joints where double and triple agents mingled with the crowd and, occasionally, were caught and shot, or turned for one more time.

Ossie had another joint in mind, further out across the river, in the darkening city. He would go alone. Buck Buckeridge was no fun at stuff like this, apt to drag out photos of his wife and get mushy, particularly after he'd hit the juice. The navigator Goodall looked as merry as a pallbearer at a wake, shrunken from malaria, still stricken by the shakes. Gellatley, who'd flown the second Hurricane, was another washout, some kind of egghead academic, obsessed with ancient tombs, more interested in dames long dead than those alive and kicking. And Tommy Hirst, the little punk, Buck's wireless operator/gunner, could hold his liquor no better than a Freshman virgin, known for sinking face-down on the bar after the merest whiff of hooch. Only Catt had known the pleasures of raising hell, and it would be a good long time before that poor sucker grabbed himself a parcel of Cairene whore.

Ossie freshened up and climbed on board a truck that took him to the city centre. Two Cairos existed, side by side. The Cairo of smart hotels, theatres, cinemas, small, intimate cafés, restaurants offering fine cuisine, nightclubs of the better sort, the galleries and museums Gellatley was so mad about, and those piles of rocks they called the Pyramids, stuck out beyond the green fringe of the Nile, where the sand began and characters got up like Valentino sold camel rides to mugs. In this Cairo Ossie did not feel at ease. His city, the second that existed beside the first, seemed to have suffered in a recent bombing raid, though no such raid had taken place. Buildings were half-finished or falling down – it was hard to tell. In the streets of this second city, flanked by concrete buildings, rubbish lay in malodorous piles. Treading sewage underfoot, drunken troops picked fights, pulled apart by Military Police patrols, or pushed away the hawkers offering silk stockings, combs, bootlaces, ties, pornographic books, sepia photographs of women coupling with beasts. Hashish dealers did their quiet, mysterious trade for those that alcohol could not soothe. And leading off the long main street, for this was Wagh El Birket, curtained alleys led to brothels where ill-printed signs echoed Churchill's words: *Give us the tools and we will finish the job.* Or boasted: *Cleanest house in town. Drinks served afterwards.* Where perfumed whores, of either sex, reclined on balconies and fanned themselves, awaiting whatever fate might bring; some-times Australians, whose fun it was to throw prostitutes and pianos out of windows, and who paid for it with the quick blade of a vengeful pimp, their passing reported as 'killed in action', to spare their grieving families; at other times, young squaddies twisting their forage caps in their crimson hands, slipping out quickly before their mates could see, with the smell of human sweat about them and the beginnings of a rash to bring back memories, in that foxhole in the desert. To the whores it was all the same: a client was a client, dealt with in their different ways, fifty in a night, faceless and forgotten.

Ossie liked this place. It resembled war: violent, unpredictable, with few laws, squalid, the kingdom of the lowest of the low, where if you entered, all men were equal, where greenhorns and phoneys were quickly fleeced, where it paid to know the score, how to handle yourself in any situation, where you could get any damned thing you ever dreamed of, if you knew where to look.

This night, though, Ossie passed on through 'the Berka' to a quieter part of town. The streets grew wide and better-tended and palm trees nodded in laid-out gardens behind tall iron railings. The houses stood part-hidden behind these gardens, substantial and discreet, their open windows shedding golden light and casting shadows on foliage stirring gently in the wafts of still-hot desert air. From one such house there came the faintest sound of shrill and unfamiliar music.

Ossie had not discovered this place himself. He and Catt, on their previous trip, had met a red-eyed, bearded tank commander who thought he was bound to die. He bought them drinks in the Continental's bar. He had already downed a few himself. 'I'm with Second Armoured,' he said. 'The footsloggers think we have it easy, dashing about in our little tin cans. They haven't seen what happens when a Crusader's hit by an armour-piercing shell. It's like a mincer, hard to tell who was who, chaps you knew just scraps. It poses the interesting problem of what one should do with what little's left. Leave the poor devils where they are, or bury them and risk them ending up as jackal bait?' He had ordered another round of Glenmorangie. 'I'm under no illusions. I imagine it's much the same with you. How did Seneca have it? "Life, if well lived, is long enough." Are you familiar with Seneca?'

Ossie had lit a cigarette. 'Don't know the guy.'

The tank commander had laughed bleakly. 'Live life to the fullest, chaps, that's my philosophy. Seize the moment and let everything else go hang.' He had paused. 'That's what I'm about to do.'

'You got me curious,' Ossie said. 'What you got in mind?'

And so the tank commander had led them to this quieter part of town, with its wider, better-tended streets where houses stood part-hidden in their gently stirring gardens, and music drifted out from the open windows. And they had gone inside, and drunk some more, big carafes of red Egyptian wine, and watched what there was to watch, their members stiff, but did not go upstairs, as the tank commander had, because they did not, at that time, share his belief that they were bound to die.

Now, for Ossie, it was different. His need was urgent. He still did not think that he was bound to die; not by any means. But nonetheless his mind was full of death, flick-flicking through those countless sights he had seen, like some crazy, bloody lantern show: men reduced to meat, killed in various grotesque ways – visions he always pushed aside but somehow spilling over, like a brim-filled cup, insidious, spreading weakness, softening his resolve. The effect was tiny, but it was there. He had to fight it, exploit his senses, know he was alive, intact; experience that moment when all that mattered was plain old dry-mouthed crummy lust.

It had been a while and, hell, wasn't he a man who liked to do it when he had the chance? Okay, so maybe this was weakness too, this giving in. For sure it held many dangers of its own. This wasn't St Louis, where Cousin Boyd hand-picked a healthy hooker to teach a just-fourteen-year-old kid the ropes. Some birthday present. Or Spain where good Republican girls, untouched until the war, gave themselves in dugouts on Mount Aragon, before they went to fight for the cause.

Ossie never liked to pay. He usually found a way to meet his needs, as long as he wasn't choosy. But now he didn't have the time or inclination to sweet-talk Red Cross nurses or flat-footed WAAFs, blasé from so many passes they'd come to believe they were Queens of the goddamned Nile. So here he was, about to shell out plenty, and probably catch a dose. But standing here, with that screwy feeling in his stomach and knowing what was going on inside the house, he reckoned it was worth every damned red cent.

The broad-built Nubian on the door, in wide trousers and an

embroidered jacket, remembered him. Ossie told him what he wanted and the Nubian nodded, as though it might be fixed. He rubbed his thumb and forefinger together and grinned. *'Baksheesh, effendi, baksheesh?'*

In an ornate room, lit by candles, four *almeh* singer-dancers were moving to the lilt of traditional strains played on a round-backed three-stringed rebec, the musicians bowing the fiddles held upright between their knees. Sometimes the pace picked up, the women's bodies naked under multicoloured gauze, necklaces of gold swinging and sliding across their tremulous breasts that swayed to the rhythm of the dance. At other times the beat was slow, individual dancers taking their turn to twist and contort their torsos in a brazen and indecent way, but their faces fixed, absorbed by the complexities of their steps.

The audience sat in shadows, 'officers only' the general rule, but exceptions made for a few civilians, their tropical suits stained with sweat, eyes bright; very different, this, from the sterile confines of Cairo GHQ or smoky newsrooms where, as corres-pondents, they telegrammed their stories through.

Ossie joined them where they stretched out awkwardly on Mameluke carpets, supported by rich cushions, adjusting their positions with grunts and smothered coughs, most sheepish and constrained, a few of the sharper souls nodding to the melodies, trying to catch the dancers' eyes. The music ceased, the *almeh* stood demurely, smiling at the ripple of applause, then slipped away. The time for other things would come but, first, to gratify a different appetite.

Low, round tables were carried in, with basins and ewers for guests to wash their hands and mouths; then silver trays with condiments and small cakes of bread. *'Bismillah,'* was mumured in self-conscious tones, prompted by the servants. 'In the name of Allah.' Then light soup was brought, taken from a great tureen with ivory spoons, the first of many courses, eaten with the fingers; stuffed poultry, stewed and boiled meats, okra tangy with lemon juice, mince and rice wrapped in vine leaves, roast lamb on skewers, fish dressed in oil, vegetables prepared in many ways, with sweets and fruit between the dishes. Throughout, wine flowed. Finally, *ruzz mufelfel,* rice boiled with butter, and *khushaf,* raisin water perfumed with the syrup of roses – all this explained with care by those who ran this uncommon bawdy house. Hands and faces washed again, and wafted with the smoke of aromatic plants, the men relaxed with coffee and cigars and European spirits, their pulses fast.

Ossie had found himself a pillar and he sat, propped up, waiting for the main event, not talking because he was not here to talk. The rebec players took their places, and began to tune their instruments, joined by a blind man with a darbukka drum who struck up an insistent beat, quiet at first, a sound that seemed as ancient as the Pharaohs. Through a curtained archway, with a rustle of silk and jingle of gold adornments on her wrists and ankles, Farida came. The rebec began to wail a tortuous refrain, but still soft and slow, like the darbukka drum, the musicians loosening a fold of their turbans across their eyes, so they would not witness Farida dance. The blind man also lowered a turban fold, as though her performance might restore his vision.

As the music gently filled the room, the woman moved among the groups of men, perfuming their hands with rosewater. She was naked to the waist, except for necklaces of precious jewels and gold piastres, full-breasted, her skin a glowing bronze and, close to, suffused with the fragrance of sandalwood and musk. Her braided hair, hennaed blue-black, was gathered up and held in place by an ornamental band of twisted gold. The men were very quiet, their closeness to this exotic creature somehow prompting a slight unease. Though close, she seemed beyond their reach: beyond the reach of any man.

Ossie had no such thoughts. When she rinsed his hands, he met her gaze. It seemed the Nubian had earned his baksheesh. Her green eyes, lids dark with kohl, were mischievous, her lips apart. He glimpsed her tongue. She moved away, half-looking at him as she went, her head inclined. She danced.

He remembered county fairs where hucksters peddled hoochie-coochie hoofers under fancy names, Cleo Patra, Little Cairo, Toots Kamun. They had been decked out with Ancient Egypt trappings, toying suggestively with a goddamned asp, pulsating their flat white Yankee Doodle bellies to convey the mysterious East, though New Jersey was the furthest east they had ever been.

Now, as Farida moved, her pelvis shaking, her arms extended above her head, advancing, falling back, stretched for a moment on the floor, her heavy bosom flattened and quivering on her ribcage, as the music pumped and pumped, eyes closed as though in ecstasy, then gracefully erect, coming towards him in little, faltering steps, the muscles of her thighs contracted, her broad gold buttocks tight, then all the signs, her every glance and gesture, showed Farida had decided. She did not do it with older men, or men too young. It was not to do with money, either. She was rich, and enjoyed an opulent and pampered life. Maybe she was led by pleasure, simple whim, indulging herself with whoever took her fancy when she felt a need. This much Ossie knew from the tank commander who had thought he was bound to die. Farida had chosen him. Ossie wondered if the tank commander still had a brain to dream of her, back with his Crusader crew. 'Life, if well lived, is long enough.' He didn't know squat, that Seneca guy. No life was long enough. And come to that, no night was long enough.

He looked at good old wiggling, golden-fuck Farida and licked his lips. She was going to cost him plenty, pretty well clean him out. But seeing her strut her stuff like this, who cared? He looked around at the other poor suckers, those with hungry eyes, who wouldn't get her tail. He pitied them, but felt a surge of satisfaction.

Then a door began to open, admitting a streak of electric light. Ossie heard the Nubian's voice, raised, indignant, mixed in with the blather of some fruity English jerk, chuckling at his objections, brushing him aside. The door pushed open wider. More light washed in. A hinge squeaked like a corny sound effect from a Boris Karloff movie, and someone murmured a protest. Farida frowned, and paused and stopped. The spell she had cast hung for a moment in the scented air, a delicate illusion, and abruptly vanished. The music wavered, and fell away. And she was gone.

In the semi-darkness a burly figure, followed by two others, smaller, blundered in, its arms held out to keep its balance. 'Good grief, it's like a blessed coal mine in here. Whoops. Pardon me, old boy. Was that your foot?' The newcomer plumped down heavily next to Ossie, releasing a surreptitious fart, shifting several times to adjust his bulk. 'Dammit, never did get the hang of lolling.' He looked across at Ossie, to see if his mild drollery had struck a chord. Then he was leaning close, mouth open, small eyes narrowed. 'I say, don't we know each other?' It was the porcine, red-veined face of Wing Commander Bernard Booth, his whisky breath assaulting Ossie's nostrils.

'Yes, by George, it's Wolf. Good God. Well, well, well. Should have known we'd find *you* in a place like this.' A hasty harrumph. 'Not that we don't appreciate your hospitality, Bakri old chap, please don't think that. Bit of local colour. Just the job.'

An Egyptian, dapper, with slicked-back hair and a European suit, leaned forward easily from the waist and shrugged his narrow shoulders. 'No need to detain you here for long, my dear Wing Commander. Besides, it seems we may have missed the best.'

The best, it seemed, at least to Booth, did not mean Farida's florid charms. 'Ah,' he said, 'the fabled feast. Pity. I'm distinctly peckish. My fault, of course. Shouldn't have tarried so long at Shepherd's. Perhaps another time.'

'I say, do you mind?' a voice called out.

Another: 'Yes. Thanks so much for barging in like that. When you people have quite finished with your gabbing, perhaps we can get on with the ruddy song-and-dance.'

'Absolutely,' said a third. 'Wrap up or bugger off.'

Bakri's thin brown fingers touched Booth's sleeve. 'On balance, Wing Commander, I suggest we bugger off.'

To his own surprise, Ossie joined them in the garden. He passed the Nubian without a word. His hunger for Farida had dissolved. It was as though he'd already had her, the primal urge diminishing, leaving just the usual ruminations about what the hell it was all about. It was a kind of craziness, that worked you up. One screw, more or less, who cared? As it was, the whole damned thing had turned out like a Laurel and Hardy short, with Farida cut down to a walk-on comedy part. Hell, maybe Booth had done him a big favour, saving him from laying out £50 and picking up a dose of clap.

Gathered with his companions near an ornamental pool, Bernard Booth was lighting a cigar. 'So, Wolf – small world, eh?'

If Ossie was grateful, he showed no sign. 'You totally English sonofabitch.'

Booth sucked wetly, and the tobacco glowed. 'I'll put that down to drink.'

'Who gives a shit?' said Ossie.

'I see you haven't mellowed,' said the small man next to Bakri. It was Rupert Pringle.

'Oh boy,' said Ossie. 'My night's complete.'

Pringle turned to Bakri. 'Meet Flight Lieutenant Wolf. Thorn in the Axis side – and everyone else's, come to that.'

'I see you haven't mellowed,' said Ossie.

'Not in your case, no.' Pringle offered Ossie a Turkish cigarette.

Ossie turned it in his fingers. 'I recall you said this was a filthy habit.'

'Life moves on. We're all a bit older, aren't we?'

'Not all.'

'Ah. A sombre reflection on the beastliness of war.'

'That's what gets me about you, Pringle. You're all heart.'

'Coming from you, that's rather rich. So why are you here? Just slumming?'

'One hell of a slum. Better than those joints in Pigalle.'

Pringle smiled thinly. 'I wouldn't know, of course. We last met, Bakri, in Paris, just before the Fall. I was doing . . . certain work, while our dashing pilot here was downing German aeroplanes. Quite a number, as I recall.'

'It was a barrel of laughs.'

'Time for a new catchphrase, Wolf. That one's a little thread-bare. Didn't you trot it out for *Picture Post*? "Our Yankee ace of Malta" and all that rot?'

'I thought all that rot was up your street.'

'One of the addresses in the street,' said Pringle. 'But I have other properties now.'

'Like Hand of Friendship, maybe?' Ossie blew blue smoke at Booth.

'No, not that. The time for AMIHOF has passed. It never quite worked out. So Bernard is helping in other ways. Bakri too.'

'You make it sound mysterious.'

'Oh, it is,' said Pringle. He looked thoughtful. 'Something strikes me. Remind me what you're up to now.'

'Ask jolly old Booth. I reckon he had a hand in it.'

'Not at all, old boy,' said Booth. 'All your own work. Make big enough waves and you end up stranded.'

'I'm on the Takoradi run,' said Ossie. 'Ferrying kites from A to B.'

'Sounds mundane,' said Pringle. 'Not exactly your line of work.'

'It has its moments.'

'How long are you here?'

'A few more days.'

'Bernard,' Pringle said, 'have you got pen and paper?' The nib scratched on the back of a Shepherd's bar receipt. He folded it and handed it to Ossie. 'You can find me here.'

'And why in hell should I want to do that?'

'You like delivering aeroplanes?'

'Okay, so what you got in mind?'

'A hare-brained scheme cooked up by madmen that will almost certainly get you killed.'

'Don't sugar-coat it, Pringle,' Ossie said. 'Give it to me straight.'

Five

On the crest of a sand dune commanding a view of the Roman fort, Beppo Lutzow braked the *Kübelwagen* to a halt, stood up, supporting himself against the windscreen, and studied the stone walls through the Leitz binoculars he had borrowed from an artilleryman in Benghazi. The building was smaller than he had expected, barely twenty metres square, but still, he whistled. 'It's amazingly well preserved, as though a Legion might march out through the gates at any moment.'

'Spare me,' said Hartmann, from the back seat. 'We've got enough damned armies in this desert already. Anyway, I thought we were hunting gazelles, not spooks.' He stretched his arms above his head, yawning. 'How not to spend a day off-duty. To think I could be sleeping in my bunk, or drinking Pilsner with the boys. Instead, I'm lost in the desert with a mad Bavarian whose head is in the past.'

'We're not lost,' said Lutzow. 'That's Gasr Haddumah. It's a well-known antiquity. It's even marked.'

Slumped in the front passenger seat, Emil Gotz lit a small cigar. 'Marked? Where? Who would bother over such a flea bite?'

Lutzow indicated the spot on the map with his forefinger, and passed the map across. Gotz did not look at it but folded it up and began to fan himself. 'I don't believe there are any damned

135

gazelles,' he said over his shoulder to Hartmann. 'It was just an excuse for Herr Professor here to pursue his interests.'

'Well,' said Hartmann, 'it makes a change from fighting Tommies.'

Lutzow sat back behind the wheel, replacing the binoculars in their leather box to protect them from the whirls of sand. 'Let's go down and take a look.'

'Wait a moment, Beppo,' said Gotz. He jumped out, walked round to the back of the field car and tilted the rear seat cushions forward. From the small storage compartment he lifted out the rolled army blanket, secured with string, that protected the three 8mm Mauser rifles they had cadged from Stores. He chose the sniper model, with telescopic sights, loaded a cartridge and threw the weapon up to his shoulder. The crack of the shot was startling in the silence, echoing round the piled-up dunes. The bullet struck a crenellation on the fort; chips of stone flew up and ricocheted away, a fading whine, puny in the vastness.

'For God's sake, Emil, what's the point?' said Lutzow. 'Why waste a shot?'

'With such a weapon, in those times, a man could have ruled the world.'

'Ah,' said Hartmann. 'Another who wants to rule the world. Leave such ambitions to our Führer and the Fat One. Stick to flying 109s, you clown.'

'Sometimes, Matthias, you make me uncomfortable,' said Gotz. 'It is a good thing you are among friends.'

'I'll tell you something,' said Beppo Lutzow. 'If there were any gazelles about, they've certainly gone now.' He turned the ignition key and pressed the starter button. The little air-cooled flat-four engine rattled alive. He engaged first gear and, with Gotz once more on board, still armed with the sniper rifle, the butt resting on his thigh, drove slowly down the steep slope of the dune towards the fort, careful to keep the vehicle straight.

Closer to, the walls seemed more imposing, formidable to an

attacking force 2,000 years ago. The three men appeared small against the ramparts, as they moved towards the gateway that did not have a gate. In their path lay curious mounds of sand, like mole hills – larger though, and more irregular in outline. Lutzow prodded one with his foot. The sand shivered and slipped away, revealing a desiccated human hand curled inward like a fist. Gotz pushed aside the sand with his Mauser butt. A buttoned khaki sleeve with yellow rank chevrons showed this was no ancient corpse.

'My God,' said Lutzow. 'What happened here?'

They cleared a few more mounds. The dead were all Italians. Behind the fort they found two Autoblinda armoured cars. Part of a motorised division then, attacked when on patrol, almost certainly from the air. The armour plating was pierced by shells, and both vehicles had burned. Beneath each chassis the sand was stained with fuel and oil, and human grease from crewmen trapped inside. Not all had died that way. Faint tracks still visible in the sand led towards the fort where, yards from cover, those few who had survived the first assault had fallen to another strafing run.

Instinctively, Lutzow raised his eyes towards the sky. Gotz grinned.

'Don't worry, Beppo. This is more ancient history. These *Makkaroni* caught it a week or so ago. Bad luck for them, and good luck for some damned Englishman.' He drew on his small cigar and blew a perfect smoke ring.

'Half right, Emil,' said Lutzow. 'Certainly unfortunate for the Italians, spotted in the open, so close to cover. But for the English flier this was more than just a lucky break. Peitsmeyer in our reconnaissance *Kampfgruppe* says his fellows are having a tough time of it. Their losses are exceptional – four aircraft in as many days. It seems the Britishers are keen to stop us seeing over the hill – even here, so far from the front line. Something big is building up.'

'Everyone knows that,' said Gotz. 'Didn't you read what

Rommel told the nation at that press conference in Berlin the other day? "We hold the gateway to Egypt, with the full intention of action. You may rely on us to hold fast to what we have conquered." This in the presence of Goebbels. So not a claim to be made lightly.'

'It certainly made the right impression on the Führer,' said Hartmann. 'I gather he presented the conqueror of Egypt with a field marshal's baton.'

Gotz flicked his dead cigar towards the silent fort. 'You suggest the honour was undeserved?'

'Somewhat premature, perhaps. To be the conqueror of Egypt, first you must conquer Egypt.'

'You sail close to the wind, my friend,' said Gotz.

'In what way? I simply state the facts. Naturally I have the greatest confidence in Command. No doubt there is a simple explanation for the enemy's sudden zeal to eliminate prying eyes. Perhaps it is a symptom of his fear of what is to come.'

'The British will not attack,' said Gotz flatly. 'We will choose the time and place to open the offensive. The smart money says the third week in November. Rommel knows that. If he expected trouble he would hardly be in Berlin.'

'I heard his health was in question,' said Hartmann. 'Jaundice, wasn't it, and other things to be expected in a man of his years? At least, that was what was rumoured – that he'd gone back home to get some treatment. Of course, now we know it was simply to receive a promotion.'

Gotz shook his head. 'You're a damned defeatist, Matti. I'm sick of your innuendos. If it's a bet you want, I'll wager one hundred marks that we will be in Cairo for Christmas.' He rubbed his hands. 'Then, we will have our reward for serving time in this godforsaken desert. I'm told that Cairo offers many amusing diversions.'

'Ah,' said Hartmann, 'is that why you're fighting the war, Emil? To bang some carpet-kissing Ali Baba whore?'

'Enough, idiots,' cut in Lutzow. 'We're here to hunt gazelles, not each other.'

'From what I've seen,' said Hartmann, nodding his head towards the dead Italians, 'we could all turn out to be the prey. May I suggest we leave the *Makkaroni* and their forebears to guard this godforsaken relic and see if we can, by some miracle, find our way back to base?'

Ten miles from Benghazi the rain began, light at first, then heavy and insistent. It was growing dark, made darker still by low grey cloud that shrouded the distant seaport. Beppo Lutzow steered off the road, close by the crumbling remnants of a goatherd's shelter. With Gotz he secured the *Kübelwagen*'s canvas hood, fastening it to the windscreen clips, but still it flapped and billowed in the rising wind, and sprays of rain drove in.

For days the weather pattern had been the same, the downpour starting with the fading light, reducing runways to a glutinous, rutted mess. No flying of any kind. Instead, the *Staffel*'s sand-coloured Messerchmitt 109Fs stood impotent in their blast-pens, draped about with camouflage netting under which the ground-crews carried on their work. Such conditions had become routine. Few bothered to complain. The desert had many moods; too hot, too cold, too wet, too dry. Never agreeable or benign, always a malignant force, exposing weakness, testing the spirit, frustrating the designs of men, hostile and impartial. And opportunities for a break from operations were scarce. That was not the Luftwaffe way. Tours of duty could last for many months and even, in some theatres, years. The pilots were compelled to devise their own diversions. Like racing camels, half-wild and desert-bred, loaned by tribesmen in exchange for twenty cigarettes. Or inter-*Staffel* football games, the Me 109 contingent against the Stuka boys. Or milder, more cerebral pursuits, like Lutzow's interest in archaeological remains, or tournaments of chess or recreating concerts – Bach, Mozart, Beethoven, Wagner, Brahms

– from scratchy records on wind-up gramophones. Or impromptu and eccentric fancies, like hunting gazelle where gazelle had long been hunted to extinction.

Lutzow reached to start the *Kübelwagen*'s engine, but paused. The wind force had increased, dispersing the low cloud. The rain had passed, a filmy steam rose from the ground and streamlets scoured out runnels in the sand. It was very quiet, just the running of the water and the moan of wind. When they heard a new and far-off sound, they thought it was just another storm. But soon they knew it was the faint, first growl of an approaching raid: many aircraft, with an unfamiliar engine note. At altitude the cloud was thinning now and very soon, through breaks, they glimpsed a sizeable formation passing towards Benghazi, unopposed, at least by air.

Lutzow was by the bonnet now, binoculars to his eyes, and began to count. 'Ten, fifteen, twenty, thirty.' Again he gave his small whistle that could convey so many things – lust, surprise, approval. This time, disbelief. 'We are well placed here, my friends. God bless all gazelles. And protect our unhappy comrades.'

Gotz took the Leitz glasses. '*Amerikaner*,' he said. 'B-24 Liberators. Unmistakable.'

'So sure, Emil?' queried Hartmann. 'Even in this murk, at twenty thousand feet?'

'Unlike some,' Gotz replied, 'I take time to study the *Gruppen*'s aircraft recognition charts.'

Hartmann sighed. 'Tell me, Emil, is there anything you don't know?'

Gotz turned his head aside and spat. 'No man can be criticised for keeping himself informed. We are officers, after all, not mere unquestioning foot-sloggers. It is important we perceive the bigger picture, and this requires an understanding of the details.'

'So,' said Hartmann innocently, 'with your grasp of the situation, what would this attack suggest?'

'Suggest?'

'A raid of such intensity is something new. Is it significant, do you think?' A crooked smile. 'I only ask.'

'As usual, you make a joke. As usual, quite misplaced.' Gotz waved an arm towards Benghazi. The seaport shook, illuminated by exploding bombs, and the wavering beams of searchlights and anti-aircraft fire. The sky above the city was livid red. 'Does that, perhaps, amuse you?'

'Not in the slightest,' Hartmann said. 'But it makes me wonder.'

'What?'

'If your hundred marks are safe.' With Lutzow, Hartmann began to lower the *Kübelwagen*'s hood. 'But then, I'm forgetting, Emil. You assure me we will choose the time and place to open the offensive. Third week in November, I think you said. I'll note it in my diary. And get our *Volkslieder* warblers to start rehearsing "Stille Nacht" for our Christmas celebrations in Shepherd's Hotel.'

That night, even Emil Gotz was unaware that massed formations of Allied bombers were striking the Panzerarmee's rear, pounding shipping, landing grounds, supply columns and troop concentrations, not only in Benghazi but other strongholds too: Tobruk, Matruh, Sollum, Bardia, as well as ports in Crete and south-west Greece.

Yet, as they watched, close by the goatherd's shelter, and saw Benghazi obscured by smoke and flame, there could be no doubt that this was more than just a routine raid. Only later did they grasp the broader picture. For now, they stood in silence, the *Kübelwagen* trembling on its springs as shock waves fanned out across the wilderness of sand and scrub, from where the bombs were whistling down.

They drove into Benghazi when the fury of the raid had passed. What they saw held no surprises. Each of them had served in Poland, France and Russia. Emil Gotz had been in Spain, where it all began. What did give pause for thought was that this devastation had been wreaked by *Amerikaner* bomber fleets. No longer could they only talk of Tommy as the enemy.

Of sixteen fighters in the *Staffel*, ten had been destroyed. Stores of spares and aviation fuel and ammunition had also gone. Nine men were dead – two pilots, Ultsch and Schmoller, and seven of the 'black men', as the Luftwaffe styled its ground-crew. Four more were in Benghazi Hospital, the building only lightly touched by the Liberators' sticks of bombs.

Opposite the hospital, the Panzerarmee's official brothel had survived unscathed. Business was brisk, quick sex a celebration of survival, and soldier clients, before or after using the Libyan whores, passed cigarettes to patients through the shattered windows of the wards, in the buoyant mood of those whom death had spared and who believed, for a while at least, that they were the chosen few.

With Matti Hartmann, Beppo Lutzow was at the hospital to find young Eisenach. It was only two weeks since he had completed advanced fighter training, and joined their combat *Gruppe*, after seven months and six hundred hours of flying and ground instruction: a methodical and thorough programme, more hard-won, the Luftwaffe claimed with pride, than that of their opposite numbers in the Royal Air Force. When British cadets were already judged fit for elementary flying training, Luftwaffe candidates were still in the classroom, learning aviation theory. From there, and finally at the controls, they faced the four-stage licence process, each grade subdivided, starting with A2, thirty hours of dual flights and thirty hours solo; then through the various levels to C2, with every kind of discipline experienced and understood: night flying, aerobatics, formation flying, cross-country work, flying on instruments alone in covered cockpits until, at last, the very best were posted to the *Jagdfliegerschule*, the advanced fighter-pilot school, to learn the final, crucial lessons on obsolete but high-performance single-seater types. And then, the last step: a posting to a combat squadron, still raw but confident that they knew their chosen trade.

Beppo too had followed such a path. It had taken him from conscript in the Reich Labour Service, in which all German youth was required to serve, to military service with the Wehrmacht. Identified in the ranks as officer material, with potential flying skills, he found, within another year, that he had exchanged his *Reichsarbeitdienst* spade, and work on civic, military and agricultural projects, for a Messerschmitt Bf 109E-3, fresh from the Regensburg production line. He, at least, in the ensuing years, had put his knowledge and ability to the test. For Eisenach it was over before it had begun. Poor devil. Already he was *hors de combat*, without a chance to prove himself, without a single kill against his name.

They found the *Leutnant* in a ward designed for twenty men but that now held forty. Their friend's face was bound with bandages, with small slits for his nose and mouth. His hands were also covered. He sat propped up but was unconscious. An orderly said he was badly burned and that his eyes had gone. He had not spoken since being brought in, but seemed untouched by pain. The orderly checked his pulse from time to time, as Lutzow watched, and each time confirmed that he was still alive.

'There's nothing to be done,' the orderly said. 'If he comes round, I'll tell him you were here.'

They left the ward and found another, where the black men were. One was Beppo's ground-crew chief, *Feldwebel* Peltz, the other an *Unteroffizier* he knew only by sight. Neither was badly hurt. Peltz was temporarily deaf from blast, his eyes as red as cherries, his face specked black with flying grit, the other cut about with shrapnel that had missed the vital parts, his wounds stitched up, both men as merry as if they were in a *Biergarten*, adrenalin still pumping through their veins. The only sign of what they had endured was Peltz's trembling hand, unable to hold a bedside tumbler. They made jokes, and talked of trivial things, and did not ask about young Eisenach in the adjoining ward, or the nine already dead.

'*Hyäne* is safe,' said Peltz. 'Have no fear of that, *Herr Oberleutnant*.'

'Far more important,' Beppo said, 'is that you rascals are still here, ready to make fresh nuisances of yourselves.'

'We hear the bordello is still in business,' said the *Unteroffizier*, half his hair burned off and an eight-inch slash running from his temple to his chin. 'How late do they stay open?'

'Not for you, my friend,' said Matti Hartmann. 'Even *Kameltreiber* tarts must draw the line. Wet dreams only, for a while.'

There was something strained about the burst of laughter, a touch too loud, too long. When Beppo Lutzow and Matti Hartmann left, the men were quieter and more reflective, as though their reserves of nervous energy were starting to seep away.

At the airfield Beppo searched out his Messerschmitt 109. None of the Liberator's eight-hundred-pounders had fallen close to its stone-walled pen. As Peltz had said, it was little damaged; punctured here and there by shrapnel and flying debris, but operational still, with a small amount of work. On the nose its name, *Hyäne*, remained unmarked, below the cartoon painting of a hyena, fangs bared, flanks mottled like those of the war machine that bore its name; a hunter with a heart as big again as that of a full-grown lion. When Peltz had first suggested the idea, Beppo had dismissed it. Such christenings, he considered, were a childish fancy. But then, why not? It amused his black men and on reflection seemed appropriate somehow, at this time and in this place. Now, it struck him as a small defiance.

Back in the tent he shared with Hartmann, Beppo said: 'Poor little Eisenach. That is the end for him.'

'Let us hope.'

'Also for Ultsch and Schmoller.'

'An excellent fellow, Ludo Ultsch. We cannot afford to lose such men. But Schmoller? One less *Nationalsozialische* toady will not be missed. He was a particular friend of Gotz, I think. I must commiserate.'

Beppo shook his head. 'Your tongue will get you into trouble, Matthias. Like today. It is unwise to provoke Emil. You know his views.'

'That is why I provoke him. We are soldiers, that is all. We do what soldiers do. We are not required to be careful in the air. Why should we be so on the ground? We fly, we fight, we do all that is required of us. That is enough. One must take on these hardline stooges, and show them there is more to the Reich than Adolf Hitler.' He pulled off his leather flying boots and stretched out on the metal bed, hands behind his head. 'Don't doubt me, Beppo. I love my country. I have found its resurgence magnificent. But now we stand to throw it all away.'

'You think we're done?'

'Don't you? You had a taste of *Amerikaner* power today. It is what the British prayed for. They no longer stand alone.'

'But Rommel—'

'Oh, Rommel, Rommel, as though to repeat the name will work a miracle. I don't deny he has great flair and daring. But he is a man like any other, and a sick one. Come now, surely you don't need me to draw a picture of our situation, low on fuel, having to conserve our stocks, losing machines we cannot replace? An army is only as good as its supply lines.'

'Ours are short,' said Beppo, 'across the Med. The enemy's lines are the longest known in war, around the Cape to Suez or by air from Africa's western coast.'

Hartmann grunted. 'Put like that, how can we lose? But, Beppo, here's the truth, straight from a contact in Command. Agreed, our routes for reinforcement may be one-tenth the length the enemy must contend with. But you forget that Malta did not fall, despite the impression Kesselring sought to give, and the

Tommies also strike, by sea and air, from their Egyptian bases. Everybody knows our convoys have been hard hit. You cannot keep such a secret, when cargoes do not arrive. But do you realise to what extent? In one month alone, eighty per cent of what was shipped from Italy and Greece was lost – twenty-four ships sunk.'

'You are too gloomy, Matti. The Führer will not permit defeat. Rommel will turn the tide. You know his genius for invention, his ruses to fool the opposition, provoke mistakes, so he can seize the moment. Not for nothing is he called the Fox.'

'Unfortunately, Beppo, it is plain the Führer considers Africa already won. And no one is prepared to contradict him, or give news of setbacks. As for the Luftwaffe, Goering dares not tell him of our difficulties. You've seen the Fat One's latest battle orders. How did it go? "The practice of breaking off the attack and seeking the horizon when warned of Spitfires is to cease forthwith." He tells us the interesting fact that a strike from superior height is not the only tactic, that we must attack from all directions, even if at a disadvantage. My God, he almost accuses us of cowardice. Spare me the old man's combat lessons. Unlike him, we do not fly Fokker Triplanes on the Western Front.'

'He was brave,' said Beppo, 'in his time. You have to give him that. Winner of the *Pour le Mérite*, appointed Commander of the Flying Circus when von Richtofen was killed. This is no desk pilot giving us our orders.'

'Oh, he is no fool,' agreed Hartmann, 'but he sees things in the simplest terms. Shoot down many enemy planes and we will win. He ignores technology, the role of the Army and the Navy. He believes air power alone will be enough. To support this theory, he cites the successes of the *Luftflotte* on the Russian front. He compares their score rates with ours, ignoring the fact that there the airfields are rarely attacked, and here we suffer eight a day; that here, to reach the bombers, we have to fight our way through escorts of thirty or forty strong. He also conveniently forgets that, two years ago, the British gave us a bloody nose, with no help from anyone. The Fat One is a plausible fellow, Beppo. You forget, I've met him. That makes him doubly dangerous. The Führer trusts him. In person, he is persuasive. His manner is enthusiastic and direct. He meets your eye and has a certain style about him. He seems sincere, an honest man. No nonsense. His record suggests otherwise.'

'And yet you had no doubts in thirty-seven, when you were part of von Blomberg's delegation to England?'

'I was just an aide with flying duties, Beppo. Imagine, guests of the Royal Air Force. They did Feldmarschall von Blomberg and his party proud. Demonstrated their latest bombers, no less. Fly-pasts of the latest Blenheims, Whitleys, Harrows – well flown but feeble machines compared to ours. Back in Berlin, the Fat One was delighted to have confirmed how far in advance we were. As I say, his enthusiasm is contagious. You feel yourself swept along.'

'What changed your mind?'

'Very simple. It was plain where things were going, although the British didn't seem aware. But even if their aeroplanes were outclassed, as a fighting force they were not to be underestimated. The Fat One would not hear of it. When von Blomberg said as much, and urged caution, he was dismissed.' Hartmann raised himself on one elbow. 'Have you been to England, Beppo?'

'Only in a 109. What is your opinion?'

'Oh, they are much like us. Foolish, at that time. Complacent, trusting. But then they were content, not let down by their politicians as we were. In 1918 they won, we lost, with much left still to fight for. For us, it did not end. For them, it did. They had a phrase: "the war to end all wars". They believed it, to their cost.'

'You have no difficulty, then, with the expansion of the Reich?'

'*Lebensraum* is a worthy concept. Space and freedom. It is one of the foundations, after all, of the British Empire. Why should we not do the same, regain our national pride, exert power and influence in the world? So, no, I do not necessarily regret this war. But that does not mean I do not question the way it is being waged, or its objectives.'

'You say you are a soldier. Is it your place to question?'

'Come now, Beppo. Our friend Emil urges me to see the bigger picture. He is a good party man. Surely I am merely following his advice?'

Beppo smiled reluctantly. 'It is not the picture he has in mind.'

'Make no mistake,' said Hartmann, 'I will always do my duty. But it's hard to trust a corporal who thinks it wise to open an offensive on two fronts, and believes he has the entire world within his grasp.'

Beppo Lutzow shook his head. 'I still maintain the Führer will not permit defeat, on any front. Here we will be supplied and strengthened, in time for our offensive in November. I will treat you to a drink in Cairo, Matti, and remind you of your doubts.'

'Don't fool yourself,' said Hartmann. 'Africa holds little interest now, for the Corporal and the Fat One. To them, it's history. Now the Führer's thoughts are in the East, and Africa is a sideshow, already in his mind just another triumph for the invincible Desert Fox. Now he is more concerned with Russian bears than home-grown foxes.'

'It is easy to find fault,' said Beppo, 'particularly in the heat of war. Much harder to suggest solutions.'

Hartmann's mouth twisted into a sardonic smile. It was hard to tell whether he was about to be serious, or make a joke. 'You want solutions? Simple. Remove control from the politicians. We are led by ideologues and opportunists, Beppo, supported by pygmies with a taste for power and a few old, deluded warhorses eager to avenge defeat of twenty years ago. But even so, I have reason to believe the bulk of military command still has integrity, and could conserve what we have gained and preserve the honour of the Reich. After all, we have dealt with the enemy within, the Communists and the Jews.'

'Reason to believe? You have talked of this?'

'To some extent,' said Hartmann, suddenly cautious. 'There are those who see our destiny in partnership with other nations, not at war, demanding that they also bend to a dictator's will.'

'So, you mean a putsch?'

'Eventually it will come – probably too late for me. I have no illusions. My mouth will hang me, if the Tommies fail to get me first.'

'And what would this partnership of nations do?'

'Why, destroy the Bolsheviks, of course! That is the common objective, is it not, once the little matter of our glorious Führer has been dealt with?'

Late that evening, Beppo Lutzow prepared to write a letter to his parents. He thought of them bustling about their small hotel in Starnberg, a few miles south of Munich, with its view of the cold blue lake fringed by white-capped mountains; the lake where he once sailed his small boat, the distant peaks he finally climbed. On one of those treks he had come across a Roman site, said to be an outpost of the crack Third Legion. It had sparked his interest. Bavaria had been important to the Empire. He visited the various remains, at Augsburg, Kempten, Regensburg. He considered archaeology as a career, before life took a different turn. Ironic to find himself invading an ancient land, part of a destructive force, instead of digging up its treasures.

Still the notepaper remained untouched. Did Starnberg still exist? It seemed a waking dream. Here was reality. There they had no understanding of the way he existed now. Certainly, they took pride in his achievements as a pilot, displayed the formal sepia print that showed him stiff, unsmiling, in crisp dress uniform. It was much admired by friends and hotel guests, who also did not comprehend the life such heroes of the Reich were required to lead. It was a gulf between them all, impossible to bridge. As usual he did not know what to write. It was too boring to consider, always the same tale of keeping spirits up despite the privations the *Staffel* faced, and quite as boring to read, no doubt, lacking any detail that might offend the censor. The page was blank. The fountain pen wavered in his hand. At least there was one detail that did not call for thought. He looked across at Hartmann. 'Matti, what's the date?'

Hartmann groaned. 'Twenty-third October. Now for God's sake, let a fellow sleep.'

But Hartmann did not sleep. No one slept that night. Approaching ten o'clock, distant guns were heard, lighting the horizon, and then fell silent, unexplained. Fifteen minutes passed, then no one was left in doubt. Along a forty-mile front, a barrage of massed artillery opened fire, on simultaneous command, launching a storm of shells on known and suspected Axis company positions. Another fifteen-minute pause, during which the defenders attempted to gather their shattered senses, and British sappers began to mark out white-taped routes across the minefields for the main advance. Then it began again, a creeping barrage, hour by hour, an avalanche of ordance, making the sky appear to burn.

Five hundred miles away, Benghazi, sheltered as it was by facing west across the Gulf of Sirte, throbbed and shivered to the impact of the multiple explosions

Hurrying to their machines, struggling into flying gear, with no orders issued yet, not knowing what to do, but feeling they should be ready to take off on the instant, Lutzow and Hartmann came up with their four remaining comrades, Korten, Rudel, Lohr and Emil Gotz.

'What says your smart money now, Emil?' said Hartmann. 'I must decide how I am to squander your hundred marks.'

Gotz did not seem to hear. His jaw was working, his eyes distended, like a man confronted by a circumstance that could not be, was unthinkable, impossible to grasp. Then, as he reached his Messerschmitt and prepared to climb up on the wing, he turned. 'Those guns you hear are ours.' His voice was thin and sounded unconvinced. But still he added: 'I'll collect your money, *Dumpfbacke*, when we land.'

Soon *Gruppe* orders were received. It seemed the main attack was in the centre and the south. The remnants of the *Staffel* were instructed to strafe advancing troops near Miteiriya Ridge. On board *Hyäne*, patched up, and answering to the controls in the normal way, Beppo Lutzow formed a finger-four at a height of four thousand metres with Hartmann, Lohr and Gotz, Rudel and Korten keeping watch above. Already the sky was streaked with vapour trails of earlier combats. Clearly the enemy was active and aggressive. Below, turbulent clouds of dust and tank tracks on the desert surface showed the many points at which the enemy had broken through.

With his thumb, Beppo flicked off the hinged metal safety guard over the red firing button on top of the control column, ready to trigger the 20mm cannon firing through the airscrew spinner. On the leading edge of the stick, his index finger rested on the buttons that, with the slightest pressure, would loose the twin 7.9mm machine guns mounted under the cowling above the engine.

He cleared his throat, like a man about to make a speech. His words were few. 'Attention. Engage at will. Going down now!' And, with this brief command, he led the dive-down to attack in line-astern, the airspeed touching 750 km/h, as usual at that velocity the controls becoming stiff, his booted foot applying slight left rudder to counteract the tendency to side-slip. It was good to be in action once again, to execute a simple task, to kill. The air was criss-crossed with rising flak, streaming towards the diving *Staffel* from all directions: ahead, to left and right, behind. But no sign yet of enemy machines.

As he prepared to open fire, Beppo remembered, for an instant, that time in Poland before he had grown comfortable with his work. A Panzer division had been attacked by Polish cavalry, halting their advance. They called up air support. The cavalry was charging over open ground, a colourful scene from the pages of a history book. With the others, Beppo had fanned out, sixty metres apart, and come in low, quite unopposed. His thumb had hesitated on the gun-button, unwilling to annihilate these tiny men on tiny horses, like models in a small boy's war game, bounding towards the Panzer positions, their sabre blades winking in the sun. But then his thumb pressed down and, across the broad expanse of ground, the men and horses fell, some struggling to their feet before a second pass cut them down. No one had spoken when they landed, all conscious that something exceptional had been destroyed, that they had played a part in extinguishing a vision from another age. It was redolent of Emil Gotz, firing his Mauser at the Roman fort at Gasr Haddumah; obscenely inappropriate and out of place.

Now, though, diving on an armoured column, Beppo did not hesitate. Sturdy as the hunter from which it took its name, *Hyäne* barely shivered to the recoil of the cannon and machine guns. Even their sound was drowned out by the thunder of the Daimler-Benz engines. And there was nothing to be seen; the rate of fire so high that shells and bullets were invisible – not even a flicker of muzzle flash. Only the stench of cordite in the cockpit spoke of action. All very clinical and clean.

But different in the ground. A British tank erupted in a burst of flame; another faltered, turned off the track and trundled a few metres, belching oily smoke before it too erupted in a ball of fire, a crewman tumbling from the turret, a fiery figure that rolled and rolled and finally was still.

In Beppo's rear-view mirror, something flashed and fell, scattering pieces across the desert floor, fragments rebounding from the armour of the surviving tanks, a wash of aviation fuel blackening the sand and igniting shrubs.

In the air the enemy did not show itself, so the *Staffel* had no need to heed the Fat One's words: to press home the attack, not turn for the horizon at the shout of 'Spitfire!' Not that they required such orders, working in a frenzy in their cockpits, aware that one of them had gone, not knowing who had in a moment passed from living, vibrant being to scraps of molten flesh mixed in with burning metal, plastic, rubber, oil and fuel spread across a broad expanse of wasteland.

Finally, as he turned for base, out of ammunition, Beppo counted the other aircraft, one by one. And knew that Matti Hartmann would not be pocketing the 100 marks owed to him by Emil Gotz. 'My mouth will hang me, if the Tommies fail to get me first.' Beppo felt an odd relief that this fellow he had served beside for nineteen months had not met his end with a noose around his neck. Such things did happen; worse, a man's last moments filmed to show the Führer a traitor's final agonies, suspended not by rope but chicken-wire. Hartmann had been careless with his talk, emboldened by his prowess and reputation as an ace. It would not have been enough to save him from betrayal by such as Emil Gotz. As it was, no doubt he would receive some posthumous honour for his sacrifice, an Aryan hero given a funeral in Berlin complete with empty coffin weighed down with stones.

Beppo touched down briefly in Benghazi, refuelled, rearmed and was assigned free-hunt patrol, a singleton, seeking targets of opportunity. He did not speak with Emil Gotz, but noticed the man walked with a springy step, as though the loss of Hartmann had proved a point, or perhaps had solved a problem. Or saved him 100 marks.

Nobody could tell Beppo how the battle went. It seemed a very big affair, likely to prove conclusive, one way or another. There was much talk of Rommel's absence. It was rumoured that General Stumme, veteran of the Russian Front, appointed Panzerarmee head by Rommel while he was on leave, was dead. Some said his car was strafed, others that it had been hit by anti-tank and machine-gun fire, straying too close to enemy ground positions. The Army was without a coordinating brain; a dangerous void at the highest level.

Beppo could not be concerned with more than what he had to do. He thought it right that Matti Hartmann should be avenged. He very much wanted that task to fall to him. He headed west and climbed to six thousand metres, twisting his head to right and left, scanning the blood-red sky for prey.

The faintest movement, two thousand metres above and to the right, caught his eye. He guided *Hyäne*'s nose into a steep and careful climbing turn, to put him on a level with the unknown machine, the sun behind him. It was a solitary Spitfire, painted pale blue, which had made it difficult to spot. It followed an unwavering, deliberate course and he knew it for what it was: a spy plane on intelligence work, photographing their positions. He also knew it was not armed. The Englishman was as good as dead. He felt a momentary qualm. Then he thought of Hartmann, and he did not care. He tried to settle himself more comfortably in the cockpit. It was cramped and his shoulders almost touched the sides. He was tall and, as usual, was conscious that his head was only inches from the flat top of the side-hinged canopy of armoured glass. Still, it was a fine machine. It enclosed him like a worn-in suit of clothes, the slightly offset control column easy in his hand, the twelve-cylinder Daimler-Benz responding instantly to the slightest pressure of his left hand on the throttle lever as he moved towards the Spitfire, still unseen in the radiant fan of sun. His heart was pounding, there was an aching in his limbs. Only seconds now. He was closing very fast on the Spitfire's starboard beam, fractionally below, to hide himself beneath that elegant wing. He throttled back a little to make certain of his aim. The outline of the Spitfire filled the Revi 16 gunsight. He knew he had this Englishman. He wondered who he was, this man about to die.

Below the closing fighters, great columns of dust and flame showed where the battle still raged, spread across the boundless tract of desert.

Six

It was what every Photographic Reconnaissance pilot hoped he would never see – an enemy aircraft approaching out of a clear sky, with no help at hand, at the controls of an aeroplane incapable of evasive aerobatics thanks to its heavy cameras, and quite unarmed, without even RT to call up base and say goodbye.

Kit had seen the mottled Messerschmitt 109 early in its wily and careful climb to put itself between him and the sun. It was nicely done, but after three years of combat flying he had an instinct for the merest movement in his field of vision; something that should not be there, something new and wrong. Not that this awareness was any comfort.

He felt a twitch of irritation. Group had been blandly reassuring about the Luftwaffe's likely strength south of Miteiriya Ridge. 'We've bombed their airfields to blazes, Curtis. Unlikely you'll encounter anything up at all. Jerries' telecommunications are generally all to hell, chopped to bits by shellfire. Added to which we've had a bunch of Wellingtons circling, stuffed with electronic gubbins that convert enemy radio transmissions into static. They're fighting blind.'

Unfortunately, thought Kit, nobody had bothered to tell this single, determined Hun.

He had few options. 'If you're bounced, keep weaving.' Yes, mordantly amusing in the tobacco-fug of one of the Benson

155

lecture huts, during training. Nothing like a touch of black humour to side-step the obvious, uncomfortable question about what an ambushed PR pilot could actually do to stay alive. Answer: very little.

As the Messerschmitt began to close, but still several miles away, Kit reviewed his three choices: run for home – but then the Hun was handily placed due east and had the speed advantage; bale out now, before the Spit was swept by the inevitable storm of fire; or put on a show of what Ossie Wolf called fancy flying, before the brace of bulky F-24s broke loose from their mountings and smashed the fuselage to shreds, or the German finally fixed this lamest of lame ducks squarely in his sights and put an end to an encounter with only one conclusion. Kit had no illusions about what faced him now. Situation none too rosy. Yes, that just about summed it up. Dry flying jargon, dismissing the approaching horror and extinction, suggesting that, even now, he might prevail. But how?

Meanwhile, he prepared for his second run across the Panzerarmee's battle lines at Miteiriya Ridge, switching on his cameras with calm deliberation, still without a plan in mind, wondering vaguely if, at last, this really was the end.

As he went about his work, his peripheral vision picked up the Me 109 half a mile away, on his starboard beam, 500 feet below, trying to conceal itself beneath his wing. Still he made no move, holding his course as though preoccupied with his task. He sensed the other man's grip tightening on the Messerschmitt's control column, thumb on the gun-button, seconds from opening fire. Reckoning himself already dead, Kit resolved to mark his exit with a final, defiant gesture.

Throttling back a little, he slid open his canopy and locked it, then on the instant kicked hard on the right rudder and pushed forward on the stick, dropping into a steep descending turn at 80 degrees of bank, wings almost vertical, long nose dropping, the whole machine shaking, flexing, the cameras sagging on their mounts and distorting trim, making it hard to keep control. The g-force from the violence of the manoeuvre forced the blood flow from his brain, denying oxygen to his lungs. Spots began to float before his eyes, the first sign of blacking out. Something cracked behind him in the fuselage and the machine began to twist and squirm as though the tailplane was loose. He was losing speed, close to a stall, still hanging in a turn but dipping into a final dive.

The Messerschmitt, surprised, had opened fire, its cannon shells and bullets whining past the vertical Spitfire's underside. With only moments to react, its pilot rolled it to the right, the aero-engine thunder reaching a crescendo as each aircraft flicked past nose by nose. Unwritten aviation law, known by all who flew in combat, dictated that in head-on attack both opponents should, in the final moment, pull into right-hand curves, belly to belly, and so be ready to bank around for another pass. This time, with a combined approach speed of 600 mph, the fighters were too close for such considerations and, with a crack like an artillery round, their port wings struck, were severed in a burst of flame and both machines fell away in violent spins.

Kit felt slight surprise to be unharmed, not touched in any way. He felt alert and in command, and very calm, hanging upside down, pinned securely in his seat by the webbing of his Sutton harness. Above his head, the desert was spinning as wildly as a top. He was pleased that he had thought to push and lock the canopy open; hard to do that in a spin, the wrong way up. The engine was still bellowing, propeller thrashing, but futile now. He reached for the control column but it felt vague and disconnected in his hand, as though every line had sheared, and seemed to make no difference to the falling fighter's attitude. The altimeter, somehow working still, showed his height: ten thousand feet. He closed the throttle and the Merlin died. Now he could only hear the shriek of wind and, far away it seemed, a muted roar where battle was still joined along a front of forty

miles, stretching from the sea of sand that was the Qattara
Depression to the Egyptian coastal plain at Mersa el Hamza; a
battle of great proportions in which he seemed required to play
a tiny and possibly short-lived part.

He saw the port wing was gone, just a stub, cut away between
the roundel and the fuselage. Down to nine thousand feet now,
and time to jump. A pity to lose the kite but at least there was
no chance of anything useful falling into enemy hands – apart
from him, of course. Dizzying though the Spitfire's gyrations
were, its descent was relatively slow, and it was spinning flat, not
quite on its back. Not like baling out in a 400 mph power dive,
when a pilot had to wait. And wait and wait, initially dropping
at the same speed as the aircraft, fighting the temptation to pull
the ripcord because, that way, brought up short by parachute and
harness, meant dislocated bones and ruptured organs. So patience
was required, and nerve; waiting, waiting for gravity to lend a
hand and slow you to the natural speed of a body falling through
the air, little more than 100 mph, when you could safely operate
your 'chute. Done right, you hardly felt a thing – just a welcome
tug and bounce.

This time, though, the risk was different: trying to float clear
of the inverted wreck without being hit or getting the parachute
harness snagged. And so Kit stamped his feet against the rudder
pedals, stamped them hard; right, left, right, left. No response,
the pedals hanging loose, as if the tailplane had gone. The ailerons
then. But only one remained, flapping in the starboard wing. He
tried the stick again and thought he felt a very slight resistance,
as though a frayed cable was scraping across a twisted metal spar.
The single aileron moved. It was enough. The drag snatched at
the airflow and flipped the Spitfire into a parody of an air-show
stunt. It snap-rolled violently through the sky, shedding pieces
as it went. Then it lost momentum, steadied, right side up,
climbed a little, banking left, and stalled. And at the point of
stall, Kit unplugged his oxygen and RT leads, let his leather helmet

fly away, released his harness and pitched himself, head first, over the cockpit side.

His parachute deployed and he drifted down, rotating slowly, the landscape passing before his eyes from left to right, like a shaky panning shot in a some early travelogue. He saw a falling aeroplane, silhouetted black against the sky, and then a ball of brilliant fire spurt up from a distant dune. Behind him came the thud and echo of a similar explosion. It seemed the Messerschmitt might have gone down too. Had its pilot also taken to the silk? If so, he might have company on the ground. Which raised the question: who would capture who?

The horizon began to flatten out, the details on the ground became more distinct. He picked out a column of tanks: Crusaders, Grants, Matildas. Not Panzers then, so some relief. Except he realised they weren't moving. Nothing moved, apart from dense black smoke drifting from the stationary column across the churned-up sand that showed the course they had taken, veering off a track marked out with stretched white tape, wide enough to take a single tank. He knew what it meant, this white-taped route, but did not care to think about it now.

He prepared himself to land. He did not want to suffer a careless injury so far from base. One hundred feet to go. He tucked in his chin, the risers of the harness grasped in an arm-bar protecting his face and throat. He noted his direction of drift, saw he would be touching down close to the burning armour. Something below, spread out on the ground, a flash of white, distracted him for a moment. He had the impression of a solitary moving figure – then it was gone. His feet and knees were pressed together tight, his legs trembling with the effort of maintaining muscular tension, to cushion the impact of the fall. As the balls of his feet touched sand he twisted his upper body against the tug of the canopy still full of air, and rolled. Dragged along for twenty feet, he pulled at the lines to gather in and collapse the 'chute, but then the billowing silk was blown against the glowing red-hot turret of the lead Crusader. The material began to melt, turned black and vanished in a puff of fire. A foul smell filled his nostrils and made him retch and choke. It was not entirely the odour of burning silk. He knew this porcine stench from seeing tanks brew up in France, when the Panzers blitzed their way to Paris through the remnants of outgunned Allied armour.

He shrugged off his harness and crouched down for a moment, to assess his situation. By the burnt-out Crusader, several bodies lay in contorted attitudes, the ground around them marked by their final struggles. Five more tanks were stretched out line astern, all destroyed, their crews either roasted in their machines or spread out on the ground, blackened figures with mouths agape, hands contracted into melted fists, giving them a pugilistic air although, for them, the fight was done.

Several hundred yards away, Kit saw the marked-out track he had picked out from the air, two lines of tape stretched between upright steel rods, the lines eight strides apart. This had been the sappers' work, inching forward behind the creeping barrage that had begun the battle fourteen hours ago, clearing a path across the Devil's Garden, the Axis minefield five miles deep, packed with anti-tank and anti-personnel devices, some designed for tanks triggered by pressure, movement, vibration, sound; others placed to kill the infantry, exploding underfoot or set off by tripwires. Not for nothing had the planners dubbed it Operation Lightfoot.

Kit remembered being in the flight tent with Pat Hallam, the Operations Officer, back at Alam el Halfa, soon after the artillery had begun its work. The noise alone was frightening. There were stories of blood running from the ears of the Allied gun-crews, of men running to the rear, driven mad by the unrelenting tumult. 'Good grief,' Kit had said. 'It almost makes you feel sorry for the Hun.'

'That's what they said about the Somme,' said Hallam. 'The

top brass couldn't imagine how anyone could survive such pounding. But they did, and cut our chaps to pieces.'

'This time it's different. We outnumber the Jerries two to one, twice as many tanks, superiority in the air. And we've taken them by surprise.'

'They've got Rommel, don't forget.'

'I heard he's in Berlin.'

'Not for long, I bet. This battle's just begun. He can turn the course of things. We know that to our cost.'

'No,' said Kit. 'This time I think we'll get him on the run. He's low on fuel, supplies of every kind. Even the Fox can't make his Panzers run on air.'

And yet the early news had been bleak. At 2.00 a.m the infantry advanced along the routes cleared through the minefields by the engineers. Behind them, between the marker tapes, trundled the tanks in single file. The moon was full that night but the columns were raising dust, so visibility was bad. Soon the lines of armour became bogged down. Some crews pulled off the tracks to by-pass jams, quickly followed by others who assumed they knew the route. The first explosions had warned of them of their mistake. There had been good illumination now, from blazing tanks. Men leaped from the turrets, their clothes alight, detonating German S-mines – 'debollockers' as the British infantry grimly dubbed them – that sprang up from the ground, level with the hip, spraying ball-bearing shrapnel across a twelve-foot radius. It was the aftermath of such devastation that now confronted Kit. One thing was certain: he could not stay where he was. Yet how to escape the trap?

He scanned the surface of the ground that lay between him and the fluttering lines of tape. It told him nothing. In places, burned and blackened indentations showed where mines had already detonated. Hundreds more might lie concealed. Then he perceived the most obvious solution. He measured his flying boot against the width of the Crusader's track: about two feet across.

Of course. He simply had to walk to safety, back to where the white tapes were, treading along one of the tracks left by the tank. A piece of cake, as long as he kept his balance. As long as, by some freak of chance, a live mine did not remain where the tank had passed.

He wiped his mouth but there was no moisture there. He steadied himself and took the first few steps, deep in the rut that rose and fell with the contours of the ground, swaying slightly, arms bent slightly outwards, elbows wavering as he tried to keep his balance, inching forward foot by foot, pausing now and then to fill his lungs, to breathe evenly and deep, and raise his head to look ahead to where the white tape fluttered. He did not know how long it took, to cover those few hundred yards; perhaps ten minutes. It seemed like many hours. Although the day was cool, he was damp with sweat. His eyes were red from glaring at the surface of the sand, to right and left, where the smallest stone or creature's burrow could be mistaken for the firing mechanism of a mine.

Finally he reached the track, his legs trembling with tension. He felt very cold and sat down in the dirt, folding his arms across his chest to generate some warmth, rocking back and forth, puffing out his cheeks, like a man who has just emerged from an icy sea. Then, back on his feet, he realised that all around the sounds of battle were very loud. But even so he heard a cry. At first he could not place it until, a long way off, he saw a figure, shimmering like a mirage – an outline of a man, standing where the white-taped track curved a little to the left. It seemed the Devil's Garden might end there.

Kit raised his head and narrowed his eyes. The man was waving. In response, he began to raise his hand. Then he realised that the man was not waving, but beckoning with a pistol. Kit's hand fell to the Webley .38, bulky in its webbing holster on his waist, the cumbersome revolver with which he had fired a round or two, at tin cans set up on the dunes behind the lines at Alam el

Halfa; had fired and missed. This was something like a joke. Except it wasn't remotely funny.

Beppo Lutzow had considered the Englishman already dead, just another Royal Air Force roundel painted on *Hyäne*'s tailfin, marking one more victory. Twenty-three now. Perhaps he would make the cover of *Signal* magazine as the latest Afrika ace. He heard it did wonders for a pilot's popularity with the Berlin *Frauenzimmer*. It was even said it guaranteed home comforts free.

He was sure he had not been seen, stealing up on this dozy snooper in his pretty blue Spitfire, intent on securing his photographs, quite unaware that he was about to be shot to bits. They were not fighter pilots, these men, more airborne boffins, with no real knowledge or understanding of man-to-man combat in the air. Courageous, or course, no doubt of that, aware that they had no means of fighting back, with vigilance and speed their only weapons. For this unlucky fellow, though, his time had come. As it had for Matti Hartmann. That was how it was. At any moment, one mistake or plain bad luck could send a pilot down. Carelessness had cost this man his life. One back for Matti, a fair exchange.

Fifty metres from the target, he readied himself to let go his cannon and machine guns as impersonally as an executioner. Just a two-second burst. No point in wasting good ammunition. He was impatient to complete the kill and move on quickly to another target of opportunity, before he was detected. Except that, in the fraction of time between his brain directing his thumb and forefinger to press the cannon and machine-gun buttons and the muscles contracting, the Spitfire suddenly screwed itself round towards him in an almost vertical diving turn, evading by perhaps eight metres the stream of shells and bullets that flashed harmlessly past its belly.

Scheisse! He had been seen, after all, his wily stalking gone for nothing. The Englishman's plan was clear. With no other options, he was prepared to kill them both. It was unbelievable, fantastic. Brave.

Instinctively Beppo snapped the Messerschmitt to the right, its windscreen full of the Spitfire's upwardly tilted elliptical wing. The details of the underside stood out plain, the blue expanse of smooth, stressed alloy skin, the neatly recessed rivets, the circular outlines of the wheel wells where the undercarriage folded in. Then, with a crack and boom that reverberated round the sky, audible even above the scream of engines, his left wing was ripped away in a flash of fire. The impact threw the Messerschmitt into a violent upwards spin, before it lost momentum, power-stalled and dropped into a vertical spiral, the g-force pinning him to his seat, his chin forced on his chest.

He clawed away the oxygen mask that swung loose and tugged free the radio lead. Then, thrusting out his left arm and grunting with the effort, he managed to close his fingers round the yellow and black lever that jettisoned the canopy, spring-loaded and designed to flip off backwards if a pilot had to exit fast. He pulled it back, the springs released, but the canopy rattled loose and for a moment did not disengage. He thumped upwards with both fists against the armoured glass, and the airflow caught the canopy's leading edge and snatched it clear.

Releasing his belts, Beppo tried to stand up on his seat, but the air pressure drove him down and made his body seem like lead. He crouched, hands on the cockpit sides, his vision blurring. He heard a crack, the screech of metal under stress and then, behind him, something sagged and broke away. He saw, to his right, through red-filmed eyes, the severed tailplane tumbling round and round, like a child's kite. Immediately *Hyäne*'s attitude changed, the spin became more horizontal. The forces on his body eased. He felt a lightness, and suddenly he was free and floating clear, his arms and legs outstretched, turning, turning, very slowly, his sight and senses sharpening with every second.

He was thinking now, and planning, no longer just reacting; in control again, master of his situation.

And so he allowed himself to fall perhaps 100 metres, wary of falling debris, before opening his 'chute. It was a pleasant moment, swimming in the air, remote from the world below where, it seemed, the far-off battle was joined between a million blacksmiths fighting it out with mighty hammers, iron on iron, shaking the very sky. At last he pulled the d-ring to release his canopy and it streamed out, filled and spread, throwing him into shadow, shielding him from the sun.

Below his dangling feet he saw *Hyäne* strike the ground quite close to where another machine was burning. A little to the right, the broken ground of minefields, the Afrika Korps' defensive line, stretched eight kilometres, west to east. He was drifting very close. He had not thought of that, surviving such a narrow escape only to be blown to pieces by the efforts of his own countrymen. At first it seemed he must land there, but then the slightest change of wind direction, thirty metres from touching down, swept him a little further west and clear. The details of the landscape became distinct. A route across the minefield had been marked with tape. Some way off the track, columns of oil-black smoke were rising from a cluster of motionless tanks. He saw where they had missed a slight curve to the left and pressed ahead, breaking through the marker tape, doomed.

He touched the ground as gently as if he had jumped down from a chair, so gently that he stayed firmly on his feet. He pulled in the lines, collapsed the canopy and released himself from his harness. A shadow passed above him, moving slowly towards the minefield; a shadow as though cast by a giant bird. He looked up, startled. A man was hanging below a parachute of unfamiliar pattern, arms folded crosswise across his chest, his legs pulled up. Beppo knew immediately who he was: the Englishman who had tried to kill them both.

He watched as the pilot came to earth and sprawled out in

the blackened sand close to the shattered tanks. He waited for the detonation, to see the distant figure enveloped in a gout of flame, but it did not come. No doubt the tanks had triggered any mines along their course until they were finally overcome, and crewmen, leaping from the turrets, had set off others buried in the sand close by. It seemed that way, the area around the column cast about with huddled and dismembered dead.

The Englishman took time to study his situation. Then, at last, having cast this way and that, he began to move along the tracks left by the tanks. A logical solution: the only one. Beppo smiled to see him move with such deliberation, like someone wading through shallow water. He realised he was willing him to survive. Strange, that. So recently he had been eager to see him die, remembered only as a victory roundel on *Hyäne*'s rudder.

He felt inside his leather flying jacket for the short-barrelled Walther PPK, stowed in its holster in his zippered pocket. Light and handy, he had obtained it through a cousin in the Munich *Polizei*, to replace the heavy Luftwaffe standard-issue Luger. He had nine rounds already loaded, nine more in a magazine stowed in the holster pouch. He might need every one, ringed around by unknown dangers, a flier without wings. Then, perhaps the Englishman was also armed. So it could come to that: two pygmy duellists fighting out their private war, unseen, surrounded by an infinity of space that echoed to their puny shots. And if one fell, or both, the sun would bleach their bones quite as well as those of long-dead Roman legionaries, their fate unknown, their tale untold, hidden finally by the sand.

The Englishman had gained the safe route marked out by the lines of tape. Still he was unaware of being watched. He sat down on the stony track and hugged himself, rocking, rocking like a child, shivering from cold or fear. Though fear did not seem likely. Far away, the fury of the battle had reached a peak. Yet here there was little noise – just the distant fluttering of the stretched white tape, the hiss of sand carried by the wind, the crackle of the burning tanks.

The Englishman stood up. Now Beppo saw the holster at his waist. Whatever weapon it contained was not in play. It would stay that way as long as he took the upper hand, and fast. He had good English, from his childhood conversations with the hotel guests at Starnberg. He gripped the Walther pistol tightly, waving it above his head. 'Hey! Hey, you! You, *Englander! Komm nur hier, komm nur hier.* Place your hands above your head.'

The Englishman, who had been moving slowly along the track towards him, paused. He seemed surprised, and for a moment hopeful. He raised his hand to wave, then saw the pistol. Lowering his head, he began to walk again, now with folded arms, a small defiance, unhurried and methodical, studying every centimetre of the ground beneath his booted feet.

'Hands above your head!' Beppo shouted out once more, but the Englishman did not comply, only continuing his slow advance, now very close. Beppo considered firing a warning shot. It struck him as rather futile, as long as the man made no move to unbutton the bulky holster on his belt. He could see him clearly now. Tall, thin and deeply tanned, soiled with dirt and oil, hair matted to his skull. Finally, he stopped, near enough to touch. In different circumstances, they would have shaken hands.

The Englishman looked Beppo in the eye, unflinching, questioning, his cracked lips showing the faintest, humorous curve. Beppo returned his gaze. He appeared a decent fellow, an experienced pilot clearly, with that slight, abstracted air of all professionals who fly, most comfortable in the cockpit, their element the sky. He had the look of any of his comrades in the *Staffel*. He looked like Matti Hartmann.

Part two

Jorrocks

Seven

Some weeks before Kit Curtis went down, a three-ton Opel Blitz truck with the palm tree and swastika symbol of the Afrika Korps on its doors and mudguards came down the final, sloping stretch towards a compact, wire-ringed camp, its gearbox whining under its load, its heavy-treaded tyres kicking up stones from the vestigial course they had followed across the desert for more than half a day.

Ossie Wolf, supporting himself by pushing his feet hard against the fascia, one hand on the open window, the other gripping the seat squab by his thigh, still could not prevent himself from being thrown around by each lurch and bounce. It had been a rugged trip. He was conscious of every bone and muscle in his body. For hours they had travelled without a stop, only halting when Chaim Herzl left the wheel, jumping down to consult his map and compass, allowing a few moments to stretch their legs. It had been a laborious process, even for an expert navigator, picking their way through the labyrinth of camel tracks that lay between them and their destination. They seemed as far from other men as it was possible to get. Once, as Herzl handed him the flask of tepid water, Ossie had spat into the sand. 'Brother,' he had said, 'I feel like a box of parts.'

'*Scheisse!*' Herzl had shaken his head in exasperation, and said in German: 'No English, you damned fool, ever. How many more times must you be told? *In Gottes Namen*, why did they pick you for this job? No, don't tell me. Just get back in the truck and shut your mouth.'

Ossie had growled: 'No one talks to me that way.'

Herzl had grinned. 'Perfect accent when provoked. That's good. At least in some regards you fit the need. And no mean pilot, so they say. Perhaps after all you will work out.' He brushed down the uniform that marked him as a Wehrmacht lance corporal. Ossie they had made a private, but in this crazy outfit ranks didn't mean a thing. So, saying nothing more, he had climbed back in the Opel's cab, assuming his position, his German field cap tilted forward, its peak across his face, pretending to be asleep, despite the breath being knocked from his lungs by every rut and rock. Now, after three more hours of slow and careful progress across the desert floor, scanning land and sky for signs of danger from any quarter, enemy or friend an equal threat, the Opel halted outside the barbed-wire gates of what Ossie knew must be Mulholland's base.

Two sentries advanced, Mauser rifles slung across their shoulders, both wearing steel helmets bearing the Afrika Korps insignia. The tall one with the broken nose waved the Opel through, calling out to Herzl as they passed: 'Hey, *Kamerad*, you have our bird?'

'*Ja, ja*. Now all he needs is wings.'

'*Sehr gut*. The *Kommandant* is waiting.'

Inside the camp, the illusion was complete, busy with twenty or thirty men, all correctly garbed as Panzerarmee soldiery, the only language heard the bark of German. Herzl parked the Opel Blitz in a compound set aside for transport; more trucks, two Volkswagen command cars, BMW motorcycle combinations with MG34 machine guns mounted on their sidecars. A few mechanics were working on the engines. Five hundred yards away, close to the perimeter fence, a squad was scrambling its way across the obstacles of an assault course: parapets, pits and horizontal poles.

Closer to, a dozen men were being instructed on how to kill an enemy hand-to-hand. And on the central, open square, ringed around by Wehrmacht-style wooden huts, more were snapping through parade-ground rituals to the usual, harsh commands. '*Das Gewehr . . . uber!*' As Ossie watched, the close-packed ranks shouldered arms together, their rifles flying into place with a simultaneous, satisying crack. Then: '*Achtung . . . Präsentiert das . . . Gewehr!*' Presenting arms, most difficult of all, but in a moment the line of upturned muzzles was perfectly aligned, only moving slightly here and there, men quivering with the effort of holding steady.

Herzl touched Ossie on the arm. '*Mitkommen, mach schnell. Der Kommandant.*'

Ossie forgot the rule. 'You sure these guys ain't kosher? They sure look right to me.'

Herzl hissed: '*Verflucht noch mal! Das Englisch ist verboten.*' Then, unexpectedly, he softened. And in English murmured; 'Oh, they're kosher all right, my friend. None more so.'

The *Kommandant* was standing by the window of his office, overlooking the parade ground, studying the marching files now moving slowly past in the goose-step. His badges of rank proclaimed him as a Wehrmacht *Oberst*. He turned, neat in his olive-green tropical tunic topped by a tartan woollen civilian scarf, the kind that Rommel wore, his sand-coloured trousers gathered at the ankle by web gaiters, above laced-up leather and canvas desert boots. When Ossie came to attention, as he had been coached to by Herzl, the *Kommandant* raised an eyebrow. 'You omitted to click your heels. Welcome to Holly Force, dear boy. You catch me watching the Tiller Girls going through their routine.'

Ossie cleared his throat. '*Das Englisch ist verboten, nein?*'

'Everywhere but in this office, Wolf. It keeps me sane.' He turned back to the window. 'I assume you're familiar with *Der Stechschritt*? We British choose to think the goose-step funny. We miss the point. As Orwell notes, it's an affirmation of naked power, a vision of a boot crashing down upon a face. Like a bully, it challenges you to laugh; the kind of military display that's only possible in a country where the common people dare not laugh at the Army.'

'I heard the Wehrmacht didn't teach it any more.'

'Correct. But here it has its purpose. Those good old Prussian virtues: discipline and superiority. The lion must also know how to play the fox.'

'Uh-huh,' said Ossie.

'Wonderfully ironic, is it not?' the *Kommandant* said. 'Every one of those Aryan heroes is really a son of Zion.'

'No kidding.'

Behind him, Ossie heard a smothered laugh. Over his shoulder Chaim Herzl said; 'Yes, they are mostly Palestinian Jews. As I told you, kosher to a man.'

The *Kommandant* was not a Wehrmacht *Kommandant*. His name was Aubrey Mulholland. Ossie Wolf had met him last in Heliopolis, two weeks before, behind an unmarked door that led to Rupert Pringle's kingdom; Pringle who, in Cairo, in the garden of the uncommon bawdy house beyond the Birka, had scratched out some directions on a Shepherd's bar receipt of Bernard Booth's. 'You can find me here.'

'What you got in mind?'

'A hare-brained scheme cooked up by madmen that will almost certainly get you killed.'

The fat man Booth had been in Heliopolis too, and Bakri, the Egyptian, his presence still unexplained. And Mulholland, in a light civilian suit, thick fair hair cropped very short. But Pringle, at that stage, had not given him a name.

'This gentleman has a proposition.'

'Oh yeah?'

'I have a certain project,' Mulholland had said, 'that needs a man like you.'

'What's a man like me?'

'An expert pilot prepared to chance his arm.'

'That's true of every flier.'

'No,' Mulholland said. 'Our last man lost his nerve.'

'You picked a deadbeat then.'

Mulholland had sat back in his chair, his hands behind his head. 'He's certainly dead.' He stared at Ossie, his face without expression. 'You have fluent German, I understand. How is that? Explain.'

Ossie jerked his head at Pringle. 'My old buddy must have filled you in.'

Pringle winced and closed his eyes.

'Explain again.'

'Third-generation Volksdeutscher family in the States, still hung up on *Heimat* bullshit. The greater Germany to come – tradition, duty, honour, all that crap.'

'Tradition, duty, honour crap?'

'In their case, absolutely.'

'Carry on.'

'In our household, German was the mother tongue. I learned it good, and everything that went with it too.'

'Elaborate. In German.'

Ossie dropped easily into his second language. 'I had a Cousin Max. He flew an Albatros Scout over the Western Front. Had quite a reputation. I soaked it all up. I wanted to be like him. My father wanted it too.'

'And so you went to Spain?'

'That's right.'

'And flew for the Fascist cause?'

Ossie switched back to English. 'Quit playing games. You know all this. You also know I wised up fast. Let's get to the point.'

'Watch yourself, Wolf,' said Pringle. 'You're addressing a senior rank.'

'He's travelling incognito, huh?'

Pringle looked at the gentleman in the light, civilian suit. 'I warned you he was a Bolshie type.'

'Jeez,' said Ossie. 'Fascist? Bolshevik? Make up your goddamned minds.'

'That's rather rich,' said Pringle. 'Surely that's been the story of your life?'

'My name is Mulholland,' said the gentleman in the civilian suit. His voice was smooth and even. He had the slightest lisp. 'I'm a serving officer with the British Army. My regiment was posted to the Western Desert in forty-one. Now I command a particular brainchild of mine, that may or may not work. But at least it's worth a try.'

'What is this brainchild?'

'That, dear boy, is the leading question. Unless you're on board, I'm not at liberty to say. Some describe it as a ragbag foreign legion of throwouts, murderers and the dangerously deranged. It suits us very well. People tend to stay away.'

'Away from where?'

'Oh,' said Mulholland, waving a languid hand. 'Out there, you know. Out there.'

'So,' said Ossie. 'More cloak-and-dagger stuff.'

'That would fairly sum it up.' Mulholland took a coin from his jacket pocket and began to spin it idly. 'So what do you say? Interested or not?'

'How does flying figure?'

'Sign on for the voyage and I'll tell you all you want to know.'

'And that's it, huh? That's all you're letting on?'

'That's all, until you report to Force HQ.'

'Holly, I'm not at all sure we've got our man,' said Pringle. 'You know what they say about the leopard. I thought perhaps that Wolf here might have dropped a spot or two, in the intervening years.'

'Oh, I don't know,' said Mulholland. 'I quite like his look. He's got a lot of what we need. He's under no illusions, and he knows the risks. I think we'd rub along just fine. Besides, time's not on our side.' He turned his head, his grey eyes studying Ossie, continuing to flip his coin. 'There is one thing, dear boy, before you give me your decision. You'll be in German uniform, so if you're caught, they'll shoot you on the spot. Does that alter things at all?'

'No,' said Ossie, 'that's fine. You can count me in.'

'That's the ticket.' Mulholland slapped his right hand on his left, trapping the spinning coin, then raised his palm. 'Ah, heads.'

'Who won?' asked Ossie.

'Both of us, I think,' said Mulholland, pocketing the coin and standing up. 'Got to dash. Delighted we've got things fixed. These chaps will sort out whatever paperwork's involved. I'll give you a detailed briefing when next we meet.'

'Out there.'

'That's it, out there.'

Pringle saw Mulholland out. He came back looking thoughtful. 'I hope we've got this right. Holly seems very keen on you. For God's sake don't let him down. He's a rather special chap.'

Ossie said: 'Who's going to tell Tim Fletcher?'

Pringle frowned. 'Did you hear what I just said? Remember, I put you up for Holly Force. You struck me as the sort of unhinged cove to fit the bill. God knows, we're rather stuck for choice. Don't make me regret it, that's all. A lot depends on this, the climax of the operation. It sounds far-fetched, but as you'll hear, it's mad enough to work. Holly's band of brigands have already proved their point. Audacious is not the word. Anyway, who's Fletcher?'

'My CO at Takoradi.'

'Oh,' said Pringle, 'Bernard will sort that out. I doubt the fellow's going to be desperately upset to let you go.'

'So tell me, Pringle,' Ossie said, 'where do you guys fit in all of this?'

'We oil the wheels for Holly Force. Make sure it gets what

it needs to do its job. Keep a track of things, as far as we are able. Keep them out of trouble with the bigwigs, when the case arises.'

'Trouble?'

'A rather grey area, Wolf – ungentlemanly warfare. The first rule is, there are no rules. The PM understands. That's good enough for us.'

Later, watching the Wing Commander shuffle through his papers, Ossie said: 'So what more can you tell me, Booth?'

'Nothing. That's not down to me.'

'Who is it down to? Pringle says it isn't him.'

'He's right. Holly's your man.'

'Level with me, Booth. I'm curious. Who is this character Mulholland?'

'An old Arab hand. You know the type. Well, possibly you don't. Bit of a mystic. Loves the desert wastes. Knows the native tribes, speaks their various lingos, rides a camel, shares their tents. Was all over this neck of the woods before the war. Wrote books. If there was bugger-all there, that's where you'd find him. Not that I'd have been looking. Mystery to me, old boy, the lure of the benighted wilderness. Can't stand the place. Like to have folk about. But there, it takes all sorts.'

'Talking of which,' said Ossie, 'is Mulholland a bachelor boy?'

'Don't worry about old Holly,' said Booth. 'He may appear a little light on his feet, but he's solid gold. Just don't cross him, that's my advice. Tales get back. Your predecessor, for example . . .'

'Oh yeah?'

'Let's say he didn't come up to scratch.'

'Are you saying what I think you're saying?'

''Nuff said, I think. You'll find out. Or rather, I suggest you don't. I wish you luck. From what I hear, you're going to need it.'

*　　*　　*

Now, in his spartan office, with its view of marching ranks, Mulholland said, 'Good show, Herzl. You can go. Wolf, sit down. So, tell me, what do you understand about the current state of play?'

'Here?' said Ossie.

'No, generally.'

'Obviously, something big's about to break. The grapevine says it's just a question of when the brass decides the time has come.'

'Our opposite numbers believe it will be November.'

'How do you know that?'

'They told us.'

Ossie grunted. 'You asked, they told you, huh?'

'Something like that. Unfortunately for them, dear boy, they're wrong. Monty will unleash a full-scale attack in a few weeks' time, in late October. The front will stretch from Alamein, on the coast, to the Qattara Depression in the south. The Eighth Army is going to hit the Hun with everything it's got. If all goes to plan, it will be the first time in this war that the Axis army has been defeated in the field. And with Rommel neutralised, it will open the way to Sicily, to Italy and beyond.'

Mulholland smiled pleasantly. 'I'm sharing this intelligence with you, Wolf, because you're one of us now. I'm backing my hunch that this time we've got the right man for a very particular job. Anyway, the pressure's on. We've got work to do. No time for more of Pringle's bureaucratic rigmarole. Besides, despite his best endeavours, the last chap he put forward turned out to be short on guts. At least, the sort of guts that we require. You may have a goodly number of black marks against your name, but lack of guts is not among them. That, with your flying skill, is good enough to for me. However,' and here his smile became more fixed, 'if at any point it seems my confidence is likely to be betrayed, or you go against my orders, I will not hesitate to take extreme measures. Every man here understands that. Achieving our objectives far outweighs all other considerations.'

'You can count on me,' said Ossie.

'Good,' said Mulholland. 'You'll have a chance to prove it very soon. I'm planning a little sideshow that needs a chap like you.'

'Suits me. I crave some action.'

'I have a feeling we might get along, dear boy,' said Mulholland. He took a rose-red pack of Sulima cigarettes from his tunic pocket and offered it across. Ossie took one and lit it from Mulholland's lighter. An obscure tobacco fragrance hung between them, exotic and sickly sweet.

Ossie studied the oval tube between his fingers. Mulholland looked amused. 'Turkish. But don't worry – German made. We're good on detail. We learned that from Bertie Buck.'

'Bertie Buck?'

'We're not unique in this line of work. Bertie was among the first to set up shop, training a similar bunch of bandits over Mersa Matruh way. Bertie's Suicide Squad. Prescient, I'm afraid. For Bertie and his boys things turned out rather badly, thanks to rotten luck and a few bad apples. Still, lessons were learned and here morale is high.'

'So where is "here" exactly?'

'Exactly I won't tell you, until we know each other better. For the moment, well, it's just a little hidey-hole I knew before the war, nicely off the beaten track as you've discovered, convenient for our operations. Naturally those who need to know are in the picture. Wouldn't do to be duffed up by our own chaps. So we're safe enough until we venture out. Then it's no holds barred, of course. We're on our own.'

'What happens if the Jerries come knocking on your door?'

'It has been known, although we're a long way south of the main event. When they did, we carried it off. You've seen, dear boy. We're more convincing than the real thing.'

'So what's your racket here? For sure it's more than checking out the Panzerarmee's movements and maybe a little sabotage.

Your guys are training hard. Looks like you got something big in mind.'

'Suffice to say it's a venture that's got the powers-that-be in something of a flutter. In fact, they're keen to wash their hands of the whole affair. They will harp on about the rules of war, as though the Geneva Convention means a fig to the house-painter's merry band, quite apart from predicting dire consequences if we end up in the bag.'

Mulholland opened a drawer in his desk, took out a folded Post Office telegram and passed it across to Ossie. It was unstamped, undated, with O.H.M.S. pencilled at its head, addressed from C to M. The single sentence read: *Good hunting*. Mulholland took the telegram back, refolded it, replaced it in the drawer. 'From Winston,' he said, 'who's not averse to dirty tricks himself. He is a politician, after all.'

Abruptly, he switched to German. 'Tell me, are you fighting fit?' He leaned forward, his eyes hard. 'I mean, really fighting fit.' He sat back, his jaw working. 'For example, have you killed a man, not in the air but on the ground?'

'Sure,' said Ossie. 'Some.'

'In Spain?'

'In Spain and after.'

'How? What methods did you use?'

'Rifle, in Catalonia. Shotgun and a pistol one time near Verdun in forty, taking out some Fifth Column sons-of-bitches.'

'Your feelings?'

'Feelings?'

'It can be different when you're close. Close enough to smell the blood and hear the final gasp.' Mulholland paused. 'So, never trained in silent killing? How to use your bare hands or a knife?' Ossie shook his head. 'I particularly like the knife,' Mulholland said. 'The knife is quick and silent, properly used. Personal, of course. An intimate experience, not to everybody's taste.'

'A stiff's a stiff.'

'You Americans have a way with words. But words are easy, deeds are hard. You have a lot to learn.'

'I'm a quick study.'

'And time's against us.'

'Not only time,' said Ossie. 'Seems you're under threat on every side.'

'Quite the joker, Wolf. Let's hope it will sustain you. You'll find our training rigorous and harsh.'

'That suits me fine. I grew fat in Cairo.'

Mulholland swivelled in his chair and looked out through the window. The square was empty. The marching ranks had been dismissed. He said in English: 'Your German is exemplary. Your family taught you well.'

'Yours ain't too shabby,' said Ossie. 'You Volksdeutscher too?'

Mulholland shook his head. 'A facility for languages, that's all. I'm fluent in eight, get by in three.' He handed Ossie another oval cigarette. 'I'm curious, Wolf. You fancy yourself a hard-boiled fellow. I wonder why. What drives you, would you say?'

'Drives me? How?'

'What is it? To banish fear, safeguard freedom, protect the individual, save the Jews, secure a better world? Or prove something to yourself?'

'Such as?'

'I wouldn't know. An inner weakness, something to be denied?'

'You lost me, pal.'

'Yes, I rather think I have.'

Ossie frowned. 'Like I said in Helio, my old man played me for a sap, just like Hitler played a nation. What did the cockeyed bastard say? "Propaganda can make a people believe Heaven is Hell, and vice versa." I hate that kind of crap, and anyone who supports it, messing with people's lives. I'll fight it any time and any place.'

'To the death, of course.'

'That's what it all comes down to. These Fascist sons-of-bitches brought it on themselves.'

'They played you for a sap.'

'That's right. They played me for a sap, and now they'll pay, for all the saps out there who can't fight back.'

'Ah, so you fight for them.'

Ossie hesitated, then shrugged. 'Okay, it's personal, if you want it straight. I'm here to get even for being suckered. I don't subscribe to filling folk's heads with garbage, pushing them around, telling them what to think and do. Brother, it's that simple.'

'Is it?' said Mulholland. 'It could be argued that a lot of the Panzerarmee chaps have been suckered, as you call it, by following the Nazi cause, inspired by the likes of Erwin Rommel and Albert Kesselring, fellows much like us, by no means all of them Fascist sons-of-bitches, simply carrying out their soldierly duty and keen to serve their country.'

'You kidding me?' said Ossie. 'That's a load of hooey. Jesus, in Spain I walked away. The writing was on the wall in letters ten foot high. These bastards could have walked away as well. That's all it takes. That's all it ever took. Instead, they let it happen. Guilty as charged, I say.'

'Step forward the self-appointed executioner.'

'Who gives a shit? I find these kinds of conversations don't help any. In the end it's all the same. We win, they lose and life goes on.'

'Perhaps,' said Mulholland. 'Perhaps not. It rather depends on the kind of world we're left with, wouldn't you say? And what you had to do to reach that point.'

Ossie stared at him blankly. 'I wouldn't know. Maybe all I want to hear right now is why I'm here. Apart from learning how to use a goddamned knife.'

Mulholland pushed back his chair. 'Quite right, dear boy. To horse, to horse. Time to introduce you to our Air Force.' At the door he turned and pointed to the floor. 'The Anglo-German border. *Vergiss nicht.*'

'*Jawohl, Herr Oberst*,' Ossie said. '*Deutsche einzig*. I won't forget again.'

Outside the perimeter fence, where the ground stretched flat and hard towards the rock-strewn hills where nothing grew except a patch or two of camel thorn, and insects bred and crawled and swarmed, and horned vipers slithered after prey, searching out small mammals like jerboa, the desert rat, deep in burrows but not safe, a camouflaged awning secured by ropes was stretched across a flying machine that also held a hint of insect. As delicate-looking as a mosquito, it was spindly and insubstantial, its tapering body narrow as a racing scull, wide wings folded back, perched whimsically on tiny tyres that might have come from a small boy's die-cast model, compressed-air oleo shock-absorbing struts angled from the wheels to wing root between the broad, glazed wind-screen and the side-glass of the cockpit. The fuselage and upper surfaces of the wings were painted a uniform sand-brown, the under-surfaces and rudder the palest blue. On its flanks it bore the German cross, bold black on white, and on its rudder the Nazi swastika. This warlike touch struck Ossie as something like a gag.

Beneath the awning, men were moving, one balanced on a metal ladder, big and bulky against the tiny plane, leaning into the engine bay, part-hidden by the stubby twin-blade prop.

'Delightful contraptions, don't you think?' Mulholland said. 'Fell into our hands intact three weeks ago, in the middle of a sandstorm. The pilot put it down, completely lost. He and his observer marvelled at their luck in stumbling on a Panzerarmee base. Asked us to inform their unit at Bab el Qattara of their little mishap and report that they expected to resume their flight when the weather lifted. Our set-up took them in completely. They swallowed our story whole. They also quite believed us when we said the sand had ruined their engine, and were touch-ingly grateful when we laid on transport to restore them to their comrades. Two happier fellows you can't imagine, waving us farewell. I gather from Herzl that it came as a dreadful shock when they arrived in Cairo, and found themselves under lock and key.

'For us, it was wonderfully providential, having a nice new Storch delivered to our door. The first, I'm afraid, picked up in the general to-and-fro of the battle around Alam el Halfa, was written off by young Dobbs when he lost his nerve with dire results. Pringle's people had done their best, trying to locate a replacement, but predictably had drawn a blank. And our technicians were up against it, trying to mend the wreck without the benefit of a manual. The Storch might appear a rudimentary if not primitive device, but the wings particularly are an ingenious design, bristling with flaps and slats, and progress was slow to say the least. Given that the little beast was vital to our enterprise, it seemed our venture might be on the rocks. Then fate, if not God, intervened, and now we have the luxury of two – the original, of course, cannibalised for spares.'

Mulholland removed his olive-cloth field cap and thrust his hand through his stubbled hair. 'Not forgetting our other windfall, finding the right man to fly the thing.' He turned his head and looked Ossie in the eye. 'Quite a run of luck. When things work out so well, it makes me nervous. Almost too good to be true. I recall that all windfalls bruise. I'd hate to find I've picked a rotten apple, like poor old Bertie Buck.'

'Is that some kind of joke?' said Ossie.

'A bad one, let us hope.'

For moments Ossie held Mulholland's unblinking gaze, then turned away, moving round the Storch saying nothing, hands deep in trouser pockets, the stub of the sickly oval cigarette dead between his lips. He knew the Storch well, of course, but only as a target – had shot them down in France. It was the Luftwaffe's general purpose workhorse, used for military liaison, reconnaissance and spotting for artillery and tanks. He nodded to the fitter and rigger, who glanced questioningly at Mulholland. Distrust was in their eyes, suspicion even, confronted with this unknown, unproven pilot who could turn out to be another Dobbs. At a sign from Mulholland they finished their work, replaced the engine cowling and pushed the pygmy aircraft out into the open. The wings were folded forward and secured.

'Time to get acquainted,' Mulholland said. 'I think you'll be amused.'

On the Storch's starboard side Ossie found the cockpit door, mostly glass, slanting outwards with the lower section angled back, almost horizontal, so the crew could survey what lay below. To Ossie it looked as quaint as an olde-worlde sweetshop window.

Though diminutive, the Storch stood tall. Ossie had to stretch to reach the door catch. The door swung upwards on its hinges, and secured beneath the wing. He used the ladder to inspect the cockpit from outside. Space was generous, big enough for a man to stand erect, if twin bucket seats hadn't been bolted to the floor, one behind the other, tandem-style, each with a large rectangular well to take a parachute.

'Jesus,' Ossie said. 'The guys who fly this thing had better be real good pals.'

He slid himself into the pilot's seat. Although he was low down because the parachute wasn't there, his forward view was unobstructed by the Storch's nose.

'The engine's mounted upside down,' said Mulholland, 'with the narrow part at the top. Helps the visibility no end.'

From his position at the controls Ossie could glance down and even see the splayed-out, toy-like wheels. The tall control column, simple as the handle of a broom, moved in front of him as he adjusted his weight, resting his feet on the broad cast-alloy rudder pedals with leather ski-type safety straps. Mounted on the tubular fuselage member on the left, the throttle control. On the grey-painted half-moon instrument panel, the usual dials: altimeter, airspeed indicator, artificial horizon, oil and fuel gauges. No surprises. Those came when Mulholland, leaning in from the ladder, pointed to a clutter of cranks and wheels and gears behind the throttle control.

'To operate the flaps,' he said. 'Teutonic ingenuity. The point at which aeroplane designer and blacksmith meet, but if your left arm's strong enough it's a doddle. Now plonk yourself in the rear seat and I'll take you for a flip.'

'You can fly this thing?' asked Ossie.

'It's easy to fly it badly. Rommel uses one to get about, bit ham-fisted by all accounts. To fly it well you need to know its quirks. It's hardly what you're used to, of course. The whole idea of aviation is getting maximum efficiency through the air, and speed. The Storch operates on the opposite principle. Drag is good. She'll cruise at eighty mph and land at twenty-five. You'll soon acquire the knack. After all, what's a string-and-sealing wax lash-up like this to an ace like you?'

With parachutes in place, and harnesses secured, Mulholland pressed the engine's electric starter button – 'a rare luxury, dear boy, eliminates the need for someone to swing your prop because, the way these things are used, there's usually nobody about' – and the air-cooled V-8 Argus fired up. It rumbled like an Indianapolis race car. Mulholland was calling back across his shoulder, but for the first few minutes Ossie could barely hear a word. It didn't bother him. Unseen, he slipped his harness so he could get a better view. His eyes would tell him most of what he had to know.

Mulholland cranked on twenty degrees of take-off flap, grunting with the effort, and turned upwind, although the breeze was slight. Forward on the throttle and the Storch began to trundle across the compounded earth, the airspeed building up. Muholland's right hand pushed forward on the control column, to raise the tail. It came up only slowly. The pressures seemed extreme. Then, at 40 mph, they suddenly eased. Stick in both hands, he pulled back hard. The effect was startling, the Storch rising almost vertically, its nose at an angle of forty-five degrees. Ossie doubted lift-off had taken more than thirty feet.

Mulholland cranked up the flaps and eased off the throttle. The airspeed settled to a burbling 60 mph. The Holly Force camp rotated slowly below them. A few men paused to watch them passing overhead. They made a little height, about 800 feet. Mulholland cut the power and the Storch seemed to hang suspended in the air. Ossie waited for the stall. Hell, relinquishing his harness hadn't been such a great idea. How competent a flier was this oddball Limey? They were flying low, too goddamned low to deliberately invite a spin. Ossie checked the airspeed: 35 mph. The guy was showing off. He'd kill them both. Except the Storch did not spin, or even approach a stall. With the stick held back and the merest trickle of power, the elevators bit. The airplane held a straight and steady course.

'I'll pop her down,' Mulholland shouted. 'Then you can show me how it should be done.'

He turned downwind. The landing area looked indistinct and very small. He came in on his final approach, a steep descent, airspeed steady at 50 mph, cranking down full flaps, the ailerons drooping, the trailing edges of the wings bent down. To Ossie it seemed they must augur in. His discarded harness clanked mockingly against the seat. Too late to fix it now. If he survived the initial impact, maybe he'd be thrown clear. He looked around for something to grab hold of, saw only Mulholland's shoulders working at the controls. Definitely not an option. They were close to the ground now, maybe twenty feet off, the desert floor a blur of tan and brown. And then Mulholland levelled off and eased the throttle. Suddenly it was quiet, just the rush of air across the huge expanse of slatted wing and flap, the propeller windmilling *whop-whop-whop*. In any other airplane, it would have been the end; a certain stall.

'Goes against every instinct,' Mulholland said, in conversational tone, 'but at this point what you want is slow, slow, slow.' He nodded at the airspeed indicator. It showed barely 25 mph. He pulled back on the stick and cut the power, and they touched down without the slightest bounce. Instead, the oleo struts of the landing gear spread out and gently cushioned the landing. The Storch stopped in three airplane lengths.

Ossie gave a low whistle. 'That's quite a trick.'

'Beguiling little beast, isn't she?' They taxied towards the makeshift hangar. One of the camouflage awning's entrance flaps had come untied and was snapping and cracking in a rising wind. Whirls of dust and sand flitted across their path like miniature tornadoes. 'Got down just in time,' said Mulholland. 'Looks as though a ghibli is blowing up from the Sahara. They can last for days. You've missed the window. You're grounded, I'm afraid. Bad luck.'

Ossie shrugged. 'I've flown in worse than this.'

'Not in a Storch, dear boy. The wind speed of a ghibli can touch 60 mph. That's about as fast as you can fly.'

'What if we get a ghibli during this stunt you're planning?' said Ossie. 'You going to ground me then? I need to know I can fly this machine in all conditions, however bad.'

'And what if you destroy it? So far you've only sat at the controls.'

'I won't.'

'I'm sorry, Wolf. The Storch is fundamental to our plan. I can't afford to take the risk. You'll have time enough to put her through her paces. For now, someone will show you to your billet and organise some food. Then I'll tell you more about the who, what, when and how of Operation Jorrocks.'

They were scrambling out of the Storch now. The ground-crew men came forward. They did not look at Ossie but listened intently to Mulholland's observations on the flight, one making notes in an oil-grimed notepad.

'Right,' said Mulholland finally. 'Let's get your accommodation sorted out.'

189

Ossie turned away. '*Ja, gewiss*, but later, after I familiarise myself some more with this little bird.'

For a moment Mulholland looked uncertain. Then he nodded brusquely. '*Sehr gut*. The fellows will tell you all you need to know. They're both ex-Palestine Airways, by the way, so you can count on them to know their stuff. Report to my office when you're done.'

The two men watched him walk away, still avoiding Ossie's eye. One turned towards the Storch. 'Hold it,' Ossie snapped in English. 'Let's get one thing straight, right off.'

The fitter with the notebook drew in breath. '*Das Englisch ist verboten.*'

'Brother, when I'm riled, I express myself better in plain American, *verstehen?* From this point on, this baby's mine and you guys work for me. I'm here to fly and that's what I intend to do. Back me up and I'll see you right. If you don't cut the mustard, I'll kick your asses all the way to a foxhole on the front line. Don't think I can't. I got influence. That's why I'm here.' The fitter, open-mouthed, eyes wide, dropped his pad. Before he could pick it up, Ossie was with him, his face so close he could see the oil-clogged pores in the fitter's nose. 'Okay, wise guy, what's your goddamned name?'

'Yosef Mintz.'

'Mintz, huh? As of now you're Pepper.' He turned to the little rigger. 'And you?'

'Haim Katz.'

'Mintz and Katz. Sounds like some crumby vaudeville act. Katz, I dub you Felix.' Ossie grinned broadly, rubbing his hands together. 'Now give this heap of shit a pre-flight check. I'm going to take her up.'

The camouflage awning was lifting in the violent gusts, like a tethered balloon. The Storch was inching forward on its kiddie-kar wheels, carried by the mounting force of the ghibli.

'The *Kommandant* forbade it.' Mintz was sore and fractious.

'Don't tell me what the *Kommandant* said or didn't say,' rapped Ossie. 'Remember this. Your orders come from *me*. It's my ass that's on the line. So button your lip and give this kite the once-over, before it takes off on its own. And Pepper, grab yourself a 'chute. You're riding shotgun. I could use some ballast.' Before either man could move, he added: 'Well, how do you like that? I reckon that old ghibli's just about blowed itself out. Nothing but a gentle breeze. Just darlin' weather for circuits and bumps.'

The three men leaned against the racking wind, unsteady on their feet. Behind them, the camouflage awning strained against its creaking tethers, threatening to fly itself.

Back in his office, Mulholland sent for Herzl. 'Chaim, our American friend should be along quite soon. Find him a billet where he won't ruffle too many feathers. He's a belligerent little type and might pick on the wrong person. Some of our chaps are on a very short fuse.'

'For a first effort, his flying didn't look too bad.'

Mulholland smiled wryly. 'That was me. Wolf was grounded by the weather. We'll have to wait and see if he's as good as he thinks he is. Which, by the way, is very, very good.'

Outside, the ghibli was gaining in strength. Particles of stone and sand were rapping against the window, fine clouds of dust curling down from the ceiling, pressing through the gaps between the eaves.

Then Herzl cocked an ear. 'Grounded, is he? I'll swear that's the Storch overhead.'

'God rot it,' Mulholland said. 'I rather think you're right.'

They went outside, hands cupped across their foreheads, squinting upwards, shielding their eyes against the stinging grit. The Storch, indistinct against the driving skeins of reddish Saharan sand, swooped overhead, its unseen pilot correcting an adverse left-hand yaw, swiftly counteracting incipient skids and sideslips with a light and expert hand, the ailerons and rudder working hard together, perfectly coordinated, the fragile-looking mono-plane banking into a neatly executed turn, smoothing a passage through the buffeting southerly blow, the yammer of its engine barely heard and, to Mulholland, gazing up stiff-necked, looking less stork than broad-winged bird of prey, balancing on the violent fluctuations of the wind, entirely at ease, equal to any test of flying skill the ghibli might care to throw its way.

Many of the Holly Force men had gathered in noisy groups, peering upwards, some open-mouthed, some grinning, others shaking heads. The Storch banked away and passed from sight, over near the landing ground.

'Get those idle beggars back to work,' Mulholland snapped at Herzl, starting off towards the hangar. 'At least the fool has had the sense to put it down.'

He had not moved two paces before they heard the rising bellow of the Storch's engine and saw it once more in the air, tossed about by gusts and thermal currents, heading back towards them. Slowly, very slowly, it battled against the rising force of wind, pitching, rolling, yawing to right and left, but always pulling back on course and pressing forward until it once more hung above them, very low, then lower still.

'Rat me,' Mulholland said. 'The madman's going to land it on the square.' The Storch seemed to hover now, sinking foot by foot, its engine screaming, throttle fully open, holding it fixed and almost stationary against the headwind's pressure. Then, as the windspeed built still more, it began to be forced back. And Ossie Wolf put it down, the wheels and tailskid striking the hard earth of the drill square precisely together in a textbook three-point landing.

'*Gevalt geshreeyeh!*' Herzl exploded in Yiddish. 'Good grief. That's the first time I've seen an aeroplane touch down back-wards.'

Two figures had jumped down from the cockpit, one beck-oning to the groups of watching men. A few of them ran across.

The wings were quickly folded back, the Storch pushed into the lee of a nearby hut.

'Place Wolf and his companion under close arrest,' said Mulholland, 'and bring them here to me.'

But the interrogation did not go entirely Mulholland's way, unlike the time with Dobbs when what had seemed so plain was swiftly proved, and matters took their inevitable course.

Now Ossie Wolf and the fitter Yosef Mintz stood silently before him, Wolf impassive, Mintz still pale and shaking from his flight.

'You defied my orders,' said Mulholland. 'I ought to have you shot.'

Wolf's expression did not change. 'You granted me permission to get to know the kite.'

'Get to know, not fly. Don't bandy words with me. My meaning was crystal clear.'

'I guess I misunderstood. I thought you'd changed your mind.' Then Ossie brightened. 'Anyways, the weather lifted so I figured it was okay to take her up. You said we could be closed down for days. I had to grab my chance.'

'The weather lifted? When?'

Ossie turned to Yosef Mintz. 'Pepper, you'll bear me out. Ain't it the truth I told you the ghibli had blowed itself out, and was nothing but a gentle breeze? Great weather for circuit and bumps?'

Mintz looked confused.

'Well?' said Mulholland. 'Answer, man.'

'Yes, he did say that.'

'And had it?'

'He's not qualified to answer that,' said Ossie. 'He's not a flier.'

'So, you reckoned it was safe?'

'Hell, I proved it, didn't I?'

'And landing in the camp?'

'First time I put her down it looked to me like your lash-up hangar was fit to bust itself apart. I didn't want to risk the airplane any, so I took her up again. I figured the drill square was the safest place, with plenty of help on hand to stow her good.'

Mulholland looked at Mintz. 'Exactly what was your part in this?'

'Ballast,' said Ossie quickly. 'I reckoned I could use a little weight. The guy was simply following orders. None of this was down to him.'

'Mintz, I want to hear from you,' said Mulholland.

'Nothing to add, *Herr Kommandant*,' said Mintz stolidly. 'Except . . .'

'Except?'

'I have never seen such flying before, and hope to never again.'

'Very well, Mintz. You can go.' A lengthy pause, then: 'Wolf, on the evidence, I have decided to accept your plea.'

'Huh? What plea is that?'

'Temporary insanity. It's the only explanation. You acted like a blind idiot, going up in those conditions. You know that quite as well as I do, and don't bother to deny it. Not only did you place yourself and our machine in jeopardy, to make some obscure point, but you recklessly risked the life of another, highly valued man.'

Ossie opened his mouth to speak. Mulholland held up his hand. 'Don't bother me to feed me the same old feeble claptrap. It just won't do. Won't do at all.' In his hollow temples, blue veins were standing out, although his voice was controlled and calm. 'I've noted a few points in your favour. You jumped to Mintz's defence. Also, you flew that Storch with the most extraordinary skill. And finally, you used your brain in choosing where to land. However, make no mistake. Defy my orders again and you'll go the way of Dobbs. Better not to have you on the operation, if you can't be trusted. If needs be, I can fly the Storch myself. Is that clearly understood?'

Jawohl, Herr Kommandant.'

Jawohl, Herr Kommandant,' Mulholland repeated drily. 'I'm

disappointed in you, Wolf. You may think you've cut something of a dash, with your flashy flying. But ability in the air is not enough. We demand much more. On the ground you also have a role to play, for which you will be trained. That role requires unquestioning obedience, loyalty to your *Kamaraden*, and mutual confidence. Have no illusions, we are playing a dangerous game, made more dangerous when an individual doesn't toe the line. Less than an hour ago you assured me I could count on you. I took you at your word. Clearly, I was wrong.' Mulholland held up a single nicotine-stained finger. 'One more chance to prove yourself, Wolf. Just one. Now it's up to you to show you're more than braggadocio and bull, a shallow little man who can fly a plane but is damn-all use for anything more. Step out of line again and you'll find yourself facing a court martial back in Cairo.'

'On what charge?'

'Serious misconduct in action, obstructing operations. Plenty to choose from, that would fit the bill.'

'Uh-huh,' said Ossie. 'Is that what happened to Dobbs?'

'Never mind what happened to Dobbs. Concern yourself with what might happen to *you*. Five years in Abbassia military prison would give you plenty of time to contemplate your misdemeanours.'

'Okay,' said Ossie flatly. 'I goofed. I'm wised up now. You got yourself a deal.'

'I don't do deals,' said Mulholland. 'It's very simple. Obey your orders, to the letter, or you're out, with everything that entails. It's up to you. Personally, I think you'll fail. You're too far gone.'

'You reckon?'

'Yes,' said Mulholland. 'I recall what Rupert Pringle said about leopards and spots, back in Heliopolis. I should have listened. He was almost certainly right.'

Ossie snorted. 'Pringle's never been right about a goddamned thing.'

'He put you up for this, despite his qualms.'

'Maybe he liked the idea of getting me killed,' said Ossie.

'Maybe I quite like that idea too,' said Mulholland. 'Herzl, find this man somewhere squalid to rest his head.'

Eight

For almost a week now Ossie had not flown the Storch, although the ghibli had long passed, heading north across the Mediterranean Sea to southern Europe, where it changed its name, depending on its landfall – *sirokos* in Greece, *sirocco* in Italy, *xlokk* in Malta, *leveche* in Spain – bringing to each country its cool, moist, violent storms and dusting of red Saharan sand.

Ossie acquired these inconsequential facts, at least to him, from *Kommandant* Mulholland, as he once more turned him down for flying. Ossie's briefings by Mulholland had, to Ossie, but a single purpose – to get back in the air. To Mulholland, they were to assess the American's reserves of physical endurance as they moved him on to learn the art of silent killing.

In these exchanges Ossie found Mulholland an enigma, one moment harsh, intolerant, quick to punish, fierce in his convictions and tough, yes, plenty tough; the next a fuzzy academic who talked of anything but war, who liked to parade his knowledge quite as much as his fake army of Palestinian volunteers.

But Ossie feigned interest in whatever turn their one-sided talks might take – the customs of the Berber tribes, Cambridge between the wars, fly-fishing on the chalk beds of the River Test in Hampshire – none of which meant a hill of beans to Ossie, intent only on putting himself in solid with the boss and getting back behind the Storch controls. And yet, despite his doglike focus, and positive reports on his stamina and staying power from those hard nuts training him to fight and kill, Mulholland did not relent and kept him firmly on the ground. Nor was Ossie 'dear boy' any longer. Now, clearly, 'Wolf' would do, until he had redeemed himself by strenuous endeavour, tested against the rigours of the camp's routine. If that was what it took, reflected Ossie, then that was what it took. Besides, he got a kick from knowing he could deal with whatever the instructors cared to throw his way, learning how to fight without the Queensberry rules, so-called 'foul methods' to help him kill more quickly, attacking an opponent's weakest points with edge of hand, thumb up, the whole hand tensed, arm bent, chopping from the elbow using his full body weight, striking a variety of points: back of neck; the head from bridge of nose to base of throat; either side of head or throat; the fore and upper arms; the kidneys and the base of the spine.

The principal instructor, Hyman Jabotinsky, was blunt. 'Kill as fast as you can. In this business, a prisoner is a handicap and a danger. He'll attack you if he has a chance. Don't give him one.'

To this deadly education was added tuition in kicks, in finger jabs, the use of knee and head and elbows; how to escape from body holds, both front and rear; the use of the fighting knife – techniques of thrust and slash; sentry killing by strangulation, the crushing of testicles and snapping of limbs. 'Cruel, maybe,' said Jabotinsky lightly, 'but not as cruel as prolonging your victim's death.' Such compassion was unconvincing when accompanied by a brutish leer.

But still, fully occupied as he was, Ossie always posed the question in Mulholland's briefings: 'Okay, so when do I get to fly again?'

And Mulholland's reply was as monotonous: 'When I decide you're ready. The real question is whether you're worthy of Holly Force. Your role is far more than acting as our tame pilot, lounging about in some comfortable mess, sipping tea and waiting for a sortie to be announced, while flunkeys polish your aeroplane. Here you're an integral part of a fighting force. If I decide you will shovel ordure, you will shovel ordure. If I require you to force-march for thirty miles in seven hours, no questions asked, then that is what you will do. Is that clearly understood?'

'*Jawohl, Herr Kommandant.*' The way the ready phrase came out did not suggest a meek compliance.

'Believe me, Wolf,' Mulholland said, 'unless you take on board the skills you are being taught, you will soon be dead. The decision is yours, and very simple. Apply yourself and live. Or fight the system and die.'

'You mean I could get knocked off,' said Ossie, 'if I don't deliver the goods?'

Mulholland smiled his thin, hard smile. 'Don't be ridiculous, Wolf. In training you've nothing to fear from us. We may flout convention, particularly of the Geneva sort, but we draw a line at popping off our own, even if they are found wanting.' He felt in his pocket for a coin and began to flip it up and down, as he had in Pringle's office. 'I simply mean that you will kill yourself, through negligence and weakness. Out there, survival is granted only to the best prepared, who know the game. We can try to teach you all we know. Whether you listen, and survive, is up to you. Is my meaning clear?'

'*Jawohl, Herr Kommandant.*' Again, that faint but insouciant twist.

'Of course,' added Mulholland, 'if, in the field, you let us down, I reserve the right to take a very different view. Nothing personal, you understand. That applies to every man under my command. But, then, you've already taken that on board, I think.'

'*Ja, Herr Kommandant.*'

'*Sehr gut.* Now report to *Unterfeldwebel* Jabotinsky for your orders. He's something of a character – ex-Foreign Legion, as you no doubt know. *La Légion Étrangère.* An evocative appellation.' The coin was spinning high. 'Have you ever read *Beau*

Geste? I fear the reality doesn't measure up to our childhood fancies. But I heartily recommend you winkle it out, when next in Cairo. An amusing read. No doubt you'll find a copy in the city library. They're surprisingly well-stocked.'

So that was how Mulholland spent his time on leave in Cairo, Ossie thought. Winkling out an amusing read, while he himself sought out his dangerous pleasures in the curtained alleys of the Burka, or maybe found that big house in the quieter part of town, with its open windows shedding light across the perfumed garden where the palm trees whispered gently in the wafts of desert air, and in the shadowed, ornate room, golden fuck Farida with her glowing skin and braided hair moved to the rhythm of the darbukka drum, her necklaces and bangles jingling to the pulsating beat as she advanced towards him, the muscles of her thighs contracted, broad, bronzed buttocks tight. He hardly heard Mulholland say: 'I have a little jaunt in mind, before we go a-huntin' in earnest. I may enter you for the meet, if Jabotinsky says you're up to scratch.'

'Flying?'

'No. Hard slog. A test of endurance, nerve and pluck. A trial of the inner man. If there is an inner man.' Mulholland trapped the spinning coin. 'Tails. That tells me that you'll fail, that my hunch was wrong in picking you, that you'll let us down. That you're just a lightweight fighter boy, a washout, light on grit and only useful when you've got a Spit to play with. Jabotinsky, on the other hand, thinks you might just make a go of it, if you really get stuck in. One of us is wrong. I'd like to think it's me. If not, you're no use to me. We'll carry on without you. Better that, than have a man we can't rely on. Very well. That is all.'

'*Jawohl, Herr Kommandant*,' said Ossie, coming to something close to attention, his fists clenched hard, a flush of scarlet across his face. For a moment he did not move.

Mulholland nodded towards the door. 'Save your venom for

the enemy, Wolf. Don't waste it on me. Store it up. Anger is ammunition to those who kill as we do.'

As Ossie had quickly learned, noiseless killing was the creed of Holly Force. And he was now proficient in the many ingenious ways to take a human life: bare hands, the dexterous use of a finely balanced fighting knife, and more fanciful methods like the crushing of a throat with a steel helmet rim or garrotting with a knotted length of paracord. Proficient, at least, in training. The real thing was yet to come. And so, for now, he listened to the yarns of this patrol or that, from his *Kamaraden* in his hut; how Bahr, Levine and Preuss dispatched three *Wehrmacht* sentries in the time it took them to draw a breath; or, more accurately, draw their last as five inches of freshly whetted double-edged steel severed their jugular veins. Or Rosheim, whose specialisation was dislocation of the spine. Or Carlebach, whose preference was the safety-razor blade.

For Ossie, one punishing physical test remained before he was judged fit for operations. Already he had completed a four-mile run and target shoot in less than seventy minutes; a nine-mile speed march in another ninety; two days in the desert, practising survival techniques, covering twenty miles with Herzl, Preuss and Jabotinsky always a quarter of a mile ahead, turning, waiting, jeering at another pansy flier who had not earned a swig of water from the canteen they passed around among themselves; the canteen he was denied. All this within the space of a single week. Now the ultimate ordeal: ten hours and forty miles alone with map and compass, navigating a course to a stash of food and water hidden in the desert, all that would sustain him for the duration of the exercise. Not that he was lightly laden. There were no rations in his kit, but he was weighed down with 100 pounds of Panzerarmee combat gear and personal weapons, and shod with military boots.

'You have it easy at this time of year,' grinned Jabotinsky, the one-time legionnaire, as Ossie prepared to leave. 'For me, it was fifty in the shade.'

'So that's what cooked your brains,' said Ossie.

'*Der Komiker, ja?*' said Jabotinsky. 'Not so funny, maybe, when you cannot find your supplies.' He leaned his head back and laughed, his big frame shaking. 'March or die, as we say in the Legion. March or die.'

'You kill me, Jabo,' Ossie said, 'you *schadenfroh* bastard.' Then, with the help of the still chuckling Jabotinsky, he struggled into the sand-drab military pack that seemed as big as himself, shouldered his Mauser 43, and passed out through the gate, between the sentries, without another word, following his compass course and heading east.

He marched, taking short paces to conserve his strength, making steady progress at first – not fast, not slow, as he had been taught. His body felt taut and fit, stronger than it had for years, honed by the Holly Force regime. The record for this endurance trial of forty miles was nine hours fifty-five minutes, achieved by wiry Willi Bahr, who had taunted him before he left. 'No pampered *Amerikaner* can do this thing, not in any time that counts. Soon we will have to come out on the BMW combo, to bring you back and dust you off and send you back to Cairo.' Ossie had said nothing, recalling Mulholland's promise. Step out of line once more and he could face a spell in an Abbassia prison cell. Maybe Mulholland couldn't make the five years stick, but life could prove uncomfortable – way more uncomfortable than this. And rugged as it was, Holly Force had the ferry business beat in spades.

As he marched, he went over in his mind what he had learned of Mulholland's so-called ragbag legion of throw-outs, murderers and the dangerously deranged. It was hardly that. Instead, the group consisted mostly of Palestinian Jews, many born and raised in Germany, some whose fathers had fought for the Fatherland in the trenches of the first Great War, hounded out of the country of their birth by the *volkisch* masters of the *Reich* who preached of Jewish 'otherness', this obstacle to the purity of the Aryan race, and were setting about the task of genocide with brisk efficiency. Mulholland's volunteers were drawn from Jewish commando units within the British Army, under Middle East command; from semi-legal Palestinian underground groups; some from the Free Forces of the Czechs and French; a few, like Jabotinsky, from the ranks of mercenaries serving with the Foreign Legion. Each man was fluent in German and carried three names: his own, and two *noms de guerre* – one non-Judaic German for operations, one English in case of capture. Yet they were united by more than this, eager to avenge the persecution of their faith, not only now, when in the greater Germany millions stood by mute and failed to raise a dissenting voice, but also for the persecutions of centuries past.

These were emotions Ossie understood. And he matched their hatred of the Fascist cause, for a jumble of reasons that boiled within him but for which he could never really find the words, except to mumble that he wouldn't play the sap for any man, and didn't respond to sons-of-bitches who pushed ordinary folk around. This, mixed in with cursing those who filled the kids' heads with garbage, and thinking, reluctantly, about the many guys he'd known, and flown with, who'd bought the farm. Reluctantly, because that was looking back, and could not be changed, unlike the future in which he could lam the Nazi bastards good.

Now, freed from the Taki run, Mulholland had given him that chance. For sure, it didn't hold a candle to flying a Spit in anger. Nothing did. But for the moment it would have to do, this secret, brutal, no-rules war they fought; tracking the movement of enemy troops and traffic, blowing up ammunition dumps, attacking aircraft on the ground, mining roads, identifying landing sites for the RAF, taking prisoners, guiding Allied stragglers to the safety of their lines. Mulholland even ventured out alone, in Arab dress, assessing the reliability of the desert tribes, convincing them to share their intimate knowledge of the land, recruiting them as scouts, building trust with his knowledge of their language and their ways; ways not generally understood by Europeans, whose lives, particularly in war, were ruled by punctuality and precision.

Ossie looked at his Hanhart watch. It showed 7.45 a.m. He had been marching for nearly three hours, had covered perhaps twelve miles. Not even a third of the way. He quickened his pace although it was heavy going, weaving a course between and over huge dunes, the surface always changing from loose fine-grained sand to fields of basalt to ankle-twisting rock. His tongue was like leather in his mouth, teeth grinding on bitter-tasting dust, but the stash of food and water, if he found it, still lay eight miles away. His compass was constantly in his hand, set against the deliberately rudimentary map, pencilled by Jabotinsky on the back of a Wehrmacht requisition form; the map that gave him only bearings, no indication of the rise and fall of the terrain, the maze of gullies that doubled back or ran out in dead ends.

He knew he had to average at least four miles an hour to complete the trial in the allotted time; time he could not waste. Yet he forced himself to stop, shrug off his rucksack and confirm his position against the stars still visible in the lightening sky. He did this as men had done it for aeons past, because on this exercise it was required, measuring with his fingers the heights of various stars above the horizon, then estimating their position against Polaris, the only one that did not move. This was how a merchant nation had navigated its camel trains across the desert oceans, and learned their latitude, when it was said that one day's travel north would raise the Pole Star by one *isba*, a single finger-width. It was a method that perfectly suited the needs of Holly Force, at times when sextants were judged inappropriate or not to be had, and they needed to read the message of the stars.

For a weakening moment Ossie felt the urge to ease himself down, lean back against the rucksack, relax his muscles, take the weight off his booted feet. Instead he heaved the rucksack onto his sweat-soaked back. Under the sudden weight he staggered for a moment, regained his balance and resumed his trek.

The sun was hanging orange to the east. He felt its growing warmth, welcome now, but later not, and thought about finding the supplies. He moistened his lips, then thought again. How would it be if he passed them by, left them there untouched? Leaving maybe just a note, in case any disbelieving sons-of-bitches claimed he'd never found the stuff. Yeah, got back to camp, beating Willi Bahr's time to hell, and let it drop he'd done it without breaking into their goddamned cache of food and drink. No bastard had done that before in Holly Force, he was pretty sure. The idea of it urged him on. He was moving smoothly now, a steady rhythm, breathing easily, feeling good, the rucksack somehow lighter, almost part of him, spread across his shoulders, bumping gently against his spine. He began to laugh. Boy, that would be one hell of a trick to pull. He laughed more deeply at the idea of Mulholland's face, and the mugs of all those other tough palookas who reckoned they could rope him in. So far they hadn't got him beat, even with their greet-the-dawn routine: '*Kompagnie anfsteher!*' 'Company, get up!' signifying thirty minutes of hard PT; forty push-ups, fifty sit-ups, twenty chin-ups on the bar, rounded off with a five-mile run. This, after being shaken awake two or three times at night, to see if, surprised and half-awake, he might forget his training and respond in English.

Pure draughts of desert air enveloped him as he marched. Refreshing, except they could not quench his thirst. Around him, silence, broken only by the crunch of sand and stone beneath his feet, the rasp of his breath across his cracking lips and the hum of flies, wheeling around his head, and settling on his face and hands, growing bold now with the coming of the day. Also, deep inside him, but surely heard, not merely sensed, the pounding of his heart.

The ground had levelled out and stretched away, featureless and bare, not even an ankle-high bush or two of camel thorn. He might have been walking on the moon, a quarter of a million miles from home, an unearthly and indifferent world, a place not fit for man. He stared up at the naked void of sky. It told him nothing, except he was of no account, as expendable as that desert flea crawling on his boot. His impulse was to crush it, but then he paused. Some primitive instinct told him that if he was merciful, then the desert might be too, as though the desert was more than just a waste of space. Jesus, he was cracking up. Nothing mattered here, nothing could make a difference. The desert was the desert, and that was all. No, not quite all. Yeah, he could make a difference. He squashed the flea.

He cleared his mind. He did not think. The swarm of flies was thicker now, an ink-black dizzying haze that spun around him as he marched. They crawled into his eyes and mouth and ears. At first he waved them off but then he let them be, unwilling to waste his energy, knowing they would only settle again. The Arabs lived like that, with flies they did not brush away, seemed not to notice. They did not notice many things, like this lousy land from which they scratched a living. They stood beside the roads and watched the armies pass, as they had for a thousand years, and did not notice who the armies fought or why. They knew that nothing mattered, nothing made a difference. The desert was the desert, a place not fit for man, unless he was an Arab who lived with flies he did not brush away.

They made good progress, the flies and him. He envied them their wings. It was the bunch he had started out with, as far as he could tell, with others joining in. Their dark and flying shapes, sharp against the glare of sun reflecting from the desert floor, reminded him of the Luftwaffe's bomber fleets in France, unflagging and malevolent of purpose, filling the air with a constant, busy drone. He began to kill a few, grabbing them with his hand, feeling them crunch between his fingers and his palm. When he looked, he saw a moisture there, a yellowish fluid mixed with blood and fragments of broken carcass. He studied it as he marched, drawing in his cheeks against his teeth, unable to summon up spit, wondering if the mess might wet his lips. Thank Christ, no need. He realised he must be closing on the stash of water.

Food was of no interest. He doubted he could get it down. But liquid was.

Pushing so hard, he felt the subtle signs of dehydration: the sweating ceased, his body became clammy, his heart and respiration rates increased, and he had a throbbing head. He felt no need to urinate and when he forced himself to try, what little came through was deepish yellow. No time to play the hero with his screwy scheme to make the bastards eat their words. 'No *Amerikaner* can do this thing, not in any time that counts.' No, they knew the score, had this thing planned real good, understood just when a guy's resources would be low, exactly when to place supplies within his reach, when he needed them and not before, if he was to complete the march in decent shape. He cursed himself for setting such a pace, losing precious fluid in the chase to beat the time of Willi Bahr.

The stash, he knew, was marked with a shallow cairn, insignificant to the casual eye. If he was on course, he would come across it soon. His eyes were red from staring. The Mauser rifle thumped against his legs. He felt the urge to throw it down, the rucksack too. Panting, he took a fly into his mouth, tried to cough it up, felt it struggling behind his tongue before it passed on down his gullet. Retching still, he saw a gathering of stones, quarter of a mile away, close to a wind-bent clump of tamarix. Nearby, as though suspended in a sea of mercury, its outline shimmering and indistinct, was the figure of a man.

It was an Arab, sunk down on his haunches, in loose-fitting, light-coloured robes, a big white turban wound around his skull. He had his back to Ossie, but he'd heard his approach all right. Something in his attitude changed; he stiffened, and inclined his head a little to the left, listening to the advancing tread of the American's heavy boots. Twenty yards away, two hobbled riding camels jinked and snorted in mild alarm. Ossie cursed. The raghead had parked his scrawny ass right next to the goddamned mother-lode, by accident or design. Either way, he could prove a threat. Who knew where the sonofabitch's loyalty lay? With the Allies, the Axis or just his stinking tribe?

Ossie unslung the Mauser 43 and then, with a contraction of his scalp, remembered that its ten-round magazine was neatly stowed in a side compartment of his pack. Too late now. He would have to bluff it out. He quickly covered the fifty yards between him and the silent Arab, the empty Mauser levelled at the nomad's upright back. He felt it was a threat that had been sensed. He came around in front. The man looked up. The lower part of his face was covered with a length of turban, wrapped about in the Tuareg style. The eyes, in shadow, were almost slits. Ossie looked for weapons. An antique long-barrelled *jezaa'r* musket protruded from the saddle pack of the nearest camel. No sign of knife or pistol at the Arab's waist. The man took in his uniform.

Ossie said roughly, to show he had control: '*Heil! Sprechen Sie Deutsch?*' No choice but to follow the pretence through, whatever side the guy was on.

The Arab shrugged, and murmured something in a thick and guttural dialect. With the Mauser, Ossie gestured for him to get to his feet, but at first the man made no attempt to move, just shifted his weight and continued to stare up through his slit eyes. Then he cleared his throat and spat into the sand.

'Spik English, maybe?' he asked. The question hung in the air like a primed grenade.

Ossie hesitated, then shook his head and gestured with the Mauser once again. '*Nein. Aufspringe, sofort! Tun Sie, was ich Ihnen sage.*'

The man may not have understood his order to obey and get to his goddamned feet, but he understood the tone, and the jerking barrel of the Mauser. He rose slowly, the palms of his hands turned outwards, his shoulders hunched, no longer a source of menace but wheedling and submissive. 'English shit. Americans shit. French shit. Fuck those who brought them into this life, the sons of dogs. Ruin to their houses. May they be swept by catastrophe. Death to Montgomery, offspring of a thousand whores. Much honour to General Rommel. May victory greet the great and glorious German Army.'

Ossie's finger trembled on the trigger of the empty Mauser. Otherwise he gave no sign of comprehension. '*Fahr zur Hölle, Kameltreiber.*' He jerked his head towards the camels. '*Leck mich!*'

'You wish one beast?' the Arab said, rubbing his hands together, trying to gain his favour. 'I give him you. Walk for fifteen days, no food, no water. Better than walk yourself.'

For a second, Ossie considered the offer. Tempting, no question of that. Hell, these desert ships could cover sixty miles a day. He could ditch the animal a mile or two from camp and saunter back through the gates as if he'd been out for an afternoon stroll, blowing old Willi's record all to hell by whatever margin he liked to choose – say thirty minutes, to make the guys believe it, just. And never let on how it had been done. What was wrong with that? You had to run with the breaks that fortune fed you. Jesus, Holly Force's whole business was dirty tricks. And yet he didn't want to win that way, he wanted to beat the bastards fair and square. In that moment, it was important. And anyways, the lousy wog probably aimed to put a bullet through him with that damned old *jezaa'r* muzzle-loader as soon as his back was turned, reclaim his property, steal his gear and leave his corpse to turn to bone and paper in the furnace of the desert, like the husks of men Gellatley, that egghead freak, had once dragged him along to see in a Luxor tomb.

And so he said again: '*Leck mich!*' And booted the Arab's ass to make his meaning doubly clear.

The Arab tottered and fell onto his kness. He was feeling inside his robe. Ossie seized the barrel of the Mauser, ready to use it as a club. He did not want to kill this sucker. It would be easy, as easy as crushing that goddamned flea. But maybe this raghead was on the level, just trying to scratch a living from this lousy wilderness, a mug who'd wound up here by chance, wrong time, wrong place. But then again, it struck him suddenly, why two riding camels? Now he scanned the area with urgent eyes, his fingers tightening on the Mauser barrel, looking for a second man, who'd maybe already got him in his sights.

He glanced down at the Arab, calculating how hard to hit him so the blow would penetrate the turban. The man had twisted round, was propped up on one elbow, oddly casual, not seeming to understand how close he was to death. There was something in his eyes that seemed familiar. He was stretching out the hand he'd dug inside his robe. Ossie saw it held a rose-red pack of cigarettes. He recognised the brand: Sulima Turkish.

'Good show, dear boy,' the Arab said. 'I'd say you've earned a smoke. I must admit you held up jolly well. Now, whet your whistle, have a spot of grub, and then we'll get cracking on Mutt and Jeff. There's been a change of plan.'

Nine

The ground rose a little to the west of the minefield where the column of British tanks still burned, but dully now, covered with a pall of oily smoke. Occasionally there was a sudden burst of flame, illuminating the wreckage and the corpses of the crews. At these moments the scene, washed overall with the gentle light of a full moon, was lent an unreal, almost artificial look, not unpleasing in its composition, like some morbid diorama in a war museum.

The dead were spread about, just as Kit Curtis had come across them hours ago, some contorted, resembling Pompeiian figures in their final agonies, others apparently resigned, stretched out or on their sides, their knees pulled up, like slumbering children. It was fanciful, of course, Kit thought, but somehow it seemed odd that they had not moved, remained there fixed and silent, just as he had seen them first, patient, waiting; waiting for a future that would never come, living only in the minds of those who loved them, knew them, imagined them safe, unable to be harmed, whatever fate might overtake the comrades they mentioned in their letters home. And yet their lives had ended here, this way, in a mess of blazing fuel and detonating mines even before the battle had been truly joined on this, the first day of the assault.

Though pressed down by fatigue, Kit compelled himself not to sleep. Oblivion might be welcome, if disturbed by dreams, but what of the silent German facing him across the narrow defile in which they had taken shelter for the night? The little Walther PPK still rested in the fellow's hand. It struck him as a nonsense, to be treated as the man's prisoner, out here, under boundless space, where a billion stars flickered with light that had begun its journey before the earth was born. And here two beings faced each other in flea-sized confrontation. He supposed the same could be said of the two great armies whose struggle lit the horizon all around, and shook the earth, and made the scree slopes hiss with falling stones and sand. Infinity suggested that nothing mattered; that existence was merely fleeting consciousness, devoid of meaning or purpose. He caught himself. Life mattered. He believed in life, if he did not believe in God. Life was all he had.

He looked across at the other man. He could not see his face, but knew that he did not sleep either. For fear of him, or to prevent his escape? Either way, it made Kit smile – until he wondered if the German was turning over in his mind whether to end it with the pistol. Not so funny, that. A rather pointless and dismal way to go, but no worse than what had befallen those poor devils in the minefield.

He breathed in deeply, despite the dust and odour hanging in the air. At least he remained alive, and conscious and alert he retained a vestige of control. Once asleep, the German might take courage and end it now. Horrid to think he might not wake. And then there was something else: it seemed that in this place, the act of sleeping was itself a kind of death, a departure from the here and now, an opting out, a small surrender.

Surrender, that hateful word. That day, he had already surrendered once, emerging from the horror of the so-called Devil's Garden to see the German waiting for him, waving his tiny pistol, bawling out his asinine commands, still sticking to the rules of war when really, it seemed to Kit, they should be celebrating their survival. He knew he was naive, but he felt there was a difference between fighting as they had been trained, pilots matching skill for skill, machine against machine, and this primitive confrontation on the ground, when the blood was cold.

Instinctively his hand had moved towards the Webley .38, heavy in its holster, the weapon he had only fired twice, as though to ape some character in a Hollywood cowboy film. Then he had raised his hand and waved, as the German yelled for him to place his hands above his head. He was damned if he would, and began to walk with folded arms, a small defiance, studying the ground in case there was a mine the sappers had missed, and as he walked he found it difficult not to laugh. Again the German had shouted: 'Hands above your head!' Again, he had ignored the shrill command and continued his slow advance. But it was not so funny as he had drawn closer to the other man, understanding what this meant, that he had yielded, ceased to resist, submitted to another's will. It was a bitter truth, not comic in the least.

It seemed to Kit that he was callow and poor-spirited, unwilling to fight as men had always fought, hand to hand, obeying no rules of decency or conduct, with no shred of honour or respect, burning with the desperate urge to kill, consumed with hate. He could only kill at second hand, not seeing the enemy's face, smelling his sweat, feeling his body writhe with pain, being confronted with the brightness of his blood. He wondered why he had not gone for the Webley on his waist. That was its purpose, after all, the very nature of war, destroying the enemy wherever he might be. This was his duty, just as it had been at 20,000 feet. He was required to destroy this man who sat so quietly, twenty feet away, nursing his pygmy pistol in his hand. He wondered if the German had similar thoughts. The war had shrunk, was now contained in this tiny space. Yet, for him to attempt to kill this man, without a weapon, in the way that he must be killed, punching, flailing, kicking, gasping, a struggle to the death, no rules, no limits, gouging an eye, tearing an ear, kneeing a crutch until somehow the job was done, was nothing more than murder and he did not want to live with that. And if the price was a bullet administered while he slept, well, it simply meant he would not wake. There were worse ways to go than that, and he had been close to many of them in his time.

So, trembling with the cold, his limbs in spasm from attacks of cramp, he shuffled himself a little deeper into the hollow he had cleared out with his hands at the base of an outcrop of wind-sculpted rock and prepared himself for sleep, a luxury the German had to deny himself, in his role as captor.

It seemed to Kit that he did not dream, but hung suspended in a void of blue where nothing changed and nothing moved, and he was nothing, an entity without a thought or purpose, unconscious of the elapse of time, the passing of a minute or a million years the same. He felt enveloped by some eternal truth that hung beyond his comprehension because, for the entity he had become, comprehension did not exist, was only sensed.

When finally he woke, this vagary stayed with him for a fleeting moment, and then was gone. He could have been asleep for hours or days, but he knew he was refreshed, alert, somehow roused to action.

By the position of the moon, he calculated it was a few hours from dawn. It had fallen oddly quiet, the desert seeming to deaden sound. To north and south the sky still flickered white, as though lit by a passing summer storm. Kit saw that the German had been unable to fend off sleep. His chin was sunk down on his chest and he was breathing deeply, head rocking slightly with each exhalation, the pistol hanging loosely in his fingers. Kit knew this was the moment to launch himself across the small divide, and try to seize the German's weapon. He had no particular wish to be the captor in this farce, but neither did he want to be the prisoner. With some distaste he recalled their brief exchange the day before, as he had walked unsteadily towards the German from the minefield, covered by the wavering muzzle of the Walther PPK.

'You are my prisoner,' the man had said, in English.

Kit had made the face of one who does not necessarily agree. 'Oh yes?'

'I have the gun.'

'Yes, you certainly have the gun.' A pause. 'Don't you think that, in the circumstances, this is faintly ridiculous?'

'Faintly ridiculous.' The German tried out the words.

'Silly.'

'Silly like you wanted to destroy us both, maybe, up there.' A jerk of the head towards the sky.

Kit had shrugged. 'I had no other weapon, except the aeroplane itself. You do these things, and think about them later. That's the game.'

'For you it is a game?'

'A form of words, an English phrase. Don't read too much into it. We're under no illusions about what it's going to take to kick you out of Africa.'

The German had tossed the pistol from hand to hand, in a taunting way. 'That is silly also. You cannot beat the Panzerarmee. Our leaders will not permit defeat. Very soon we will be in Cairo. Already we hold the gateway to Egypt.'

'But can you get the gate open?'

'Oh, I think you will find out soon enough. Now, you must obey. If not I will be compelled to shoot.' Somehow the threat was unconvincing, something in the German's eyes suggesting he was not ready to pull the trigger.

Kit said: 'Why don't you, then?'

For a moment the German hesitated. Then: 'You have useful information. Soon I will deliver you to the Abwehr and you can tell them what you know.' Now he was more assured. 'You see, I have a purpose. Not so silly, perhaps.'

After that, they had said very little, finding shelter for the night among the tumbled rocks of the pinched defile that, to the west of the Devil's Garden, cut down through the rising ground. There they listened to the sounds of distant battle, fought down the tightening dryness in the throat that presaged thirst, but silent still, both preoccupied with their private thoughts.

Now, Kit's hand fell easily to a fist-sized stone with a jagged edge. It was cold and hard. His fingers closed around it. It was as handy as any man-made weapon. He might need it if he failed to seize the pistol, and found himself in an unseemly brawl. Yet even then, could he smash the fellow's skull? He stared at the sleeping man. The German's lips were slightly open, a bead of dribble in the corner of his mouth. Kit imagined him as a child. Somewhere parents fretted for his safety. He saw them studying his image in the family album, their heads together, moving their fingers over the sepia prints, marvelling at how their boy had grown from swaddled infant to bright-eyed scholar to fighter pilot of the Reich, stiff and formal in his Luftwaffe uniform, one of the chosen ones, proud to serve the Fatherland, one of the elite fighting for the greater Germany. Kit possessed the means to end such dreams. It was his purpose, after all, to kill.

His fingers tightened on the jagged stone. He stood up and began to move towards the German, his heartbeat pounding, drawing in rapid, shallow gulps of air, the cold stone balanced in his hand, placing his feet with care, not wanting to slip on the yielding scree. At last he stood above the man. Still the German had not moved. Flies were crawling on his hair; hair that was dark with brilliantine, though tumbled now; a fellow who cared for his appearance.

From the east, a wave of sound began to build, rhythmic and unmistakeable: the throb of many aero-engines. The German stirred at that and groaned, came half-awake. Kit threw down the stone, no longer caring about the noise he made, and bent and snatched the pistol from the German's open hand. The crash of the falling stone echoed round the crevice like a shot. The German sat up, startled, frowning as though he had imagined himself somewhere else. At first he did not notice Kit, slightly to his right. He began a yawn that stopped halfway when, in his peripheral vision, he glimpsed the Walther pistol inches from his temple.

Kit said with heavy irony: 'You are my prisoner. I have the gun.'

'*Ach so!*' The German nodded. '*Ja*, you have the gun. May I ask you, do you not consider this faintly ridiculous?' He laboured over the unfamiliar words.

'Not in the slightest. Now, where's that bloody Webley?'

The German pointed to the webbing belt and holster around his waist.

'All right,' said Kit. 'Chuck it over here.'

Resigned, the German unbuckled the belt and, still sitting, tossed it awkwardly in Kit's direction. It landed in a spray of dust. Kit picked it up, flicked open the holster flap and removed the big old Webley. Standing with a weapon in either hand he had to suppress a grin, feeling again, for a fleeting moment, like some Western desperado. The German regarded him quizzically, seeing no possible humour in the situation. Then Kit began to shake the bullets from the chambers of the Webley and throw them down, with great deliberation, one by one, watching them bounce and rattle against the stones before being lost to sight in the cracks on the crevice floor. Finally, he tossed away the Webley itself.

The German had sprung to his feet. '*Hör auf damit!* Stop that now. We have need of ammunition.'

'We?' said Kit. He waved the Walther PPK towards him, forcing him to halt, trying the various buttons on the stock until, with a click, the magazine of .32 bullets ejected itself from inside the wood-faced grip. This he also hurled away, then bent and hammered the pistol's barrel against a rock until the muzzle was distorted.

By now the German had advanced a pace or two. '*Verflucht noch mal! In Gottes Namen*, we could have shot ourselves some food.'

'What, from the abundant game?' said Kit.

Above them, the noise of engines was very great. A formation of bombers was heading west at 18,000 feet, Martin Baltimores packed in tight and, behind, another group, this time Douglas Bostons. Kit counted thirty aircraft altogether, and looked at the German who was also staring up.

'Looks as though you've got us on the run,' said Kit.

'*Was bedeutet das*? An English joke?'

Kit appeared not to hear. 'Tell me, what plan did you have in mind?'

'Plan?'

'To get us out of here. Or was it only you? Did you have something else lined up for me?'

'Ah, I see, to finish you here? Hah! Maybe not such a bad idea. You are a big trouble to me. But no,' the German slowly shook his head, 'I tell you before, you have useful information. I wished to deliver you to the Abwehr. That was my intention. It does not matter now, unless we choose to fight like crazy men.'

'That had crossed my mind.'

'Mine also. But not the pilot's way, perhaps.' The man seemed more rational now, without the pistol, no longer the contemptuous Aryan warrior, as though the adrenalin that had sustained him had finally drained away. If he was prepared to listen, it seemed to Kit worth trying the direct approach.

'It appears to me,' Kit said, 'that we have three choices – assuming we don't intend to beat the living daylights out of each other.'

'Living daylights?'

'First choice, to stay exactly where we are and wait for someone to turn up, friend or foe depending on which side you're on. Take pot luck, as it were.'

'Your English phrases . . .'

'Second choice, head east, back through the minefield towards the British lines.'

'But are they still the British lines?' the German said quickly. 'I believe the Panzerarmee would have counter-attacked in strength and pushed you back.'

'Not likely,' said Kit, 'but I suppose you have a point. Third choice, head west and link up with the first fighting outfit we come across. Pot luck again. If it's your people, I'm in the bag. If it's mine, then you are.'

'You damned Tommies have mounted a big attack,' said the German. 'It sounds to me like *die Hölle auf Erden*, like hell on earth out there. In the open, I do not believe we have a chance.' A shadow passed across his face. 'Particularly unarmed.'

'I don't think those popguns amounted to very much,' said Kit. 'Worse than having nothing at all. Just get you into trouble.' He looked thoughtful. 'There is a fourth option.'

'Yes?'

'You go your way, I go mine.'

'That too is possible. But it seems to me, in that case, we turn our backs on duty. I say the situation must be resolved, one way or the other. Otherwise, what purpose have we served?'

'Very well, we stay.'

'Unless you wish to battle to the death with rocks.'

'Later, perhaps,' said Kit. 'When we've had a rest.'

The German grunted, in amusement or derision, and scrambled back to his position on the rock-strewn slope. There he sat, forearms resting on raised knees, hands clasped, gazing towards the minefield where the tanks still smouldered and the bodies lay. Kit wondered what was going through his mind: reflections on the senselessness of war perhaps, the squandering of youthful promise, the extinguishing of the best of the very best.

Beppo Lutzow was, in fact, worrying about his nose. It put him at a further disadvantage to this curious Englishman who seemed determined to play his pacifist games, and made an already serious situation worse. He felt the fleshy area around his nostrils. It was tender to the touch and, by squinting, he could see it was red and bulbous, like the nose of an *Auguste* clown he had once found sinister and unfunny in a Munich circus. A tiny yellow-backed fly had bitten the skin, the seeping puncture attracting larger flies, some landing unobserved, feeding stealthily on the wound and creating a ring-shaped, itching crater that threatened to make his whole face a sore.

He did not like his situation. He had displayed great weakness, yielding to fatigue like that, allowing the Englishman to seize his weapons without the least resistance. He felt ashamed, and shocked. He had betrayed the trust invested in him as a German officer. However, a different adversary might have ended it there, with a bullet in the head before he was properly awake. He had been contemplating such a thing himself, when he held the initiative, but had not quite reached the point at which such a decision could be made; it had something to do with the Englishman's likeness to Matti Hartmann, perhaps. He knew he was very fortunate. At least he had lived, could try his luck again when the moment came. It should not prove too difficult. The Englishman did not strike him as a fighter.

Meanwhile, it was perhaps better not to be the jailer, burdened with the need for constant vigilance. Such strain had led to his humiliation. Now he could recover his strength, await the time to act. Such thoughts provided him with a shred or two of consolation. No doubt things would work for him, even now. They usually did. In the *Staffel* the Lutzow luck had become something of a joke. Whatever misfortunes befell his comrades, Beppo Lutzow always came through. So it would prove now, he was sure of it. The Englishman had made good work of rendering the Walther PPK quite useless, but that fat old Webley was probably still in working order, lying where it had been hurled away, beyond the crest of the slanting gully in which they sheltered. No bullets were to be seen, lost among the rocks, but he only needed one. Yes, the Lutzow luck would probably grant him one, when the Englishman moved away to piss or shit, those acts not willingly done before an audience.

But could he, in reality, shoot this man, who sat so quietly a metre or two away, staring at the sky and thinking, what? Beppo felt confused, light-headed, as though he was starved of air. More likely short on food and drink, not oxygen. But still, his airways did feel pinched, as though there was an obstruction there. Automatically, he pushed a finger into his right nostril, to clear any dried-up mucus. He had forgotten his raw nose, and yelped with pain.

The Englishman glanced across at him, quick, alert, the speed of his reaction suggesting that, after all, he might not be so easily overcome. Unwise, perhaps, to underestimate him, despite his nonchalant manner.

'Problem?' he asked.

'Insect bite,' Beppo replied. 'My nose.'

'Bad luck.'

Luck again. Did the desert flies not know about the Lutzow luck? Beppo did not reply directly. Then: 'We cannot remain here very long.'

'I know. A few hours more, perhaps.'

'Do not give me orders.'

'Not orders, old boy, an observation. Go, if you wish. What's to stop you?'

'You, perhaps?'

'You've nothing to fear from me. This whole damned thing's a nonsense.'

'*Sehr gut*. I will go when I am ready.'

'What better time?'

Beppo seethed. In the war of words, at least, he always seemed to lose. He gave himself the thin excuse that English was not his mother tongue. It was as if the Englishman read his mind. 'I say, your English isn't half bad.'

'My people have a hotel.'

'Ah. I wondered if you'd been to England.'

'Only in my Emil.'

'Your Emil?'

'My Me 109. Emil after Herr Professor Messerschmitt, Wilhelm Emil Messerschmitt.'

'Of course, I forgot it was a general term. I thought perhaps it was a pet name for your machine.'

'Such things are stupid,' said Beppo, at the same time reflecting guiltily on *Hyäne*'s smouldering remains.

'Of course.' The Englishman paused. 'I once gave my Hurricane a nickname. Stupid, as you say. Didn't bring me any luck.'

'What was the name?'

'*Epicurus.*'

'Ah, the Greek.'

'You're familiar with him?' The Englishman appeared surprised.

'That period is of interest to me, yes.'

'"Skilful pilots gain their reputation from storms and tempests." At the time I thought it rather neat. Seems childish now.'

Beppo felt a spark of liking for this man, prepared to admit his frailties, unlike himself. Which of them was most childish? The Englishman, plain-spoken, unabashed, smiling at his own mild foolishness? Or him, denying his affection for the hardy little aeroplane he had dubbed *Hyäne*. Still, he could not bring himself to admit this to the Englishman who sat, apparently relaxed, as though on some damned picnic.

'What's your name?' the Englishman said.

'Lutzow. You?'

'Curtis.'

'Rank?'

'Flying Officer. You?'

'*Oberleutnant.*'

'Same difference.'

'*Was sagen Sie?* I do not understand.'

'Same thing, no difference.'

'*So.*'

'I'm curious, Lutzow. What's it like to fly an Emil?'

'I believe it is the finest *Jagdflugzeug* in the world. It responds like lightning to the controls. The armament is mighty. *Perfekt.*' Beppo felt a surge of satisfaction, sensing he had scored a point. 'Against the Spitfire, for example, the Messerschmitt is much the better plane.'

'Oh yes, the Spitfire is vastly overrated.'

'You think so, truly?'

'No.'

Beppo shook his head, irritated by the Englishman's verbal games. His voice was sharp. 'At the controls of the 109, *mein Freund*, one feels invincible.'

'Not quite invincible, of course. You didn't do so well in 1940, or Malta in forty-one, and here you're taking something of a drubbing. Drubbing – you are familiar with the word?'

Beppo snapped: 'No matter. I know your purpose. You cannot question the valour of the Luftwaffe.'

'Only its motivation, perhaps,' said the Englishman.

Beppo lapsed into a sullen silence. He did not have the words to express his frustration. Perhaps it was just as well. He might have demeaned himself in this man's eyes. His emotions boiled within. He thought again about the Webley lying out there somewhere, in the sand; about the bullets that might lie beneath the rocks and stones. So easy to end it thus, as simple as picking off a squirrel in the wooded hills behind the hotel in Starnberg, above the cold blue lake; just the thump of the bullet striking home, the futile squirms and scrabbles, the stiffening of the body and the film of death spreading across the sightless eyes; then all was over. No more words to twist his meaning, leaving him feeling impotent and enraged. *Jawohl*, so easy to end it thus.

He wondered if he could. He had not killed a man, in such a way. He had seen some things in Poland and elsewhere that he wished he had not seen, towns and villages burned by

Verfgungstruppe divisions of the Waffen SS; the people too. He supposed such methods were necessary. How else to teach the population the price of cowardly attacks by terrorist partisans on German troops? But certain images were imprinted on his mind: a mother in an execution pit cradling two young children, an officer of the Polish Army shouting *'Niech żyje Polska!'* – 'Long live Poland!' – as the death squad placed the noose around his neck on the gallows in a pretty, tree-lined public square, an ancient peasant couple, clinging together, booted through the door of the burning church where perhaps, fifty years before, they had been joined as man and wife.

Such was the inevitable price of war, at least this war, the smaller horrors for the greater good, required to achieve the just expansion of the *Reich*, when all would be accepted and understood, even by the most resolute of enemies, like this Englishman, so quick with words when what was required was deeds; deeds conceived through the exercise of logic – if necessary merciless and cold, not improvised in the crimson heat of combat, like trying to ram your enemy and kill you both. That was no way to win a war; that was merely desperation. It was so much harder to weigh up all the facts and devise a plan, to find an inner strength, to steel oneself to act in ways that, at another time, might be thought unthinkable. That was indeed true courage, a *Triumph des Willens*, a triumph of the will, asserting one's firm belief in the Fatherland's right to exercise the power of life and death. Only by compliance would peace be granted, and then on terms dictated by the Reich; a sweet revenge for twenty years of penury and humiliation.

Yet doubts still lingered. He and the Englishman clearly shared a bond, the love of aeroplanes and flying, both happier aloft, traversing the limitless sky, those rolling vistas of light and shade, where the brilliance of the sun touched cloud massifs dwarfing any earth-bound mountain range, where the aviator seemed close to some elusive truth, far beyond the comprehension of the common man, a truth incapable of expression, known only to the very few who blended intellect with skill and daring and hung, as though suspended in time and space, far above the grubby, brutal world below. Typically, it was an obsession born in youth. No doubt this Curtis had also built his models of balsawood and paper, and learned the principles of flight by watching their erratic path. As boys they could have played together. Later, he too had embarked on that initial, shaky solo flight, when the dream turned real. They had much in common. What had the Englishman said? 'Same difference.' Yes, same thing, no difference. It applied to more than rank. It was a perplexing truth. And now, what faced him was a test. He had failed once. Would he fail again?

Kit Curtis tried to gauge the brooding Lutzow, who would not look him him in the eye. He was under no illusions. The German was clearly playing a waiting game. He felt disappointment. He had expected more of a fellow pilot, although on opposing sides. But whatever his scruples, he was damned if he was going to die at this man's hand, in this benighted hole, stretched out near those other British corpses, as yet unburied and unmourned.

His lips were bleeding now and he could find no soothing wetness in his tongue. He thought about cool water, tumbling from a tap, filling that half-pint tankard they used to keep for him behind the bar at the Cat & Custard Pot near Hawkinge. He smiled a little at the imagined comments of the other chaps. 'Hold hard, Kit. Have you gone round the bend? Bloody water?' And instantly, he knew where water might be found. He stood up, brushing off the sand. The German, Lutzow, started and half-rose himself. Kit waved him down. 'Don't fuss yourself, but I've just had a rather good idea.' Not that it was anything to do with the ruddy Hun, but even now he retained the impulse to be polite.

Without saying more, he started off unsteadily down the hill towards the entrance to the minefield. The German had made no attempt to argue or interfere; had sat back down, apparently preoccupied and unconcerned, but still shooting out those little glances when he thought he wasn't watched. Odd that, bloody odd. After all, Kit thought, he could just keep on walking, following the white-taped path leading east through the Devil's Garden to the Allied lines, assuming of course that Monty's boys were gaining the upper hand. The trouble was, this was by no means certain in such a fluid war. The carnage in the minefield suggested that not everything had gone to plan. In which case, of course, he might walk slap-bang into the clutches of the Panzerarmee, returning triumphant from yet another Rommel masterstroke. The man had done it plenty of times before, giving the Eighth Army a bloody nose at Tobruk and El Agheila. No doubt that shifty little Hun had worked that out. To hell with him. He'd stick to his plan. It was a good one. Though, as he drew closer to the shattered tanks and their decomposing crews, it seemed one heck of a price to pay.

Something was droning across the sky, quite high, a Storch reconnaissance plane, and heading north. It seemed an evil omen.

Ten

Mulholland's riding camels padded along at a steady pace, covering the ground somewhat faster than a man, an easy jog, unvarying and sustained, their soft broad feet hardly marking the surface of the sand. Ossie's mount, kneeling to let him clamber into the Tuareg saddle, fancy with its coloured leather and embellishments of copper, brass and silver, had turned to fix him with thick-lashed eyes as Mulholland had shown him how to position himself cross-legged, both feet resting on the animal's neck, ready to apply the pressure to make it start and stop, and turn to right or left. The eyes, as dark and glistening as ripened plums, reminded him of Farida, his golden fuck, until the camel yawned and folded back its lips, displaying a mouthful of crooked teeth cloaked in a mist of foul breath.

When they moved off, Ossie found it tough to keep his balance in the narrow saddle cushioned by layers of cloth in front of the camel's hump. He was riding high, higher than on any horse, and the ground looked a long way down, and hard. But quickly he learned to let his body roll to the rhythm of the beast's strong shoulders.

He also had to get accustomed to the Tuareg gear that Mulholland had ordered him to wear, covering his Wehrmacht uniform with an ankle-length blue-black linen robe and swathing his head and lower face with the windings of a twenty-foot-long scarf. His kit he stowed in leather saddlebags, durable and light, and fancy too, decked out with geometric shapes in tans and yellows and opal green, something like the Navajo designs he'd come across in Arizona when brushing up his flying skills pre-war by hanging out with sun-creased commercial stick'n'rudder jocks at the old Davis-Monthan field. It made him twist a grin behind the muslin *tagilmust* scarf to think of how those guys would greet him now, decked out like some faggot movie sheikh, perched at the controls of a very different ship to a Stearman PT-13; a desert ship that grumbled quietly to itself, maybe a little like a 200-horsepower Lycoming at that, but throttled back, inexorably closing down the twenty miles that lay between the stash of food and drink where he'd been offered a Sulima Turkish cigarette and been caught good, and the base of Holly Force where the phoney raghead told him things were bubbling up quite nicely.

They moved along, flank to flank, him and the phoney raghead, the camels content and easy in their nearness, the scuffing of their feet like whispers in the heavy silence. Ossie pulled down his wrap-round scarf, snorted back a gob of phlegm and spat it clear, watching it arc away and kick up a spurt of sand. Mulholland caught him hawking up and Ossie saw a momentary distaste reflected in his eyes. That was rich, he reckoned, the way the ragheads carried on – those Tuareg sons-of-bitches the Englishman so much admired. He'd heard some tales of nomad ways that stood a guy's hair on end. Maybe that was what drew in Mulholland and his kind, the oddballs they called 'old desert hands', who travelled with the tribesmen and spoke their mumbo-jumbo and shared their bitter water and unleavened bread and spouted bull about the hard and simple life as though they'd discovered some universal truth. Hell, there was nothing those primitive bastards could teach a white man, living a life that wasn't a life in the goddamned boondocks, a no-man's-land that wasn't worth a dime.

Mulholland was riding on, nodding to the gentle motion of his camel. Ossie felt compelled to break the silence.

'I figure it's time you put me in the picture,' he said.

'What picture's that?'

'Jesus, Mulholland, we're in the middle of nowhere. Cut me a little slack.'

'The Bedu don't indulge in idle chat,' said Mulholland. 'We might be watched, and out here voices carry. The less you know and say, the better.'

'That's all you're letting on?'

'That's all.' Mulholland was staring straight ahead. 'Enjoy the peace and quiet. It's likely to be the last you'll get.'

For Ossie the time passed slowly. Something had come up, something big enough to abort his march. Something that called for flying, otherwise they'd never have called him back. He wanted to learn more, but knew Mulholland would keep it buttoned.

After another hour or so, shuffling across the flattened plain, the ground began to rise and seem familiar. Occasional vehicle tracks began to show on the flattened earth. It was oddly cold and the wind blew from the west, whipping swirls of sand against any exposed skin. It stung like shot on Ossie's hands and the soft flesh round his eyes, though elsewhere he was well protected by his enveloping Tuareg gear. In that, he had to hand it to the ragheads. When it came to desert gear, they knew a thing or two.

Somewhere, very high and to the north, he heard the growl of engines, big Bristol radials with their trademark oscillating *woo-woo-woo*. Wellingtons, he guessed, a sizeable formation, growing fainter now yet still no crump of bombs. He figured he might know their mission. In Cairo he'd met a couple of bomber-boys based in the Suez zone, members of a Wimpey squadron flying from Tikrit, specialists in jamming German radio communications whenever the Axis fan was about to be hit by shit. Like Mulholland said, things were bubbling up quite nicely.

They heard the camp before they saw it, obscured by a final ridge that made the camels lean forward a little against the slope, but breathing smooth and even, taking it in their loping stride.

Their ears were pricked, picking up the sounds of men: shouts of command, the stamp of boots, the revving motor of a truck, the rattle of live rounds from over by the *Hindernisparcours*, the bruising assault course laid out by Jabotinsky on Foreign Legion lines, and everything overlaid by the general din of dissonant noise that hung above any military base busy with its daily tasks.

They went on down, Ossie suddenly awkward in his Tuareg robe and feeling like a mug, astride his goofy mount that now and then turned its head and fixed him with a plum-eyed gaze so like Farida's he wondered if he could ever look on her again without remembering this goddamned bad-breathed beast. As they moved towards the guards on the barbed-wire gates he waited for the wisecracks but they didn't come. Instead, the sentries waved them through without a word. Clearly small potatoes, mere routine, to see two extras from *The Desert Song* emerge from nowhere, with just the slightest nod to indicate the *Kommandant* was back from picking up that damned stray *Flieger* who seemed to be more trouble than the last sad case who let them down, now buried deep, close to the cannibalised carcass of his Storch, in a rough-and-ready plain-marked grave.

The sun shone yellow-gold through the window of Mulholland's office, picking up glinting particles of dust hanging in the air. The *Kommandant* was sitting on the corner of his desk, one leg dangling, crisp once more in his *Oberst* uniform, checking documents and, as he moved, the particles of dust moved with him, eddying around his angular frame. The cloud of tiny golden specks gave Mulholland an unworldly look, lending him a weirdly saint-like aura, as though he was some bony mystic, the kind who holed up in a hermit cave someplace for fifty years and pondered on the meaning of existence. So Ossie thought, standing roughly at ease, and waiting for Mulholland to finish his scrutiny of his papers. Finally Mulholland looked up.

'Lucky you fly better than you ride a camel, otherwise you'd be on your way back to Cairo. You're the most tottery Tuareg I ever saw.'

'Maybe, but it sure beats walking,' said Ossie. Then he shrugged. 'Why camels?'

'A useful test, dear boy. As I said out there, you held up well. Didn't break your cover.'

'I damned near broke your head.'

'Oh,' said Mulholland vaguely, 'I don't think it would have come to that.' He felt in the breast pocket of his tropical *Feldbluse*, took out a coin and began to spin it in his usual, casual way. 'There were other reasons, too. For camels, I mean.' The coin was catching the golden light. 'The game will soon be afoot, in earnest.' He jerked his head towards the busy scene outside his office window. 'The chaps are up to their ears right now, carrying out my orders, so they've got better things to do than pick up strays. As for me, well, for the moment I'd done my bit. And I like to polish my desert skills. Besides, you were in tricky terrain, decidedly dodgy for motorised transport, but perfect for the dear old dromedary. Marvellous creatures, don't you think? Don't leave tracks, don't waste fuel and can go for a week without water. Nice natures too.'

'You're cracking me up.'

'I can see that, Wolf. You need to overcome that sentimental streak.'

There was a knock on the door. Chaim Herzl came in, a radio transcript in his hand, carefully written out in pencil on an authentic Wehrmacht form. He and Mulholland exchanged a significant glance.

'It's on?' Mulholland asked. He caught the coin and placed it on his desk.

Herzl nodded. '*Ja*. It starts tonight.'

'Get Bahr and Jabotinsky. And organise some coffee.' Mulholland went around the desk and eased down in his chair. 'Wolf, take a pew.' He read the radio transcript in silence, then tore it into pieces with great care. He looked up. There was an odd light in his eyes. 'Do you know what day it is?'

'I kinda lost track.'

'Friday the twenty-third of October. A date you won't forget.'

Bahr and Jabotinsky came in with Herzl, carrying mugs of coffee which they passed around. 'That's all, Herzl,' Mulholland said. 'No interruptions, clear?'

The legionnaire Jabotinsky nudged Ossie in the ribs and murmured: 'March and die, or march and catch a camel, huh?'

Willi Bahr leaned across. 'Hey, Jabo, remember what I said? No *Amerikaner* could do that thing, in any time that counts.'

'The camel saved your bacon,' Ossie said. 'I had you beat to hell.'

Jabotinsky laughed. 'Willi here's a good Jewish boy. No point in saving bacon for him.'

'I eat bacon, you bet,' said Bahr defiantly. 'Except at Passover.'

'I hear pork kills Jews as sure as Nazis,' said Ossie.

Bahr started breathing deeply. 'Whose war you fighting, you Gentile schmuck?'

'Yours,' said Ossie, 'you bacon-eating tough palooka.'

He grinned and Willi Bahr and Jabotinsky grinned, and they drank their coffee, and waited for Mulholland to begin. It started slowly, as though what Mulholland had to say was too big for words.

'Quite finished bickering, children? Good. Bahr and Jabotinsky know what this is about. You're the only man here, Wolf, still in the dark. The rest of Holly Force has been fully briefed.' Mulholland felt for his coin, still lying on the desk, then pushed it away as though he wanted no distractions. 'A while ago we had a conversation. What I told you then is happening tonight. At 21.40 hours the Eighth Army will launch Operation Lightfoot with the biggest artillery bombardment since the Great War. Axis positions will be attacked along a forty-mile front, from the sea to the Qattara Depression. It's going to be a bloody business, driving corridors through the minefields for our tanks in the north, pouring through our troops supported by a creeping barrage, and lots of fighting hand-to-hand. Montgomery is confident we'll win. He believes that Rommel is on the back foot, his supply lines overstretched and short on reinforcements. Monty's prediction is that we'll have the whole thing wrapped up in twelve days.'

Ossie glanced at Bahr and Jabotinsky. 'That's swell. So where do does Holly Force come in?'

'Various operations. But for you, as I indicated some time ago, I have a very particular job in mind.'

'A sideshow, as I recall.'

'All our operations are sideshows, Wolf. Full-scale battles aren't our style. But this particular sideshow offers the star prize. Or did.' Mulholland pulled open a desk drawer and took out a brown envelope. 'Are you familiar with Heracles?'

Ossie nodded at the envelope. 'That his dossier?'

Mulholland sighed. 'What passes for education on your side of the Atlantic? No time to teach you classics now. Heracles was a mythological Greek hero. He had to perform twelve labours to atone for a crime I won't bore you with now. The second task was kill the Hydra, a monster with many heads – but only one head was immortal. That was the key. Once Heracles had lopped that off, the beast died.' Mulholland began to slip a photograph out of the envelope. 'Regrettably, our Hydra's immortal head is currently sick in Germany, so this fellow will have to do.' He held up a grainy black and white print. 'General Georg Stumme, commander of Panzer Group Africa in Erwin Rommel's absence. The Panzerarmee is already demoralised without its *Wustenfuchs*, its Desert Fox, in control. Remove Stumme and we could help to turn the tide of the battle, whether he's the genuine immortal head or not. In Berlin's eyes he has assumed that role and that's enough for us.'

'If you take out Stumme, won't Rommel return?'

'Perhaps. But how long would that take? Days. In war, a day lost can make the difference between victory and defeat. Besides, the intelligence types report that Rommel's suffering from everything but the bubonic plague. Stomach and liver ailments, bad circulation, high blood pressure, nasal diphtheria. The man's a wreck, which is hardly surprising. He's fifty years old, never sleeps for more than five hours and exists entirely on adrenalin.'

'Could be another of his little tricks,' said Ossie. 'I heard he looked bright enough when he got his field marshal's baton from Goebbels and said he held the key to goddamned Egypt. I mean, he's the guy who ran his tanks round and round the city when he landed in Tripoli, to fool us into thinking he had a much larger force, and there was that time he got trucks to follow behind his armour to raise so much dust we thought it was one giant tank column. He's not called the Fox for nothing. Could be this whole sickness thing's another hoax, to catch Montgomery off his guard.'

'Intelligence says not, and I believe them,' said Mulholland. 'Far more likely that in Berlin he simply made the effort to convince the world he's in the pink. No, he's crocked all right. The only question is how serious his condition might be. It certainly seems it was bad enough to send him home four weeks ago. Being the man he is, he'd hardly choose to absent himself from his command at such a time, and for so long, unless it was for something more important than picking up a gong from Goebbels. It was an obvious risk, and Rommel hasn't made his reputation by being caught with his trousers down. It's entirely untypical. The logical explanation is he's under doctor's orders to get himself fighting fit before the attack he anticipates in late November.' Mulholland paused. 'As far as we're concerned, one thing's sure. Rommel's still in Hunland and fat little Georg is here. As I say, not quite the quarry we were after, but he'll have to do. Remove him from the equation and we'll sow confusion in the Panzerarmee at the highest level, and at the crucial moment. And that's where you chaps come in.'

Ossie leaned forward, elbows on his knees, hands clasped. 'So how do you propose we rub him out?'

'You don't,' said Mulholland. 'Your job is to find him. Piece of cake for undercover pros like you. Like all the Desert Army high-ups, Stumme stands in awe of Rommel. He'll be keen to prove his boss chose the right man for the job. When the attack begins he'll try to act like him, visiting key positions at the Front, meeting his commanders face to face, setting an example to the men. Whatever other qualities Stumme may lack, courage isn't one of them. So he won't be kicking his heels and waiting for reports at Deutsche Afrika Korps headquarters in El Daba. Not that he's likely to receive many, anyway. The artillery johnnies confidently predict that his landline communications will be smashed by the bombardment. So, even if he is tempted to lurk in his HQ he'll be forced to get out and about, by road or air, to find out what the devil's going on. I guarantee the fellow's going to be riding off madly in all directions, as Stephen Leacock put it. And that's our chance, while he's exposed and vulnerable.'

Mulholland replaced the photograph of Stumme in the brown envelope and handed it to Ossie. 'You will take the Storch, along with Behr and Jabotinsky here, leaving at first light. You will be in the uniform of a Luftwaffe reconnaissance pilot. Bahr and Jabotinsky will be dressed as members of the *Feldgendarmerie* for reasons that will become plain. It's a role they have played many times before. They will explain their needs and the role they expect you to play. Together you will prepare a plan of operations to be run past me, a plan that will give you the best possible chance of pinpointing Stumme's position. When he is found – and note that I say *when* not *if* – you will radio through precise coordinates and someone else will do the rest.'

'Put like that it sounds a cinch,' said Ossie. 'But hell, a forty-mile-long front's a lot of ground to cover. The guy could turn up anywhere at any time.'

'It's a question of psychology, Wolf. If you were Stumme, and under attack, where would you choose to show yourself, bearing in mind the kind of battle under way?'

'With the Panzer armour, I guess.'

'Precisely. So that narrows it down. The Italians are concentrated in the south. The German tank formations are to the north, grouped around Deir el Qatani and Tel el Eisa. We'll back those two particular horses. Sooner or later Stumme's bound to show himself at one or t'other. All you need is patience, guile, sharp eyes and a modicum of luck.'

'Uh-huh,' said Ossie. 'So how do we stop ourselves being shot up by our own people? There's going to be a lot of trigger-happy sons-of-bitches out there.'

'You spotted that. Well, regrettably that's the nature of our business. As I say, you'll need some luck. As usual we'll do our best to spread the word among the powers-that-be that we're likely to be stooging about in the general area. And we'll give the Storch a distinctive touch or two. But, you know, heat of battle and all that sort of thing. Mistakes will happen. Just try and make sure they don't happen to you.' Mulholland reached for his coin and balanced it on his thumb. 'However, if you do have the misfortune to get the chop, please make sure it's after you've located Stumme and radioed in and not before. I'd hate to send you all on a wasted journey.' He flicked the coin. 'Now, if there are no further questions, I suggest you go and inspect that flying pram of yours and get down to working out your modus operandi.'

'I got a question,' said Ossie. 'Who's in command?'

'Jabotinsky, though in matters of airmanship, you'll call the shots.'

When Ossie went to check the Storch he noticed that Jabotinsky and Bahr trailed along a few paces behind, as though deferring to him in some unstated way. He recognised the look they gave him as they approached the canvas hangar, the look of men confronted with something they did not understand, the mysterious world of flight, exercised by very few, that small percentage that possessed the brains, the nerve, the reflexes, the self-belief to control an intricate and bewildering machine in an element as wildly unpredictable as the air. He liked the feeling that he could do what other men could not, or did not care to. All the elements of his being came together in this, the summation of his skills, expressed in the readiness to lay his hide on the line, time and time again, and not just go up but go up and fight in that arcing blue arena where he took on other men, that small percentage that had followed the same path as him.

In that moment, as he walked towards the little Storch standing in the shadow of the hangar, he knew in a single flash of comprehension, too swift to express in words, that he was living out a time he would remember and look back on all his life; a time experienced by the chosen ones who lived to fly and, best of all, to fly in war and maybe die – but that was all right too, because that was the price they were all prepared to pay. And that was why Jabotinsky and Bahr looked at him the way they did, the look that said, 'You do what we cannot do ourselves; you fly, we cannot fly.' So Ossie understood the look. Accepted it, took it like a medal, a mark of approbation even if unconsciously bestowed. And sureness of himself rushed through him like a shot of rye. 'In matters of airmanship, you'll call the shots.' He would make sure of that, and more.

He recalled a maxim from the cocksure pilot's book of golden rules, that sounded as if it was some kind of joke, but wasn't, like all the other maxims there, learned by tyro fliers at their instructor's knee. 'There's the pilot and then there's the guys in the back.' In the back of the airplane, or back at base, it made no difference. When it came down to it, the guys in the back were of no account. The pilot was all. Ossie felt the power grow within him. He experienced a tangible throb of pleasure, somewhere around his solar plexus, at the prospect of flying again. He was back in control once more. He reckoned this little operation sounded like a million laughs. And he was out to enjoy it all he could.

He took his time inspect the Storch. He wanted to rub it in, make Behr and Jabotinsky witness the cool routine, the methodical preparation, the mysterious process to the earthbound of checking this and testing that, before you put a machine in the air, even an elementary tinpot crate like this. The ground-crew had been pleased to see him, partly because with Ossie grounded they had been assigned to working on the unit's transport, as well as polishing their combat skills alongside the rest of the fighting force. Under Mulholland's command, no one was allowed a narrow specialisation, each man required to be as adept at killing in a variety of ways as driving a truck, operating a field radio, wielding a spanner or, as Ossie had quickly learned, piloting an airplane.

Now he relished being back among familiar things – sniffing in the blend of aviation fuel, hot oil and dope, the lacquer that stiffened the fabric of the Storch's fuselage and wings, relishing that special feeling he got when he looked at a machine he would soon take up.

For what seemed like weeks he'd barely had time to visit the hangar, told by Mulholland to stay away and so resist temptation. On principle he had defied the order a time or two, but only briefly, as the rigours of his training permitted few distractions. As well, he had found he did not care to come too close to this silent bird he was not allowed to fly. And so he had walked around it, saying little to the ground-crew guys because there was nothing to be said that meant a damn. He did not want to reveal to them his anger and frustration, or show that Mulholland had got to him. But now was different. It was heady to run through pre-flight checks, trying to catch them out, find out what they'd missed, digging into that knowledge they shared, that intimate understanding, that affinity that came from living aviation in all its forms, that narrow, cabalistic world of flying.

Already Mintz, the fitter, had run up the big lump of inverted 200-horsepower Argus. The shut-down engine was still clicking and ticking, radiating heat like a dormant heart, ready to revitalise this slight and spiky joke of a machine that stood propped up on its strutted, tiny wheels like some plaything of a giant kid.

'Hey, Pepper,' Ossie said, not bothering to speak in German in front of Bahr and Jabotinsky. 'You mean you've passed this heap of shit as airworthy?'

Mintz was beaming, once more happy in his work. 'Don't blame me. Take your complaints to Adolf Hitler, why don't you?'

'That's not a bad idea,' said Ossie. 'I could fly this baby clear across Europe, put her down outside the Reich Chancellery and deliver my opinions to the *Drecksack* in person. And put a slug through the sonofabitch's pump.'

Mintz wiped his hands on a grease-stained rag. 'She get you there. She is a good machine.'

'Even if she was put together by Fascist assholes,' said Ossie.

Mintz glanced at Bahr and Jabotinsky. 'Better in German, please, I think. You make me plenty trouble.'

'Sure thing. What's *Deutsch* for Fascist assholes?'

Ossie gave Bahr and Jabotinsky the entire show, a copybook pre-flight drill, starting with the twin-blade wooden propeller that looked as though it might be connected to an elastic band. He moved on to the landing gear, the wings and tail, testing the ailerons, elevators and rudder for full, free, unrestricted movement, each procedure methodical and slow just like the manual said. He stepped up on the starboard undercarriage strut and secured the top-hinged door underneath the wing, then swung himself into the cockpit. Bahr and Jabotinsky were getting restive, shuffling their feet and murmuring to each other.

Ossie called across, 'No use hurrying this stuff. Besides, I gotta remind myself how to fly this crazy kite.' He saw in their faces a flash of doubt. It evened up the score a little, for all the stuff they'd thrown at him. Comfortable in the snug tin bucket seat he turned his attention, with great deliberation, to the cockpit check.

Mintz was on a small inspection ladder, leaning in. *'Alles in Ordnung?'* he asked.

'Nicht so schnell,' said Ossie. 'Let's keep Frankenstein and his monster guessing for a while.'

Yeah, he thought, there's the pilot and then there's the guys in the back. The pilot is all. Then he paused. Not every pilot, though. There was that poor bastard, Dobbs. A pilot who was nothing. The man that Mulholland said hadn't come up to scratch. The stiff who lay not 200 yards away, under piled stones to keep away the feral dogs that seemed to appear from nowhere and hung around any military base, both sides of the line, scavenging for scraps or, on a lucky day, at some fresh site of war, feasting on new-killed corpses, unburied or vulnerable in shallow graves; the only creatures eating well in this lousy zero of a place. So what had Mulholland said about the guy? 'Defy my orders again and you'll go the way of Dobbs.' Was he really nuts enough to knock off some poor slob who didn't cut the mustard?

'Say, Pepper,' Ossie said, 'tell me what happened to that feller Dobbs.'

Mintz avoided his eye. He shook his head. *'Ich weiss nicht. Einen Unfall.'*

'What kind of goddamned accident?'

Mintz shook his head again. 'Ask anyone. Not me. The man is dead.'

'Jesus,' Ossie said. 'Being dead don't mean end of story. What kind of guy was Dobbs when he was alive and kicking?'

'I cannot say.'

'You cannot say what kind of guy he was, and you don't know how he died.'

'Recht so.'

'I told you once to back me up or I'd kick your ass all the way to a front-line foxhole. I wasn't kidding, brother.'

'What you ask, only the *Kommandant* can tell you.'

'I had you pitching for my team, Pepper. Looks like I was wrong.'

Mintz shrugged. 'You want we should complete your pre-flight now?'

'Hell, yes,' said Ossie. 'Seems we're just about finished here.'

Fuelled up and every system checked, Ossie bundled Bahr and Jabotinsky on board the Storch to see how the buoyancy and trim were affected by their weight. He cranked out the barn-door take-off flaps, which increased the area of the wings by almost 20 per cent, and taxied out at little more than walking speed, s-bending the machine with rudder and an occasional touch of brakes to see around the narrow, tilted nose, the roar of engine almost painful to ears that had gotten used to desert silence. He had the stick full-back, though heavily laden as it was there was little chance of nosing over. Even so, Mintz and the rigger Katz were stationed at each wing-tip, holding on, and trotting now. His passengers crouched behind him, their callused mitts wrapped round the cockpit tubing for support, looking apprehensive, like hard-ass punks he'd seen on board the roller-coaster car at the Chain of Rocks amusement park in west St Louis, trundling down the tracks, eyes wide and faces frozen, cut down to size, heading for unknown terrors.

The propwash was raising vortices of dust and, as he throttled up and headed down the strip, the tailplane felt like lead. He pushed forward on the broom-handle of a stick but the needle of the airspeed indicator was only showing 30 knots. The stick was as firm as an iron rod. He knew he had to wait, wondering if the two great lunks behind him would mean he wouldn't get the ship unstuck at all. His right arm was getting stiff, and shaking with the strain. Then, with the ASI at 40 knots, the pressure on the stick eased off and he pulled it fully and easily back. He was off the ground in less than 150 feet and climbing at an angle of 45 degrees. He wound off the flaps, cruising now at 60 knots, and banked around the base, the fuselage creaking, rocking as Bahr and Jabotinsky adjusted their positions.

'Steady, guys,' he shouted across his shoulder. 'You're unsettling her. Hang on now. I'm going to try to get her back on the deck. This is where it gets real tricky.' It was hard to keep from laughing as he felt them tense behind him, cranking down the flaps and dropping the Storch on the ground in a perfect wings-level stall-down landing, floating in and holding off, with power shut down, moving so slow it seemed they were hanging in the air though airspeed was showing 25 knots. Even at that, she wouldn't stall. Slower then, and finally, after the briefest hesitation, with stick right back, she settled, the landing-gear legs spreading out and cushioning the airplane's weight so she didn't even bounce. They'd stopped in the space of fifty feet.

'Hot dog,' said Ossie, throttling up. 'Damned if I didn't get it right. Let's see if I can do it all again.'

It was on his approach for the third and final time that he saw below an Opel Blitz heading out of the camp's main gates and turning north, with a small field gun hitched on behind. The rear canopy of the truck was folded back and on the benches eight men sat, four each side, helmeted and fully armed, neat as lead figures in a war game. Out to the left, the two-man crew of a BMW motorcycle combo with an MG-34 machine gun mounted on the snub nose of its sidecar was avoiding the dust storm kicked up by the Blitz.

Ossie turned around to Jabotinsky, squatting in the tandem seat behind him like a captured bear, and pointed down. Another of Mulholland's sideshows, he reckoned, ready to make a nuisance of itself when Montgomery lit the fuse that night.

Jabotinsky nodded, exposing his camel teeth in a grimace that might have been approval, or something else. His voice was weak and shaky. '*Ja*,' he quavered, 'we teach the bastards good.' Against his yellow teeth, his face had a greenish tinge. It was a hectic combination.

Ossie knew the look. 'Oh, shit,' he said. 'Hang on, Jabo. We're going down.'

He took the Storch low over the BMW combo's head, waggling his wings. The goggled crew looked up and waved, their bodies moving to the contours of the rough terrain, and Ossie banked away towards the landing strip, waiting for Jabotinsky to throw up on his back. The Legion man was groaning quietly now, but held it in. On the ground he clambered out and weaved towards the hangar, clawing at his gut. Standing by the Storch with Willi Bahr, Ossie watched him go with something close to satisfaction.

'Lucky the Legion's a bunch of foot-sloggers. If they'd been an air force, old Jabo there would have been all washed up.'

'Maybe it's you who will be washed up, if you can't do more than fly a fugging plane,' said Bahr. 'You fight sitting down, like you're at the movies, nothing real. You wait until we get among the *Panzergrenadiers*, so close you can smell their sausage breath. Then we see how tough you are.'

'Say, you got a Kleenex handy, Willi boy?' Ossie said. 'Your buddy needs someone to wipe his mouth.'

In an office Mulholland had set aside, they worked out their plan of operation, spreading across a table the *Kommandant*'s map that showed the Allied and Axis dispositions, as far as they were known, stretching from Alamein near the coast to Qaret el Himeimat in the south. Ossie was reluctantly impressed. He could see that Bahr and Jabotinsky knew their business, as he knew his. He did not have a lot to say. His job was simple. Fly the Storch to certain points and land where he was told, stay at the controls ready to take off, and only join the others if he got a sign. One sign meant he was to join the bluff, help brazen things out. The other, and there were only two, meant that it was all up with them and the time had come to sell their hides as dearly as they could, knowing they could expect no mercy. The odds on being taken prisoner, wearing Wehrmacht uniforms behind Panzerarmee lines, were zilch. Less than zilch if it was discovered that two of them were Jews. In this situation Ossie was to destroy the Storch with a grenade and support the others in the final action. The prospect didn't worry him unduly. He had no doubt he'd be up to snuff, if it came down to that. Whatever they believed, he had seen and done his share of killing close at hand, though with a less than expert hand, in Spain and France. And if it meant promotion to the harp farm now instead of later, well, it made no real difference. But it didn't stop him thinking, as Bahr and Jabotinsky folded up their map, that, hell, he'd come this far in this lousy war that somehow he'd survive. He always did.

Mulholland approved the plan. He issued each of them with a *Soldbuch*, the leather-covered paybook that proved the identity of every German soldier, containing his service number, the unit in which he served, his rate of pay, equipment and clothing issued, some medical information. For Bahr and Jabotinsky there was more: the *Feldgendarmerie Ausweis*, the identification card that confirmed the holder had authority over all non-tactical decisions, answerable only to the regional *Kommandeur*; the pale green *Tachebuch*, the pocket notebook carried by every member of the force, and various forms.

The fakes were accurate enough to fool the sharpest eye, particularly on the field of battle. They had been doctored by little Leo Szryk, a forger of some notoriety before the war, deported by the Reich which, ironically, had saved his skin. And now he was recruited to a more honourable line of work, kept busy by the ingenious demands of Holly Force.

Szryk had also created three *Erkennungsmarke*, the regulation oval metal dog tags stamped with the matching service number, name and unit, worn around the neck. Like the others, Ossie found he had some personal items too – a crimp-edged photograph of a hefty, smiling Fräulein, a postcard of the Unter den Linden in carefree times, the beginnings of a letter home. The *Soldbuch* showed that each of them had been freshly christened with solid, Aryan names. Jabotinsky was *Stabsfeldwebel* Kroseberg, a warrant officer in the *Feldgendarmerie*, Bahr was *Gefreiter* Freytag. His lowly rank, lance corporal, made Jabotinsky cuff him playfully round the ear. Ossie was Heinz-Horst Schroer, a *Luftwaffe Aufklärungsflieger*, reconnaissance pilot with the rank of *Leutnant*.

'Don't get no ideas, *Amerikaner*,' said Bahr. 'You're still a fugging taxi-driver, just the same.'

'Pipe down, wise guy,' Ossie said, 'or I'll put you on a goddamned charge.'

The uniforms, brought in by Herzl on Mulholland's order, were similarly authentic, in the case of Bahr and Jabotinsky accurate down to the kidney-shaped duty gorget of metal that rested on a *Feldgendarm*'s chest, suspended on a chain. A faint fleck of blood and a carefully mended, odd incision in the back of Ossie's leather flying jacket suggested how Holly Force might have acquired such gear.

'You also have Allied service names,' Mulholland told them. He glanced at Bahr and Jabotinsky. 'In the event of capture and interrogation, you may admit to being Srenkiewicz and Janicki, NCOs with the First Polish Armoured Division. Wolf, you're Irwin Burrard, Royal Canadian Air Force. No papers, of course, to support those claims, but I doubt you'll need 'em. If you're bagged in fancy dress, they'll almost certainly dispatch you on the spot.'

'Suits me,' said Ossie. 'I was getting kinda confused, trying to remember all this stuff.'

'I leave it to you, Jabotinsky, to make your final preparations,' said Mulholland. 'Anything you need, Herzl will sort out. I may not be along to see you off.' He nodded through the window, where men were mounting a *Granatwerfer* light mortar onto the back of a seven-ton Opel half-track. 'We're teed up to give the Eyeties a little surprise. The Regia Aeronautica are flying Fiat CR.42 fighters out of a temporary airfield close to the El Taqa

Plateau, doing intercepts and strafing sorties, thirty or so miles from here. They don't think they've been spotted yet. They're about to discover how wrong they are. As soon as the artillery opens up tonight, we're off. Useful cover, Monty's Brock's Benefit.' At that he got blank looks but did not bother to explain. 'Any questions?'

'*Ja, Herr Kommandant,*' said Jabotinsky. 'Our secondary targets?'

'Obvious. Act the pest. Make a thoroughgoing nuisance of yourselves.'

'I got a question,' Ossie said. 'There's one guy missing from this mission. I reckon it's time I knew the reason why.'

Mulholland frowned, then understood. 'Ah, Dobbs.'

'Yeah, Dobbs.'

'All right, Jabotinsky, Bahr,' said Mulholland. 'Wolf will catch you up.'

The others gone, Mulholland sat back in his chair with folded arms. 'A fellow, name of Surtees, once said that it's better to be killed than frightened to death. He was writing about fox-hunting, but naturally it also applies to war.' He paused. 'It applied to Dobbs.'

'You saying the guy was yellow?'

'That's a harsh judgement on any man. He possessed his own brand of courage. Unfortunately it wasn't ours.'

'Back in Helio you didn't mince your words. You said he was short on guts.'

'Did I? Yes, I imagine I would have put it that way. Time was running short. It was important to get you on board without delay. I saw you were the kind of chap who couldn't resist a challenge to his manhood.'

Ossie's scalp contracted. 'How'd you figure that?'

'No matter,' said Mulholland. 'As for Dobbs, at first he was the same. We thought we'd got our man. Bravado, I assume, because when we tested him he failed. He couldn't live with that, and ended it. Frightened to death, as you might say. The pity was, he not only wrote himself off but also an invaluable machine. Opting out is down to the individual, of course, but to jeopardise an entire operation is inexcusable.'

'You saying he knocked himself off? I got the impression you might have helped him out.'

'It suited my purpose. It doesn't hurt to keep a new boy off-balance, particularly a recalcitrant type like you. A rough-and-ready lot like this needs to know how far you'll go to get the results you want.'

'You mean, you might have gone that far?'

'Dear boy, here's hoping you'll never know.' Mulholland sighed. 'War is a filthy business. You don't need me to tell you that. It brutalises us all. It makes unreal demands. It's not enough to screw up your courage, rise to the occasion, once, twice, a hundred times. You've got to have the will, the absence of imagination, the blunted senses to reach the point where it's possible to go on indefinitely, not caring whether you live or die. If, however, you still value life, it means you want to live. And that, ironically, is often fatal.'

'Like it was for Dobbs?'

'He'd proved his mettle many times, flying a reconnaissance Mosquito over the Norwegian ports, photographing targets in northern France, piloting a Maryland out of Malta to snap the Italian battle fleet gathered in Taranto. Came highly recommended with a good degree of nerve and skill. He even had proficient German, thanks to an Austrian mama. But here he faced a different test. Trouble was, he preferred to fly. Ground ops was quite another thing. We soon found out he was apt to get rattled under fire. Some it takes that way – there's nothing you can do. In his previous line of work no one had ever known. Says something for his gumption. He also found our training hard. His fitness let him down. He failed to complete a desert march, and had to be brought in. The men, as you can imagine, were merciless. It all conspired to make him an outsider.'

'You could have sent him back.'

'Not an option, I'm afraid. Might have blabbed – couldn't take the risk. I took the decision to force the fellow's hand. Make or break. It was in his interests, after all. I explained it all. The only decent thing to do. He understood. We gave him this final test, to land the Storch under intensive fire, pop out, detonate a charge, knife a couple of dummy sentries and exit sharp left. Quite a little pantomime, alarming to a greenhorn – the whole idea, of course. The fellows were going to cut it very fine. Mausers, mortars, MG34s, grenades, the whole shebang. Naturally, they planned to pile it on with the greatest glee, and made sure he knew all about it. Risky to the aeroplane, of course, but Dobbs himself was the greater risk. We had to know how he'd stand up.'

'He pranged it, huh?'

'No, not then. He funked it, turned away. Couldn't bring himself to put the Storch down. After that, he didn't exist. The man was on his own. Nothing I could do. Not that I tried. Like the men, I'd made my judgement.' Mulholland sat back in his chair, hands clasped behind his head. 'Dobbs had too. He took the Storch up a few days after that. Climbed to five thousand feet, cut the engine and despite the Storch's very best efforts to save him from calamity, nose-dived in.' Mulholland stood up. 'You're a very different proposition, Wolf. I wonder where you'd be without this war? It's meat and drink to you, whatever form it takes.'

'Looking for another one, I guess,' said Ossie.

'I don't believe you give a tuppenny damn for anyone but yourself.'

'Look out for Number One,' said Ossie. 'No one else gives a shit.'

'I'll get my favourite aunt to embroider that on a sampler for my bedroom,' said Mulholland. 'By the way, you're part of Operation Jorrocks. More Surtees, I confess. Jorrocks was the character who said "My soul's on fire, I'm eager for the chase." In the circumstances most appropriate, wouldn't you agree?'

'What's this Jorrocks guy's claim to fame?' said Ossie.

'Oh, he was a huntin' feller. An eccentric and extravagant Englishman devoted to dangerous pastimes and fond of causing trouble,' said Mulholland. 'Fictional, of course. Nobody like that could possibly exist in real life.'

Eleven

Beppo Lutzow watched the Englishman go. Of course he had not deigned to explain himself. He could not imagine what he had in mind. And what was it to him? The fool could try walking to Cairo if he wished. Very soon he would find himself staring down the barrel of a Tiger tank. Beppo did not doubt that the Allied attack had been repulsed. It had to be so. What had General Rommel told the nation? 'You may rely on us to hold fast to what we have conquered.' Such a man could not be pushed back.

However, to more personal matters. Now was the time to consider his own position, whether the Englishman returned or not. Without a weapon in this no-man's-land, where danger could lie hidden behind every dune, he felt uneasy and exposed. This was his chance to recover the Webley and its ammunition.

The revolver was easily found, fifteen metres distant, caught in a single, spiky shrub. Clearly Curtis had a good, strong arm. The weapon seemed undamaged. Beppo checked the barrel and the chambers, blowing away the dust and grit. He felt restored by the weight of the Webley in his hand. From the top of the rise he saw that the Englishman had almost reached the place where the white tapes began. Perhaps he would step on a handy mine and solve both their problems. Perhaps, for that purpose at least, he would not need the Webley after all.

He skittered down the slope and began to drag aside the rocks and stones in the crevice bed, probing with his fingers down the many holes like burrows, anticipating the cool feel of a metal cartridge case. One of the larger slabs of rocks proved hard to shift. Then it moved and he heard a rasping sound, not stone on stone but made by some living thing. Looking down he saw, close by his right leg, a large brown snake, dark blotches running along its length, rubbing its coils together as it slid towards him, the friction creating the rasping sound he'd heard. It gathered itself, and struck.

He felt the fangs sink into his flesh, below and behind his knee. There was a fierce pain, like two sharp needles driven deep, and then a burning sensation, of something spreading outwards from the lacerations. Dropping the Webley, he reeled away. He could only stare ahead, eyes wild, not focusing, mouth open with the shock, stumbling up the slope. Far off he saw the Englishman close by the tanks. Instinctively, he raised an arm. The Englishman, surprised, waved back, holding something above his head, pointing at it, shouting out like a cheery friend.

Beppo slumped down, unbuttoning the ankle strap of his loose-fitting cotton trousers. He saw that his calf was already red and swollen. Nausea overcame him, whether from the venom spreading through his system or the vivid image of the dark-blotched snake he could not tell. Nor did he care. His body was not his own. He began to vomit. He thought that perhaps he was dying. No man should go this way. It was very stupid, to survive so much in the air and catch it from some *schmutzig* reptile hiding under a stinking stone. No hero's death, as he had expected, extinguished in a blaze of fire or blown to atoms in a moment. Instead, a wretched exit, painful and prolonged; alone, unless the Englishman came back. He hoped for that. It was ironic. Minutes ago, he had wished him gone.

He tried to rise, to see beyond a rocky outcrop to where the Devil's Garden lay, but found it difficult to move, a creeping numbness in his lower limbs. He tried to shout but nothing came; only a rasping sound, rasping like the coils of the dark-blotched snake, rubbing together as it moved towards him, before it struck.

Kit saw the distant figure of the German disappear. What on earth was the fellow about? Perhaps rescue was on the way. If so, he wondered what uniform it would wear. No way of knowing any of this, of course, until he made it back. So he put such speculation out of his mind and concentrated on the job in hand.

This was neither easy nor pleasant. Already he had recovered one water bottle from the charred remains of a corporal spread-eagled in the shadow of a blackened tank of the Royal Armoured Corps. The khaki felt cover had been partially burned away and, when touched, the webbing straps crumbled to a silvery ash. But the metal-topped cork was still intact and when, finally, he managed to tug the bottle free from beneath the exposed ribcage of the crewman, he found it was almost full. The sloshing of its contents made him gulp and lick his lips. He removed the cork and raised the bottle to his lips. The water was warm, like blood, and when the thought occurred to him he coughed and spluttered, and was almost sick.

Close by was the body of a young officer. His face, which had escaped the flames, was bony and beardless, very English; probably one of the fox-hunting classes, imbued with the cavalry tradition – the type who talked of tanks as chargers, their garages as stables. He had been denied the chance to ride into action in his armoured steed, the enemy in sight, crying: 'Tally-ho!' His passing had been devoid of glory, part-roasted in the confines of his Crusader II, destroyed by an unseen foe. His expression was oddly peaceful, eyes closed, small mouth slightly open, as though he was about to speak. Two feet away, near his outstretched hand, lay a second water bottle, quite intact, not touched by fire. It seemed the beardless officer had reached towards it as he died. It, too, was full.

It was the last. And on the tanks the radiators had boiled dry. Kit turned towards the Crusader track that would lead him back to the white-taped route across the minefield, and safety. He felt he should do something for the dead, but to bury them, single-handed, was a hopeless task. There were too many, and he was weak. Nor could he bring himself to intone some half-remembered religious mumbo-jumbo that, alive, these men would probably have scorned. And so he began to retrace his steps, swaying so that his heart started to pound, put off-balance by the water bottles' weight, once more damp with sweat and tension, scanning every inch of ground for a mine that had been missed; one of those bloody Bouncing Betties that could cut a man in half. He hoped the German would appreciate his effort. He looked towards the rising ground. No sign of the bugger now. Bloody rum. Perhaps he did have something up his sleeve. Pity he couldn't trust the chap. Their chances were much better if they stuck together and saw this business through.

Beppo Lutzow, prone and shivering, heard the crunch of the Englishman's boots as he mounted the slope beyond the rocky outcrop. The pain was extreme now, but he struggled to fight it down. He did not want to admit his weakness. Then the Englishman was standing over him, cradling water bottles in his arms.

'What have you been up to?' Kit Curtis asked. 'You look like bloody hell.'

'*Eine Schlange* – a snake. Down there.' Beppo pointed to the crevice floor.

'Down there?' Kit took in the area where the stones and rocks had been displaced, then saw the Webley. 'Ah, I get it now.' He placed the water bottles on the ground, but not where Beppo could reach them. 'You've been bitten, I assume. What sort of snake? Did you get a look?'

'*Braun*, like earth. Dark patches on the back.'

'Small horns? Just here?' Kit pointed to his temples.

'*Ja*, exactly so.'

'Horned viper. They're actually quite rare. Nasty bite, but probably not lethal, unless complications set in.' He paused. 'Serves you bloody well right.'

'Thank you,' Beppo said. He licked his lips. 'You have water.'

'Yes. British water carried by chaps your people killed.'

'*Das geht mir am Arsch vorbei!* I don't give a shit! Keep your *Scheisswasser!*'

'I intend to, old boy. It suits me just fine to have you laid low for a bit. Gives me a chance to think, without you prowling about getting up to mischief.'

Beppo said dully: 'What can I expect?'

'From the bite, you mean? Oh, swelling, nausea, some haemorrhaging from the mouth and bowels, possible necrosis. That's death of tissue around the wound. One of my blokes was bitten, so I know.'

'How long to recover?'

'No idea. Our chap kicked the bucket, but I recall the medico said that wasn't usual.' Kit relented. 'Actually, he didn't. Kick the bucket, I mean. He was back on his feet in a matter of days, but then, he had the advantage of serum to help the treatment along. Not that it helped much in the long run. He got bounced by a 109 near Mersa el Hamza a week or so later. Struck by another reptile, you might say.'

'Is there nothing to be done? For me?'

'I'm afraid there is, and believe me I don't relish the thought.'

'I do not understand.'

'I need a knife, preferably sharp and sterile. You haven't got one hidden, I suppose, waiting for me to turn my back?'

'No, I have no knife.'

'Otherwise you'd have used it, no doubt. Well,' said Kit, 'I'd better get my skates on. The longer the wound's untreated, the worse it will be for you.' He handed Beppo one of the water bottles, twisting out the cork.

'Here. I suppose after all you'd better have a swig.'

'Thank you.'

'That's all right. Naturally you'd do the same for me, wouldn't you?'

Beppo Lutzow did not reply. His leg was very swollen now, and he had to force himself not to cry out as waves of pain seemed to engulf his body.

The Englishman was moving away, slipping back down the slope, almost lost to sight. Beppo, his senses distorted by the spread of venom in his tissues, forgot to speak in English, and called out: '*Wohin gehen Sie?*'

The Englishman simply waved a dismissive hand. 'Don't guzzle too much of that ruddy water. It's got to last.'

Among the tanks once more, treading as carefully as before, Kit could find no suitable weapons on or near the dead – no combat knives, no bayonets. Perhaps the Tank Corps types did not expect to fight their war that way. But then, close by a Crusader, he found a handy shard of steel, cauterised by the inferno. He tested the edge against his thumb. It was as sharp as an open razor and left a fine incision. He sucked away the beads of blood and set off back along the tank track to the white-taped safe route and the rising ground where, hidden from sight, the German lay. When he reached him, he was barely conscious, and murmuring to himself, delirious.

Kit shook him roughly. 'Snap out of it, man. I need you *compos mentis.*'

The German opened and closed his eyes, once, twice, screwing up his face, trying to clear his brain. '*Mir ist kalt.*' His teeth were chattering.

Kit ignored him. He pulled him into a sitting position, took the material of the trouser leg in both hands and ripped it apart. It was soaked in pale blood running from the bulging puncture wound in the German's calf. Kit grimaced. 'Christ, what a ghastly mess.'

'Not good?'

'Not good.' Still, Kit forced a reassuring grin. 'First, that comic nose and now bitten by a snake. These things go in threes. I wonder what comes next?'

He tore two strips from the olive cotton of Lutzow's ruined trousers and tied them around his lower leg, above and below the wound, quite lightly, but enough to slow the flow of body fluids and the creeping venom. Then he held up the shard of blackened steel. 'This is where it gets interesting. Ever heard of cut and suck?' The German shook his head. 'Really?' said Kit, feigning surprise. 'I thought the Deutsche Afrika Korps covered every eventuality.' He paused. 'I can't promise this is going to work, but it's all I can do for you, lacking a nice cold compress or some handy snake-bite serum. It's going to hurt like the devil, I'm afraid. All I can say is, thank God you weren't bitten somewhere else.'

Holding the shard firmly, he cut into Beppo Lutzow's leg, across the swollen area of the wound. The man's yelp of pain was startling in its shrillness. The incision was deep, but not deep enough to interfere with nerves, veins, tendons, ligaments and muscles. The rush of blood increased, not dense and bright as normal, but pallid and thinned to the consistency of water by the anti-coagulant in the serpent's venom.

Kit bent and sucked hard at the laceration. He could feel the wetness flowing round his mouth. It had no taste or odour. He knew that it could not harm him, was hazardous only when in contact with the internal fluids of the body. This knowledge did not suppress his instinctive fear, and disgust at what he was required to do, to try and save this man.

At last he pushed the leg away, and rinsed his mouth with water from the bottle he had given the German. He spat into the dust, nauseous but unable to be sick because there was nothing in his stomach.

'That's it,' he said. 'A long shot, but it might just help. I'll have another go in a few minutes' time. Filthy business, isn't it?'

256

The German nodded slowly. His face was white. He tried to put firmness in his voice, but it came out as a whisper. 'Where did you learn such things?'

'Our medico filled me in, when that chap in my flight got bitten. Lucky for you I'm the attentive type.'

'It is dangerous for you, I think,'

Kit shook his head. 'No, not for me. The poison would have to enter my bloodstream. I could even drink the stuff, and suffer no ill effects. More risky for you, actually. My spit's not sterile. Could be complications. Be ironic, wouldn't it, if you bought it because of my spit? When I had another Spit in mind.'

Beppo did not understand the joke and Kit could not be bothered to explain. Besides, it seemed a facile jibe.

'What chance do I have?' said Beppo.

'No idea, old boy,' said Kit. He took the German's foot and rested it on a piece of rock, to elevate the leg. 'All you can do is wait. If you're lucky, that ruddy snake's just eaten, in which case it will have used up most of its venom.'

'If not?'

'I'd say you're in for a pretty uncomfortable time. But if our squadron quack has got it right, you'll probably live.'

Twelve

Over by the hangar the rigger, Haim Katz, was painting a narrow crimson band around the fuselage of the Storch, just ahead of the German cross. As Ossie Wolf came up, he paused in his work, the dripping brush resting in his hand, spots of paint specking the sand. He stepped back a pace or two, head angled, like an artist contemplating a half-completed canvas.

'That's real fancy, Felix,' Ossie said. 'Great brushwork.' With action imminent, his mood was good.

'I think maybe it take more than a little paint to show the British who you are,' said Katz.

'Oh brother,' snapped Ossie, 'meet the prophet of fucking doom. I got news for you, you dismal sonofabitch. Montgomery mentioned us in his order of the day. "On no account attack the little Storch with a red ring round its ass".'

'Ah,' said Katz. 'Well, that is very good.'

'Yeah,' said Ossie. 'Wouldn't it be?'

Mintz came across, carrying a jerrycan of fuel. 'The tank is about half full, to save unnecessary weight. You have a range of two hundred kilometres if you are not too heavy on the throttle and the prevailing wind is favourable.'

Ossie was still sore. 'Pepper, here's the deal,' he said. 'I won't tell you how to be an airplane mechanic. Don't tell me how to handle a ship.'

Mintz flushed. '*Es war nicht meine Absicht zu . . .*'

'Yeah, yeah, you didn't mean to. Just stick to topping up the goddamned gasoline, brother. Spare me tips on how to use it.'

Mintz put the jerrycan on the ground, as though he had something to say, but bit his lip, staring at his feet. In the silence, Katz called out: 'Hey, Yosef. Have you heard? General Monty has personally forbidden attacks on *unser kleiner Flugzeug.*'

Mintz stared at Ossie. 'Truly?'

'What do you think?' said Ossie. 'Just levelling the score with our sadsack over there.' Maybe he'd been a little rough. Mintz was an okay guy but most of all he needed him on side. He tried a grin and a playful shove towards the jerrycan standing by Mintz's feet. It didn't work. Mintz scowled.

'Haim and me, we know our stuff. You have no cause to doubt us. Palestine Airways had many machines – de Havilland Rapides, Short Scions. We turned our hand to all of them and never a complaint. No problem here, as well. Flying Officer Dobbs, he trusted us . . .'

'Uh-huh,' said Ossie. 'I guess you oughta know. Mulholland's filled me in on that poor mug Dobbs.'

Mintz picked up the can, still sour. 'He was a good fellow. Proud. An excellent pilot.'

'Is that a fact?'

'But not as good as you. You got him beat, in all departments except one.'

'Oh yeah?'

'He was a man who cared.'

'Jesus,' Ossie said. 'What is it today? The Feast of Saint Powderpuff, the patron saint of sensitive souls?'

'I do not understand.'

'The way I heard it,' Ossie said, 'Dobbs cared all right. He cared about his hide.'

'This butchery takes men in many ways. He had already done

259

very much. He understood his weakness. He was one of the bravest men I knew.'

'Sure. So brave he quit because he couldn't take it and compromised an operation.' Ossie was angry now, veins on his temples standing out, his face thrust inches from the fitter's. 'Jesus, you guys. I've been places. I've seen things. I could tell you stuff. Don't talk to me about humanity. Humanity's out of fashion. This is a battle for survival, fellers. Last bastard standing wins. Anyone with a yellow streak better step aside. Dobbs did us all a favour, except the thoughtless sonofabitch wrecked an airplane in the process. Hell, if he felt that way, he could just as easily have put a bullet through his brain.'

'Maybe it was an impulse, what he did,' said Mintz. 'He wasn't thinking straight.'

'No doubt of that,' said Ossie. 'I tell you, Pepper, don't waste your sympathy on a guy who couldn't make it to second base. What makes him so all-fired special? Why should he escape? Able to choose the time and place, when so many other suckers never get the chance?' He kicked out at the jerrycan. 'Now stick that goddamned gasoline in the tank and let's run through those engine checks. If there's one thing I can't stomach, Pepper, it's a sentimental Jew.' He said it with a twisted smile, but his eyes were hard.

That night, they sat outside the rudimentary hangar, the camouflage awning lashed down with ropes secured with metal pins hammered into the hard, flat ground that lay outside the camp's perimeter fence; ground where nothing lived except for a patch or two of camel thorn, a million bugs, a starving snake hunting the few *jerboas* hiding in their burrows and, for this night only, the members of an operation named for a man called Jorrocks who didn't exist and meant nothing at all to any of them.

They sat, not talking for the moment, staring at the sky – like kids, thought Ossie, like a bunch of expectant kids waiting for a

Fourth of July fireworks spectacular. The heavy silence was heightened by the emptiness of the Holly Force camp a few hundred yards distant; a camp without men or machines, except for a skeleton staff in touch with the various missions already under way. Close by, the Storch waited too, awkward-looking, less stork than gadfly, white moonlight reflecting on its skinny fuselage and the fabric surfaces of its wings. For the moon was full and shining very bright, strong enough to cast a shadow; shadows of the silent, almost immobile men, the angular machine, the canvas hangar whose outline on the dirt resembled a crouching beast.

Ossie was impatient. 'Jabo, what time you got?'

Jabotinsky squinted at his wrist. It was light enough to see the dial. 'Is coming up to 20.30 hours.'

'Fingers in your ears, boys,' Ossie said. 'The gunners are about to press the tits.'

As though on cue, they heard the crack of distant shells, high-air bursts to test the meteorological conditions and help the artillery plot its trajectories. A pause, and then at 20.30 field and medium guns opened fire along the entire front for fifteen minutes. The ground beneath them shivered and, where the horizon had shown as delicate silver, now it burned a livid scarlet streaked with yellow. Again, an interval of ringing silence. '*Bei Gott*,' said Willi Bahr, 'I would not be in a Panzerarmee foxhole now.'

'Let's hope they paste the suckers good,' said Ossie. 'Last bastard standing wins. That's what this show's about.' He glanced at Josef Mintz, crouching in the semi-darkness to his left, in case the guy had something on his mind, but Mintz said nothing and looked away.

At 22.00, to the minute according to Jabotinsky's watch, the rolling barrage was unleashed. It seemed to burst the sky apart, seemed too terrible a force to be man-made. A storm of shells from eight hundred guns that stretched along a line of forty miles began to pound all known and suspected enemy concentrations; gatherings of Panzer armour, Axis airfields, anti-tank-gun positions, trench complexes, stores of ammunition, transport and supplies, strategic strong-points of every kind.

In the Devil's Garden, the explosions of the shells mingled with the crump of detonating mines as the Allied gunners blew to pieces tracts of tangled wire and lethal ground, and the engineers moved forward to begin their work of clearance, marking out safe routes for tanks and men with tape stretched taut between iron stakes. Overhead, and barely heard above the tumult of the guns, formations of Wellingtons and Halifaxes moved steadily towards their objectives, largely unopposed, unloading their tons of bombs on targets already lit by flames.

No one in the little group close by the canvas hangar, outside the perimeter of Holly Force camp, had slept, or even talked, each man preoccupied with his inner thoughts, imagining how it might be to find yourself pinned down beneath a storm of ordnance with nothing to be done but pray to God that you might survive, if you believed in God, or if you didn't, pray to something, anything that might help you live. Nothing to be done but wait; wait to find out if you would be left intact while all around you others were shredded, minced and mangled, burned and blown to fragments, decapitated and disembowelled, rendered a smudge of blood and flesh or reduced to an oily pool; others you had known, from the heady days in Poland, France and here where, led by Rommel, victory had seemed assured, except that Rommel was not here to quell your fear and instead the Afrika Korps was led by tubby General Stumme, court-martialled by the Führer for blunders on the Eastern Front, but given another chance when the Army found that experienced commanders were, thanks to Russia, in rather short supply. No, Stumme would not soothe your fears, reassure you by his presence that this was not the end, that somehow you and your comrades would come through, that even now the Reich would still prevail. Such doubts had been unthinkable, a few short months ago, when the prize of Egypt had seemed within DAK's grasp, but now they entered the mind of every man who witnessed the Allied might, assembled to throw them back.

For five hours the barrage was sustained without a pause and then, at 03.00, it ceased. The smell of cordite filled the air. Still no one spoke outside the hangar. Then Jabotinsky delivered a prolonged, low fart, a puny sound, and comic compared to the thunder of the cannonade. It provoked a burst of laughter mixed with groans. Bahr, propped up next to Jabotinsky, fanned away the stench. '*In Gottes Namen*, Jabo, spare us your poison gas.'

'The Jabo bomb,' said Ossie. 'Monty's secret weapon.'

'We have four hours,' said Jabotinsky. 'At 07.00 the guns will start again. If the *Kommandant* is right, Stumme will be leaving his headquarters to assess the situation. We know his communications have been damaged, possibly destroyed. For sure, he will be confused. He may suspect this is the beginning of a big offensive, but he will not know. The only way he can learn the truth is by talking to his commanders face to face.' He studied the sky and nodded at Ossie and Willi Bahr. '*Sich vorbereiten*. Make ready. Now we go.'

Ossie stood up and brushed himself down. He banged his temple with the heel of his right hand and shook his head. A tinny resonance persisted in his ears, as if the noise of guns refused to go away. In the south-west sky, towards the void that was the Qattara Depression, the moon hung seemingly unchanged, but when he looked again, he saw it was less brilliant now, more indistinct, occasionally obscured by drifting veils of smoke, tarnished by what was happening here, a conflict on another planet, a mortal struggle, mightily important to the men who fought but quite invisible across the gulf of space.

He got into his flying gear – the black hide zippered jacket with the curious incision in the back, fine quality, expensive, no doubt a private purchase by its one-time owner, as was the service practice, with added shoulder boards to show the rank of *Leutnant*:

sand-coloured life-vest, tight-fitting leather helmet, soft leather boots. No oxygen mask required as, Storch-style, they would be flying low; no RT leads to be plugged in as wireless silence was to be observed, except for the coded message tapped out in Morse on a Wehrmacht field radio by Willi Bahr, providing the coordinates of General Stumme's position, when he was located. *If* he was located. Otherwise, there was no one back at base to listen or respond. If things went wrong, their fate would be unknown. They would simply disappear.

Ossie walked around the Storch, doing the routine external inspection with Mintz and Katz. Then he pulled himself into the pilot's seat. All controls responded, full and free. He gave a sign to Mintz and pressed the electric start button. The Argus engine churned and coughed and came alive. The stick of a propeller vanished in a silver whirl. He ran the Argus until it was good and hot. All engine instruments were showing what they should. He raised his thumb and killed the power and slid back out.

By the hangar Bahr was checking the grey-painted field radio, bulky in its webbing case.

'Holy cow,' said Ossie. 'It's a goddamned Frigidaire. You want we should leave the ground?'

'You think we land at Stumme's feet, *Amerikaner*?' said Bahr. 'We will have to march a little, I bet.' He patted the radio set. 'This we can carry with us, and also leave behind.' He pointed at the Storch. 'Better than transmit from that little bird. The Boche have keen ears, they listen out for things that do not fit. Better they find this box of tricks than spoil our travel plans.'

Nearby, on a bench, were laid out various weapons: sheathed fighting knives, greased and fiercely sharp, some lengths of paracord, a pair of MP38/40 machine pistols, a wooden box of half a dozen stick grenades and three holstered Walther P38 pistols. Jabotinsky took one of the pistols and handed it to Ossie who, before he fixed it to his belt, removed it from its holster and weighed it in his hand. 'I sure would like to get the Fat Boy in the sights of this little toy.'

Jabotinsky brushed away the thought. 'No, not our job. *Das Hund der den Hasen auspurt, ist so gut wie das der ihn fangt.* You are familiar with this saying?'

'You got me there.'

'The dog that starts the hare is as good as the one that catches it. We start the hare. The rest we leave to your Royal Air Force.'

'They won't let you down.'

'Is better not,' said the Legionnaire. 'Old Jabo does not care to risk his ass for nothing.' With Bahr he gathered up the rest of his *Feldgendarmerie* kit – the leather dispatch case, wooden baton and traffic wand with its big red disc. They climbed on board the Storch, Jabotinsky at the back, Bahr positioned behind the pilot's seat with his heavy radio at his feet, and Ossie last.

Yosef Mintz secured the cabin door, peering in, not seeing well because of the reflection and bad light. Through the scratched, refracting glass his features looked distorted, glossy, with the sheen of melting wax, like a man with burns, before the flesh begins to dry and pucker up. Ossie gave him one of his special signs – right thumb up and then the index finger jabbing forward, a cocky line-shoot that usually raised a nod and smile, but Mintz did not respond, turning and walking back towards the wingtip, ready, with Katz, to help guide the Storch as it taxied to its take-off point.

On the airstrip Ossie turned upwind and applied the brakes, the Storch shaking under power. He cranked the take-off flaps to *Aus*, the oiled chains meshing smoothly with the gears, throttled up and released the brakes. The machine began to move, clearly heavier than before, sluggish and protesting, sagging on its undercarriage, engine straining, flames spitting back from its stub exhausts. Ossie took his time, allowing the speed to gradually climb towards 40 knots, then pushed forward on the stick. Nothing doing. Okay, more speed. Now nearly 50 knots. It seemed this mission might end right here, buried in a dune. He pushed on the stick some more. At last the resistance began to ease. It was lighter now. He felt the tail begin to rise. He pulled the stick back hard. At 60 knots the Storch pointed up and climbed. He heard his passengers' curses turn to chuckles of relief. He made some height and levelled out, winding off the flaps. Then he set his course and put the Storch into a shallow climb, smoothing its passage through the air, conscious that with the weight it carried, the slightest updraught was enough to flex its wings. A moderate angle of attack was also good for speed.

He flew at first on instruments though able to see outside quite well, the landscape washed with a lunar glow, looking like the moon itself. At 4,000 feet he throttled back to a cruising speed of 80 knots. It was peaceful at this height, and yet not. Great flashes and explosions still lit the northern sky, although by now the barrels of the Allies' massed artillery had already begun to cool. But this was just an interval in the symphony of slaughter. Already the gun-crews, intent as musicians in an orchestra tuning up, were tending to their instruments of death, adjusting, cleaning, oiling; stockpiling fresh supplies of shells, preparing for the final movement, the crescendo, the climax to a singular first night that, for many thousands, would also be their last. The performance would resume in three hours' time. Three hours to find a single, small plump general among 100,000 men.

Until they picked out some passing feature on the ground, an ancient camel route winding through the desert, dust clouds raised by convoys crawling nose to tail, jagged lines of trenches exposed by fresh-dug sand, the telltale tracks of Panzer tanks criss-crossing the terrain like tangled string, it seemed they did not move, fixed motionless in the air, a tempting target for anti-aircraft guns. It was not unknown for gunners of either side to loose off at anything that caught their eye. Would the black crosses on the crawling Storch's wings be plain enough, in this faint light, for the hard-pressed crews of 88mm *Fliegerabwehrkanone*, faced by massed attack from many points, to look again and hold their fire? To Ossie it felt cock-eyed to fly above the Boche positions, slow and low, expecting the zip of flak at any moment, despite the Storch's markings. But nothing came. It seemed the Eighty-Eights had plenty more targets to the east, where a heavy darkness clung to the ground despite the silver-brightness of the sky, a darkness pierced by spurts of flame and pillars of oil-black smoke, like the eruptions of lava, hot ash and gas viewed from a volcano rim.

Ossie checked his watch and compass. The time showed 03.30, the compass was steady on its bearing of 342 degrees. Deir el Qatani would show up to starboard very soon, the first concentration of enemy armour that lay close enough to DAK headquarters at El Daba, on the coast, to be within reach of its commander *General der Kavallerie* Georg Stumme. If he followed the pattern predicted by Mulholland, he would venture out to assess, first-hand, the battle situation. The man could turn up anywhere, on a defensive line that stretched for twenty miles, and travel by land or air, maybe in a Storch, like Rommel the Fox himself, who flew his own machine and had been known to swoop down on a Panzer column and demand to know why its advance had stalled. The odds on nailing Stumme, Ossie figured, were worse than winning a multi-roll bet in a game of craps. But it looked like fun to try.

Then Willi Bahr banged him on the shoulder. 'Put us down! Put us down right there.' He was leaning forward, gesturing at a string of vehicles moving along a well-worn track in the early light of dawn, trailing dust that spread out behind the convoy like giant yellow feathers: tanks, half-tracks towing field guns, trucks loaded tight with men. 'The surface is clearly good,' Bahr said. 'Land three hundred metres ahead and to the right of the leading Panzer, *Herr Taxifahre*.'

Ossie nodded. 'Willi, I hope you tip real good.' He reduced power and came around towards the convoy downwind in a shallow turn, winding out the flaps, feeling the drag pull them back like a monster hand, upwind now, watching the attitude of the nose, keeping it raised to kill the speed, 50 knots too fast to land, but slowing, slowing, airspeed now barely 30 knots, right off the throttle, air shrieking through the wing struts. For a long moment they were flying parallel with the leading tank, and from its turret its commander studied them through his field glasses. Then, with Ossie holding the stick right back, the Storch's spongy tyres finally kissed the dirt, bounced a little on the ruts and started to roll. The tail came down and the skid dug in, flicking up stones against the drooping elevators, rattling like a tattoo on a tin drum.

'*Ausziehen!*' Bahr shouted, reaching for the handle of the door. 'Move!' His voice was strained. So, Ossie thought, this wasn't quite the routine mission these intrepid warriors wanted him to think.

He cut the engine, pushed up the door, secured it under the wing and jumped down. Bahr and Jabotinsky pushed past him without a word, the machine pistols slung across their chests scratching against their *Feldgendarmerie* gorgets, grasping their traffic wands, breathing hard and looking tough, the peaks of their steel helmets low above their eyes; eyes narrowed against the enveloping dust that swept across them from the convoy as it began to slow and pull abreast, separated by no more than fifty metres. The tank commander was out of his turret now and men were running forward from the trucks. Ossie watched Bahr and Jabotinsky march towards them, come smartly to attention and salute, present their papers for the *Hauptmann*'s scrutiny, then start to wave their arms around as if they ran the whole damned German army.

To Ossie it seemed the conversation lasted a long, long time. More men had joined the group. At any moment he expected Bahr and Jabotinsky to be exposed, disarmed and beaten down or shot. If so, for sure he would be next. He unbuttoned the holster strap of his Walther P38. The pistol's range was barely thirty yards. He would have to let them get real close.

Turning around, he reached inside the cockpit for one of the stick grenades and placed it very carefully out of sight behind the Storch's wheel, where he could snatch it up and take some sons-of-bitches with him and the Storch too. The idea that this might be the end gave him an odd charge, a pulse of adrenalin running through his veins. His body ached for action. If it had to finish, he thought, then this was as good a time and place as any.

But still the talk went on. The tank commander was not as tall as Bahr and Jabotinsky, and he had to stand back a pace or two, with folded arms and jutting chin to reduce the angle of his head and make himself look a big shot to his men. From this distance it was hard to read his face, but he showed no sign of doubting that these burly and assertive *Feldgendarmes* were who they claimed to be. And he was nodding now, saluting, turning back towards his tank, the group around him starting to disperse. So it seemed that after all this was not the time and place. Ossie picked up the stick grenade and replaced it in its wooden box. Jabotinsky saw him do it as he came up. 'Got you anxious, *ja*?'

'Thought I might have to bale you out.'

'*Ach so!*' Jabotinsky grinned and shook his head. 'It was like you say in the Royal Air Force, a bit of cake.'

They climbed back in the Storch and Ossie pulled down the door. 'So they didn't see through a couple of phoneys, huh? What in hell did you tell them you were doing?'

'The truth,' said Jabotinsky, from the back. 'That we were looking for General Stumme.'

'Jesus. Didn't they wonder why?'

'Of course. It's classified information. What do you think – that we trumpet our business to the world? But we drop the name of Rommel, tell them we can't say more. You see their eyes

269

light up at the magic word. He is their talisman, their idol. They would do anything for Rommel, hence anything for us.'

'Of Stumme they have no firm information,' said Bahr. 'The rumours are, he is near the coast – but nobody knows for certain. Communications are badly damaged, headquarters difficult to raise. They make reports but get nothing back. To them it does not matter. These men are Panzer grouped with Italian armour, to give the *Makkaroni* backbone as the *Hauptmann* put it. They know their orders and will carry out their battle plan, general or no general, unless he is the Fox.' Bahr leaned forward and tapped the chart on Ossie's knee. 'Set a course for Tel el Eisa, north-west of Alam Nayil, *Herr Taxifahrer*. That is the location of 15 Panzer and there we will demand more information. At least this time we have the password of the day.'

'Oh yeah?' said Ossie. 'You asked, they told you?'

'Correct,' said Bahr, 'thanks to the *Hauptmann*, our Rommel-loving friend. You must understand, if a *Feldgendarme* demands of you the password of the day, you do not hesitate to prove your identity.'

'That simple, huh?' Ossie asked.

'*Natürlich*. In these treacherous times, *Amerikaner*, no one can be trusted.'

'As I told you,' grinned Jabotinsky, 'a bit of cake.'

'So what is this goddamned password,' Ossie said, 'just in case I'm caught flat-footed?'

'Wotan,' said Bahr, 'chief among the gods. They love their Nordic mumbo-jumbo, these stinking Boche.'

Once in the air, Ossie turned downwind and made a low-level pass along the length of the Panzer column, waggling his wings. He thought it a neat touch. The men waved back, resuming their advance towards the east where the darkness lay, but it was greyer now, still shot through with bursts of fire and towers of smoke but spread about with the orange glow of the rising sun. Already there was the promise of cloying desert heat, despite the hour.

The flies would feast well today, gathering in black clouds on the bodies of the dead and wounded, dipping into their sweat and blood and excrement, gorging on the mounds of spilled internal organs and severed limbs; the only multitude whose victory was assured.

The time was close to 04.15, more than sixty minutes since they had taken off from base, when Ossie picked out the western fringe of the Devil's Garden. In the minefield tanks were burning, a straggling line of Crusaders, Grants and a few Matildas with their distinctive slotted flanks. Nearby were the wrecks of what looked like two fighter planes, their markings gone, but one a Spitfire, identifiable even from its twisted frame. He doubted the pilots had survived. It was no place to find yourself in trouble, even if you baled. Some kind of dogfight, maybe, in the early dawn, one to one, a test of skill and guile, yeah, fighting how it ought to be, not as it was below, where men were being blown to shreds by other men they never saw, or battled hand to hand in trenches slippery with blood, watched by ghosts who had killed each other in just this way for a thousand lousy years. He felt a moment's envy for the pilot of the Spit, free to engage in combat in that peach of a machine, on this bright clear morning with the whole damned sky as his arena. Then he snapped back to the present.

One thing he knew for sure: he wasn't quite where he was meant to be. The Devil's Garden told him that. Somehow he had allowed the Storch to veer marginally off course. Bahr's metal radio screwing up the compass's magnetic north, maybe, or his fault for not applying a touch more starboard rudder to counteract the crosswind that barely stirred the thick, almost fluid air; gentle but still strong enough to play tricks with this heavily laden toy machine. He recalculated their position south-west of Miteiriya Ridge, the deviation no more than a few degrees, and fed in subtle corrections through stick and rudder to restore them to their heading for Alam Nayil, the stronghold of 15 Panzer.

Willi Bahr had also seen the pulverised British armour, but his eyes were not as sharp as Ossie's, and at first he did not recognise it for what it was.

'*Was ist das?* Panzer?'

'Not unless they're in retreat,' said Ossie. 'They're heading west. Or were. They're our people. Nothing moving, that I can see. Looks like they took a wrong turn.'

'Looks like you took a wrong turn also, *Herr Taxifahrer*,' said Bahr. 'We should not be so close to *das Teufelsgarten*.'

'This is the scenic route,' said Ossie. 'If you don't like it, Willi boy, find yourself another ride.'

Keen as his eyes were, Ossie did not notice, 1,000 feet below, a single slow-moving figure descending a slight slope where a crevice cut into the desert floor, making for the minefield. If he had, he might have wondered what would motivate a man to enter such a place alone.

Thirteen

A day passed, and a night. The moon was on the wane, blurred at its outer edge, the craters showing clearly in the crystal air. The din of battle was constant, lighting the horizon, but very far away. Both men shook with cold but, for Beppo Lutzow, it was more than coldness that gripped his bony frame. Unlike the Englishman he could not sleep, tormented by the toxin that had filtered through his veins and organs, rendering his entire body as sensitive as an exposed nerve. Occasionally his head began to nod, only for the smallest movement to jerk him back, wincing with the burning pain that seemed to have reached his brain, inducing a rising panic close to fear. In the semi-darkness he was like a child, sensing nameless threats concealed by the shadows, waiting to pounce behind the rocks; like the bogeyman beneath the bed, the ogre hiding in the pattern of the wallpaper. Like a viper sliding unseen towards him, poised to strike.

Dawn came as a relief, but with it a lowering fatigue that made oblivion, or at least insensibility, a time of non-existence, seem attractive. It made him think that this must be like dying, and then he wondered if he was, and forced himself to shake off his exhaustion, so the Englishman would not see.

Water was very low, only half a bottle now, and neither man had eaten for several days. The Englishman had even pulled aside the rock, searching for the viper, ready to pound it with a stone, but it had gone.

'Pity,' the Englishman had said. 'I'm told they taste like chicken. Cooked, of course. We'd have had to eat it raw. Perhaps not such a loss.'

On the wound in Beppo's calf, a crust had formed. A little fluid seeped around the edges of the scab but still, the swelling had reduced. 'Perhaps after all you've saved me,' he told the Englishman, 'but only so I can starve to death.'

'Someone will be along.'

'Too damned late, I think. We'll be like those *Makkaroni* at the Gasr Haddumah fort, shapes in the sand, nothing to show how we came to be here or the manner of our death.' Beppo's words were slurred. He felt light-headed and half-believed that this was Matti Hartmann sitting by him, watching the sun begin to spill its copper light across the land; a land where beauty did not matter because there was no human here to see it, or rather, would not be soon.

Kit saw the man was feverish still. There was nothing he could do. Perhaps the fellow had it right. Perhaps it had been a waste of time, pulling him round from the viper bite to suffer a slower fate, tortured by thirst and starvation, a prolonged and painful exit, expiring bit by bit, weaker hour by hour and day by day. How long would it take? He hoped he would be able to go out remembering good times – those summers at Trebetherick, the careless days at Trinity, the flying, of course, at Kidlington and after, always flying; the day he gained his wings, that little embroidered brevet that meant so much; then Hurricanes in France, the battles over Malta in his Spitfire, that beautiful machine. And softer things: the touch of Juliette Garencière's hand upon his face, her voice, the promises they made, that, yes, they would survive and be together – thin hopes that now seemed thinner, her vanished in France, him here, perhaps about to vanish too.

He pushed all this aside. 'We're not dead yet, my friend. Tell me about your people, this hotel they run.'

A change came over the German's face, as though he had come back from another place. He stared at Kit as though surprised to see him. He fingered his suppurating nose, a minor ill he had forgotten. They talked . . .

They talked of flying, but in guarded terms, vague about the machines they knew. Easier to speak of Starnberg, where the wooded hills ran down to the cold blue lake; of Cornwall, where the surf curled into the golden coves; of student days, Kit's time as stroke in an Oxford eight, skipping yet another lecture, Beppo's spell in Munich at the hotel school, but drinking too much with a footloose crowd in the Marienplatz bars.

The memories created a momentary, slender bond, but Beppo's thoughts were still in Munich. '*Ah, München,*' he said. '*Hauptstadt der Bewegung.* You know this phrase?'

'No.'

'Capital of the Movement. Where it all began, in 1923 when they jailed the Führer. But they could not keep him down. Ten years later, he was back, and Munich became the headquarters of the *Nationalsozialistische Deutsche Arbeiterpartei.*'

'Ah, yes, the Nazis.' To Kit the mere sound of the words was distasteful. Now he wished to end the conversation. This man with whom he had shared some common ground seemed suddenly a stranger; an enemy once more.

'Just so. That is where I began to be aware.'

'Aware?'

'Where I began to understand.' Beppo frowned. 'You English, you are such hypocrites. No country but yours must spread its influence across the world, it seems. You forget this Empire you are so proud of was built on the backs of a subjugated people whose rights you pretend to respect. And now you call on them to sacrifice themselves in a war they did not want.'

Kit fought down his indignation. 'Ridiculous. They joined us willingly. They know very well the hellish world you people are out to create.'

'That is ridiculous also. We wish only to re-establish a nation betrayed by its politicians in 1918, those defeatists who failed the German Army, and allowed the Fatherland to be sliced up and disposed of like so much cake by a conspiracy of the so-called victors.'

'That all trips very easily off the tongue. Where did you learn such claptrap? From Doctor Goebbels's broadcasts?'

'It is the duty of the Reich to bring together all the Germans of Central Europe. To unite them in a single state. Not just populations with a German culture, like Austria, the Sudetenland, and Poland, but everyone of Germano-Nordic descent – the Scandinavians, the Dutch . . .'

Kit cut in. 'Do you actually believe this tosh?'

Beppo seemed to hear the mordant tones of Matti Hartmann, talking of Siegfried Schmoller, particular friend of Emil Gotz. 'One less *Nationalsozialische* toady will not be missed. One must take on these hardline stooges, and show there is more to the Reich than Adolf Hitler.' Had he become such a creature, then, a deluded stooge, parroting rhetoric? He shook his head, confounded. 'The pity is, we share many virtues with the English. Pride in nationhood, order, respect for authority, industriousness. Surely you cannot deny, we are much the same?' Hadn't Matti Hartmann said this also? Yes, he heard his voice. 'They are much like us.' Somehow, it was a comfort to know that at least he and Matti shared a point of view.

The Englishman was saying: 'No Briton would have voted Nazi, knowing what they stood for. You wouldn't find us so passive and complicit, ready to knuckle under to such a war-mongering bunch of racist thugs.'

Beppo knew he should not permit the Englishman to speak of the Reich this way but, though provoked, he experienced a kind of thrill to hear such condemnation, even from an adversary's mouth. It muddled his response, and he could only say: 'You mean our attitude to the Jews?'

'To anyone who threatens the purity of the so-called Aryan race.'

'You fail to understand. The Jews are not like us. They are a mobile nation – Jewish first, and German second. Their God is Mammon. They are a malignant force, in every country. They stick together, on a global scale, working against the national culture wherever they may be, siding with the Left to foment revolution and dissent.'

'What utter rot.'

'It has been proved beyond question that the Jews are a political, economic and cultural threat,' said Beppo, with more conviction now. His family had always disliked their wealthy Jewish guests who snapped their orders for food and drink, constantly demanding the very best, and strode about the lakeside grounds as though they owned the place, quick to complain and dispute the bill. 'Nothing would suit them better than to instigate a Jewish war, amassing profits and setting nations that resist their influence at each other's throats.'

Kit's face was pale. 'I wonder that viper wasn't sick. That the poison didn't flow the other way.'

'You will see,' said Beppo. 'You will better understand, when we occupy your country. At present you only see our warlike face. Our destiny is to be in partnership with other nations.' This talk was becoming tiresome. His head was throbbing; he found it hard to think. The shade of Matti Hartmann whispered in his ear, 'We are soldiers, Beppo, that is all. We fly, we fight.' But then came the insidious afterthought: 'However, it's hard to trust a corporal who believes he has the world within his grasp.'

Maybe Matti had it right. It was hard to trust. Hard to trust in anything. What had seemed so clear, so few years ago, was blurred now. He saw again the strafing of the Polish cavalry, gallant, doomed, the officer on the gallows in the pretty, tree-lined square, defiant and erect, the mother with two children in the execution pit, the ancient peasants shrieking as a Waffen SS *Sturmscharführer* booted them inside the blazing church. The price of war, the smaller horrors for the greater good?

'We are soldiers, Beppo, that is all.' That was better. That, at least, was a constant truth, and indisputable. He must hold on to that. To do one's duty would bring its own reward, would help to reassert the Fatherland's power and pride. It was all the Fatherland could expect of him and he would not fail.

The Englishman was smiling in his infuriating way, superior and assured. 'Occupy our country? Don't make me laugh. You had your chance in 1940, and couldn't make it stick. There's no hope for you now. Your mighty Führer's led you up the garden path. You've had it, old boy. It's just a matter of time.'

Fourteen

They did not need to navigate their way to the location of 15 Panzer at Tel el Eisa. It revealed itself by great rolling clouds of dust, flashes of high explosive and tracer flicking across the sky, white, red and green. To Ossie the desert looked like a giant parking lot, littered with German and Italian tanks, some *Panzerkampwagen IVs* still in action, pumping out shells from their 78-mm guns, others engulfed in burning diesel fuel, hit by fire from unseen Allied anti-tank positions and artillery support. In between the tanks rushed ambulances and trucks. When one was struck it kept on rolling for a time, small shapes leaping out, alight like candle flames, and squirming in the dirt.

They put down well behind the action, in a shallow depression 1,000 feet across, fringed by tamarisk bushes and camel thorn. Nowhere was it more than four feet deep, but it gave the fragile Storch some protection from the flying shards of metal that keened across from where the engagement was being fought, and might prevent it from being seen and singled out for attack.

A dugout was close by, about ten foot square, sunk into the eastern side of the depression, with railway sleepers for a roof and observation slits all round. Men were moving about inside, shouting, roused. Climbing out of the Storch, Ossie saw the outlines of machine guns, heard the metallic clank of weapons being prepared for action. It looked like a battalion headquarters that expected to be overrun. Further along the bank, to right and left, part-buried with only their barrels showing, two 88-mm artillery pieces were being readied by their crews. They showed no interest in the two *Feldgendarmes* who had jumped down from the tiny plane and were marching across the open space towards them. Men who expect to die have other things on their mind than *Kettenhunde* – 'chain dogs' in Wehrmacht slang – overbearing, bureaucratic, meddlesome even under fire, who might distract them from the task in hand.

A Panzer regiment *Oberfeldwebel* came through the dugout doorway. From where he stood, Ossie could see the man's face was contorted with a kind of screwy joy, his eyeballs bulging, his whole frame shaking with anticipation. Tucked into the belt of his camouflage smock were two grenades. A meat-red paw was wrapped around an MP38 sub-machine gun. He was all hopped-up, ready to loose off at anything on sight that seemed to represent a threat – like a couple of fake field cops who didn't get their story straight. Jabotinsky was giving it to him good, talking calm and reasonable, as if there was nothing going on, as if it was just some conversation in a city street, but all the time the NCO's sweaty hand was clasping and unclasping the butt of his machine-pistol.

'Stumme, you say?' he shouted. 'In all of this, you look for Stumme?'

Jabotinsky shrugged dismissively, like any *Feldgendarme* who did not care to bandy words. 'We have dispatches. That is all you need to know.'

The *Oberfeldwebel* was scornful. 'You think *uns alter Hasen*, us old hares, know what is in a general's mind, where he might turn up? If he has any sense he will stay well away from here. It is too hot for generals, unless he remembers how to use a Karbine 98. Unless, of course, he is the *Wüstenfuchs* himself.' The *Oberfeldwebel* nodded proudly. 'Then you would locate your general! Where Rommel is, there you will find the Front.'

Jabotinsky seized his opportunity. 'Believe me, *Kamerad*, the *Generalfeldmarschall* is here in spirit. And he has full confidence in General Stumme.' He narrowed his eyes. 'Don't you?'

The *Oberfeldwebel* looked surprised, and then defensive. 'I am a soldier. I have no opinions – I do what I am told.' He rallied. 'You puzzle me, *Stabsfeldwebel*. How is it you do not have accurate intelligence on General Stumme's position? Surely the *Feldgendarmerie* knows everything. That is what you would have us *Kanonenfutter* believe.'

'The General is on the move continually,' said Jabotinsky, 'as Rommel has ordered him to be. As he would be himself. Besides, he has no choice. Radio communications have been badly damaged.'

'I am well aware of that!' snapped the *Oberfeldwebel*. 'Who can tell what our situation is? Who can be believed? Like you – you drop in from nowhere to seek out information. We hear many stories about the Tommies' tricks.' He leaned in, suddenly suspicious, his finger moving on the trigger of the MP38. 'Show me your papers once again. Something is not right here.'

'*Recht so!*' said Jabotinsky. 'You forget your duty, *Soldat*, which is to obey. The *Feldgendarmerie* answers only to the regional *Kommandeur*. Now get back to your men. Clearly you know nothing of any use to us. We have no further questions.'

The *Oberfeldwebel* was not so easily brushed aside. 'Don't try to teach me lessons. I know how far your authority extends: non-tactical decisions. Non-tactical, *ja*?' He waved an arm. 'I am in sole command here. Our officer is dead. I do not take orders from *Etappenschwein*, rearguard swine. I demand your papers. If you refuse, I will assume there is a reason. Something smells. I have no time for this. Soon I must welcome Tommy.'

The barrel of his MP38 came up. Then, behind them, one of the Eighty Eights opened fire. The *Oberfeldwebel* turned his head. Shells were coming in. From the dugout rang the chatter of machine guns, nearby the dull thud of a grenade. The

Oberfeldwebel's mouth was open. He gaped as though this could not be.

There was a heavy report, a good way off, the six-pounder of a Crusader III, firing on a flat trajectory. Something burst ahead of the depression's forward rim. A spray of blood spattered Jabotinsky's chest. The *Oberfeldwebel* had lost half his face to a jagged lump of red-hot steel that flew on to miss the Storch by a foot and slashed down stalks of camel thorn on the depression's furthest bank. He staggered and dropped his weapon, staring at Jabotinsky with his single eye; his brains were resting on his shoulder. He took a single forward pace and began to fall, clutching at Jabotinsky's shoulders.

Jabotinsky pushed him off. 'Thank you for your help, *Herr Oberfeldwebel*.' With Bahr he walked back slowly to the Storch and Ossie acted casual too, though now the Eighty Eights were heavily engaged, and shouts and screams were coming from the dugout where the machine-gun fire had stopped, and underneath their feet the earth was quaking from the pounding of artillery and the clank and grind of tanks.

'Another bit of cake?' said Ossie.

Jabotinsky grimaced. '*Das Schwein* has spoiled my uniform.'

Ossie swung the Storch around at the far end of the dip in the desert floor, the bark of its engine barely heard above the storm of battle. Holes began to show in the fabric of the fuselage and wings, but although they sat exposed in the hothouse of a cabin, all angled glass, perched high inline like riders on a three-man bike, somehow they were not hit. The ground beneath the wheels was rough, but as the Storch gathered speed, its widespread gear legs and spongy tyres smoothed out the rocky, uneven surface and in the cabin they hardly felt a thing. At 50 knots the pressure on the stick began to ease and then, with the trademark Storch lunge, they were climbing almost vertically away but this time quickly diving down and hugging the contours of the terrain, using every rise and fall for cover.

For a long while no one said a word, Ossie flying due west to put some distance between them and where the action was, to give them thinking time, except he wasn't sure who was doing the thinking now. In the rear seat, Jabotinsky was trying to clean his tunic, using his fighting knife to scrape away the *Oberfeldwebel*'s blood and brains. Bahr had twisted in his seat, pointing out bits he had missed.

'Yeah,' said Ossie finally, 'well, that could have gone a whole lot better.' He moved the stick and made a shallow turn to starboard, going north once more, lacking any orders from the back. 'What made that sonofabitch so sore?'

Jabotinsky gave a bitter laugh, his fingers sticky, crimson. 'He told me that something smelled. Maybe he could smell a Jew. He had a Nazi nose.'

At that Bahr laughed as well. 'He got no nose, no more.'

'Hell, Jabo,' Ossie said, 'you smell as bad as any man, but not so I'd know your damned religion.'

He started to gain height. Below, more Axis armour was moving east, fanned out line abreast so the crewmen wouldn't eat each other's dirt, stirring up great drifting clouds of yellow powdery dust, something like the Harmattan haze that had swept across Fort-Lamy, hiding the Heinkel 111 that did for Tony Page. Jesus, Ossie thought, it seemed like years ago but was really only months. He felt a rage. He wanted to dive down but not in this apology for an airplane, instead in a Mark V Spit armed with guns and cannon, so he could get one back for Tony, and all the other guys who had died that day, and all the other days stretching back through Malta, Britain, France and Spain, any place where folks had stood up and fought the Fascist sons-of-bitches. His hatred was refreshed. He'd grown accustomed to the ways of the Boche, speaking their language every day, training as they trained, perceiving them as men. This was destructive to his cause. The Germans talked of *Untermenschen*. This was how he must see them too – sub human. He must not forget again.

Twice more they landed, each time closer to the coast. The sun was higher in the sky but still the desert lay obscured beneath a black-brown blanket of greasy smoke. The acrid smell of cordite filled their nostrils. The German guns were active now, matching the Allies shell for shell, understanding what they had to do, knowing this was no feint, no probing of their strength, no rehearsal for a later, bigger show, but the show itself.

Stumme would be a busy man, trying to make sense of that which made no sense, deprived of the fullest information, learning of some successes but also breaches in his defences where the Tommies were breaking through. More often hearing nothing, unable to form a view, to frame a strategy to throw the Allies back, apart from fight, not yield a metre of ground, as the Führer ordered, by throwing into battle every gun and every man, and standing fast because there was no other road than that which led to victory or death.

The sentries outside the Panzer fuel store on the Rahman track, where they next put down, did not share that view. They had not seen an officer or an NCO since the barrage had begun and did not know the password of the day. The four green recruits, fresh from patrolling the Comiso docks and eyeing up the Sicilian whores, were not interested in victory or death. They wished to live. This detail had helped them to escape the Front. But now they were consumed by fear, seeing the horizon lit by fire, ears ringing from the counter-barrage, trying to make sense of that which made no sense, like General Stumme, and statements like the Führer's, passed on slyly by Jabotinsky, that also made no sense. They were eager for news from the *Feldgendarmes*, but not that kind of news.

'Are things that bad?' said one, who was very young, a boy, sunk deep into the tropical greatcoat that had protected him against the cold of the desert night. His helmet, that seemed too big and wobbled on his head, was camouflaged with sand-coloured paint, but its badge with swastika and eagle had been left uncovered, carefully painted round. A cautious fellow, respectful of authority.

Jabotinsky ignored the question. '*Hören Siezu*,' he said. 'Listen to me. What traffic on this route?'

'Nothing so far. We are well behind the lines.'

'Aircraft, then?'

'Yours only, and some bombers, very high. Not ours.'

'No other machine like that?' Jabotinsky nodded towards the Storch. The sentry shook his head. 'Tell me,' said Jabotinsky, 'what orders were you given?'

'To await the arrival of *Panzertruppen* and help them to refuel.'

'You wait in vain. The Tommies are pouring through at many points. Now you have new orders. Destroy this fuel, before it falls into enemy hands.'

The lad was not a fool. 'Such an order must be in writing, *Herr Stabsfeldwebel*.'

'Of course,' said Jabotinsky. He opened his dispatch case, took out a pad of message forms and, with a pencil, scribbled out his order. He signed it with a flourish. The sentry took it, read it slowly, then folded it and slipped it into his greatcoat pocket, watched by his companions who had said nothing, apparently content for him to speak for them.

'You have explosives?' Jabotinsky said.

'We have *Stielhandgranate*.'

'That will do.'

'And after?'

'Remember what the Führer said. There is no other road but that to victory or death.' The sentry scrutinised his face anxiously, to see how serious he was, but Jabotinsky's expression did not change. 'It is for the Fatherland, *Junge*. Stand fast and, if you must, die on the field of honour. It is your duty to *der Grosster Feldherr aller Zeiten*, the greatest warlord of all time.'

Ossie, by the Storch, waited for the kid to burst out laughing. He knew, and surely everybody knew, since prisoners had been taken, that the phrase was common among the ranks of the dis-affected in the German Army who, since the Eastern Front, had begun to doubt the Führer's strategic grasp on the complex busi-ness of waging war. 'No other road but that to victory or death!' It was a nonsense, a melodramatic folly that could squander the Desert Army. So *Grossfaz*, the shortened version, was familiar to every man in every foxhole, even the staunchest Nazi. But not, it seemed, to this beardless youth. Instead he seemed inspired. His jaw set firm, he clicked his heels and shot Jabotinsky a crisp salute. Then he and the others turned and hurried off to find their stock of hand grenades and blow up what they had been ordered to protect.

Ossie watched them go, the *Untermensch*, the hated Boche, chattering in low, excited voices like children. He knew their dreams of glory were bound to end up on the wrong side of a firing squad, unable to explain, Jabotinsky's piece of paper screwed up and tossed aside, branded traitors to the Reich. Not under-standing, to the last. He surprised himself by feeling a moment's pity, but remembered that bright-eyed, obedient punks like these levelled towns and villages on the personal orders of the Führer, shot the men and transported the women and children to the death camps, because it was said the people were in sympathy with the partisans.

Back in the air, he said: 'Jabo, you should be on the goddamned stage.'

'An excellent performance, *ja*?'

'Better than the last. You reckon they'll blow the dump?'

'*Natürlich*. He was a good young soldier, that one.'

'Was.'

Jabotinsky laughed. 'Those schmucks, they are in big trouble, I think.'

'You've done for them, that's for sure.'

'Why waste our bullets?' said Willi Bahr. 'It suits us fine the Boche save us the job.'

Below, not far away, they heard the crackle of detonations and then the crump of diesel fuel igniting.

Jabotinsky grinned. 'What did I tell you? That good young soldier carries out his orders.'

'Okay, *Grossfaz*,' Ossie said, his hands and feet light on the Storch's controls. 'While you're in the mood, dish out some more.'

'You fly this course, I tell you when and where to land.'

'I've had it with this Russian roulette,' said Ossie. 'We've spun the chamber three times now. Pretty soon, you big ham, you're going to find yourself making your farewell appearance. I don't want to be at that curtain call.'

Jabotinsky's voice was thick with sudden anger. 'I am in command.'

'Sure,' said Ossie easily. 'But hear me out. You guys ever heard of Charlie Chan – the Chinese private eye? He say, "when searching for needle in haystack, haystack only possible location".'

Jabotinsky glowered. '*Ich verstehe nich.*'

'It's simple,' Ossie said. 'Let's go find the goddamned haystack.'

At 06.15 they reached the Luftwaffe landing ground close to Deutsche Afrika Korps headquarters at El Daba, on the Libyan coast. It was easy to identify, strewn about with the remains of wrecked and burning aircraft; mostly transports, but whether shelled or strafed or bombed impossible to tell. Others stood intact, or were in the air, setting off on sorties, or returning. The airfield had that universal look that airfields always have: an un-natural flatness stretching to a far horizon and set against a giant sky, deep blue without a hint of cloud but streaked with vapour trails, the signature of battles in the air. Beyond the landing ground's levelled surface of fine-grained sand, across the worn black tarmac of a highway thick with vehicles and troops, the Mediterranean, calm and deep blue also, licked empty beaches stained with oil and debris and, further out, were ships, haphazardly spread about, at every angle, spilled matchsticks on an azure carpet. Great twists of smoke were rising where several had been hit and smaller craft were circling round to pick up the survivors.

Other vessels were under way, trailing wakes that mimicked the vapour trails that hung above them, showing where the danger lay.

Further along the coast, about a mile away, a jumble of low-lying buildings identified El Daba itself, the site of DAK head-quarters, until now little more than a scratch on the map.

Few on the ground took any notice of the solitary Storch, approaching the airfield from the south. It was the usual work-horse, usual markings apart from the odd band of red ahead of the German cross, and no doubt the usual mundane mission. What could be of interest? It put down close to a machine-gunned Junkers Ju 52, upwind although the air was barely stirring in the rising heat, a nearby windsock, merrily striped in red and white, sagging against its pole. No interest, either, in the three small figures who jumped down from the Storch cockpit and paused for a moment, taking in their situation.

The snub-nosed Ju 52 transport lay with a broken back, its triple engines tilted to the sky. It had not burned but its fuse-lage of corrugated metal was perforated by countless bullet holes, and by the port-side exit door a body dressed in flying clothes lay face down, surrounded by a circle of drying blood. The door hung half-open on its hinges. The interior was dark, but shot through with tiny beams of light shining through the apertures like stars, and there more men were sprawled. Their blood had flowed along the sloping floor, in a rush at first, and then more slowly, seeping through the many holes and trickling down the aircraft's metal skin in coagulating beads.

Work parties had not reached this corner of the field, a quarter mile from where a cluster of military tents was gathered round a single-storey building, colonial-style, dirty white with tall arched windows and, for a backdrop, half a dozen drooping palms. Once picturesque but battered now, its thick adobe walls had been pierced by shells and cannon fire. There was much activity there. Ossie could tell the latest raid had been a very recent thing and, even as he looked, the leaves of several of the palms caught fire, ignited by a spray of aviation fuel from an exploding bowser. For an instant each palm-top created a perfect flame, pendulous and bright, like a birthday candle.

They took their weapons and set off together towards the building. Ossie came along, as they had grudgingly agreed. No hanging back this time. He was there as extra eyes and ears, and also as an extra fighting man. Either that, he'd said, or they could fly the goddamned plane themselves. They'd had their chance. This time, as Ossie had put it, 'was the last spin of the chamber'. This time it *had* to work. If not, it meant they'd failed, and all that was left to do was act the pest, like Mulholland had said – make nuisances of themselves. Strictly small potatoes.

They saw no signs of panic. The men they passed were disciplined and worked with purpose, many wearing only shorts and boots, their bodies tanned dark brown, veterans of the desert, ignoring the searing heat of wrecks, pulling at tangled spars to drag out the dead and injured, working in chains with pails of water to douse down fires, in teams to move aeroplanes, trucks and cars to safe positions, not hearing the sounds of agony and torment all around, heeding only orders, oblivious to the hum of exploding ammunition, the possibility of a fresh attack. Half-naked, with blackened faces, lit by bilious flame, they resembled a primitive tribe, united by a common purpose, driven beyond fear.

Ossie and the others approached the adobe building by the burning palms. The signs beside the entrance with its splintered door told them it was the administration block of a Luftwaffe *Geschwader*, a transport wing.

Ossie and Willi Bahr let Jabotinsky go ahead, and head on down a corridor towards an office where telephones were ringing and officers were jostling each other round a table, pointing at a large-scale map, shouting at staff across their shoulders, snatching reports and scanning them with bloodshot eyes. On their faces, mingled with tension and fatigue, was that same screwy joy of the Panzer man, understanding that the time had come, the time when everything must come together, everything for which they had trained and worked and planned; the ultimate test of their beliefs, their expert skills and nerve; the consummation of their careers; a battle to be fought and won, as they had always won. This time would be no different. They knew this. And in their faces, that certainty was clear.

Jabotinsky stood outside the door, as though awaiting orders. This time, he and the others would listen, pick up information at its source. This time they would say nothing, unless approached. Then offer very little. If it all went wrong, their only hope was a single word – Wotan – the password of the day, to turn aside a challenge. For in this place, a veritable eagle's nest, mere bluff could not be counted on for long. With each step, they knew, each passing moment, death was at their shoulder. But then they had understood that all along. At Holly Force base, they had been dubbed *ein Himmelsfahrtkommando*, a trip-to-heaven unit, a suicide squad, a black joke borrowed from the Wehrmacht.

The corridor was narrow. Men pushed past Jabotinsky, cursing. A Luftwaffe *Hauptmann* wearing a crumpled service cap thrust him roughly to one side. 'Get your great carcass out of the way, you oaf. Why block the door? There is hardly air to breathe. What business have you here?'

Jabotinsky opened his mouth as if to speak, but the Hauptmann waved a hand. '*Kettenhund*, don't waste my time. Make yourself useful. Go arrest some Tommies for wilful damage.' The Hauptmann slammed the office door behind him. The voices could no longer be clearly heard.

Jabotinsky came back down the corridor, he looking aggrieved. 'Those Luftwaffe sons-of-bitches. What they know?' He strode past Ossie and Willi Bahr, staring straight ahead, heading towards a broad rutted track lined with oil drums that led away from the landing ground in the direction of El Daba. He was walking quickly and the others had to half-run to catch him up. When they did, the man was convulsed with anger.

'That fugging *Hauptmann* better watch his step,' he seethed. 'He got no right to address a *Feldgendarme* like that.'

'You dumb bastard,' said Ossie, out of breath from keeping up. 'You're forgetting who you are. Or who you're not.' He began to laugh, and so did Bahr. They had to stop walking – they could not move for laughing. Reluctantly, Jabotinsky began to laugh as well. The three men stood there on the rutted track lined with oil drums, leaning against each other, laughing. They would pause and fight for breath and start to laugh again.

'It's really not that funny,' Ossie would groan, and it would set them off again. 'Jesus,' he would gasp, 'it's really not that funny.' The laughing was more than laughing at a gag, or even a comic situation. Its cause had been forgotten. They could not look at each other without being racked by mirth that wasn't mirthful any more, but sinister and dangerous, and hard to bottle up, like trying to get a malicious genie stuck back inside its jar.

Jabotinsky straightened up at last. 'Those *Transportgeschwader* sons-of-bitches, they don't know nothing.'

'Okay, Jabo,' Ossie said. 'We got the picture.'

Jabotinsky spat. 'We got no fugging picture. We waste our time. To hell with fugging Stumme. No chance of Stumme. Never any chance of Stumme. We – what you say? – we kid us. We go back now, pay Herr Hauptmann a visit. A *Stielhandgranate* or two, in that little room, do a very good job I think.'

'That's nickel-and-dime stuff,' said Ossie. 'We're out of time. I say we head on into El Daba. It's the only place there's an outside chance of picking up stuff on Stumme. Jesus, Jabo, what's your problem? Nothing's changed. We always knew the odds. They're stacked against us, sure, but I haven't come this far to settle a score with a guy who's put your fat nose out of joint.'

'I put your fugging nose out of joint, *Amerikaner*,' said Jabotinsky. 'How many times I tell you? *I* am in command!'

'Oh yeah?' said Ossie. 'Maybe we'd better have this out, right here and now, before you get us killed for no damned purpose I can see.'

They faced each other, not knowing if they were serious or not, and in that sudden silence came the rasp of a motorcycle exhaust. A Zündapp combination was bouncing along the track towards them. It wheeled around in a neat slide and stopped beside them with a shriek of brakes. The steel-helmeted rider pulled down his dark goggles so they hung around his neck. They could see he had spent a long time motorcycling in the desert because the goggles had left a permanent lighter mark around his eyes. He twisted the throttle to make the engine roar and die away.

'You are the fellows who flew in on the Storch?' he shouted. So they had been seen. The rider looked at Ossie. 'And you, *Herr Leutnant*, I see you are the pilot.'

Jabotinsky intervened. 'Identify yourself.'

'*Obergefreiter Frölich*,' said the rider. 'Of the *Aufklärungs-Abteilung*.'

'You have the password of the day?' demanded Jabotinsky.

'Wotan.' But the rider did not look at Jabotinsky. Instead he addressed Ossie. '*Herr Leutnant*, if you please, you and your comrades must come with me. The *Major* wants to see you without delay.'

As they talked, Bahr had moved slowly around the combination. Unseen, he was poised a pace or two behind the *Obergefreiter* seated on his saddle. His right hand grasped the handle of his fighting knife, his left secured the sheath. Across the *Obergefreiter*'s shoulder he stared at Jabotinsky, his mouth stretched tight in a feral smile, waiting for a sign. He teetered slightly, like an athlete anticipating the crack of the starter's pistol. The signal did not come.

Instead they heard the rumble of many engines. A convoy of trucks came slowly round a distant bend, carrying troops and heading for the landing ground; mostly three-ton Opel Blitz but interspersed with captured Fords and Austins. At their head, in an open Kübelwagen, a young officer stood upright beside the driver, gripping the windscreen with a leather-gloved hand, and staring eagerly ahead. He saw the small group by the Zündapp combination and threw them a spirited salute, which they all returned.

'Hah!' said the *Obergerfreiter*. 'He plays at being Rommel.' He nodded towards the soldiers in the convoy, packed in ranks. '*Fallsschirmjager*. Paratroop battalion. Tough devils. Soon they will be dropping on the Tommies.' He revved the Zündapp's motor, repositioned his goggles over his eyes and jerked a thumb at Ossie. 'The *Major* is an impatient man. You on the back, *Herr Leutnant*, the others in the chair.' He grinned. 'A tight fit, but it can be done.'

The *Obergerfreiter* did not spare his passengers, wheels often off the ground together, the Zündapp bounding across the ruts, squirming under power, only easing off his throttle as they reached the outskirts of El Daba where robed Arabs astride tiny mules mingled with the constant flow of traffic, mostly trucks and tanks, or herded goats across their path, cursed from every side, or squatted outside mud houses, shaded by the walls or clumps of palms, silent figures from a distant past, passive and incurious. Packs of half-wild dogs fought over scraps of garbage in the narrow streets. Stirred by the passing transport the humid air was heavy with the smell of diesel, cheap coffee and tobacco, animal dung and the excrement of man.

Some buildings had been destroyed. A sign hung crookedly outside a mound of rubble – *Bar-Ristorante Nazionale* – a relic of the Italian occupation, when El Daba had rested in the hands of General Graziani's desert army, urged by Il Duce to believe that war was beautiful, all that made life worth living: a belief not shared by many of his soldiers, some buried in the ruins of the bar where they had drunk bad wine and tried to remember, or forget, what quirk of fate had brought them to this place.

Close by, fenced off with posts and wire, were other dead, but these lay in well-dug graves, the fallen of the Fatherland laid out in neatly ordered rows as if still on parade, each marked by a wooden cross and gathered below the Nazi flag, hoisted on a lofty pole, but hanging limp, its swastika unseen.

Beyond the cemetery, a man was working on a patch of scrubby land, guiding a wooden plough pulled by a single camel, raising a drift of dust, preparing to sow an unknown crop for a harvest that might never come. They had time to note all this because, by now, the combination had joined the slow-moving line of vehicles on the coastal road. Once, they halted altogether, smothered in the fumes of a Maybach personnel carrier. The soldiers on the halftrack laughed to see them choke.

Despite the Obergefreiter's protests, Ossie swung off the pillion seat and walked a few paces into cleaner air. To his left, a dark alley led off the main highway. Arches ran along its shadowed length, before it twisted out of sight. Outside a coffee house, three old men were huddled over dominoes, absorbed, and further down, small kids were playing *isseren*, the Libyan game of sticks, throwing six split sticks in the air and scoring points for how they fell. A fat man in a djellabah and a crimson fez stood watching them, correcting their adding up. The sound of women's voices drifted down from shuttered upper windows, and on the roof tiles unseen doves clattered their wings and exchanged soft calls. The image fixed itself in Ossie's mind. It was as if the coast road was a river, this alley an undisturbed backwater, where old men and children still played their ancient games, and women found time to talk, heedless of that other world that shook the ground 100 yards away and filled the air with thunder.

They found the *Major* in his tent, between El Daba and the sea, one among a hundred tents, spaced out to reduce the risk of aerial attack, but this one large enough to contain a staff of more than twenty men. The *Major* was short and stout. Sweat stained the armpits of his *Feldbluse*. Steel spectacles gave him an academic air but his eyes were unblinking, cold: a teacher no pupil would care to cross. Two privates were snatching up field telephones that rang again as soon as they were replaced. Officers and NCOs were studying charts laid out on tables or conferring in small groups, raising their voices to be heard above the jangle of phones, the thud of boots and, outside the tent, the grumble of the convoys, the sound of aircraft overhead and the pounding of artillery to the east.

The *Major* made them wait, receiving written reports from every side. He read them quickly, selected a few with care and thrust them into a leather dispatch case open on his desk. The *Obergefreiter* cleared his throat.

'Ah, Frölich,' said the *Major*, looking up at last. 'Stand by outside. You will be needed very soon.' He stared at Ossie, Bahr and Jabotinsky. His gaze was penetrating, shrewd, as though somehow he knew them for what they were. Impossible, of course. Ossie returned his stare.

'Your papers,' said the *Major*. He took them and half-sat on the corner of his desk, checking each one with care.

'Schroer, I see you are one of us,' he said abruptly. For a moment Ossie did not respond, until he realised the *Major* was talking to him – *Leutnant* Heinz-Horst Schroer, reconnaissance pilot, in the same line of work.

'Yes, *Major*. *Aufklarungsflieger*.' He gave the *Geschwader* the details Mulholland had given to him.

The *Major* removed his spectacles and began to clean the lenses with a cloth. 'Then you must know *Oberleutnant* Kropp.'

A trap? Ossie shook his head. 'No, I am not familiar with that name.'

'Ah,' the *Major* said. 'Now I recall – Kropp was killed six months ago, after you were posted in. How quickly one is forgotten, eh?' He replaced his spectacles and added, musingly, 'Still, one would have thought . . .'

The danger was not past.

'I am not familiar with the name,' Ossie said again. 'Attrition has been high.'

'Attrition, you call it? You sound like a politician. Here death is death.' There was bitterness in the *Major*'s tone. He paused, then rapped out: 'What is the nature of your assignment?'

Jabotinsky stiffened. '*Feldgendarmerie* business, *Herr Major*.'

'Silence!' snapped the *Major*. 'I addressed the senior rank.'

'With respect, *Herr Major*,' persisted Jabotinsky, '*Leutnant* Schroer is under my direction.'

'Damn you, *Stabsfeldwebel*,' said the *Major*. 'Hold your tongue. That is an order. Speak again and I'll have you placed under close arrest.' At that moment, a *Hauptmann* took him to one side, handing him another document and whispering urgently in his ear.

Jabotinsky looked across at Ossie and Willi Bahr, and nodded at the MP38 machine-pistols hanging at their sides, his meaning clear. Ossie shook his head.

The *Major* dismissed the *Hauptmann* and handed back their papers. His anger had subsided a little.

'I have no time for pedantic *Polizei* nonsense, *Stabsfeldwebel*,' he said, 'nor do I have any interest in your assignment. It can hardly be more important than mine, so don't try my patience with details. I am countermanding whatever orders you have received with immediate effect. Any trouble with your superiors, get them to talk to me.' He gave a sardonic laugh. 'If they can get through, that is.'

Adding the *Hauptmann*'s document to the others in his case, he snapped shut the clasp and locked it with a key. Then he glanced up at Jabotinsky, this solid fellow, this good old soldier on whom, perhaps, he had been too hard.

'You understand, of course, the importance of *Aufklarung*

reconnaissance. We pride ourselves on moving fast. Light armour, halftracks, fast vehicles designed for the terrain, mad fellows like Frölich on his Zundapp. We are attached to DAK headquarters, its eyes and ears. Except the British have made it hard to see and hear. Their infernal barrage has knocked out much of our field-telephone system. In many places we are fighting blind.' He tapped the dispatch case. 'We are down to this, delivering vital information face to face, the only method that offers at least some hope of it reaching the right hands.' He lifted the case, as though testing its weight. 'This batch has particular importance, on which the outcome of the battle might turn. That is why I have taken it on myself to act as postman. I do not care to entrust the task to anybody else. But every minute counts, and setting off by road is not an option. Even Frölich cannot make our armoured columns disappear. That is why the report of your arrival was providential. The Luftwaffe's Storchs are either missing or destroyed. Now *Leutnant* Schroer can fly me to my rendezvous.'

The *Major* called for Frölich and handed him the case. Jabotinsky had not said a word, had barely moved, apart from flexing his fingers on his MP38. The *Major* pulled on his field cap. 'Don't look so perplexed, *Stabsfeldwebel*. Rest assured, my decisions enjoy the full support of the highest authority.'

'The highest, *Herr Major*?' Jabotinsky repeated.

'In Deutsche Afrika Korps, the very highest.'

It came to Ossie, and the others, what this meant. The *Major* was talking of General Stumme. He knew him as a man. Suddenly Stumme was real, no longer just a name, a grainy image in *Signal* magazine, elusive and remote, but tangible and even close. So close he might walk into the tent at any moment. But then the *Major* added: 'You, Schroer, may have a chance to confirm this for yourself.' His meaning was plain. Stumme was not here. As Mulholland had predicted, he was out there somewhere, assessing the situation at first hand as Rommel would have done. These despatches could be for him. It seemed they might even be heading for an appointment with Stumme himself.

The *Major* had a final order. 'You, *Stabsfeldwebel* – remind me of your name.'

'Kroseberg,' said Jabotinsky.

'Well, Kroseberg, your sense of duty does you credit. I have no wish to get you into hot water. One of my men will escort you to the commander of our *Feldgendarmerie* battalion. You can explain yourself to him. I am sure he will quickly sort things out.'

'With respect, *Herr Major* . . .'

'Damn it, man, I'm doing you a favour,' said the *Major*. 'You look as though you've come here from an abbatoir. Get yourself cleaned up. The *Gefreiter* here can come along, in case we run into any difficulties on the ground.' A private handed him a message form. He studied some scribbled figures. 'Our rendezvous has been confirmed, the time and place. These are the coordinates.' He stretched out his hand and snapped his fingers. 'Your flight plan, Schroer.'

Ossie hesitated. He had it tucked inside his leather jacket. But it did not show departure and arrival points, in the usual way, just pencilled lines to plot a simple course with added notes about the ETA en route. Authentic Luftwaffe issue though it was, it had been left unmarked. But now he knew he had no choice. He took it from his jacket and passed it to the *Major*.

'*So?*' said the *Major*. He raised an eyebrow in enquiry.

'Given the nature of our mission, *Herr Major*, and the situation in which positions can be attacked or overrun at any minute, it was decided that nothing should be written down.'

'Hmm.' The *Major* weighed the point. 'And the position of your base?'

Ossie spread out the chart. 'Due south of Deir el Qatani, not far from 15 Panzer.' He pointed with a vague and filthy finger at a featureless area near the Rahman track.

'You might as well tell me you are stationed on the moon,'

said the *Major*, shaking his head. 'What a place this is. When we get to Cairo, the *Kameltreiber* can have it back with pleasure.' He folded the chart and put it in his tunic pocket and then, with great deliberation, tore the message form into tiny pieces. 'I am also prudent. I will hold the coordinates in my head and plot them in the air. Frölich, kick some life into that oily beast of yours and take us to the landing ground. Time is short.'

Ossie looked at Jabotinsky and held out a hand. '*Hals-und Beinbruch*, Jabo. Break a leg.'

They froze. So natural to use the name like that, easy on the tongue, one word enough to end it all. It passed unnoticed by the *Major* and his men. Jabotinsky, eyes accusing, did not reply. There was nothing to be said. Besides, he understood his situation. Soon he would find himself being questioned once again, no doubt in an easy way at first, but that would quickly change. His story would not stand up. It would not take them long to find the holes. His papers would be checked again, and exposed as fakes. If it had been an ordinary Panzer unit, he might have had a chance. But the *Feldgendarmerie* knew its job, was thorough and suspicious, trained to sense when the pieces did not fit. He was doomed and could not even fight, because the others had to reach the Storch, be safely in the air and out of reach, before he was discovered.

That was his only objective now, to string things out by any means, to give the others time. Then, well, he hoped it would be quick, kicked along to where they did such things, given a bullet in the head, rolled into some shallow, unmarked pit. It seemed a stupid way to go, but these days most ways of going were stupid, so how could he complain? A soldier led a soldier's life, and often died a messy death. That was how it was. At least they'd had uncommon luck, with this twist of fate that had led them to the *Major*. If Willi and the *Amerikaner* could flush out their little fox, his death might have some value, even now. Perhaps it was not so stupid, after all.

He did not want to see the others any more. He wanted them to go. He turned away without another glance, he heard the shuffle of their boots, the motorcycle's roar, the spin of tyres. He was alone, but not alone because a soldier, nervous and respectful, as soldiers often were towards the field police, said: 'If you're ready, *Herr Stabsfeldwebel*, I will escort you to the *Feldgendarmerie* battalion.' He was keen to please. His attitude would alter soon enough, thought Jabotinsky. He might even be the man they picked to pull the trigger, by that fugging unmarked pit.

'This is your lucky day,' the soldier said, as they headed away from the *Major*'s tent. In the distance they could hear the Zundapp, revving hard.

'How's that?'

'While your comrades take off for the Front, you can have a breather.'

Jawohl,' said Jabotinsky. 'Yes, you're right. A breather would be good.'

Hardly had he said the words than a wash of vivid light lit up the sky. A wave of sound ripped across the desert from the east, as loud as a clap of thunder, but thunder that did not pass.

The soldier flinched. *'Mein Gott.'* He did not notice that the *Feldgendarme*'s face had broken into a jubilant grin.

It seemed to Jabotinsky that every Allied gun in all the world was firing. By his watch it was precisely 07.00 hours.

Fifteen

Conscious of his status, the *Major* was unwilling to share the sidecar of the Zundapp, He leaned back against the squab with his dispatch case clasped against his chest, his head held high, ignoring the occasional sprays of grit and stone that flew up from the front wheel and struck his face. His only protection was a pair of British Army-issue gas goggles, worn over his spectacles, the type adopted by the Desert Fox himself. Rommel had taken his from a captured British general and now they were much-prized booty, quite the fashion with DAK's senior command.

Ossie's rank as *Leutnant* had earned him the pillion seat while Bahr half-crouched on a footrest by the rear wheel, hands gripping the tubular metal frame. The outfit looked, to Ossie, like a stunt about to happen, an act put on by Putt Mossman's motorcycle circus. As before, the mercurial Frölich made few concessions to his passengers, inspired it seemed to even greater feats of daring by the savagery of the Allied barrage that lit up the horizon and pressed upon their ears, as if he had to prove himself, to show he had no want of courage although he was merely the rider of a Zundapp and not commander of a Panzer tank.

They jolted along the rutted track, past the Luftwaffe building with its now blackened palms, and slithered to a halt between the Storch and the carcass of the Junkers Ju 52. A Luftwaffe ambulance was parked close by, its rear doors open.

The *Major* eased himself stiffly out of the sidecar and brushed himself down. 'Next time, Frölich,' he said straight-faced, 'you must show me your paces when we are really in a hurry.' He was not without a touch of humour and Ossie felt a momentary disquiet. *Der Untermensch*? These lousy contradictions. Even Frölich had his points, the madman who only knew one speed, now roaring back towards El Daba.

The last few corpses of the bomber crew, on bloody stretchers, were being pushed on board the ambulance. 'Poor devils,' said a *Feldwebel* with the badge of driver. 'Not one escaped.' He saw them moving towards the Storch . 'Ah, so it is yours, *Herr Major*,' he said. 'The mystery plane.'

'Why so?'

'No one has seen the crew.'

The *Major* frowned. 'They reported to me in El Daba and are under my command.'

'*Ah, alles gut*. The *Geschwader Kommodore* is a stickler for procedure, even in the middle of all this. He went through the roof when he was told an unknown aircraft had landed here without permission.'

'Unknown?'

'Well, unknown to us, *Herr Major*,' said the *Feldwebel*. 'They say a check accounted for all Storchs in this sector, except for yours. And apparently no one reported in on touching down. Not my business though.' He climbed behind the wheel and engaged first gear. 'Well, at least the mystery has been solved.'

'Inform the *Geschwaderkommodore* that I will report to him when I return,' said the *Major*. He watched the ambulance move away and turned to Ossie. 'So, a Storch that does not exist. Can you explain?'

Ossie looked surprised. 'What is there to explain, *Herr Major*?' He pointed to the building by the palms. 'We reported there. They had no time for us. The place was in an uproar. No wonder they've bungled things and got their numbers muddled. We lost our patience and set off for El Daba. Luckily, Frölich saved us a long walk. At least, we thought it lucky until he touched the throttle.'

At that the *Major* smiled a little, but it quickly faded. 'Your objective was El Daba then?'

Ossie breathed in hard. This was getting tough. 'So we understood. Only *Stabsfeldwebel* Kroseberg knows the purpose of our trip. No doubt he would have told you as much as his orders permitted, *Herr Major*, but you said there was no time.' He was sweating, trying to work things out before the *Major* fired another question. He felt as though he was being hunted down. But then he realised it did not matter what he said. He was talking to a dead man. Except the *Major* did not know it yet.

'Yes,' said the *Major*, 'that is true. Time was not on my side.' But still he was uncertain. 'It is curious that we were not warned of your arrival, if your mission was so important. I am very near the top and get to hear most things.'

'You know the *Feldgendarmerie*, *Herr Major*,' said Ossie, with a glance at Bahr. 'They have their methods. Sometimes they are closer than the Abwehr.'

'Well,' said the *Major*, apparently dismissing the matter from his mind at last, 'nothing can be more important than this task.' He tapped his case. 'You see, I carry history in my hands.' He gave a little laugh to show he was half-joking but Ossie could see he liked the phrase.

The Storch was as they had left it, less than an hour before. Or almost, Ossie realised. The cabin door hung loose, unlatched. With manpower short, no doubt the ambulance crew had been ordered to inspect the little machine while they were on the spot. He wondered what they had made of the radio behind the pilot's seat, the stock of hand grenades. He swung up and secured the Storch door beneath the wing. He saw that the radio and grenades were still in place. That figured. No junior ranks would take it on themselves to remove such things. All would be reported.

Shove the decision up the line, that was the German way. It suited Ossie fine, and bought them time.

The *Major* was pacing about some yards away, his arms behind his back, his fingers hooked around the handle of his case, history bumping against his calves.

Bahr leaned in close to Ossie. 'You think Jabo has a chance?'

'No. He's a goner, that's for sure. Let's hope he stalls things long enough for us to fly this sucker where the *Major* wants to go.'

'You think it is also where we want to go?'

'Maybe. Maybe not. But the way I see it, it's the only game in town. Sounds like we could be rubbing shoulders with the brass. I say we play it to the end.'

Bahr shrugged. 'No problem for the *Himmelsfahrtkommando*.'

'No problem,' Ossie agreed. 'Now get on up there, Willi boy, and get those goddamned *Stielhandgranate* stowed out of this sonofabitch's sight.'

The *Major* saw Bahr settling in the rear seat and ducked under the Storch's wing. He saw the man-pack radio at once. 'This radio. What purpose does it serve?'

'*Stabsfeldwebel* Kroseberg thought it wise to bring our own equipment,' said Ossie quickly, 'to improve our chances of reporting back to base.'

'Commendable,' said the *Major*, pulling himself on board. 'But reporting what to where? As you say, your Kroseberg is as tight-lipped as an Abwehr agent. You would think we were on different sides.'

Ossie laughed at that. He slipped into the pilot's seat and, from his position at the controls, secured the door. The engine churned, and coughed and burst alive. He cranked the flaps, released the brakes and the Storch began to move. To his left, along the rutted track a good way off, he saw a half-track raising dust. It was moving fast, armed men on board. The airplane took its usual time to get to 40 knots, but now that time seemed stretched. The tail was heavy and the prop blast on the elevators froze the stick. In Ossie's hand it felt like a steel rod set into cement. He pushed forward hard, the muscles of his right shoulder straining, taut. The tail came up a little and then, reluctantly, a little more. The tyres began to skip across the ground. There was that buoyancy, that sensation of floating free that always made a pilot's spirits lift a little too. And then Ossie felt a hint of looseness about the stick. He pulled hard back and the ground began to drop away. Cranking up the flaps, he eased the power, fighting his instinct to push the throttle lever through the gate. At a cruising speed of 80 knots, the Storch began to claw its way to 1,500 feet.

Ossie looked down and watched the racing half-track through the starboard window. It had reached the shattered Ju 52 where it slewed around. The men jumped down and ran about, checking out the bomber, before they gathered in a group. They were staring up against the sun that made it hard to see the tiny plane that droned east towards the Front. He saw them get back in the half-track and set off for the Luftwaffe building by the blackened palms.

He grinned at that. They'd be lucky to find someone to give them the time of day, let alone an airplane to put up, forty minutes into a fresh artillery assault.

Ossie did not mention the half-track to the *Major*, busy with the map and chewing on a pencil-end. Hell, why should he? There was no damned reason to think it had anything at all to do with them.

Sixteen

The nervous soldier had taken Jabotinsky to an open-sided tent where a young *Feldgendarmerie* officer was pacing to and fro, shouting into a field telephone. The sound of the Allied artillery was very loud. The ground vibrated gently beneath their feet and dust was drifting down from the canvas above their heads. The officer was having trouble understanding and making himself understood. Occasionally, he would hold the handset at arm's length and stare at it accusingly, as though the piece of Bakelite in his hand was responsible for the bad communications. He took no notice of the nervous soldier or Jabotinsky, apart from shooting them a quick glance and turning away, the receiver pressed hard against his ear, presenting them with his back. Finally he slammed the handset down. His mood was bad. 'No sense,' he muttered. 'No sense, no orders, no information. Chaos, only chaos.'

'*Herr Oberleutnant*,' began the nervous soldier.

'I'll speak for myself,' said Jabotinsky. 'You can go.'

The nervous soldier hesitated, staring from face to face, but did not move.

'What is this?' the officer said. 'Can't you see? My hands are full. Go and bother someone else.'

Jabotinsky turned to go. The telephone rang. This time, when the *Oberleutnant* picked it up, it was plain he could hear clearly what was being said. He listened with care, eyes fixed on

Jabotinsky, nodding and chewing at his lower lip. Jabotinsky had moved away.

'Wait!' called the officer, the phone still to his ear. 'You there, *Stabsfeldwebel*. A moment, please.' He replaced the phone. 'I am told you wish to report in to your unit.' He sniffed. 'I cannot promise much, but at least we can have a try. Your papers, please.'

'This can wait,' said Jabotinsky. 'You're occupied with more important matters.'

'No, no,' said the *Oberleutnant*. 'I am sick of trying to make sense of garbled nonsense. A simple task will be a welcome break. Besides, I would not dream of turning away a fellow member of our force.' He held out his hand and beckoned with his fingers. 'Your papers now. I will see what I can do.'

Jabotinsky had moved back towards the desk. He had slipped the safety catch on his MP38 and his forefinger was resting lightly on the trigger. But then he thought about the others at the landing ground. He eased back the catch to safe and rested the weapon on a chair so he could reach the documents in his *Feldbluse* pocket. He passed across his leather paybook and *Feldgendarmerie* identification card.

The *Oberleutnant* flicked through them with little interest. 'All seems to be in order.' He pushed them to one side. 'I understand, Kroseberg, that some questions have been raised about the nature of your mission.'

'Questions? Well, it is of a secret nature, that much is true.'

'I see,' said the *Oberleutnant*. With a jerk of his head he dismissed the nervous soldier who saluted and hurried out. '*So*, Kroseberg, now you can relax. You are no longer dealing with the Boy Scouts of the *Aufklarung*. You are back among your friends. However, you must be plain with me if you want my help.'

'I would like that,' said Jabotinsky doggedly. 'I would like that very much. But I have my orders.' He could see no other way than to spin things out, and hope an opportunity might present itself to work his way out of this sorry mess. Perhaps the *Oberleutnant*'s phone would ring again, or urgent orders would come in, or El Daba would be subject to a new attack – anything to distract the man from his fleeting interest in the minor matter of an NCO engaged on confidential business who only wanted to check in with his unit.

'Your objective was El Daba, I understand?'

'That is what I told the *Aufklarung*.'

'Is it or is it not true?'

'*Herr Oberleutnant*, I have my orders.'

'I see. A moment please.' The *Oberleutnant* dialled a number. 'Wendt, report to me immediately.' He smiled across at Jabotinsky and neither of them spoke. The MP38 was resting on the chair, just out of reach. An *Unterfeldwebel* hurried in. 'I have a headache for you,' said the *Oberleutnant*. 'Try to raise the commander of this unit.' He gave the man Jabotinsky's *Soldbuch* and identification card.

'It may prove difficult, *Herr Oberleutnant*,' said the NCO. 'The situation is changing by the minute.'

'Really, this is not the time,' said Jabotinsky. He took up the MP38 as casually as he could and slung the strap across his shoulder, so the weapon rested easily across his waist.

'No excuses, Wendt,' snapped the *Oberleutnant*. 'This *Stabsfeldwebel* is engaged on a special mission. For the present, his orders prevent him from saying more. Such discipline is to be admired. Advise his commander that he has reached his objective in El Daba. Then put him on the line.' He grinned at Jabotinsky in a friendly way. 'Your commander will be pleased to hear you are safe. He can confirm to me your mission in the broadest terms while I can reassure him that we are doing everything in our power to support you in your task. Then you can speak to him yourself.'

He paused, gestured to Jabotinsky to sit down and offered him a cigarette from a silver case. 'You understand, of course, that this is not entirely altrustic. I realise your orders are explicit, but obviously I must satisfy myself that things are, what shall we say, entirely as they appear? A formality, of course, but strange things have been known in this desert war. Both sides play games, practise sleight of hand, what the British call dirty tricks. One should never be surprised. Complacency and carelessness are our enemies as well.'

Jabotinsky strained to catch the sound of an aero-engine starting up. It emitted a distinctive growl, that big V8 Argus, but the landing ground was a good way off and he knew it was unlikely to be heard against the general uproar. Anyway, he doubted the others would have reached the Storch yet. He glanced at his watch and was surprised how little time had passed since he last checked it. The second hand seemed to hesitate before it moved. It was no longer merely measuring time. It was counting down.

He looked at the *Oberleutnant* drawing contentedly on his cigarette, his booted legs stretched out. He studied him as a hunter regards a kill – impassive, calm, considering where the shot should strike. He doubted he would have the chance. Yes, spin things out, that was the only option. He was still involved, still playing his part, still fighting, even by doing nothing.

The *Oberleutnant* began to talk of before the war, his comfortable family home in Leipzig, his admiration for the Führer, his recruitment to the *Hitler-Jugend*, his abhorrence of the Jews. It followed a predictable path.

Jabotinsky ceased to listen, remembering the white light of Sidi-bel-Abbes when he signed on for the Legion, the bugle blowing *Réveil* at 5.00 a.m to herald another brutal day, the human dross that was the average legionnaire, drawn from among outcasts of every creed and colour, the pledge to serve France with honour and fidelity, knowing he was there because he had killed a man who took his wife, the woman to whom he had made a similar pledge, his rise to *caporal-chef* before he killed another man, a *sous-lieutenant* who kicked and cursed him as the bastard of a filthy Jewish whore, and something went inside his head, one curse too many in a lifetime's curses, echoing down the years. He had got away that time, helped by those the *sous-lieutenant* had also kicked and cursed, and worked his way to Palestine on merchantmen that plied their trade along the North African coast. But there was no one to help him now.

The *Unterfeldwebel*, Wendt, came back in. Without looking at Jabotinsky, he placed a written note in front of the *Oberleutnant* and murmured in his ear. The officer read the note with care, glanced up at Wendt, and read it a second time, his face quite without expression. He did not look at Jabotinsky either. Pointing to something written on the note, he nodded his agreement. Wendt saluted and left.

'Well,' said the *Oberleutnant*, 'that's that.' He stood up and began to walk about, rubbing his hands together as though he was cold. He paused. 'Surprisingly enough, we have managed to get through to your unit.' He paused again. 'Or rather, the unit you claim to be part of. They have never heard of you. Can you explain?'

'Impossible,' said Jabotinsky. 'Is this a joke?'

'I am not laughing, as you see. Is there anything you wish to say?'

'*Herr Oberleutnant*, I protest. This is wasting time.'

'Time is certainly running out,' said the *Oberleutant*. 'Look, may I suggest we cut things short? Tell us who you really are. It will save us all a good deal of trouble, and you'll make things easier for yourself in the end.'

'I must speak to my unit personally,' Jabotinsky persisted. 'I am in a secret detachment. It is quite possible that whoever the *Unterfeldwebel* talked to was not aware of its existence.'

'Your commander, for example? For that is who we talked to.'

Jabotinsky heard the scrape of feet behind him. His MP38 was snatched away and his arms were wrenched behind his back. He tried to stand but lost his balance, falling face down on the dirty floor. The cigarette he had been holding between his lips was crushed and burned his mouth. Men were dragging him to his feet. He spat away the smouldering fragments. The *Oberleutnant* misunderstood.

'Defiance, I see. Not sensible in the circumstances.'

'This is ridiculous,' Jabotinsky protested. 'You are creating a lot of trouble for yourself.'

The *Oberleutnant* came up very close. 'So, you continue your charade? Well, I suppose you have little choice. This must be a bad moment for you – the worst. You must feel very lonely now, but don't worry. Soon you will have company. We will reunite you with your comrades. They have not been gone so long. I have already dispatched a vehicle to the landing ground to pick them up. I am a thoughtful fellow. It will save them all a walk.' He placed his hand on Jabotinsky's stubbled jowl, like a concerned friend. 'I'm afraid you're in for an unpleasant time. You will tell us all we need to know.' He drew his hand away, then brought it back sharply, something between a slap and a blow. 'It's just a matter of time. How long is up to you. But of course, you realise this, being in the trade you are. Excellently done, I must admit.' He nodded at the men who had pinioned Jabotinsky's arms. 'It's all right. You can loose your hold. He knows it is all over.' He held out the silver case once again. 'While we wait for confirmation, perhaps you would like another cigarette? It may be your last.'

Jabotinsky wiped his mouth and took the cigarette. As he inclined his head to accept the *Oberleutnant*'s light he thought he made out the distant throb of a big V8, so faint it might have been imagination, his mind playing tricks. But instinctively he knew it wasn't. The *Oberleutnant* had not counted on that lunatic Frölich and his Zundapp, covering the ground as though the devil was on his heels. He grunted at that, the picture of Frölich beating the fugging devil. He'd beaten him all right. He knew because now he could hear an aeroplane climbing under power, in a sudden lull. Its engine note was quite distinct. He inhaled the tobacco deep into his lungs. It gave him a moment of euphoria. He felt alive and strong and able to bear pain. What faced him seemed a pity. But with the others gone, nothing that happened here mattered any more. That knowledge also gave him strength.

Seventeen

The *Major* had come well equipped; with a hand-held marching compass, a pair of hefty Panzer-issue binoculars, painted yellow tan, that hung around his neck, a pistol in a leather holster at his waist, its butt towards the front, and stowed in his dispatch case a wooden map board complete with metal clip and lengths of elastic to hold a chart in place. To this he had secured the map and, pushing his spectacles back onto the bridge of his nose, he quickly plotted the location of their rendezvous from the co-ordinates he had memorised. Their current position was easily confirmed. The railway station at El Daba was still in sight, a stop on the single-track line that ran from Alexandria, 120 miles to the east, all the way to the terminus at Mersa Matruh, sixty miles west.

The *Major* reached forward and banged the back of Ossie's seat. 'Continue as we are. Keep the railway line in sight. Soon we will reach another station, Sidi Abdel Rahman. I will give you a bearing then.'

Ossie called back over his shoulder, 'Don't rely too much on that footslogger's instrument of yours, *Herr Major*. The metal radio by your feet might throw your readings out.'

The *Major* did not reply. They were flying parallel with the coastal road and below stretched a long line of trucks loaded with men and supplies, or towing artillery pieces. Heavy and medium

313

tanks had taken to the flat scrub on either side, fanning out like competitors in an overland race. Ossie could not hear the racket of the Storch's engine because of the noise of guns, although they were nearly twenty miles from the Front. The plane did not appear to move against the thin ribbon of track below, seeming to hang suspended like a model aircraft on a piece of wire. Only the needle of the airspeed indicator marked their sluggish progress.

Five miles from Sidi Abdel Rahman they came upon a considerable armoured force, stationary and gathered in neat ranks, mostly Panzer IIs and armoured cars. Ossie pointed down.

The *Major* nodded enthusiastically. 'The Ninetieth Light Division, waiting in reserve.' Puffs of exhaust smoke showed they had their motors running. 'You see,' he went on, 'they will not be waiting long. Soon they will advance. We're told they will face an Australian division. Our Panzer boys will quickly teach those kangaroos a lesson.'

Ossie had an image of a piano flying through a window, bars broken up, skulls cracked, whole areas of the Birka transformed into one vast brawl. And that was simply what the Aussies did for relaxation. The stories of their relish for a fight, with fists or weapons, in beer-fuelled high spirits or to the death in battle, inspired or prompted dread, depending on what uniform you wore; not always an Axis one. He reckoned the *Major*'s Panzer boys could be heading for a lesson or two themselves.

Quite soon they came on Sidi Abdel Rahman itself, a scatter of Bedouin dwellings close to a curving beach of white sand that ran down to a transparent sea, a band of opal close to the shore, hard blue further out, bland waters that rose in a gentle swell and broke in tiny waves. But moving with the waves, imitating life, were the shapes of men, and parts of men, nudged and bumped by drifting flotsam: fuel cans, lifebelts, clothing, shards of wood, all black with oil that spread across the surface like ink blots on a sheet of green-blue paper. Where the flotsam had reached the beach, groups of Arabs were picking busily through the mess. To Ossie, from the height of 1,000 feet, they looked like the Coney Island crowd, any summer Sunday.

The *Major* banged the back of Ossie's seat again. 'The station. Circle here. I will give you your bearing now.' They banked around the small white building with its single platform. The tracks shone silver in the sun. The Arabs on the beach began to scatter, as if they feared attack.

The *Major* passed forward a piece of paper. 'Here is your bearing, *Leutnant*. One seventy-four degrees south-south-east. ETA fifteen minutes. Mind, I expect precision now.'

Ossie checked his watch. It was 08.00 hours. They held the course for five minutes, then the *Major* took up his big binoculars and began to scan the terrain uneasily, working them jerkily from side to side. 'Reduce your height to one hundred and fifty metres. And keep us steady, damn it, so I can see.'

Ossie put the Storch into a shallow glide, reducing power, speed eased back to less than 50 knots. Gradually the ground became criss-crossed with tyre- and track-marks, some routes more worn than others, and pock-marked with fresh craters left by many shells. The confusion of tracks grew dense. Ossie could see dugouts now, men firing from entrenched positions, some Eighty Eights in action, a Panzer brewing up, a crewman struggling in its turret engulfed in burning diesel fuel. Lazy blobs of coloured lights curled up from the left, slow at first then zipping past, so close the Storch rocked. Ossie heard the familiar crack of flak and something struck the steel tubing inches from his head and ricocheted away.

'*Verdammter Mist!*' the *Major* shouted. 'We are too far south and east, you blockhead. That rising ground is Miteiriya Ridge. You've taken us into the thick of the fight.' At the same moment there was a crash like someone dropping a box of tools, followed by a torrent of expletives. The steel cockpit filled with metallic fumes.

The *Major* was writhing in his seat, clutching at his legs. '*Mein*

Gott, mein Gott.' Blood was oozing from a spatter of little wounds, but he quickly gathered himself. 'It's nothing, nothing,' he rasped. 'I'm only lightly peppered. Flak fragments have pierced the floor. Your radio took the impact. It won't be broadcasting "Das Mädchen unter der Laterne" for a while.' That little touch of humour that hinted at the man within was not welcome, given what they had to do.

The sky was smudged with dark clouds of bursting flak. Ossie half-rolled and dived to a safer height, pulling back on the stick and levelling out. He didn't like to pop a guy who could raise a smile. He had to goad the *Major* into anger. Insolence should do it. 'Didn't I tell you to watch out for deviations on that toy compass?'

Instantly the *Major* was incensed. 'Watch your tongue, you insolent pup. Don't blame my compass for your mistakes. Obviously your flying is at fault. Now take us out of here, before you kill us all.' He bent his head over the map. 'Here is another bearing. Three thirty-eight degrees north-north-west. That will take us precisely to the spot, but not if you continue to handle the controls in such a slapdash manner.' He leaned forward. 'A warning, *Leutnant*. Do not provoke me. I am a dangerous enemy to have. If you value your skin, you will remember that.'

That was better, thought Ossie, much better. 'Don't worry,' he said. 'I do and I will.' Then he added, in a more conciliatory tone: '*Herr Major*, can you at least tell me and the *Gefreiter* what we're looking for now, so we can keep our eyes skinned also?'

'Very well,' said the *Major*. 'No reason now that you should not know. Our rendezvous is with a single staff car on a minor track, in a sector less exposed to enemy attack. It will be travelling south with three men on board – a driver and two others. We should come upon it very soon. Despite your little diversion, our timing is good, just four minutes from our ETA. When you sight this vehicle, waggle your wings and land as quickly and as close to it as the terrain and situation permit. The enemy may be closer than we think, so do not shut down. I will not be detained long, just long enough to deliver this.' He touched the dispatch case on his knees.

Ossie spotted the dust trail first, a vehicle moving fast, too fast to be a truck and raising insufficient dust to be a tank, a half-track or an armoured car. Closer to, they saw it was an open Horch, containing two officers in the back, both moving with the pitch and roll, the driver energetic at the wheel, avoiding the bigger potholes on the broken surface of the track, correcting slides with an expert touch. No Panzer pennant was showing on the offside wing, no flash of red and black and white, to denote a general on the move. But Ossie's stab of disappointment was quickly gone. At this place and time, insignias of rank would not be wise. It did not mean a general was not on board, even Stumme himself. Then he pushed the idea from his mind. Experience told him luck didn't work that way.

He came in diagonally across the Horch, at a height of 90 feet, air speed less than 30 knots, rocking the Storch's wings. The car had slowed, the driver still alert, watching the track ahead, the officers looking up from the rear seat, one angular and tall, the other short and portly, a swoop-fronted grey-green field cap angled over one eye. Something glinted on that eye, a wink of glass.

Sonofabitch, thought Ossie, could it be? By all that's holy, could it be that this is the monocled Stumme? Now, drifting over-head and very close, he made out touches of gold to the man's *Schirmmütze* cap, to the collar patches and shoulder boards of his tropical tunic. No mistake. No mistake at all. The guy was a goddamned general, all right, a top banana making his presence known, someone doing it Rommel-style. Even if it wasn't Stumme, Ossie reckoned, here was a target of opportunity worth laying his butt on the line for. He knew that Bahr would feel the same. But with the radio wrecked by flak, calling up the fighter boys was out. They'd have to come at it a different way. Somehow they had to work things out, improvise as they went along. For that they needed time. He'd hoped it might prove tough to land, rough ground maybe or coming under fire, so he could put some distance between the Storch and the staff car, but the track below was broad and flat, apparently unthreatened, so there was no excuse not to put the Storch down real close.

By now the car had stopped, the driver jumping down and swinging open the big rear door like a slick chauffeur arriving outside the Cotton Club on Broadway and 48th. The general descended stiffly, stretching out his arms and stumping about to restore the circulation in his legs. The tall officer was leaning forward from the rear seat, giving orders to the driver. The general paused in his exertions to watch the Storch bank around, its big flaps down, and drop towards the track behind the Horch at its usual steep and crazy angle so it seemed that it must crash, but touching down without a bounce and trickling along towards the waiting car, its tiny propeller a shining disc. Until, well short, Ossie applied the right rudder, gave the V8 a burst of throttle to generate some prop blast and swung the Storch abruptly round in its own length. The manoeuvre, sudden and unexplained, bought them space to plan their move.

Bahr knew what he had to do, and everything happened fast. The *Major* began to shout to move up close. Bahr rose up behind him, stooping a little because of the low cockpit roof. He had a length of paracord stretched taut between his hands. He slipped it over the *Major*'s head and tightened it against his neck, his face set in a triumphant grin. '*Ich bin ein Jude!*' Bahr screamed in the *Major*'s ear. Dry croaks were coming from the man's throat. His hands were scrabbling at the cord but quite soon fell away, still twitching slightly, palms upwards, resting on his case. His spectacles had been twisted in the struggle and lay across his cheek, the lenses blind.

From his training, Ossie had known it would be quick. But even so he was startled by the speed with which a simple cord could sever the trachea, crush carotid arteries, jugular veins and vagus nerve, and break a neck. The *Major* had been startled too. His crimson face was frozen in disbelief, eyes bulging, mouth agape, tongue flat against his lower lip. When the paracord slipped free, his chin fell forward on his chest.

Pushing the lolling head aside, Bahr fumbled in the *Major*'s pockets and held up the dispatch-case key. Ossie had opened and secured the cockpit door and stood beside the Storch, its engine running slow, the propeller making lazy circles, staring across towards the Horch 100 yards away, where the portly general was standing feet apart, hands on his hips, and glaring back. The unlocked case fell open. Bahr pulled out the sheaf of papers contained in a cardboard file and laid them to one side. He reached down for a *Stielhandgranate* and pointed at the leather case. Ossie understood, and nodded, tapping on his watch and jerking his head towards the Horch. Bahr held the wooden handle of the stick grenade and undid the screw cap on its base. A porcelain ball fell out, attached to a loop of cord. He mimed a tug and extended the fingers and thumb of his right hand. 'Five seconds.' Then he stuffed the case with crumpled sheets of paper from the file, enough to support the grenade laying slantwise with its pull-cord dangling down outside. His eyes met Ossie's. 'Beware of messengers, yes?' He unslung the machine-pistol from around his neck and passed it across to Ossie, who cocked the weapon and rested it against his waist. Ossie thought of saying something, it seemed that kind of moment, but he couldn't think of anything.

Bahr climbed out of the Storch with the case and they began to walk towards the Horch. The general did not move. To Ossie he certainly looked like Stumme, but then most German brass affected that haughty Prussian mien. It was clear they had him puzzled, hardly a big surprise. He'd been expecting a *Major* of the *Aufklarung*, a man he knew. Instead he'd got a flying jock and a military cop. But Ossie saw no sign of weapons raised. Why should there be? The *Major*'s absence could be down to many things: a casualty of war, a justifiable change of plan, a crisis at El Daba, the usual lousy communications situation. No reason to suspect that these two men were not what they appeared to be.

The MP38 was swinging on Ossie's hip and he steadied it with his hand, but slowly, wary of any action that, even now, might prompt suspicion. He heard the creaking handle of the leather case swinging at Bahr's side, the crunch of gravel underfoot, the thrum of flies wheeling round their heads, the thrashing of the Storch's prop and beat of its idling engine. He had gotten so used to the cacophony of battle that he barely noticed it any more; instead was conscious of these smaller, more subtle sounds.

They were close now, twenty yards. The driver of the Horch was gunning the engine, keen to be away. Propped up against the back of the driver's seat, the tall officer had fixed them with a pair of field glasses, his cap pushed back. The general maintained his martial pose, arms folded on his chest, only the tapping forefinger of his right hand betraying his impatience. To Ossie the scene seemed fixed in time, imprinted on his retina like a photo in a Nazi propaganda sheet.

Walking steadily, breathing hard. Just ten yards now. And then they heard a distinctive thud, less than a mile away. 'Mortar,' muttered Willi Bahr. But whose? Another thud. If they were the target under fire, that was all they'd hear. No whistle of descending shells, as Joe Public always thought. The mortar was like a tossed grenade, its velocity too slow to create a rush of noise, arriving as a deafening blast that seemed to come from nowhere. But mortar fire was not precise. It took the crews a round or two to get the range. The first shell burst far short, blowing a shallow crater in the track 400 yards away. But it left no doubt about the target. Bahr and Ossie were prone, faces in the dirt. Hot shrapnel fizzed above their heads. They heard it bouncing off the armour-plating of the Horch, dull clunks like rocks being thrown against an empty metal drum.

Ossie craned his neck. The Horch was already on the move, but a rear wheel caught a jagged rut. The heavy-treaded tyres began to spin in a fog of rubber smoke. The general had ducked towards the car, in a creaky grandpa's lope, miraculously untouched. The tall officer was crouching down between the seats, holding open the rear door. Another detonation – the second shell – closer by 100 yards but landing in ground that sloped away and absorbed its force.

Bahr sprang up as the echoes died and began to run towards the Horch, his arm extended, holding out the case, with Ossie on his heels. But now the car was in reverse and moving fast, its gearbox whining with the strain. Then the driver disengaged the gear, put full lock on the wheel and hit the brakes. The engine screamed as the Horch slid round in a bouncing arc, caught in a cloud of drifting dust, neatly facing the way that it had come. The manoeuvre caught the general by surprise, one moment about to climb on board, the next exposed, alone, and thirty yards back along the track. He did not move, too proud perhaps, requiring the Horch to reverse again and pick him up. Coolness under fire, that was the Erwin Rommel way. And so he stood, like any solid burgher waiting for a taxicab.

Bahr was close, calling to the general, gesturing urgently with the case. He was putting on quite a show. The Horch was coming backwards down the track. It stopped between them. The general raised himself onto the far-side running board, then beckoned for Bahr to continue round and deliver the case. He looked approving, as if impressed by such soldierly zeal.

Ossie had been fumbling with his weapon as he ran. No need for caution now. In minutes it would all be done, one way or another. His mouth was dry from running. He felt the urge to laugh. The safety catch of the MP38 was stiff. As his eyes flicked down he stumbled on a rock. He rolled and landed on his back. He heard again the thud of mortars, once, twice. On his knees, about to rise, he saw Bahr tug the pull-cord of the stick grenade.

His arm went back to toss the case towards the general, half-hidden by the Horch. Five seconds. At four, the first mortar shell hit quite close. Bahr was struck before he could complete the throw. Three seconds. He wavered stiffly, his arm locked back, the handle slipping from his fingers. He lost his grip. The dispatch case hit the ground behind him. Two seconds. Bahr, back arched, was falling, falling. One second. He hit the ground in a puff of dust, stretched out for a moment on the case. Time out. The burning fuse ignited the grenade's explosive head. Bahr's body lifted to the muffled blast. When Ossie reached him, he moved his lips. His voice was faint. '*Mutti, mutti.*' Some burning papers had escaped and flew about like frightened birds. The second shell came down, but further off. It didn't worry Bahr. He gave a final sigh. A small blood-streaked bubble quivered on his lips and burst. He looked like a kid who'd drifted off to sleep.

Ossie snapped off Bahr's *Erkennungsmarke* dog tag and as he thrust it in his pocket he heard the grate of gears, a burst of revs. The Horch was accelerating hard, but the general was still outside, straddling the running board, gripping the coachwork and the fabric of the folded hood. He had lost his general's cap. A small, bald man on a wild ride. The tall officer was struggling with the door but it opened at the rear and the general's body was in the way.

Back on his feet, Ossie threw up the MP38, flicked off the safety catch and squeezed the trigger. Nothing. One of the Parabellum cartridges had jammed, through sand or grit or any goddamned thing; the weapon's most common fault. He threw it down and snatched the Walther P38 from the leather holster at his waist, the piece he'd balanced in his hand that day he'd told old Jabo he'd like to get the Fat Boy in its sights.

The Horch was swerving round the Storch in a well-held slide, and moving fast, but Ossie knew this could not be rushed. No longer an idle notion, he had the Fat Boy in his sights but the Walther's effective range was little more than fifty yards. He steadied himself, hands cupped around the pistol's butt, the muzzle slightly raised, and emptied the eight-round magazine, spacing the shots from right to left, allowing for deflection. He fired without much hope. The Walther seemed as puny as a pop-gun at a county fair. But something flew up from the tall officer's head, and he fell back in the car. Ossie felt no satisfaction. The general was still there, hanging on like a Keystone Cop. It was kind of a funny sight, except he couldn't raise a smile. He'd gotten that close, within a pistol shot, but no use beefing now. That little old window of opportunity had creaked open a tad when, if a guy was ready, he might seize his chance. Now it was slammed firm shut, the moment lost for good. Bahr had ridden on ahead, and Jabo too. And all Operation Jorrocks had got to show was a Panzer officer winged and an airplane full of holes.

Was it Stumme, that distant tubby figure without a cap, hauling his ass to safety? He hoped not, strongly. Jesus, he thought again, to come that close . . . He stared after the receding Horch as it mounted a crest where the track cut between two dunes and caught his breath. The running-board was clear. No damned general. The guy was gone. He wondered what it meant. Maybe he'd tumbled in the car, fixed the door somehow. By now, the Horch had dipped behind the rise, making for the coast. Then on the track, before the crest, veiled by settling dust, he saw a sprawled-out shape, what looked like arms and legs flung wide; no movement, just that unnatural stillness that even from a distance tells the fighting man he's looking at a stiff.

The mortar fire had ceased. The action had moved elsewhere, the advance thrown back or ordered to a fresh objective, some-thing more important than the lobbing of a shell or two at a Jerry staff car caught in the open; a sideshow so the mortar crews could polish up their aim.

Ossie picked up the MP38. He didn't try to clear the maga-zine; something told him not to bother. He raised the barrel in the air and squeezed the trigger. This time it fired. He had known it would. It was Murphy's Law. Anything that can go wrong will, at the worst time, in the worst way. But still there was that shred of hope, that maybe that bundle of something on the track would turn out to be a man. Could it be he'd bagged a general, after all? Although the more he looked, the more indistinct the shape became, now just a shimmering outline in a pool of silver, seeming to sink slowly, about to disappear, imagined, an illusion. The flies were already gathering on Willi Bahr, dense round his eyes and in his slightly open mouth. Ossie closed his lids. The flies rose up, noisily disturbed, but quickly settled back.

The propeller of the Storch was still thumping the air with a beat as regular as a timepiece. Ossie's watch showed 08.26. Sixteen minutes from touch down. Sixteen minutes from the paracord tightening round the *Major*'s neck; the *Major* who still moved to the engine's throb. From Willi Bahr being alive and dead. From a Panzer staff officer standing confident and assured beside his commander, on a tour of inspection, to lying in his own blood in the back of a bucking Horch. From a general acting the big shot to acting like an extra in a Mack Sennett short. The question was . . .

Ossie not only knew the question. Now he knew the answer. He had shut off the Storch's power and headed up the track towards the place where it cut between two dunes; where, a little before that point, something was stretched out on the ground, not a bunch of rocks or a shell crater caught in shadow, playing tricks, but getting sharper, clearer now, certainly a man, a corpulent man, a man flat on his back with touches of gold on his collar patches and shoulder boards. The insignia of a general.

Ossie knew the man for who he was. He recognised him from his photos, even without the monocle that had left a mark around the prominent right eye. Sparse hair, close-cropped; well-shaved heavy jowls; a cheery sort, the kind who was popular with the troops until he sent them forward. But not so cheery now, his features chalky, his lips and ears dark blue.

Ossie felt for a pulse in the pudgy neck. The flesh was already cool. He could find no wound. He turned him over and the corpse emitted a long and lingering fart. No sign of injuries on the ample back. Ossie pulled him back. General der Kavallerie Georg Stumme, commander of Panzer Group Africa, successor to Rommel the Fox. His mouth was pinched in, giving him a senile look, just some old feller who'd had a fall and, along with his dignity, had lost his dentures. Ossie remembered, back in St Louis, the ancient fossil Mr Krapf who taught them math in the fifth grade and dropped down dead, right in front of the class. Later, they were told his heart had given out. But when he was lying there, the deadest thing they could imagine, it was as if he'd performed some kind of trick, had vanished and left this husk, like the larva of a dragonfly shrugging off its skin and flying some other place. So with Stumme, not hit by bullets or flying shards of mortar shell but a victim to a faulty pump. Nobody could touch him now. He'd flown some other place. Ossie had come to see him dead. He'd got his wish, but not as he imagined.

He wondered how long it would be before the driver of the Horch realised he had lost a passenger. He could go miles before he hit a Panzer stronghold. He imagined the situation. 'Hold up, driver. What's the rush? Have you got the Tommies on your tail?' 'Clear the way. This is the transport of *Herr General* Stumme.' '*Herr General* Nobody, surely? We see only a *Hauptmann* with his brains blown out.'

Ossie bent down and, with his fighting knife, cut the ribbon of the Knight's Cross that rested at the general's throat. He slipped it in his pocket where it clinked against Bahr's metal dog tag. He left the body where it was. No doubt they'd ship it to Berlin for some fancy Nazi ritual to mark a hero's death in action and hush up the fact that they were planting a greybeard with a bum ticker who'd fallen off a speeding car.

The area was quiet now, just Ossie, an airplane and three fresh corpses. He went back to the Storch and pulled out the *Major*'s body. The man's spectacles were still hooked around an ear. The blood had crusted on a dozen flak punctures in his pants. In his breast pocket there was a photograph of a nice-looking woman and two nice-looking kids outside a nice-looking house. Not fake, like Ossie's. Stuff was written on the back but Ossie didn't read it. He tore it up and let the pieces fall away. He kept the *Major*'s pistol, his Panzer binoculars and his marching compass. The bust-up field radio was harder to shift. When, finally, it moved it left a trail of broken valves, pieces of twisted metal frame and shattered dials; and revealed a hole in the floor six inches wide. Several of the airframe tubes showed damage, one almost sliced in two. When he reached in to remove the crate of stick grenades for lightness, he thought he felt the fuselage flex. What else was hit?

Ossie walked around the Storch, looking for more strikes on the propeller, the wings and tail plane; checking the ailerons, elevators, rudder, expecting them to be loose or stiff, both bad, but finding them moving free; seeing the place where the chunk of metal that missed his head had punched a hole in the windscreen glass, just below the leading edge of the starboard wing. There were plenty more holes in the fabric, but mostly small and nothing structural. He climbed up on the landing gear and inspected the engine bay. The Argus was still hot and burning off a film of surface oil, the kind you got when a line developed a hairline crack. Nothing he could do, apart from measure the lubricant level in the tank; it was down a little, but not so much he'd got to be concerned.

Ossie was feeling a little heady. Maybe it was the pre-flight check, same old routine, everything familiar, methodical and calm; stark contrast to the crazy spell when any moment could be your last. He jumped down and fetched a water flask from under the pilot's seat, running the warm, stale liquid round his mouth, swallowing a little, some escaping from the corners of his cracked lips and trickling down his neck. He savoured the wetness on his skin. To feel such things, you had to be alive.

He did not have long to make a move. The hunt for Stumme would soon be under way. To lose a general was bad enough. To lose the commander-in-chief could get you strung up in the Berlin-Plötzensee execution hut.

It occurred to him to leave a little surprise, something from the Holly Force box of tricks that would catch the attention of the search party and help settle the score for Bahr and Jabotinsky. Taking the remaining five grenades in their crate, he laboured back up the slope. There was a narrow, wind-eroded gully by the track, quite close to where the general lay. He undid the screw-caps on each wooden handle, extracted the pull-cords and set out the grenades in a neat row in the bottom of the gully, covering them with a layer of dirt. With particular care he threaded a length of paracord through the pull-cords, knotting it in a non-slip loop, leaving the other end free, then went back down the slope, heaved up what he could carry of the field radio's distorted carcass and laid it across the gully, shielding the grenades. Then, reaching underneath, he secured the loose end of the paracord to the radio's frame, adjusting it to make it good and tight, so the slightest movement would start the fuses burning.

Back at the Storch he checked the map, still secured to the *Major*'s board, and worked out a course due west, to take him away from the immediate scene of action, across the eastern fringe of the Libyan Plateau. It was a risk for sure in a potentially sick machine, overflying a region hostile and unforgiving. But after the rigours of the Takoradi Run it was hardly a new prospect. Better that than plod across the sky at 60 knots, unarmed, a sitting duck to any trigger-happy sonofabitch caught up in one of the biggest battles in the history of the world.

He'd hold the course for ten miles or so, then take a dog-leg on a fresh bearing a few degrees west of south that should land him right at Holly Force's front door. A piece of cake, he told himself automatically. That useful phrase, nicely British, tongue-in-cheek, uttered more in hope than expectation but always unadmitted, as was the flier's way.

The Storch was reluctant to fire up. The engine was already hot, the ambient temperature 30 degrees and rising. Gas vaporising in the fuel line, Ossie guessed. Then, at the third attempt, the engine caught and he was quickly in the air.

At first the routes below were solid with men and machines moving up to reinforce the troops in the long front line where, even in the searing light of morning, the sky was still dark and hung with smoke, lit up from underneath by brilliant flashes and rolling thunder from the barrage that, unlike a natural storm, did not die away. Then the traffic began to thin, an occasional bunch of speeding trucks or half-tracks towing field guns, a company of Panzer tanks moving line abreast, throwing up bow-waves of sand like fast boats cutting through a placid sea.

Quite soon there was nothing, only the sand-brown surface of the plateau stretching as far as Ossie could see, way out to the horizon, expanding all the time as he struggled to gain height. The engine was running a little rough and lacking power. The oil pressure was down to 40 pounds, the temperature nudging 32 degrees. A piece of cake? The phrase came back to taunt him. He did not care to think about setting the Storch down, not here. The plateau was as big as Switzerland and as varied, some regions mountainous, incised by rocky wadis that only ran with water in the rainy season; some, closer to the coast, fertile enough to sustain crops and herds of cattle, goats and sheep; but here, an arid and featureless tract of shifting, fine-grained sand, known only to jackals and nomad bands until the Europeans came to fight a war. The warriors saw this place with different eyes, perfect terrain for tanks, but the marks they made upon the surface were quickly gone, like a slate wiped clean, leaving only silence, a quivering void beneath a blue bowl of sky where nothing lived for long and the lost were hardly ever found, even after death.

The Storch was handling oddly, crabbing through the air, the airframe no longer stiff, calling for constant corrections on the controls as though the tailplane was askew and creating drag. Then, five minutes from his turn-off point, a haze of oil began to flow back from the engine cowl, at first as fine as airbrushed paint, no more than a shadow on the windscreen, but darkening by the minute, specks blending into blobs that wriggled upwards, wormlike, driven by the propeller blast. In places the screen was almost black. The pressure had fallen to 30 pounds. Ossie had no choice. He had to get her on the deck while he could still see, before he cooked the engine, while he retained control, before he bought the farm. Or worse, walked or crawled away from a wreck, left to kick his heels until the desert bogies got him, drying him out just as surely as those husks of mummies the Hurry pilot Gellatley had gloated over in Cairo's ancient tombs.

He cranked down the flaps and reduced the power, stretching in his seat so he could see through the areas of screen where the oil wasn't spread so thick, straining for a clear glimpse of the ground. His vision seemed blurred. There was a film of something hot and sticky in his eyes. He screwed them up once, twice, but it only made them worse. With his right hand shaking on the stick he raised his left and touched his face. His fingers came away coated with viscous fluid. Oil was spraying through the hole in the screen punched out by the chunk of flak. Soon he was flying almost blind, as shut away as a student in a Link trainer, trusting to the instruments he could only dimly see. Airspeed under 30 knots, with flaps full out. He felt the Storch sinking, but couldn't make out the ground. He sensed he was very close, thought he could hear the whisper of the prop across the rising ground. Suddenly, he'd had enough, impatient at the suspense. Hell, let see how things turn out.

Ossie pulled back on the stick and, for a second, thought he'd got it wrong. The Storch hit quite hard but its oleo struts sucked up the bounce. The tailskid bit and he hit the brakes and cut the engine before he'd ceased to roll. All he could smell was burning oil. The screen was covered, the cockpit dripping with the stuff. He pushed open the door, missed his footing and half-tumbled out, sprawling in dust as fine as powder. It rose around him like a filmy shroud, entering his mouth and ears and eyes. Each time he blinked, small particles of grit, mixed in with oil, scratched across his eyeballs. He fumbled for the water bottle beneath the seat, cupped a little liquid in his hand and rinsed each eye in turn. It gave him some relief, but didn't improve his vision.

He stood there by the airplane, his hand still cupped, head bowed, dead ringer for some Birka beggar seeking alms who'd picked a lousy pitch. He straightened up and pressed his wet palm to his lips, but tasted only oil. He thought about those desert bogies, waiting out there somewhere, biding their time, in no hurry, knowing the way of these things; the gradual weakening, the wearing down, the giving up, the eagerness for it to be over; drifting, drifting, remembering then not remembering, forgetting, forgetting everything except the pain and heat; waiting. Waiting for oblivion which, like the desert bogeys, might be a long time coming.

He sat down under the shade of the Storch's broad wing. He had forgotten to crank off the flaps, and was glad of it. When he stepped outside, the sun hit him like a hammer. He picked at the corners of his eyes, extracting the grit that gathered there and rubbing it between his fingers. He thought he could see those fingers a little better now. It was just a matter of waiting. He'd never been good at waiting. Not waiting had gotten him into a mess of trouble in his time. He started to think about the times he'd gotten into trouble by not waiting. Remembering, drifting, waiting . . .

He snapped alert. He held up his fingers and counted them aloud, all the way up to ten. He tried to make out the graphite mark where that punk Todd Wormer once jabbed a pencil in his palm in English class instead of learning about Walt Whitman. He knew the spot but couldn't focus. He felt the lifeline, long and deep, traced by a witch in Paris, before the Hun marched into town. He held up his fingers and counted them again, ten, twenty, thirty, focusing hard, eyes weeping. Everything was blurred. He kept on staring, counting, his voice a croak. When he paused to run his tongue across his lips the silence was profound.

He went on counting fingers, hour by hour, chanting out the numbers, changing targets: five hundred, one thousand, two thousand, always higher, forcing himself to concentrate, test if his sight was coming back, even by degrees. He was in a fix, no question, a carousel of lousy luck that kept on going round and round inside his brain. He had no eyes to locate the fracture in the line which kept on leaking vital oil; no way to catch and save the oil except maybe in his water bottle, but the water bottle was still a quarter full and there was no place else to put the water but down his gullet. Meanwhile, the oil drained steadily away. A lousy carousel. But he'd known the risk, accepted it, screwed up. There was no one else to blame, no point in getting mad. So keep on counting. Don't think about what can't be changed. Just start again. One, two, three, four, five six . . .

About midday he fell asleep. He did not dream of good things: instead, he dreamed of old Dinghy, the buddy he used to hit the Paris nightspots with, burning in his shot-up Hurricane on the forward field at Revigncourt in November 1939, the day the war turned real; of Blitzkrieg and the French colonial troops who dealt with a captured German bomber crew by lopping off their heads; of Malta and that girl he knew, Claudia Farinacci, dead outside the Mellieha church, killed by a Junkers jettisoning a bomb; of Giorgio, her kid brother, who'd seen it all, saying, 'You get those devils, you make them pay'; him promising he would; airplanes falling from a crowded sky, an anywhere sky at any time in the past four years, and men, some swinging under 'chutes, some not, some men he'd known.

Ossie woke up in a sweat. He'd been asleep five hours. His

lids were sealed together with oily stuff but when he prised them open he found his sight was marginally improved – still fogged, but he could make out Todd Wormer's graphite mark and, when he raised his head, he could see the Storch quaking in the heat. Beneath its engine bay lay a broad, dark patch in the powdery sand. When he pushed himself up and went over for a closer look he saw the oil had ceased to drip, though whether that was good or bad he didn't know.

Away from the shelter of the wing he felt like a bug on a red-hot griddle, the temperature 40 degrees or more. Work would have to wait. But the mere thought of work gave him some hope. Taking a sip of water, he felt it course down to his empty stomach. He sat back down but fought off sleep. He did not want to dream again. Nor did he want to count his fingers any more. He'd got to twenty thousand – enough fingers for any mug. Instead, he would study the unchanging landscape laid out in front of him, as bland as a beige blanket; study how it didn't change, remained the same. Like him, hunkered down, leaning back against the oleo strut, flies crawling disregarded in his eyes, his ears, his mouth, his hair, him not bothering to brush them off, listening to their hum, like a tiny orchestra tuning up, seeming louder than the noise of battle that never ceased, but now a good way off. And so he studied the desert, thinking how it stayed the same, had stayed this way for a thousand years, a million – who could tell how long? His eyes felt better now. Not completely right but good enough for a little work, but this was not the time. And so he waited in a place he'd never been before, a place inside his head, a timeless place where it seemed a million years could pass in the space of a breath or two; waited until the heat let up and the sun began to sink and swell into a monstrous ball of rolling orange fire, opposite a rising near-full moon. Then, moving slow and careful, he raised himself up on the Storch's starboard oleo strut and opened up the engine bay, not sure what he'd discover, not sure if he wanted to know.

Full, the oil tank held eleven litres. Only a third was gone. It seemed he'd put the bitch down in time. He had a chance, if he could find and fix the problem. The light was adequate, his vision was holding up.

He worked his way through the Argus lump from front to back, on top and underneath, checking every line he could. He identified only two areas of doubt, a loose connection that he tightened, using parts of weapons as improvised tools, and what felt like a pinhead puncture probably caused by flak. With his fighting knife he cut off strips of leather from the sleeve of his fancy jacket and bound them tightly round the place, moistening them with the dripping oil to bed them in. He punched the starter, took the power up to idling revs, then climbed back on the oleo strut and looked around for flying oil. It seemed okay. He could do no more, other than try to scrape the windscreen clear of crud, worth doing only if it seemed he had a chance. Now, it seemed he might. Next day he'd know. Know if he would finish here, or somewhere else along the route, or defy the odds and deliver this baby back to base.

In the cockpit, working out his course, his eyes gave pain and their focus came and went, but he was in a familiar place, sat at the controls working on a pre-flight plan, calculating his ETA at various points, assuming without question that tomorrow he would fly. One way or another, he would fly.

Through the oil-smeared screen the sky had grown dark. He took a stroll across the powdery sand, silvered by the moon. Further off, the plain was vaporous blue and where it met the sky it shaded into deepest black. The air was cold; cold enough for his breath to show. A tracery of stars and planets glittered above his head. And still the sounds of war drifted across the empty land. He zipped his leather jacket with its ripped-up sleeve. Tomorrow it would serve a different purpose, sealing up the flak hole in the windscreen where the oil came in. One hell of a way to treat a swell jacket.

For a moment he wasn't sure what day it was. It seemed they'd taken off from Holly Force many weeks ago. It took him a second or two to figure out it had been that morning, the first day of the battle they were calling Alamein. He climbed back in the cockpit shivering with cold and tried to get some sleep, ready for the flight.

Eighteen

Beppo Lutzow noticed it first. Sometime after dawn on the second day of the British attack he heard the low growl of an aero-engine approaching from the north. He was still shaking with fever from the horned viper's venom in his system and thought at first it was his imagination. He had not spoken to the Englishman since their argument about the Jewish question. He had been angered by the man's refusal to understand, even to the slightest degree, that the policies of the Reich might be reasonable and defensive; that the final reckoning with Jewry had begun and could not be diverted from its course. He was troubled, also, by that ridiculous English taunt that kept repeating itself in his head about the Führer leading his nation 'up the garden path'. It evoked a grotesque picture, the Führer tripping along in cap and bells like the Pied Piper of Hamelin, who agreed to rid the town of rats and lured them to the River Weser where they drowned. But when the townsfolk broke their bargain and would not pay, the Piper stole their children – and Hamelin's future.

It was a notion Beppo could not shift from his mind. It fed upon itself. Instead of rats, the Jews – an image familiar from Party films. Instead of Hamelin, the Reich – pledged to unconditional obedience to the Führer and the state. A bargain was a bargain. Rid the town of rats, carriers of plague; cleanse the greater Reich of Jews, impediment to the expansion of the Aryan race. The price was to obey. But if the German people failed to honour the pledge, lost faith, began to doubt, would future generations pay the price? When men like Matti Hartmann voiced dissent, it gave one pause for thought. What had he said? 'One must take on these hardline stooges, Beppo, and show there is more to the Reich than Adolf Hitler. Yes, I love my country. But we stand to throw it all away.'

Beppo stood up. This was no time to waver. He squinted up against the glare, towards the north, and picked out a small monoplane working its way across the desert like a hesitant moth, barely thirty metres above the ground. Its silhouette was unmistakable. He saw that its course would bring it very close to their position. For the first time in many hours, he addressed the Englishman Curtis. 'Look! That is a Luftwaffe Storch, my friend. It cannot miss us.'

He staggered to the summit of the rising ground and began to wave. Kit did not speak or move. No point. So it was going to finish this way, with him in the bag, perhaps for years. Nothing to be done. Just wait. He sat where he was and watched the little aeroplane approach. He noticed it was trailing smoke, a ribbon of white that curled behind it like a streamer. It struck him, then, that he might not be in the bag after all. If it was in trouble, why should they take him with them? Weight counted in a flimsy crate like that and he knew the Storch could only carry three. Perhaps they would abandon or kill him here.

The Storch passed directly overhead, very low. Kit could see the pilot clearly, and was surprised. The man was black. It made no sense, a negro flying for the Fascists.

The machine was soon lost to sight, touching down on a flat expanse beyond the rise. Still Kit did not move, even when he heard its engine die. The German had run forward. In the sudden silence he heard him shouting with elation. He could only make out one other voice. It wasn't saying much, just grunts in answer to a rapid string of questions. They seemed to be about the plane.

'Storch' was mentioned many times. Soon there came the scuff of boots, and two figures came towards him down the slope, slipping a little on the scree. The German was still weak, unsteady on his feet, and his suppurating crimson nose made him look like Grock the clown. The black man was no better, gaunt in a filthy long-sleeved shirt and loose trousers with ripped knees. They made a sorry pair. But Beppo Lutzow's spirits were high.

'This fellow has hit trouble,' he cried in English. 'Bad luck for him. Good luck for us.'

'Us?'

Beppo ignored the point. 'Surely you must be pleased? This is our ticket out of this place.'

Kit did not reply. He studied the silent pilot as he came forward and saw he was not a negro after all. His face was simply crusted with hard, black oil, his thick hair matted on to his skull. Against the blackness of his skin his eyes were startlingly red. There was something familiar about the way he held himself, as though he was about to launch a punch; familiar, too, the shrewd and hostile gaze, despite the corneal fluid seeping down his cheeks, tracing faint lines like tribal markings, giving him more than ever a native look.

'Hier ist der Engländer,' Beppo said. The oily pilot only frowned and nodded, looked down at his boots for a moment, then quickly looked up again, red eyes on Kit, his teeth showing white in a faint and unaccountable smile, as though enjoying some private joke. 'This is Leutnant Schroer,' continued Beppo. 'He was much surprised to see me. He expected only English dead. He is an *Aufklärungsflieger.'*

'What's that?' said Kit, irritated by the smirk.

'Reconnaissance, like you.'

'Not like me,' said Kit. 'I fly a Spitfire. Quite a different thing to poodling about in that weird device, running errands.'

'Field Marshal Rommel flies such an aircraft,' said Beppo, stiffly.

'My point exactly,' said Kit. 'General Montgomery does *not* fly a Spitfire.' He cupped his hands behind his head, leaned back a little and yawned. 'So what quirk of fate delivered this chap here?'

'His engine is losing oil,'

'I'd gathered that,' said Kit.

'He hopes to find a fresh supply in the British tanks.'

'Fat chance.' Kit yawned again. The oily pilot continued to regard him with a sardonic air, but still said nothing. 'Why doesn't your pal speak up for himself?' Kit found the man's stare annoying.

'He has no English.'

'I see,' said Kit. 'So what happens now?'

'First, we look for oil.'

'You look,' Kit told him. 'I went down there last time.'

Beppo hesitated, conscious of the new arrival at his side. He shrugged. 'Perhaps it is only fair. The airframe of the Storch is badly damaged. It could fail at any moment. Less chance if it only carries one. As the senior rank, and a front-line fighter pilot, naturally I will take that place. It is a risk I am prepared to take.'

'Decent of you,' said Kit. He paused. 'Doesn't your chum have an opinion on that?'

'You forget, he does not speak English. I will inform him when the time comes. He will understand. He is a German officer. But of course,' Beppo added, 'you may rely on me to arrange for you both to be picked up without delay, assuming I reach safety.'

'Of course,' said Kit. He and the oily pilot exchanged a glance. It was almost as if the man had understood.

Beppo did not notice. He took the pilot aside and they had a brief discussion in murmured German. 'It is decided,' he said finally. 'Fresh oil is essential. Even a little will be of use. Without it, Schroer doubts the engine will survive for long. He has tried repairs but they have not worked. That is why he was forced to land. I have explained that I will search for the oil myself. The Devil's Garden is no place for a fellow whose eyes are bad.' Beppo sucked a tooth. 'He asked me why I do not insist you carry out this task.'

'Really? How would you propose to do that?'

'The matter does not arise. You might not search so carefully, to get me on my way. You will stay here. But do nothing hasty. The *Leutnant* has his orders and will not hesitate to carry them out.'

Kit smiled wryly. 'Very sensible. I'm always interested in trying out a new machine.'

Beppo raised a quizzical eyebrow. 'What? Surely you would not lower yourself to fly such a weird device?'

'Better than walking,' said Kit. 'Just.' He noticed now that the oily pilot had a Walther pistol in his hand. 'But I see I won't get the chance.'

Beppo started off towards the minefield and Kit stretched out and closed his eyes, ignoring the presence of the other man, trying to look resigned, as though he had given up. His mind was racing, thinking how he could catch this little sod off guard, disarm him, lay him out and seize the kite. It was the same conundrum he had faced a day or two ago, come back to whisper in his ear like some malignant spirit. *Lay him out.* An easy phrase, but what exactly did it mean? Knock him cold? Not quite so simple, as he had learned from college boxing bouts, the only knowledge he had of fighting hand to hand. There was only one certain way – to grab the pistol and end it with a bullet. Why so squeamish? He had killed so many men. But never face to face, never in cold blood. That was the difference.

He wondered where the oily pilot was. He peered around through narrowed lids and saw that the man had sat himself down nearby, the little pistol swinging by its trigger-guard from a filthy finger. There was no point in talking. His smattering of German would put him at a disadvantage, make him look a bumbling clot. Anyway, why pass the time of day with someone he might have to murder? For in his mind, that was what it was.

The man was humming quietly to himself, in gravelly and erratic tones, some tune Kit thought he recognised. Confounded, he realised he could place the tune – 'Sur les quais du vieux Paris'. Lucienne Delyle. Instantly he was back in France on the eve of war. The melody of a Paris spring, leaves breaking on the trees along *les grands boulevards*, the pavement cafés busy with the usual crowd, the Revigncourt chaps on leave and heading for their favourite bars, unaware of what the future held, thinking only of a pretty tune and pretty women in this prettiest of cities.

The oily pilot stopped humming and cleared his throat. 'So how's the recce racket then?' he said. 'Enjoying a vacation?'

Beppo had reached the edge of the minefield. He could see the boot-marks of the Englishman on the safe ground between the stretched white tapes. Standing there, he understood the courage it had taken to go back in to look for water. He had to match that courage now. And also match the Englishman's longer stride, which put him off his balance. Still, he had no choice but to go ahead, dizzy from fever and dank with sweat. At the point where the British armour had lost its way he went more slowly, treading gingerly along the tracks left by the tanks, as the Englishman had before him. He began to smell the corpses, hear the hum of feasting flies. He thought he had developed a strong stomach, after so many years of war, but this was new: a butcher's shop, a random display of parts of men, a head, a leg, a shoulder, internal organs draped about as if for sale; inside the hulks a mess of fat and bone.

Beppo forced himself to make a thorough search, moving things he did not care to touch. But everything was consumed. Certainly there was no possibility of finding oil. Then, slipping down from a shattered hull and trying to wipe his fingers clean of human grease, he saw a metal container by his feet, half-buried by the churned-up soil. He thought it was a can until he dragged it clear, and found it was a heavy box of tools. The lid was warped by fire but he kicked it open. The contents were intact. He took as many items as he could safely carry: screwdrivers, spanners, wrenches, pliers, metal shears, a good-sized hammer, a metal-cutting saw. About to move away, he stopped and turned and looked at the nearest tank. The discovery of the tools had suggested something else to him, something that might, perhaps, prove as useful as finding a can of oil.

'I got to admit,' said Ossie Wolf, 'I thought my eyes were playing tricks. I guess you've noticed, they're nothing to write home about.' He pushed the pistol back in its holster on his waist but left the flap undone.

'Small world,' said Kit.

'Someone had to say it.'

'Care to tell me what brings you here in Nazi uniform?'

'Aw gee, you'd be bored.'

'Where were you bound?'

'I can't tell you that.'

'I saw you last in London – Kingsway – in a corridor, with some other American type. Hush-hush work?'

'They tried to keep that quiet, that's for sure. Care to tell me how you wound up with this jerk?'

'Not really. You'd be bored.'

'Uh-huh. So what now? Got anything in mind?'

'I had. I was thinking of ways to bump you off.'

'Good thing I spoke up.'

'You didn't. You hummed.'

'Yeah, I don't know why I did that. Maybe to break it to you gently.'

'That's not like you. Don't tell me you've developed a sensitive streak.'

'Not so's you'd notice.'

'Your Al Jolson disguise works very well. More hush-hush stuff?'

'That's courtesy of a fucked-up motor.'

'Talking of motors, is it really?'

'Near as dammit, yeah.'

'Near as? That means not quite.'

'It's spewing oil. I've tried to fix it best I can, but nothing doing. The pressure's through the floor. The whole damned unit's about to seize, unless we top it up or stop the leaks. Both, for preference.' Ossie stood up and looked towards the distant mine-field. 'Maybe Fritz will come up with the goods.'

Kit shook his head. 'I doubt it. I've been down there. Pretty well everything that could burn did. Oil has a tendency that way, you know.'

'Don't give me that patronising shit, you supercilious Limey sonofabitch,' said Ossie, but without much feeling.

'It's reassuring to know that some things remain constant in a changing world,' said Kit. 'That you're still the same crass, boorish, foul-mouthed Yank you always were. Now,' he continued, 'with that out of the way, perhaps we can get on.'

'Get on? Get on with what? No one's going any place without that goddamned Storch.' Ossie paused. 'Any sign of Fritz? I can't see too good.'

Kit stood up. 'He's on his way. Looks like we're dead ducks. No oil, unless it's in his pockets.'

'Funny guy. Now what?'

'You tell me.'

'Got any water?'

'No. Not now.'

'I have. Not much – but it should last the two of us a couple of days. Won't be too long before someone pays us a call. That little ship's parked up as plain as day.'

'The water will last the two of us, you say?'

'Sure,' said Ossie. 'Don't worry, Fritz won't feel a thing. I've been back to college, and learned a trick or two.'

'No,' said Kit. 'We outnumber him two to one, although he doesn't know it yet. That makes him a prisoner of war.'

'Been boning up on the Geneva Convention, huh? You ever hear of something Churchill calls "ungentlemanly warfare"?'

'No.'

'You're looking at it.'

'That's hardly news.'

'Oh, it's official, I'm an expert now.' Ossie kicked the dirt in exasperation. 'Jesus Christ, you said yourself you were thinking of ways to knock me off.'

'Thinking's one thing,' said Kit.

'You always were a squeamish bastard,' said Ossie. 'I guess it suits you fine, tooling around the sky, happy snapping in your nice blue Spit, way above the action.'

Kit's jaw was working. 'Like Warburton at Taranto, photographing the Italian fleet at zero feet? Like my chaps at Alam el Halfa doing low-level trips over the flak batteries at Miteiriya Ridge? You ignorant little sod. This Jerry brought me down in a fair fight, and you won't lay a finger on him. That's an order. And before you say another word, remember you're wearing the uniform of a ruddy spy.'

'This ruddy spy has just rubbed out the boss of the whole damned Afrika Korps,' said Ossie.

'What – Rommel?'

'Stumme.'

'First reserve,' said Kit. 'It doesn't count.'

'You don't know squat. Two guys died on that operation.'

'Our side or theirs?'

'That tears it,' said Ossie. He looked towards the slope. 'Fritz is almost here. Time to pretend we hate each other's guts.'

'What do you think of his notion to liberate the kite?'

'Remember, I don't speak English. He hasn't told me yet. But I guess we play along until the moment comes.'

'That doesn't mean until *his* moment comes. I draw a line at that. Is that absolutely clear?'

'You're crazy,' said Ossie. 'The sonofabitch would ditch us here without a second thought.'

'I think you're wrong. I believe he'd do the decent thing. Not, of course, that we'll give him the chance to prove it.'

'I guess even you wouldn't be that big a mug.'

'It's somewhat academic, wouldn't you say?' said Kit. 'It seems unlikely that anyone will get the chance to fly out of here if the Storch's as clapped out as you say.'

Ossie nodded. 'For sure I brought her in on a wing and a prayer. That baby's going nowhere, outside a miracle. She'd dump you on your ass after you'd gone a mile. Tough to say what'd happen first; a toss-up between the engine quitting or the fuselage collapsing like a goddamned deck-chair. Whichever way, it's so long, folks.'

'Don't write the kite off quite so soon,' said Kit. 'You never know what Teutonic ingenuity might have come up with.'

Beppo Lutzow's head was coming slowly into view, circled by a halo of flies. Streams of sweat were running from his crown. His breathing was fast and shallow, resembling that of a fagged-out dog. He was exhausted but triumphant. In his hands he held a hammer and a saw. More implements protruded from his pockets. When he reached the others he threw the collection on the ground. They clanked dully against each other, like the cast-down weapons of a defeated warrior. But Beppo was not defeated. He felt an inner strength, remaining on his feet to prove his stamina was good. 'There was no oil, *Leutnant*,' he said in German to Ossie, ignoring Kit, 'but proper tools will help prevent us losing more. I also discovered these.' He held up a bunch of sheared-off braided metal lines. 'A little scorched but quite intact, and useful as replacements. Now, let us set to work.' To Kit he said in English: 'You are not needed.' He avoided looking him in the eye.

'Good,' said Kit. 'I hate to get my hands dirty.'

Over by the Storch, Ossie climbed up and threw back the engine cowling, releasing a pungent stench of baked steel, fuel and oil, everything ticking and hissing as it cooled. 'We need to wait,' he said, 'unless you want to burn your hands.'

Beppo was peering in the cockpit. 'Ah, you have water, I see.'

'Enough for a day or so.'

Beppo saw the damage to the floor behind the pilot's seat, the twisted tubing of the frame. He pushed at the fuselage and whistled, but made no observation. He had something else in mind.

'We have a moment then,' he said. 'Tell me, Schroer, I know little of your mission. Why were you flying south? Surely El Daba would have been a more sensible objective, as you were in trouble?'

'I was bound for 15 Panzer and Littorio at Deir el Qatani,' said Ossie, 'to report to General Stumme and receive further orders.'

'Stumme, you say?' Beppo was surprised. 'He strays that far from DAK headquarters?'

'He follows the Rommel pattern – a front-line general who likes to drop in on his troops unannounced. He flew there in another Storch but after landing it was destroyed on the ground. The fighting is fierce in that sector. I was detailed to rendezvous with the General and his staff at a certain place and return him to El Daba. Regrettably I also encountered ground fire, as you can see. I had reached the point of no return and, anyway, to turn back did not suit me, as long as there was a chance.' The details were convincing; the knowledge of 15 Panzer's position, the easy mention of General Stumme.

Beppo nodded, satisfied. 'Very well. Come down from there. Let someone with good eyes see what can be done.' But as Ossie jumped back down, Beppo paused. 'This is an awkward situation, Schroer.'

'In what way?'

'Even if we are successful in making a temporary repair to this machine, it is clear it will not carry three, without great risk. The damage is severe.' He rested his hand on Ossie's shoulder. 'You and I, of course, but as for the Englishman . . .'

'You intend to abandon him here?'

'We have no choice. Naturally we will provide the coordinates of his position when we land, but I'm afraid the Panzerarmee has more important things to do than look out for an Englishman who has been spying on their positions. Of course,' he confided, 'there is another way. In the circumstances, it could be considered merciful.' But he did not feel remotely merciful. He experienced a certain satisfaction at the coldness of his words. It was like a test, to push away the small considerations of right and wrong. He heard no gentle voice of mundane conscience whispering in his ear.

He recalled the Englishman's insults to the Reich, his softness towards the Jews, his taunt about the Führer leading the German people up the so-called garden path. Well, now he might discover where such mockery led, not up the garden path, but to a grimmer place.

Beppo felt a surge of strength within him. It was a turning point. All doubt had gone. He knew he could accomplish many things, hard things, required by logic and the Reich. He wondered at his weakness. He thought of Matti Hartmann, who had filled his head with uncertainty and lack of faith – telling him that Rommel was a man like any other, and a sick one, whose strategy was flawed; that the army's supply lines were stretched to breaking point, with vital convoys sent to the bottom of the sea; that though the Führer believed the desert battle already won it was, in Hartmann's insidious view, already lost. If Matti had lived, thought Beppo, he would have been compelled to act, denounce him to the Gestapo. He, Matti, would have lost, not Rommel, the master of surprise, rewriter of the rules of war, audacious, quick to act, and undefeated. There was no doubting now, no question of the outcome. He knew that victory was assured. All the Reich required of him was to remain firm, clear of purpose and play his part.

He laboured on the Storch engine for two hours, tightening junctions, replacing lines, careful to conserve the seeping oil as best he could. He felt it was going well, derived deep satisfaction from doing something positive at last, acting instead of waiting. There was only room for one to work. It suited him well. He wanted to be sure that everything was done correctly. Schroer with his seeping eyes was of little use, incapable of more than passing up the tools. He was literally a dead weight, an encumbrance that could make the difference between reaching El Daba and not. Beppo had no intention of taking him along. It would be a difficult moment. He would expect the fellow to understand. Somehow he doubted if he would. He sensed an innate hostility in Schroer that made him feel uneasy. It was as if he was holding something back, as though behind that blackened face he held a secret. He had said nothing when he made that significant remark about the Englishman, only glaring back with something close to accusation in those red-veined eyes that made him look more than a little mad. Perhaps he had gone too far, enlivened by the moment. He must be wary. Clearly Schroer was known to senior command, a telling witness to any transgressions here. Such things were generally not the Desert Army style. He had a dangerous thought: eliminate them both. It was so outrageous, he almost laughed. But then he thought again. Why not?

He went over every change he had made, and could see no leaking oil.

'I am finished here,' he shouted, throwing down the tools. 'I cannot do more. Now let us run her up, and see how good an engineer I am.'

As he began to ease himself off the oleo strut, he noticed a bundle of something stuffed into a hole high up on the windscreen. He tried to free it from outside but it was wedged tight. Swinging himself around, he slipped into the cockpit, reaching up to pull it down. Suddenly it came away, slimy with oil, and he saw it was a jacket. He threw it out of the cockpit door and it hit the ground with a flopping sound like a saturated towel. Beppo climbed out and looked around for Schroer. He touched the jacket with his boot. Despite its condition he could see that it was of excellent quality, the kind that wealthy pilots purchased for themselves to private order. He crouched down, spreading out the jacket on its back, admiring the cut. He heard a movement behind him – Schroer.

'Yours?' he asked, without looking round. True to type the man did not reply. Beppo wiped away a little of the oil, feeling the fineness of the leather grain. His fingers brushed a pocket and something clinked; metal on metal. 'Schroer, you should be more careful with your marks,' he said, and felt inside. It was not coins. He stood up, staring at the two objects in his palm, one an *Erkennungsmarke*, and tangled in the oval dog-tag's broken chain was something else, something he recognised immediately although he had never seen the real thing: the black and silver outline of a Knight's Cross.

Puzzled, he looked around for Schroer and as he did so, a hand was clamped across his mouth, the thumb pressed painfully against his nose. Off-balance, he felt himself falling to the left, half-supported, his head pulled straight across his shoulder by the grasping hand, and where his neck was taut and bulging with the strain the flesh was suddenly pierced by something sharp and cold, driven in so deep it seemed to pierce his soul, severing his windpipe so he could not even scream.

Kit had slept a little, despite the constant noise of battle to the east, the flies, the rising heat, the ring and scrape of tools over by the Storch, an occasional snatch of German that made him think, swimming in a semi-dream, that he was already in the bag. But most of all he slept because he did not feel the constant presence of Beppo Lutzow. At first he had thought he understood this fellow pilot, with whom he shared a love of flying, a love of country, duty, honour. Those qualities Lutzow still possessed but, to Kit, they had been warped. It was a relief not to have him close, as though a shadow had been lifted from his mind, dark, distasteful, a spectre of a loathsome world to come, if this war was lost.

Something woke him, a scuffle happening somewhere very close. Instantly he was awake, alert, his senses clear, as surely as if he had been roused by the clanging of that old brass bell at Revigncourt, the Hun in sight, the orderly yelling out a squadron scramble.

He was on his feet, narrowing his eyes against the glare. He looked towards the Storch. Two figures were moving there, locked together in a parody of a dance, scuffing up the dust. He began to run towards them, knowing he had to stop this thing, not understanding what he saw, but knowing somehow what it meant. An arm was raised. Something caught the sun, a flash of steel. The figures broke apart. A man was sinking to his knees, head bowed as though in the act of worship, but his hands were not clasped in prayer. Instead they were clutching aimlessly at his throat. Kit was quite close now. He found himself staring at the top of Beppo Lutzow's head. He noted the starting bald patch on the crown of blondish, bristly hair, the baby-pinkness of the scalp. The head was jerking up and down, nodding to a pulsing beat, quite fast at first and then more slowly until it ceased. The body stiffened, then relaxed and Lutzow toppled sideways, blood pumping from a narrow incision in his neck, startling red against the tawny ground.

Ossie Wolf had stepped back a pace or two. There was no expression on his face. He threw down a long-bladed knife, not with revulsion but carelessly, as though its job was done.

'My God,' said Kit. 'My God.'

Ossie was almost grinning, no more concerned, it seemed, than if he had been caught fighting in the schoolyard. 'The bastard had it coming.'

'You murdering bloody swine.'

Ossie stared back at him with a half-smile on his face. 'You sorry sonofabitch. You don't get it, do you? Your buddy here expected me to knock you off.' He held out two fingers and mimicked a closing hammer with his thumb. 'You know – Nazi-

349

style? "A mercy" was the way he put it, like he was kidding anybody. Some pal.'

'I don't believe you.'

'Yeah, it's hard for you to believe anyone could wish you harm. Let me disabuse you. Stuck in the desert with Holy Joe, I'd have probably come to the same conclusion.' Ossie wiped his mouth with the back of his hand. Kit made no move, staring at Lutzow's body.

'When he blabbed to you about pulling rank to grab the only seat in town,' said Ossie, 'he thought I couldn't understand. "He has no English." Right up to the last he was playing me for a sucker, kidding me I'd go along. And all the time he planned to dump me here. For sure he knew I'd have something to say about it. He probably had a way to deal with that too. Follow it through and you'll see the nature of his problem, me alive and sore and kicking and, if I survived, ready to take the shine off whatever bull he spun them in El Daba. There had to be a better way, like wait for me to deal with you, then pop me also. Or if I didn't, pop us both himself. Everything wrapped up neat and tidy. No witnesses, no boring explanations. A hero of the Reich in line for a Nazi gong. And us? Just two more nameless stiffs. It was a cinch. Except we beat him to the punch.'

'Not we,' said Kit. 'Whatever he had in mind, I believe he'd have drawn a line at cold-blooded murder.' Kit turned away. 'Unlike you.'

Ossie pulled him round. 'Jesus, what he had in mind was me putting a bullet in your brain.'

'I've only got your word for that.'

'You cock-eyed bastard. You'd take the word of that Nazi lunkhead over mine?'

'It's hard to believe, that's all. We talked—'

'Uh-huh, you won him round – that it? He'd have rubbed you out as soon as spit. That's what this is all about, the whole damned show. "Get in our way and down you go – you're history, brother." Instead of which we've got ourselves a chance.' Ossie grunted. 'You got me curious,' he said. 'How did you see this panning out? Apart from waving the sonofabitch a fond farewell?'

'Straightforward enough,' said Kit. 'Let you sort out the aircraft as best you could, then come clean about who you were, so he understood his situation.'

'Our prisoner, right?'

'Correct.'

'And then?'

'You fly on to your destination and, if you make it, let someone know we're here. If not, we're no worse off. I think that about sums it up.'

'It's simple,' said Ossie, 'I'll give you that. And Fritz? Where was he supposed to figure in all this? Quietly stand by sucking his thumb? You got to be kidding. I can see it now. While I'm warming up the Storch, you've got him covered, a real Dick Tracy. Except he'd know you couldn't pull the trigger. He'd have jumped you for sure, and I'd be next in line. It'd be us stretched out there, not him. Great plan, Curtis. But I'll take mine any day of the week.'

Bending down, he picked up something close to Beppo Lutzow's feet and brushed away the sand. He held two pieces of metal in his palm, a dog-tag and an Iron Cross. He dangled the dog-tag by its cord. 'This one's to remember a guy.' He held up the cross. 'And this one's proof.'

Nineteen

In a corridor of the German field hospital, Kit occupied a stretcher below a shattered window, through which a little salt air drifted in from the sea a mile or two away. Despite the heat he was covered with a thin blanket to keep the flies off his wounds. On the opposite side of the corridor the Australian corporal groaned in fitful sleep, trying to shift his weight but hampered by the splints strapped to his right leg. Further down, the young German crewman burned in his tank had just died. The orderlies carried him out on his stretcher and returned quite quickly with another man, unconscious, to take his place. The stench of sweat, excreta and disinfectant was so all-pervading that it seemed, to Kit, that he would never clear it from his lungs, that it would always linger there to remind him of this time.

The hospital was not a hospital, instead a blockhouse once used by railway workers, but now a place of shelter, an island surrounded by a rolling and turbulent sea, a tide of battle that came and went, throwing up new wrecks of men. Inside its walls the medics fought to save a life, regardless of what uniform the victim wore. Outside, it was a different game – the aim to kill and maim.

Above the blockhouse hung a bedraggled Red Cross flag and, although some shells had landed close, the place had not been hit.

The corridor contained perhaps a dozen men. In rooms leading off, the doctors were carrying out surgical operations. In such a room they had assessed Kit's burns. They said they had seen worse and dressed his legs as best they could. He had just been returned to his place.

The corridor was busy with doctors in blood-streaked gowns, orderlies carrying trays of instruments, metal buckets and severed limbs wrapped in cloth, stretcher-bearers fresh from the battle-field, shouting for instructions about where they should dump their loads.

Kit stretched his neck back, chin raised, so he could look behind him. The view was odd. Ossie Wolf's stretcher showed upside down, as though suspended from the ceiling. The American lay quietly with his hands at his sides, a length of bandage wound around his head, covering his eyes. The skin that showed was still dark with ingrained oil.

'Wolf,' said Kit.

'Yeah?'

'I'm back from the theatre.'

'Enjoy the show?'

'No comic turns.'

'That's the Hun for you. No sense of humour.'

'How are you bearing up?'

'Terrific, except I'm blind. They've cleared my eyes of crap, but they reckon it'll be a while before I know if it's anything permanent.'

'I suppose I should say thanks.'

'For what?'

'Well, saving my neck.'

'I thought twice, I got to admit.'

'That's not like you.'

'Been kicking myself ever since.'

'Shouldn't do that,' said Kit. 'You've got enough problems.'

The Australian corporal was awake. 'Here, you blokes. Either of you got a fag?'

The orderly they knew as Voss heard him, fumbled in his pocket and produced a pack. The Australian took a cigarette, looked at it for a moment, then looked at Voss. 'Thanks, mate.'

The orderly flicked a lighter. *'Nichts zu danken.'*

'Eh?' said the Australian.

'He says you're welcome,' said Ossie.

'You speak Kraut?'

'Some.'

''Ere, are you a plant?'

'A spy who can't see? Even the Jerries aren't that dumb.'

The Australian laughed. 'Okay, but you hear some tales. Clandestine warfare and all that bollocks. It's got so as you don't know who you're talking to.'

'That's for sure,' said Ossie.

'Still,' said the Australian, 'wait long enough and you might find yourself talking to my mates, from what I saw out on the two-way rifle range.'

'The what?'

'The battle, mate. It was going back and forth like the Don between the bloody wickets.'

'You got me, pal,' said Ossie.

'He means we could be overrun at any minute,' said Kit.

'What happens then?'

'Your language skills will no longer be required.'

The Storch had been in the air for less than twenty minutes before the engine had stopped. Ossie had scrapped his hope of reaching Holly Force, resigned instead to aiming for the front-line sector near the coast. They had no firm plan apart from trying to identify an Allied position, landing close but not close enough to be blown to pieces, and walking in. Put like that, it sounded almost feasible. They even agreed it was, but inwardly both knew that very soon they would almost certainly be dead, in any of a dozen ways.

With this scheme in mind, Ossie had gone down to the mine-field, refusing with a single curse Kit Curtis's offer to go in his place because of his lousy eyes, and collected various remnants of tank crew clothing. Turning the rank cadavers this way and that, to free the less scorched and stained items, was a ghoulish task. Yes, ghoulish. The word came naturally, familiar somehow, as though he knew its proper meaning. Then he remembered Gellatley, that morbid bastard who haunted ancient tombs, saying a ghoul was a spirit from Muslim folklore that preyed on corpses, a desert demon.

He had looked up at that, and stared around, but not sure why. Maybe looking for a desert demon. Maybe fearing it was him.

He had changed his Luftwaffe uniform for an assemblage of stained and ragged garments that didn't fit, and were mostly too big. He seemed to be a sergeant. With some regret he wrapped Bahr's dog-tag and Stumme's Knight's Cross in a strip of material and buried them under a little pile of stones, close to where the rocky defile cut down through the rising ground. Some headache trying to explain how he came by such things if he fell into German hands.

When they took off, with Kit crouched as far forward as he could, to reduce the stress on the flexing fuselage, the engine sounded strong. But then it began to falter, trailing fine white smoke that gradually turned grey and finally shaded into black.

'That's the last time I use that engine shop,' shouted Ossie.

'I hear they've gone bust,' said Kit.

'I'm putting her down,' said Ossie. 'We'll have to hoof it.'

'Suits me. I could do with some exercise.'

They were ten miles from the coast, and as far as they could make out, a little to the west of the principal action. They didn't talk again. They knew their situation.

They were hit when they were twenty feet from the ground, the flaps extended, the engine running rough, likely to cut at any moment. Until they heard the crackle of small-arms fire from the direction of the Allied lines, a good way off, and the heavier thud of an anti-aircraft piece, they thought they had a chance. If Kit had not been leaning forward, he would have been cut in half by the spray of bullets and steel fragments that sliced through the fuselage just behind his seat. The airframe sagged, the tailplane twisted upwards, almost severed, and the stick went loose in Ossie's hands as the control lines snapped.

The Storch had not been moving fast, little more than 30 knots. That helped. It struck the ground nose first, pivoted onto its back and came to rest, balanced on its wings. Bullets were zipping through the fabric and bouncing off the twisted metal tubing. Fuel was running from the ruptured forward tank. Ossie began to crawl along the upturned roof towards a man-sized gap in the shattered windscreen. He looked back, expecting to see Kit Curtis close behind. He wasn't there, but ten feet away, flat against the Plexiglas of the cabin roof, lying on his back, his head towards him, mouth moving, trying to speak, make sense of where he was, acting foggy like a fighter trying to beat the count.

Ossie scrabbled round and crawled on back. The smell of fuel was very strong. He could hear the fuel pump clicking, clicking fast, spewing out the contents of the tank. Everything was running with the stuff, him choking on the fumes. He reached along and seized Kit by the collar of his shirt. The material began to tear, but Ossie went on pulling anyway. At first he couldn't shift the weight but then Kit's body began to slide along, and as he slid he began to move, to flail about, trying to roll over, pushing with his legs against the side panels of the cabin, starting to help a little, until Ossie could let him go, could hear him scrambling along behind, panting, towards the gap in the shattered screen. And still the bullets were humming and pinging all around them. Then Ossie was out through the jagged gap, the engine cowling above his head, his fingers digging in sand.

He turned, and as he made to reach for Kit and drag him out, the fuel ignited. He heard him hollering, not human sounds, not words but animal cries of pain. 'Ahhh, ahhh, ahhh.' Fire was dropping all round them. Something in the Storch cracked. The nose went up above their heads, the fuselage tilted down. It gave them space to crawl away. Kit was beating at his legs. 'Oh Christ, oh Christ.' The stuff of his trousers was alight. Ossie was scooping up handfuls of sand, piling it on Kit's legs, damping down the flames. The rubber toecaps of his flying boots had bubbled and melted in the heat.

The Storch began to settle, the way a bonfire does, sometimes collapsing gently, sometimes in a rush that threw up sparks and gushed out a wave of heat. Once there was a salvo of sharp reports, a whining in the air: the ammunition of the MP38 exploding in its magazine. Elsewhere, the firing had stopped. They thought they heard a distant cheer. Against the desert floor the little Storch had etched the shape of a blackened cross.

Kit was writhing in the dirt, eyes screwed shut, teeth clenched, sweat droplets running down his face. Ossie pulled him further from the wreck. Each slight jarring made Kit yelp, then laugh a little weakly because he couldn't hold it in. 'Sorry,' he kept on saying. 'Sorry.'

'For crying out loud,' said Ossie, 'squawk all you want. But for Jesus' sake stop saying sorry.'

'Sorry,' said Kit.

It was only when Ossie went to check Kit's burns that he realised his eyes had gotten worse. There was a kind of stinging, as though a film of fuel had overlaid the oil and dirt. The focus kept shifting in and out, the way binoculars did when you turned the little wheel. He couldn't get it sharp.

'What time you got?' he asked. 'It's getting kind of dark.' His sight was going fast, as though someone was drawing the blinds against the glare.

He heard Kit's voice. 'Oh-twelve-hundred hours. Time for a nice cold beer.'

Ossie felt the sun against his face. 'This is screwy. I'm flying blind.'

Two hours later they were picked up by a Panzer munitions half-track returning from the Front. The crew were friendly. One spoke English and said they would be taken to a field hospital. They were loaded carefully into the space left by the shells. The soldier who spoke English said the battle was going well.

'That so?' said Ossie, as they bumped along.

'How could it not?' said the German. 'Rommel has returned.'

Twenty

For two days they remained in the corridor of the field hospital because there was no room for them anywhere else. They heard the battle all around them but still the building wasn't shelled. More wounded were being carried in every hour, or managed to walk in on their own. Voss the orderly thought perhaps the blockhouse contained two hundred injured, mostly Germans but many Australians and some British too. 'We have three doctors,' he told them, 'and nine of us. Some men die but always the living outnumber the dead.' He smiled ruefully. 'We are too good at our job, I think. Soon we will be treating patients on the roof.'

Kit was interested that Voss called them patients. This desert war was different, he reflected. In France, in Poland, and now on the Eastern Front no wounded enemy would be treated in this way, and take up space that might be occupied by a German soldier.

There was much talk of Rommel's return. The Germans were buoyant at the news. It was known that he had travelled for fifteen hours, flying from Germany via Rome and Crete to his headquarters at El Daba. At midnight on the day of his arrival, forty-eight hours after the battle had begun, a signal had gone out to all units. *I have taken command of the Army again. Rommel.*

There was also mystery about the death of General Stumme. 'Nobody knows what happened,' said Voss. 'Some say his car was shot at by British fighter planes, others that he came under fire from the Australians who were active in that sector. The driver took evasive action, although a staff officer was killed, and did not realise the General was missing until too late. When they discovered him he was dead, but it seems of natural causes – heart failure brought on by the attack.'

Ossie, on his stretcher, only grinned, his mouth stretched wide below his bandage. Then he said: 'Hey, Voss, any talk of booby traps when they found old Stumme?'

'Booby trap?'

'Die Schreckladung.'

Voss started. 'You know this word?'

'All tank crews know this word.'

'Ah,' said Voss. 'It is most odd you ask this question. A comrade was in the ambulance that collected the General's body. He says that close to it was a dead hyena, blown to pieces by a device made of German grenades. Another mystery.'

'A hyena, huh?' said Ossie. 'I hate to see dumb animals mixed up in this thing.'

The doctor pronounced himself satisfied with the state of Kit's burns. The flesh on his legs was raw and blistered, but the flames had not penetrated the nerves, muscles and fatty tissue. 'There is no infection and such injuries usually heal quite well. You are lucky. If you had been burned more deeply I would not have given much for your chances. We are not equipped to deal with such things.'

'Thank you, Doctor,' said Kit.

The doctor smiled. 'Doctor, patient. Patient, doctor. It is quite a normal situation, yes?' He shook his head. 'Strange world.'

'And the sergeant?' said Kit.

'That may take a little more time. We will know when the

bandages come off. But you understand that, Sergeant, do you not?'

'Who said that?' asked Ossie.

It was on the fourth day, by Kit's reckoning the twenty-seventh of October, that there was some kind of commotion amongst the medical staff. This communicated itself to the German patients, although nothing was explained to the others.

All night there had been heavy bombing and the artillery fire was as intense as ever. Tanks could be heard close by, the block-house shaking to the rumble of their tracks and the pounding of their guns. A rumour went round that a Panzer ambulance had been destroyed and with it six wounded, some of them Allied infantrymen. A shell was not particular.

No one could tell which way the battle might be going. There was a dull acceptance that there would be no easy victory for either side. But for the Afrika Korps there was a single word that gave them hope and strength, talismanic – murmured like a prayer. *Rommel* . . .

On this fourth day, Kit heard what sounded like a large vehicle draw up outside the blockhouse. Its throbbing engine note was distinctive – a heavy armoured car of some kind. When the motor was turned off there was a flurry of commands in German, a general air of expectancy and excitement.

'What's going on?' said Ossie.

'Search me,' said Kit. 'Whoever it is, they're creating a heck of a flap.'

The corridor darkened as a group of figures moved slowly between the stretchers ranged along the walls.

In the centre, left a little space by the officers around him, was a man of stocky build wearing a long, dust-covered leather great-coat. A plaid woollen scarf was twisted round his neck, and above the peak of his cap with the gold eagle on its crown rested a pair of light plastic anti-gas goggles. When he removed his cap to wipe his brow with a square of cloth, his high forehead, protected from the sun by his headgear, was marble white against the deep tan of his face. His expression was shrewd, impatient and determined. Kit did not need the discreet twisted-braid insignia on his shoulder boards to tell him who this officer was.

The group turned into one of the operating theatres. Not much was said. When the stocky officer reappeared he looked sombre and thoughtful. He came on down the corridor. When he saw Kit he nodded curtly, a formal jerk of the head. Then he gestured at Ossie Wolf with his field marshal's baton and said something in German to one of the doctors. The doctor murmured a reply. The stocky officer leaned forward and said in English: 'I hear you are a British Panzer.'

'Huh?' said Ossie.

'You are fighting well. You are receiving good attention here?'

'It's no hotel, but I've been in worse places.'

'Your eyes, I am told, will recover.'

'So they say.'

'Sergeant,' said the doctor. 'Please, extend your hand.'

Ossie hesitated for a moment, then with a grunt did as he was told. His hand was grasped in a cool, firm grip, the skin worn hard. 'I wish you good luck.' A pause. 'But not too much.' There was a ripple of laughter and the group moved on.

'Who in hell was that?' said Ossie.

'I'll tell you some time,' said Kit, 'when you're stronger.'

He thought about that moment, with the Fox so close. What did the rules have to say about such a situation? What was permitted, how far could you go? What were the limits? Now, facing Rommel, should he have seized a pistol from one of his entourage and shot him down, as dispassionately as Ossie Wolf had dealt with Stumme and Lutzow? Wasn't it Clausewitz who said that ethics on the battlefield were akin to having one hand tied behind your back? Ossie understood that. Why didn't he?

He saw again the Field Marshal's face. A face you could believe in. The face of a man that other men could follow. What was his view on Clausewitz? Did he understand and fight within the limits, as some people – even his enemies – said?

Among the Germans, the elation at Rommel's visit soon faded. Voss came to them the next morning, looking grey with fatigue and fear. 'The fighting is very close now,' said the orderly. 'We have seen Tommy infantry moving towards this position. It is said that our men are falling back, but we have orders to remain here, and continue to tend to the wounded. What will become of us?'

'If you're overrun,' said Kit, 'I'm pretty certain you and your colleagues will be safe enough. Don't forget, there's a big Red Cross up there, showing what this place is. That flag has been honoured by both sides so far. Why should it be different now? Our chaps will understand quickly enough what work you've been doing here.'

'You will speak for us?'

'Of course,' said Kit.

The next day the ground shook to heavy armour, very close. Men were shouting, boots rasping on the corridor's concrete floor. They were talking in English. The Australians had arrived.

Voss's fears proved unnecessary. Quickly the medical staff of both sides began to work together. And within days, Kit and Ossie, along with many others, were evacuated in ambulances and found themselves savouring crisp white sheets and pretty WAAF nurses in a Cairo ward.

Twenty-one

They met in the Long Bar of Shepherd's Hotel. Kit had not been keen but it was the only place he could think of. They were about to fly him home, to take up an instructor's job with the PRU training unit at Benson. Non-operational until his legs healed properly. After that, if the medical board graded him A1.B, there was talk of a squadron, perhaps out East. But no squadron here. No squadron either for Percy Briggs – No Pix Percy – the old Hendon hand, killed taking off in coarse pitch after a heavy night buttering up some top brass at Heliopolis to further his career. They had brought in someone from outside to command the combined flights, someone Kit didn't know and didn't want to. If he hadn't been burned, the promotion would have been his. Now he was back to square one. Well, not square one exactly – square two or three – but at least alive, which was more than could be said for No Pix Percy. For this, he supposed, he owed Wolf that promised beer.

Ossie Wolf was late. When he strolled in, his eyes were shaded by anti-glare spectacles, the nickel-framed teardrop lenses that American pilots wore. He held out a steady hand.

'The hand that Rommel shook,' said Kit.

'I'm leaving now,' said Ossie, pretending to turn round.

'Not many chaps can say that,' said Kit. 'Particularly on our side.'

'I should've—'

'Well, you didn't.'

'I didn't know.'

'Better that way. Anyway, I think our Fox has got more serious problems on his mind right now, without being assaulted by a blind bugger like you. How are the peepers, by the way? I see you're affecting the mysterious look.'

Ossie tapped his glasses. 'Bausch & Lomb. They rest the eyes. I won them in a crap game. Better than those RAF jobs that make you look like grandma.'

'Back to caring what you look like then?'

'In Cairo? Oh, you bet.' Ossie beckoned to the barman. 'Hey, boy, two beers. Jesus, Curtis, if I waited for you I'd die of goddamned thirst.'

'I hear there's been a big tank battle at El Akatir.'

'Yeah. The word is, three-quarters of Rommel's tanks are burning or wrecked. They say he's falling back.'

'So Monty's hit the Fox for six,' said Kit, 'just like he said he would.'

'Sounds that way.'

'Reported back to that hush-hush gang of yours?'

'Not exactly,' Ossie said.

'What does that mean?'

'They're kinda dispersed. Remember Pringle?'

'What? That dodgy Ministry type we met in Paris?'

'That's him.' The beers arrived. Ossie drank his down in one and shouted for another. 'Yeah, Pringle was involved. Still is. I saw him at Helio yesterday. They've wound up Holly Force. "Job done" is the way he put it.'

'Stumme, you mean?'

'Oh, it was more than that. A whole lot more. You'd never believe.' Ossie paused. 'Dirty tricks, ungentlemanly warfare. Not your style, old boy. But it could catch on.'

'It already has,' said Kit.

Ossie wrapped his hand round his ice-cold second glass. 'They're boarding me at the Central Medical Establishment a week from now. My eyes are good. Pringle's going to pull some strings, get me back in fighters.'

'Decent of him.'

'Oh, I don't think decency's got a whole lot to do with it. Pringle's been checking the statistics. There's an outfit where the strike rate's down. They don't know why – lousy flying, bad marksmanship, lack of the killer instinct, a soft CO. Pringle reckons I could make a difference.'

'A squadron then?'

'You kidding? No, a pain-in-the-ass flight commander creating hell.'

'Sounds just the ticket.'

'Or maybe Pringle just wants to get me killed.'

'I can't believe that,' said Kit. 'He always spoke so highly of you.'

'Really?'

'No.'

Ossie took a gulp of beer and swirled it round his mouth. 'Yeah, well, it could be a barrel of laughs.' He upturned his glass. 'Say, want to help me celebrate? I'll show you a little local colour.'

He led Kit through the Birka, the hawkers still proffering pornographic goods, the hashish dealers still plying their trade, past the curtained alleys where the brothels were, the whores still lolling on their balconies as if there was no war, still the sound of fighting, breaking furniture, the pounding of MPs' boots. Screams, music, laughter, the aroma of food and exotic scents mixed in with the reek of sewage underfoot. To Ossie it was like coming home.

'If this is your idea of local colour,' said Kit, 'I don't think much of it. I've seen British troops here. Why do they allow it?'

'Kind of a safety valve, I guess.'

'Where exactly are we heading? I've got to pack. I'm flying out in the morning.'

Gradually the streets began to widen, the gardens became well-tended. There was a quietness. Palm trees nodded in the sultry breeze. Behind tall iron railings large houses stood part-hidden, gold light spilling from their windows, and somewhere soft music and the murmur of voices.

Ossie reached the particular house that the bearded, red-eyed tank commander had brought him and Catt to so long ago; the tank commander who knew he was bound to die and drank much red wine from big carafes and went upstairs in that particular house because it didn't matter any more.

'What is this place?' Kit Curtis was saying.

Ossie knew this was a big mistake. He had drunk whisky before arriving at the Long Bar. Now he wanted to be here, in front of the particular house, with Catt, or the red-eyed tank commander, who had drunk much red wine, not this stuffed shirt who wanted to get back to pack. He didn't know why he had come up with the idea. Maybe they had shared so much, he thought they could share this too. But really they didn't share a thing.

The sonofabitch Nubian was still on the door, same wide trousers, embroidered jacket. '*Baksheesh, effendi, baksheesh?*'

They went inside, into the ornate room. The food had been cleared away. The wail of the rebec was matching the soft, slow beat of the darbukka drum and the *almeh* dancers wiggled their butts, watched by the usual bunch, sitting in the shadows, wanting to see and not be seen.

When Farida came in, she was not quite as Ossie remembered her – more florid, not moving so sinuously, as though she was tired or bored. As she went through her routine, Ossie wondered who she'd choose. Maybe tonight she wouldn't choose anybody, because she was tired or bored or because she was rich and they all knew it was not to do with money, whatever the Nubian said. But then she became more animated, dancing faster, shaking her golden pelvis, her arms above her head, advancing and falling back in little steps, her jewellery flashing in the light of a hundred candles; dancing for a silent, squatting English major who took her in with hungry eyes. Now she wasn't tired or bored any more. It was this sucker's lucky night.

Ossie suddenly realised that he knew the sucker. He was wearing an unfamiliar uniform. Last time he had been sat behind a desk at Holly Force base, dressed as a Wehrmacht Kommandant. It was Aubrey Mulholland.

'Well, I'll be damned,' said Ossie. 'Dear boy or what?'

He recalled that little pile of stones, out there in the desert by that slash of crevice near the Devil's Garden; the cairn that hid two objects rolled in cloth. He'd pick them up some time, and give them to Mulholland. Not as a gift but because they belonged to him and no one else.

He turned around to tell Kit Curtis what he had decided, but found that he had gone.

Kit was walking quickly, not seeing his surroundings, not thinking about where he was. He was in some other place – a greener place. A gentler place. There was a woman, and a boy. An old man waiting, hoping. There was still war, of course. But it could not last. Surely it could not last. In this barren land of heat and sand they had glimpsed the end. It would not be long in coming. Surely?

Acknowledgements

Setting a fictional story in the context of one of World War Two's major conflicts was a daunting prospect. The Battle of Alamein was waged over huge tracts of desert terrain and every service on both sides, air, sea and land, was fully employed on often complex and fast-shifting attacks, feints and retreats.

To help achieve what someone once described as 'that clinching detail', that sense of authenticity so vital to any novel of this kind, I found myself consulting the following books on many occasions, to build my knowledge and understanding:

Alamein by Jon Latimer, *War Without Hate* by John Bierman and Colin Smith, *The Rommel Papers* edited by B.H. Liddell-Hart, *The Desert War* by George Forty, *The Luftwaffe in the North African Campaign* by Werner Held and Ernst Obermaier, *Panzer Battles* by Major General F.W. von Mellenthin, *Rommel and The Secret Services in North Africa* by Janusz Piekalkiewicz, *Eyes of the RAF* by Roy Conyers Nesbit, *Adventures on the Infinite Highway* by Peter Rivington and *A Green Hill Far Away* by Fred Hirst.

On aspects of flying, *Stick and Rudder* by Wolfgang Langewiesche and *Basic Aerobatics* by R.D. Campbell and B. Tempest were invaluable.

On the personal level I am indebted to Squadron Leader Tom Rosser OBE, DFC for advising on technical aspects of flying, particularly the operations of the RAF's Photo Reconnaissance branch, with which he served; and to Martin Fletcher, my editor at Headline Review, who was key in launching me on a new career and who always provides a clear-eyed and constructive view of my work. Most of all, I thank my wife Jan, also a first-class editor, for her unfailing support throughout the long haul of the creative process.

FRANK BARNARD

Blue Man Falling

In September 1939, World War Two is declared and
Europe holds its breath. When will the Third Reich strike
west across France and the Low Countries? For RAF
fighter pilots patrolling the Franco-German border it
is a bizarre time: one moment they are chasing an
elusive Luftwaffe, the next ordering champagne in Paris.
Then, in May 1940, Hitler launches Blitzkrieg and the
Hurricane squadrons find themselves engulfed in battle.

From the cockpit of a Hurricane fighter plane to the
louche salons of Parisian society, *Blue Man Falling* follows
the fortunes of two RAF pilots, an Englishman, Kit Curtis,
and an American, Ossie Wolf, during the Battle of France
1939–40. Capturing the startling contradictions of a time
when people were at their best and their worst, it brings
to life the exhilaration and fear of aerial warfare with
astonishing power and narrative skill. Above all, it lays
bare the meaning of war, and the selflessness of those
prepared to fight until the end.

Praise for Frank Barnard:

'A gripping fusion of thrills and historical plausibility . . .
A fine balance of freshness and authenticity . . .' *Daily
Telegraph*

'Fantastic writing. Terrific, atmospheric' Peter James

978 0 7553 2555 9

headline
review

FRANK BARNARD

Band of Eagles

Summer 1941. The tiny island of Malta, held by the British, has become the most bombed place on earth. It is a crucial supply point for the Allies. The Germans and Italians want to destroy it.

For the fighter pilots of the RAF defeat seems almost certain. They are outnumbered in the air, short of food and drink and weakened by tropical disease.

Two flight commanders, Englishman Kit Curtis and American Ossie Wolf, make an unlikely alliance. Curtis is idealistic while Wolf, by contrast, is ruthless, a gifted ace thriving in the chaos of imminent invasion. But as each man is tested to the limit, they come to share a common purpose and fresh understanding.

The experiences of these pilots and their comrades are vividly conveyed in a novel of compelling pace and power. By turns brutal, funny, tragic and heroic, this is a spell-binding tour de force, a brilliant sequel to the bestselling *Blue Man Falling*.

Praise for Frank Barnard:

'A gripping fusion of thrills and historical plausibility . . . a fine balance of freshness and authenticity' *Daily Telegraph*

'A brilliantly observed, structured and informed novel. I hugely enjoyed it. The plot is gripping' Raymond Baxter (Spitfire Pilot)

978 0 7553 2558 0

headline
review

Now you can buy any of these other bestselling
Headline books from your bookshop
or *direct from the publisher*.

Envoy of the Black Pine	Clio Gray	£7.99
A Carrion Death	Michael Stanley	£7.99
The Eagle's Prey	Simon Scarrow	£7.99
A Mortal Curiosity	Ann Granger	£7.99
The Tomb of Hercules	Andy McDermott	£6.99
Nightshade	Paul Doherty	£7.99
Private Eyes	Jonathan Kellerman	£7.99